For Claudia and Alan.

BIG SKY

BIG SKY

A novel
by

TIMOTHY RYAN DAY

Adelaide Books
New York / Lisbon
2020

BIG SKY

A novel

By Timothy Ryan Day

Published by Adelaide Books, New York / Lisbon
adelaidebooks.org

Editor-in-Chief
Stevan V. Nikolic

For any information, please address Adelaide Books
at info@adelaidebooks.org

or write to:

Adelaide Books
244 Fifth Ave. Suite D27
New York, NY, 10001

ISBN: 978-1-953510-80-8

Printed in the United States of America

Contents

PART 1

1

Me

As I imagine it, the painting was changing. Each brush stroke was an organism with a set of intentions, somehow locked into a rational relationship with the composition. The colors, thick-textured oils, moved like a colony of amoebas as the whole somehow managed to maintain coherence. The image made sense even as the process of its creation evaded any rational explanation. The media picked up on the story quickly. First it was the Christian Times, then the tabloids, then the major papers reported on the media attention as a phenomenon in and of itself. It began trending on social media, going viral, spreading across the web like rivers across landscapes, like synapses forming minds, like roots laying claim to some plot of land. The phenomenon grew like everything grows: mimetically. The notoriety of the painting increased exponentially until what began as an imperceptible motion had a certain weight, a certain body. A comment became an observation, an observation the source of analysis, the analysis international news, and international news a new shared reality. There was no reason, no ends, no rationale, just an emergence. That's the way of evolution whether it's our bodies, our minds, our stories… Play and chance define the process, the unanswered question is where the process is heading…

So, someone noticed the painting. Someone noticed that it had changed, and in the course of three or four nights, Jared Rowland became a household name, a painter who everyone thought they had always known. An artist that painted a forgotten moment in America's history, and his own.

It had to be this way, I think. As Heidegger might have said, the world was always meant to emerge from the Earth. I think of Adam and Eve, working away in the garden, part of the whole that proceeded the fall, when the world and the Earth were one and the same, when gender was a meaningless distinction and all of the heavens could be crossed in a single breath. Mind and body moved in and out of one another like words in the cavern of a sleeping ear. No place such as Eden ever existed. It's a metaphor. Then, maybe metaphors are just as real as places. Eden speaks of a world that preceded the dualities: light and dark, good and evil, male and female, black and white, real and ideal. They were all tied together in a space that refused the easy distinctions, the meaningless differences that have come to be inscribed with scientific and cultural weight. Maybe as evolution plays its games of chance, the bodies and minds we become move slowly towards the capacity to bridge the divides all over again. Maybe we have never left Eden. Maybe we have just forgotten how to see it…

The painting's subject is a young black man embracing a young white woman on a corner. The woman, Patricia Stamford, is a purely fictional character. I made her up. He is real though. Or, he is a character based on someone real I should say. He's 19 years old. An orphan born Jimmie Jones. He goes by Dick, and takes the surname of his adopted family, the Rowlands. Jimmie Jones becomes Dick Rowland. He works as a shoeshine boy in downtown Tulsa. Jim Crow Tulsa. The closest bathroom that a black man can use is on the top floor of the Drexel building. On May 31, 1921, the urge strikes. He has to walk a block squeezing the muscles around his groin and abdomen before he takes the elevator to the top floor. Sarah Page is 17. She works as an elevator operator at the Drexel Building. She's new in town. A Kansas City transplant with a checkered past. She's real too.

The elevator ride is a black box. She claimed assault, though later, after the fires stopped, she dropped the charges. He said he tripped and stepped on her toe. Dick was arrested. The paper called for a lynching. An armed white mob marched to the courthouse where Dick sat alone in a cell. An armed black mob of vets from WWI went to meet them.

Who shot first? Another black box. But shots were fired and they didn't stop for two days. Fires were set. The mechanic's, the movie theater, the jazz club where even whites came to skirt the laws of prohibition era Oklahoma, they were all burned to the ground.

Private planes were equipped with bombs and the national guard assisted in the elimination of targets.

Targets.

Black owned businesses. Black owned homes. Black bodies.

Somewhere between 75 and 300 people died and 35 blocks of black wealth, generations of wealth, evaporated into the smoke-filled sky. Sarah seems to have evaporated too, and Dick along with her. Just two people, tender awaiting a spark to ignite into flames wafting up into the Oklahoma sky.

Nearly one hundred years later, what's changed?

The man and the woman from the painting, the real man and the fictional woman, produce a child, the aforementioned artist Jared Rowland. That child has a child, a daughter. Nearly 60 years after the violence in Tulsa, she has two boys. So, the boys are two generations removed from their only relative who ever really lived. The rest is pure fiction. I can see the two of them as children. Adam, I think, sang Tommy to sleep at night. Tommy's love of music, as I imagine it, was really just the offspring of Adam's voice which had been in his ear since the beginning. Voices change the trajectories of those around us. The meaning of the words, of course, but also the intonation that communicates that we are not alone, the support that allows us to push into unknown futures and the sympathy that supports the challenges of the past. They tended to each other as their mother, recently divorced and transplanted from her native Oklahoma, poured over texts in a library on the South side of Chicago. She emerges to me clearly: Graying hair pulled back tightly, straggling strands resisting the gravitational pull of the hair band and becoming tangled with the translucent red frames of her glasses. Her face is ageing but still somehow immature, naive. She clings to her past, or it clings to her. Her mind won't stop for long enough to allow her to see the world around her. She's blind to the present. I imagine the two boys were inseparable when they were young. Adam, even years before the operation that made him biologically female, years before she became Eve, was feminine, motherly, to his younger brother. He watched over him so closely that they were destined to grow apart. Music bound them for as long as it could. Their father was white, and they are lighter skinned than their mother who was herself of mixed race. Tommy is lighter skinned than Eve. Eve could be from the Mediterranean or the Carribean. Definitely somewhere with islands. Tommy has blue eyes that make him look like a Cuban Frank Sinatra. His race is fluid. If he told you he was African American, you would believe him, but if he said he was Irish, you would believe that too. The hue of his skin seemed to lighten and darken with the psychological needs of the onlooker. His hair, curled and slightly red at the roots before darkening as it rose into a wavy bush fell somewhere between Bob Dylan and Jimi Hendrix.

I imagine them as pieces in some greater sweep, as genes in an evolutionary gambit that they can never be fully conscious of… Evolution itself seems to be unconscious of its own machinations as it grinds and leaps incrementally into the future, so why should they, the results of that distant, pulsating, process be any more aware of their intentions, their motions, their meaning amongst the countless signs that flutter across the face of the planet and the universe beyond it. Their consciousness amounted to one momentary flash of a lightning bug across a continent covered in rainforests: Beautiful to those lucky enough to have perceived it, but incidental at best in the face of life creeping its way across the planet.

They are unaware of their own genesis, I think. Do I write them that way because I choose to? Or do they just appear? What right do I have to even tell this story, their story? This half-breed between history and fiction? Maybe none…

2

Us

"We're going to sit down and you're going to tell me everything, Tommy."

"But, I don't know who you are." The gun, or at least he thought it was a gun, was poking into his side. The old man was white and lifeless on the floor. The blue orb didn't look like much more than a tanning bed with a few fancy medical devices hooked up to it now that the power had been drained.

"I need to hear the story, Tommy."

"Who…"

The man predicted the end of the question. "I'm Dr. Kane, Tommy."

The repetition of his name was unnerving. It always made him feel like he was talking to a salesman or a guidance counselor, someone whose profession told them that serious people remember the names of those who they are talking to, and that repeating the name over and over was the best way to prove to the other person that you took an active interest. For Tommy it only served to remind that the person in front of him had a very structured sense of social interaction.

"He thought I could save him," said Kane gesturing towards the body on the floor. His glasses slid down his nose when he smiled.

"Seems to have been mistaken," said Tommy.

Kane squeezed the bridge of his nose. "Seems so."

Tommy nodded. "What is it that you think I can tell you?"

"You just start producing words. They will tell me what I need to know."

Tommy got the impression that Kane hadn't slept in days, maybe weeks. "You look tired. Your eyes..."

Kane moved the fingers of the non-gun hand from the bridge of his nose to his temples. "Tommy, talk, Tommy."

Two times. He fit his name twice into the same sentence. "Please stop saying my name."

"Why?"

"It bothers me."

"And the gun?"

So it was a gun.

"Does the gun bother you?"

"Of course… but for some reason not as much as the name."

"Your name is everything, Tommy," he smiled like an aggressive older sibling. "Everything you will ever be starts with your name. It's that first sign that all the others will attach themselves to throughout your life. It's the base of the model."

"Well, then definitely stop saying it."

Kane chuckled. "Just talk."

"I don't know anything."

"You know everything. You just haven't put the signs in order."

"The signs. I've always had a gift for getting the signs all mixed up," Tommy said.

"It *is* a gift."

"I'd be glad to give it to you if I could."

"I'd be glad to have it."

Tommy let the silence speak for him.

"Signs are life, Tommy." The room's already dim lights flickered. "There is the world that interprets messages and responds, and there's death. Those are your choices."

"Well, when you put it like that..."

"I want you to close your eyes, go back to the beginning, and tell me what you see. When did you first see the painting?"

Suddenly it was like he was lying on a psychiatrist's couch, recounting a dream from some state of deep hypnosis rather than remembering the events of the past few days. He felt like he was falling, peacefully, into some endless well that would not end until he reached the center of the Earth.

"Just speak," said Kane.

He began to speak:

3

I

I walk out of the noisy club. I stumble. I fumble for my cell phone and dial Missy. Each tone is a color. I get the signals mixed up in my brain. I hear a sound and it triggers a color. That's not quite right, but it's the only way I know how to explain it. Playing a concert for me is like standing before a giant canvas that the colors won't stick to. They move around, they drip and swirl with reverb and flange, they stretch, sustain, shake with distortion. I'm not being poetic. It's a disease… Or a disorder… Or whatever… My senses are all out of whack is the long and short of it. They have been as long as I can remember. I guess that's what you think is a gift, right, Doc? Maybe. Missy wants a rockstar for a boyfriend. It is becoming all too clear that I am not a rockstar. I am a barista, at best a barkeep. Whatever I am, it is almost sure to involve beverages. I sit on the couch playing video games in which I mimic criminal acts. Even being a criminal would be better. Real. I read comics. I wouldn't date me. I walk by a Tribune machine. The headline reads: 'Worst month for violence in Iraq since 2008.' I should have been a soldier. I spent my twenties bitching about, not protesting mind you, just bitching about, the war and the people who made it possible, and now I am beginning to see that it was me who was apathetic, not the world. I wanted to be a poet with a guitar. Then, songwriters aren't like novelists. Hemingway and Orwell came back from war. Not Bowie. Not Lennon. Not even Cash, really. Elvis, I guess. But how many songs did he really write? I dial Missy. No answer. Missy is a bitch. The phone vibrates in my pocket and I fumble for it again. It's Missy. Thank God.

'Where are you?' She says.

'Heading home. You?'

'Not home.' Missy is short. She's Korean. An Orphan. One of a set of twins adopted at birth. I love her. Most of the time.

'The moon is full.'

'Would you shut the fuck up about the moon already.'

I hate her.

'You sound drunk,' she says.

'Could be.' I look up at the moon. It's actually not quite full. 'I did drink a lot.'

'Surprise.'

She likes irony.

'Are you going home?' she asks.

'Later.'

She hangs up. Fair is fair.

I wander to a diner near the corner of Ashland and Lawrence. I eat eggs. Hashbrowns. Drink coffee in a brown leather booth. The waitress, whose name tag says Pam refills my cup. Even though I don't want more coffee, I stay.

'How are you tonight, Pam?'

'I've been worse,' she says with a smile overwrought with red lipstick. She has dull brown hair and two fingers with bandages on them.

She reminds me of Sue. Sue is dead. I learned that earlier this evening in a phone call from my brother, or, I should say, my sister, whose voice I hadn't heard in five years until I heard it today on the answering machine. I loved my brother, Adam. My sister, Eve, insists that he is dead. I know, Adam and Eve… Real cute. I miss my brother. I notice a man at a booth in the corner of the restaurant counting a giant pile of pennies and nickels. A teenage couple sits in the window, both half standing to engage in a very wet kiss across a pancake-filled table. The boy has a pierced eyebrow and a red streak in his hair. She looks like she may be an accountant with Price Waterhouse. Pam is lingering. She wants me to respond. I don't know how I can. A bell dings. She pivots, looks back at my blank stare, offers me one more moment in which to utter something, anything, but when I don't she's left with no options, and heads for the kitchen. The diner, I notice suddenly, is old. The polished wood bar might have been built in the twenties. I wonder if Al Capone ever ate here? It's not too far from the Green Mill where they say he spent a lot of time. I imagine him sitting at the bar, his fork picking through some scrambled eggs without much consideration for actually putting them in his mouth.

'What you think about eggs, kid?' asks Al.

'Me?' I ask Mr. Capone.

'Yeah, you, who else?' He says twirling a finger beside his temple.

'I, uh, well, I like them sometimes.'

'Chicken foetuses. Nasty, but delicious. Life is strange,' he sings it like a line from a Sinatra song.

I nod along to the rhythm.

Pam returns, interrupting my exchange with Chicago's most notorious deceased. 'You alright?' She refills my cup again. I stare towards the empty bar.

'Are you alright?' she asks again, fiddling with the bandage on one of her fingers.

'Too much to drink.'

She sits. 'You remind me of my son.' I feel 30 is too old to remind her of her son, but she reminds me of my stepmother, so... 'He passed on a couple years back.'

I don't know what to say. I don't want to remind her of a dead person, but I imagine she doesn't want to remind me of one either.

'I'm sorry,' and I think I am.

'Sorry that he passed, or that you remind me of him?'

'I dunno.' I don't. 'Both, I guess.'

'Well, on the first count, don't be. It wasn't your fault he used. On the second, don't be. I like to be reminded of him.'

'Why?'

'I loved him. Why wouldn't I want to be reminded of that?' She puts her bandaged fingertips on my hand. 'Will you do something for me?'

'Maybe.'

'Will you wait here for a half hour and then come have a drink with me?'

I nod. The half hour flies by. We go for a drink. She stares into my eyes in a way that makes me uncomfortable. We order drink after drink. It must be four or five AM by the time we get the taxi back to her place. The door has barely closed when she throws off her clothes and pulls me on top of her. The room spins, the walls dissolve and I am back in the diner. She is staring at me.

'Check?'

'Excuse me?'

'My shift is over. Do you mind if we settle up?'

Capone laughs. The man in the corner has piled up his pennies into ten or fifteen realms. The couple at the front is still kissing. She looks less like an accountant and more like a stripper playing an accountant.

Death always makes me think of Donnan. I go to Montrose Harbor instead of home. I watch the sunrise. It's warm out. Summertime. I imagine Donnan, face down in the snow on his hundredth birthday. Ten years ago now. We're ten years into the new millennium. Donnan would have been one-hundred and ten. Too old. Why mourn such an old man? He's dead, and that's that. I mourn him and I celebrate him, just like I mourn and celebrate Sue, just like I mourn and celebrate my mother, just like I mourn and celebrate myself. I never know better from worse. I never know right from wrong. I'm not a sociopath or anything. I just can't see how it all unfolds in the long run. No one can. The best we can do is understand that any given event has the ability to unfold in any number of ways. Any event has the ability to wind up good or bad.

I watch the moon give way to the sun as the lake takes on its early morning orange glimmer. The yellow of the moon feels like a feather being pulled across the grooves in my spine.

Missy is home when I get back.

"Good morning, my poet," she says. I close the door quietly. She doesn't sound angry, which almost makes me angry. How could she possibly not be pissed (American) that I'm coming home pissed (Brit) after dawn.

"Morning, indeed. Good, uff, not so sure."

"Did you have a nice night?" she is sitting on the couch in her underwear with a half finished bottle of pink champagne. The underwear is pink too.

"I wouldn't go so far as good." That's ridiculous. No one matches their underpants to their drink. "Shitty. I might call it that."

"Did you enjoy your full moon, at least?" She sounds conciliatory.

"Wasn't full after all."

"I'm sorry, by the way, that I told you to shut up about the moon. I was fucking with you, but you went and hung up, so..."

Photographs of bands cover the apartment walls. There are none of my band. She keeps those in her studio.

"Ah... I missed the punch. It happens, I guess."

"I was quoting you, you know."

"Quoting me?"

"About the moon."

Right. It was a line from a song I'd written years ago.

"Are you okay?"

"Why wouldn't I be?"

"That's not an answer." She looks towards the phone that sits on the bar that separates the kitchen from the living room. I notice that the seams on our couch were coming apart. We bought it at massive furniture warehouse out in the burbs, the Swedish empire of style contagion, when we first moved in together. Their products touch everything: my food, my clothes, my personal grooming goods. Even our most intimate moments are tagged with that little blue label dangling off the back of the mattress or sofa. Disposable furniture… How did we get here?

"I heard your brother's message."

Why did we buy a brown couch?

"I don't have a brother."

She is wearing a black T-shirt along with her underwear, swigging the champagne from the bottle.

"He has a nice voice. I would have liked to have met him."

Why was she using the past tense already? Don't we have to have a conversation before we transition to the past tense?

"Her. You could still meet her."

She frowns and swigs. "I'd like that."

"Guess you won't ever meet Sue, though."

"No, I don't suppose I will."

"That's alright," I say. I lay down next to her on the couch and she runs her fingers through my hair. I don't mean it, but I say it because it's easier than the truth: "I hated her anyway."

4

They

The boardroom was built around a long wooden table and lined by a window that overlooked downtown Oklahoma City. A projector mounted from the ceiling was aimed towards a retractable white screen. Triangular phones specifically geared towards conference calls sat on the table, evenly spaced between the overstuffed black leather chairs.

"No one cares what your grandfather did. It's a non-issue," said one of the men.

The men, all draped in suits of slightly varied greys and blues, sat around the table. The mildest distinctions in hairstyle, height, facial shape, were all that prevented one man from blending straight into the next. None were more than two hours past their last shave. The aroma of cologne mixed with various creams saturated the space like whiskey and tobacco might have in previous decades. A black woman in an olive green dress sat at the table's far corner.

Willard Stamford III looked out over the memorial. He was grateful that he hadn't been at work the day the bomb went off. Though had he been there, and had he survived, it would have made great politics.

"I wouldn't be here if it weren't for what my grandfather did," said Willard still staring over the clock, halted at 9:02. "Of course people care. One way or another it's all they care about."

He blinked and held his eyes shut for a moment capturing an image of the memorial, and letting it go as he opened his eyes again, letting reality overtake his impression. He tried to imagine the toppled buildings, the beleaguered rescue workers, the flashing lights, but the serene Oklahoma City morning would not let him bring all of that to mind. It shook him to think that the individualism, that rugged American independence that his grandfather had so championed had this darker side. It could just as easily be a McVeigh as a Rockefeller or a Jobs. All sociopaths in their way, he supposed.

"I don't think most people even remember what happened. It's not an event that is very strongly engrained in the public mind," said a blue suit.

Stamford tried to bring that other violence to mind. 90 miles and as many years down the road: Tulsa in 1921. "There's a reason for that," he said. He squinted his eyes and scrunched his nose. "Is this going to effect us or not?"

"Absolutely not," came the voice of a man in a deeper blue.

"No," parroted a light grey.

The black woman in the olive green suit moved her hand forward on the desk.

"Karen, can I assume you disagree?" asked Stamford.

"Yes, sir. I disagree. This is a huge problem."

Stamford nodded, eyes closed. "How huge?"

"Huge, you-lose-the-election-if-the-story-breaks, huge. It's not just Tulsa. Not just that your grandfather engineered race riots, which in a more civilised state would probably be enough. It's the connection to the oil that's pumping into the gulf. It's Katrina being in the recent past. It's you looking like heir to the causes of all of it. American's want fresh blood, and yours is, frankly, about as fresh as cottage cheese."

"He didn't cause the damned hurricane," said a navy, pin-striped.

"No, but his party didn't respond to save the lives of black citizens, either."

"He's not running for governor of Louisiana, Karen."

"And that's a plus for us, but unfortunately, a handful of Oklahomans have heard of Louisiana, and even more of them have heard of Stamford Oil, which is covering the coast in oil as we speak."

"He doesn't have a stake in the company."

"But the company has a stake in him. It's his last name that sits on those broken rigs."

"Maybe we should change your name," said a checked gray suit, smiling.

"Or the company's," said a faded gray.

"That might save your kid's political aspirations, but short term you're screwed," said Karen. "We can work with the oil. You can create distance. Reiterate that you sold your shares. Come out hard against the board. Demand that they take financial responsibility. But, your grandfather? There we have a lose-lose. You can't condemn your elders and you can't double down on an old racist..."

"Careful," said a dark gray.

Stamford lifted a hand to quiet him. "It's OK."

"I'm sorry, but that's what it is," said Karen.

"Since when does being related to an old racist hurt you in Oklahoma politics?" The dark gray suit chuckled.

Karen set her eyes on him, "since the younger generation started reading the bible that their parents spent so many years thumping on. Since latinos started voting. Since schools started teaching American history instead of just reading odes to George Washington."

"Don't you work for that oil company that's shitting all over the coast?"

"I work for the Stamford family, and I'm informing them that, yes, the role of Willard Stamford I in the riots of 1921 becoming public creates problems for Willard Stamford III in his attempt to win the governorship of Oklahoma."

Stamford looked once more over the memorial. "What do we do?" asked Stamford.

"I'd rather discuss that in private."

Karen stood and headed for the door. Stamford opened it for her and followed her down a long gray carpeted hallway that was lined with abstract, corporate art. Yellow triangles leaning towards blue circles inside of silver frames. The men in the boardroom stayed seated, sipping coffee from identical mugs with corporate logos, doing their best to appear as if there were thoughts circling around in their heads when in truth they were like cells in the corporate organism: replicating exactly as they were programmed to do, and rarely producing anything so free as an idea.

"So what do we do?" He asked, trailing behind her.

"For now, nothing."

"Nothing?"

"Nothing." She looked at him over the thin metal rims of her glasses.

He stood, arms apart, shaking his head.

"We've had a stroke of luck."

"Luck?"

"The reporter," she looked down at her clipboard, "Sue Shells."

"What about her?"

"She's dead."

"Jesus, Karen, tell me we didn't have anything to do with this."

She shrugged off his objection, and then broke into a smile. "Of course not, Will. Just a bit of luck."

"Luck? Christ, Karen."

"Listen, I'm not glad she's dead, but as long as things have played out this way, I'm going to look towards the not at all insubstantial silver-lining, which is maybe, just maybe, if we play this right you still get to be the Governor of this shit hole state."

He moved into the office and plopped into the red leather chair behind his desk. "What happened?"

"Do you really want to know?"

"Yes, Karen. I really want to know."

She sat in the green leather chair in front of the desk and clutched the arm rests.

"Car accident. She was on I44 between OKC and Tulsa a couple nights ago. Researching your grandfather, no doubt. A trucker passed out at the wheel and wiped out six cars on his way to the ditch."

"This isn't the first time we've had a stroke of 'luck' like this," said Stamford, his eyes focussed on some point beyond his office wall.

"You have nothing to worry about," said Karen.

"I'm not worried about getting caught."

"Then what are you worried about?"

"Being responsible."

"Your not."

He adjusted his line of sight so that she was fixed before him.

"It was a car accident. They happen all the time, Will. She was just unlucky."

"And we were..."

"Lucky."

She moved around the desk and put her hand on top of his. "If you don't trust me, this doesn't work."

"I trust you."

5

I

When I wake up she's gone. So are the photos and all of her clothes. Black jeans, military green hats, knee-high boots. All gone.

The band is finished. There are no low-rent midwestern tours to put on hold. There are no recording sessions to cancel. Missy is gone. The best thing I can do is disappear.

I go to the phone and listen to Eve's voicemail again.

"Tommy, it's Eve. Sue is dead. I don't know if you care or not, but I, for one, would like to see you. You know where to find me."

Her voice is deep and feminine. It reminds me of when he sang me to sleep as a child. Before his non-death death. He isn't exactly trans, because he was born a hermaphrodite. He just didn't agree with the choice my parents made to make him a boy. He disappeared around the same time mom died. He was singing in a jazz bar on the South side that was a famous mobster hang out. These mobsters weren't like the ones in the movies. They were just slightly sleazier than normal businessmen. Something went wrong. I never knew what. One day I got a letter. It started out as a suicide letter from Adam, but slowly transitioned into an introduction. It was signed by Eve. I didn't handle the transition well. I don't know what well would look like, but I know the way I handled it was wrong. I don't know if she's forgiven me. She says she has, but I don't know... She lives in St. Louis now. That is about the only thing I know about her life. For a millisecond I think of suicide. Maybe I could end Tommy and start anew as someone else? Or maybe I could just use a gun... It sends a shiver down my spine. What a mess. Anyway, I don't have a gun, and I'm way too much of a narcissist for suicide. I want to see my sister.

I see a picture on the refrigerator of Missy and I feel something like pain shoot through my chest and stomach. I try to distinguish heart from ego, love from desire, but I can't decide which was wounded. I pass out watching the news. They have been talking about the painting in Oklahoma for days. The name, Jared Rowland, my grandfather's name, makes me wince. They say the painting is changing right in front of everyone's eyes. It must be a hoax, but no one seems to have figured out how just yet. It is probably that English guy. He found another way to turn a prank into a million dollars. I just don't know why he chose my family.

I feel human when I wake up. I need to get to St. Louis, but money is a problem. The lease is in my name and I'm freshly unemployed. There are three weeks until rent is due. I grab a backpack with a couple extra T-shirts, a change of jeans, and my telecaster and head for the pawn shop.

They cough up enough for a ticket on the Megabus to St. Louis in return for the guitar. My sister can get me moving from there. I hope.

6

Him

Words. It all started with words. If words were capable of carrying messages, of encoding information in impossibly complex ways, of colonizing the minds of entire nations and even extending beyond them, of storing themselves remotely in amorphous cultural memories, adapting over generations, dictating the behaviors of humanity by defining the very limits of what they could imagine, articulate, *be*... Well, then words must possess some sort of being. Maybe physical, maybe spiritual. Maybe concrete, maybe abstract. But they *existed* words did. They inhabited us just as little strands of mitochondria. They determined our being, our capacity to navigate reality, just as this or that gene determined the color of our eyes, the length of our toes, the limits of our libidos. Then, Dr. Kane knew full well that genes were not as determinative as the popular imagination wished they were. They were suggestions, signs that pointed in a certain direction. They were police on the road to try and enforce the rules of circulation, but they could not stop every passing car. Some travelers were sure to make unscheduled turns, to interpret the signs more freely. These rebellious drivers were the forces behind change, the engines of instability that made evolutions ally, adaptation, and its less affable associate—disease—possible. He thought of them as tiny unconscious geniuses, of Nietzchean supermen who disregarded the law and changed everything, though these individuals could only access their will as a network, a superorganism. Words and genes were both units in systems of signs, systems of meaning, systems marked by life.

Even death was a ritual bathed in signs. The oil that clung to the stork's skin could be described: shiny, black, sticky, viscous. But, it also played into a network of ideas one held about oil, even experiences with it. It was tied to words like foreign, independent, renewable, pipeline, wealth, smog, Islam, war, disaster, efficient, energy, clean, Christianity, progress, reincarnation, evolution, disintegration, nationalization, privatization, child soldier, Communist, Capitalist, plastic, cancer, innovation, exploitation, life, and of course, as always, death. And, then there were personal associations. The smell of the gas can Father Dimitri, the long departed priest who had raised Dr. Eli Kane, had used to fill the lawn mower in Georgia. The feeling of leaning against the pump as he filled the car on his first cross-country road trip when he went to Wisconsin to study Biology, his paychecks that bore the Stamford Oil logo, his first sight of the ocean as slick and black as a frozen pond at midnight. Oil was no doubt a substance with some substantial reality independent of Dr. Kane, but he would never be able to interact with that substance from any context but that which his circumstance had created. Yes, death was a ritual bathed in signs. The oil covers the animal, blinding it until its predators, by necessity vigilant observers of signs, sense erratic behavior and attack. Then the predator absorbs the oil soaked carcass into its liver. The liver reacts to signs of poisonous content by increasing its enzymes, then swells in its battle to expel the poisons. Ammonia fills the brain and symptoms set in: confusion, blurred vision, undirected locomotion, perhaps sounds meant to express distress. If the animal is lucky, the signs of its weakness are spotted by still another predator further up the line, or an opportunistic scavenger who can expedite the process. If it suffers the misfortune of being a top predator, and no human is nearby to end its misery, it is condemned to thrash about until the nervous system is sent the signal that pain is no longer a conversation worth having with the body, and shock and dementia are allowed to carry what is soon to be a corpse through the home stretch, preparing it for its life beyond any need for conscious interpretation of signs in the world.

He thought of Dimitri in his last stages. He had not thought of Dimitri in years. He remembered that panicked look that he had since seen in the eyes of so many birds, seals, even turtles. That look, if nothing else, was proof enough to him that people shared something with their animal predecessors. That look reminded him that no matter what we added on top of it, deep down our reptilian brains were still sending pulses through our nightmares. Of course, Eli was not having nightmares anymore. Not in the traditional sense. There was no such thing as nightmares for the sleepless.

And so, as he looked out over all of that oil coating all of that ocean, he thought of Father Dimitri. He knew how it was going to end. Stamford would not provide him with the cure. He was going to die just as his father had. The least he could do was help to right a wrong before he went.

Just a day before, Dr. Kane stood at the shore in front of his cottage on Grand Lake watching a rattler scuttle into the bushes, a rifle cocked against his shoulder, a scaly finger on the trigger. He had no real interest in shooting the snake, he just wanted to be sure the thing moved in the other direction, into the water, away from him. A Diamondback releases a hemotoxic venom composed of 5-15 enzymes, metal ions, biogenic amines, lipids, free amino acids, proteins and polypeptides. When they enter your system they cause necrosis and coagulopathy. They break down tissue and make your body digestable. Some snakes can even induce paralysis, but not this one.

Dr. Kane was fascinated by the way a substance could enter the body and translate itself into effects. It was a malicious element in a complex communications network. A venom could be thought of as a lie, an impurity in a system, a computer virus… a real virus. Then, sometimes impurities lead to unforeseen benefits. More often not. That was the funny thing about evolution. It was effective so infrequently on the local level, and yet so damned effective on the global. It was a cruel system.

He walked up the steep hill from the lakeshore to the cottage. The Poison Ivy was growing back at the edges of his property. Urishiol comes into contact with the skin and causes a rash in up to 85% of people. Now that is effective communication. But, why are the others immune? He looked at the root system from the old Oak in the center of his yard. It had begun to pop up under his front porch, deforming the concrete base. He would move the porch when he had time. The tree had more right to the space than his porch, and one always had to give a little in a negotiation.

He heard the phone ringing inside and he hurried a little. Like a dog drooling for his dinner bell, he thought, his adrenoline levels raised, knowing that the call would be from work.

The brain can be chemically affected by remote. A sound can start processes throughout the body.

"Kane?" came the voice on the other end of the line. It was Karen, the third in command at Stamford.

"Speaking."

"We need you in Shreveport."

"For?"

"There's been an explosion at an offshore rig."

"Damage?"

"3 dead. Pretty hefty product loss."

They always thought that way. Product losses. Employees and goods that would not be available to increase their margins. Next she would make some reference to the environmental damage as if it were just bad PR.

"If that oil hits the beaches we're gonna have a PR nightmare on our hands."

"I'm on my way."

The inside of Kane's cottage was almost as lush as the woods outside of it. He had an herb garden, a collection of rare orchids, ivy climbing wooden tracks built around his walls, and the centerpiece, two exceptionally rare flowers: the Tacca Chantrieri, or 'black bat flower', and the Titan Arum, which translated to the 'titanic penis'. The black bat, a flower known for its incredible beauty, looked like a purple faced tiger complete with long drooping whiskers. The Titan Arum, which was famous for smelling like raw meat, looked like a swollen whale's member emerging from a splash in the ocean. The reason he kept the Tacca Chantrieri was simple: its beauty. But, the Titan Arum? It was a more complex plant. Kane did not mind the smell. It was a mystery to him. What purpose could the aroma of raw flesh serve for a flower? Maybe that was why it was so rare. A plant that slid into evolution's margin of error.

On the back wall of the cottage was a painting of a dark-green-leafed plant with little white berries. Mistletoe Phoradendron Serotinum. The State flower of Oklahoma. In the foreground the plant's leaves drooped towards the ground. Two young, black bodies came close beneath the berries as if they might kiss. In the distance a plane flew over a burning row of buildings. The eyes were led naturally from the foreground to the background and back again, revising what first seemed to be passion in the eyes of two young lovers into a shimmering terror of two young people hiding from a massacre. The artist, Jared Rowland, was one of Dr. Kane's favorites. Rowland had used the leaves of the plant itself to create the hue with which he painted. Whenever possible, Rowland had used the material of his subject in the creation of its image.

He stuffed his things into his travel bag, a couple of suits, toothbrush, shaving kit, a little leather bound book that he took with him everywhere. He jumped into his hybrid and headed for the Oklahoma City airport, which was at least a couple hours drive. He would get there and assess the damage. It would be unimaginable, as it always was. He remembered the Alaskan spill from a few years back. The news had said five-hundred thousand barrels, but it was easily more than a million. Birds covered in crude made the news, but not the plants whose stomata, or pores, were suffocated, leading them to slow, breathless deaths.

It is true, Dr. Kane had explained to a then green Karen, that plants do not have a central nervous system. To talk about pain does not really make sense, but their destruction is inseparable from our pain, so if we cannot talk of their demise as a painful process at least we can talk of how theirs demise is our own. Plants are the distant cousins that unite intelligent, purposed life forms to their unconscious universe. All the parts of this widespread family are in constant conversation through biological processes and physical laws. Kane knew this. Oil, then, was a religious matter. The real biological material of past times laying under ground as potential energy. The world's own hue from which it could construct new paintings. Or, maybe it had some other purpose, some purpose that a short-sighted humanity had yet to discover. Maybe the bodies of long dead species were destined to become cellphones, laptops, garbage bags, exhaust from the tailpipes of cars. Maybe they were meant for some less human purpose. Maybe they were meant for nothing at all, just the remnants of millions of years that housed nothing but a series of accidents, catastrophes that varied only in degree.

Karen had listened intently, something she no longer feigned to do, before asking him for a report, and handing him the findings.

Dr. Kane was no determinist. The report could say whatever they wanted it to. He gathered the real data. Performed the important work. They paid for it. He would let them say whatever they so pleased.

7

Her

Singing keeps her alive. It is as if she is hooked up intravenously to some mysteriously sustained note moved by a celestial foot on a brass pedal, rocking to pull out every last straining syllable. The voice is crackling by the time it leaves her lips, almost out of breath, pausing at nearly imperceptible intervals, but it keeps emanating from an invisible diaphragm that expands and contracts far beyond the horizons of the Earth, and tunnels its way through space and time up from her core, lungs, esophagus, mouth, to be sung in startling, cracked imperfection.

It was morning. Late morning. The sun peaked through faded curtains and illuminated the paisley-patterned table top which she slumped over in her kitchen. The television played in the background. The image of a long line in front of a Tulsa museum. A painting that seemed to be changing before the world's eyes, years after the disappearance of its creator who was also her grandfather. She held the phone in her left hand and with her right maintained pressure on the button in the handset's cradle so that the dial tone was silenced. The spring-loaded button pressed up against her finger as if it aspired towards release, towards serving its only purpose. It was an old phone with a long cream-colored spiral cord. She was in no hurry to update it. She had to call Tommy, to let him know about Sue, about the accident, about the letters, about their grandfather… She hadn't spoken to him in years, though she had seen him play once when he came to St. Louis. It was at a small club filled with cigarette smoke and the smell of stale beer and bleach. She stayed in the back of the room while his band played, his hair curling towards the roof like smoke signals that were redirected by each emphatic strike of his nails against the strings of his telecaster. He never used a pick. He had always said he needed to feel his skin against the metal and wood. She did not stay around to talk. She loved her brother. She loved his music. It was less complex than her own, rougher, but she could relate to its rawness. She loved him so much that she thought it better to stay away.

She sat there at the kitchen table, pressure against the button. All she had to do was lift her finger and the tone would emerge, like magic, but she held it down even as her past pushed up from somewhere deep under the rug and tried to sound a tone of its own.

She had given up the drugs years ago. After the trouble in Chicago. After Kim disappeared. She had always thought she'd end like her hero, Charlie Parker. She almost succeeded. She had dreamed of taking the world into her veins and liver until it made her cheeks collapse and her organs explode. She made good progress for a while. What surprised her was how much strength it took to be truly self-destructive. You had to ignore, or better yet, cherish, the contempt of those nearest you. You had to ignore, or better yet, relish, the signs your body sent to you: mucous, puss, odors, swelling, bursting, scabbing, excreting. Even other junkies would cast off those truly nearest the end. Not even those bent on destroying themselves like to be reminded of what the end looks like up close. Finally, she had given it all up. It was part of the deal. It was how she got him to pay for the surgery.

His name was Mirko, but she called him Luigi because of the moustache, thick like the tips of two paintbrushes. He was half Polish and half Lithuanian, but she called him Italian. He was a trader, but she called him a gangster. Maybe he was a gangster in some sense. He did all of the things a gangster would have done: extorted, threatened, brutalized, stole, protected, redistributed, prayed. But, he was not affiliated with any group. Not as far as Eve could tell. No group would have him.

"How do you get to be a trader?" Adam (she was still Adam when they met) asked him one day after Luigi had brought him to see the roiling sea of screams that was the Chicago stock exchange. Funny, how much it resembled a prison riot, or a union protest about to get out of hand. Criminals, the exploited, businessmen: they all seem to make the same broad motions when their livelihoods were at stake.

"You just have to learn to ask the right people the right questions in the right way. You do that and you'll always know where to put the money," he answered. Asking the right questions of the right people in the right way involved the operation of a business that allowed the powerful and monied to delve into their deepest desires. It offered Luigi the opportunity to engage in the collection of photos.

Adam wore a lyre on a chain around his neck. It had been a gift from Kim, his high school boyfriend. Once, so they had been told, it had belonged to Neal Cassidy. The other half, the grapes of Bacchus, had belonged to Ginsberg. That seemed backwards, but the clerk at the little shop in Denver had said it was so. Best to just believe what cannot be validated and is not of much significance anyway. You can waste a lifetime trying to validate the insignificant, thought Eve. That might be the most common way of wasting a lifetime.

Adam did not want to be a trader. What could possibly be more meaningless than the global economy. He recognized that its ups and down impacted billions of people's welfare, but to him this was just evidence that billions of people had forgotten how to measure. Maybe they had never known. They had become so obsessed with value that there was none left. They had become so obsessed with quality of life that no one knew what life, or the quality in it, was anymore.

He heard the song there at the exchange, too. It was tribal: the chaos, the battle cry. Somewhere deep in all that noise was a rhythm that would have to reemerge, to wreak havoc on the more civilized decor that humans had draped haphazardly across the planet.

He had begun to hum as they looked out over the pit. A low, guttural hum.

"You alright?" Luigi had asked.

Adam smiled, that soft, half-smile that was so often mistaken for condescension. "I'm fine, honey. It's them I'm worried about."

Luigi pressed the front of his thigh against the back of Adam's. "I wouldn't worry about them. They know what they're doing."

"It doesn't look like it."

Luigi smiled as he sniffed Adam's closely cropped hair. "No. It doesn't."

Men in blue jackets, some on ladders, most with hands waving in the air, shouted incoherently as numbers flittered across screens at an incomprehensible pace. This, Adam thought, is the descendant of the silk road. This is how we keep it all together. A sea of incomprehensible shouts.

Mirko owned the bar where Adam sang. A place called the Siren on South Halsted. There were no windows. The deep stain of the wood reflected the yellow bulbs that imitated candle light. The bottles that stood five rows tall behind the bar were covered in dust. The patrons were old. Mostly Polish. Mostly men. Mirko was not the jealous type.

"Adam, I want you to meet my friend, Kristof," he would say. "Kristof is a big fan of Nina Simone. Why don't you take him upstairs after your set and show him your records?"

A part of him always thought they would really listen to records when they got upstairs into the one bedroom apartment above the bar, at least one or two songs before ripping off layers of aged polyester. At the top of the staircase, knowing he had precious little time, Adam always went straight for the record player. He couldn't manage without the music. Without a soundtrack, it would just be life. He would lower the needle onto whatever happened to be there on the player. He would feel hands, rough with labor, on the back of his neck, or maybe they preferred to start lower. He would close his eyes and start to hum along.

Eve's finger began to ache against the pressure of the little plastic button which pressed against the gravity like a tiny rocket chained to its launch pad against its will. Her memories, and any nostalgia she could muster seemed to be pushing against gravity too. She felt it in her stomach and at the bottom of her lungs, the strange and sudden presence of all that she usually kept deep in some emotional bunker. She lifted her finger and the tone, like a forest full of monastic frogs, sounded in her ear. She dialled Tommy's number in Chicago, hoping that it had not changed. It rang… And as it rang she remembered…

"Luigi," Adam asked Mirko, "how much longer will it take to pay for the surgery."

"Not much longer," said Mirko.

'Not much longer' was always the answer. For six months, and then a year, and then two years. It was always 'not much longer'. Mirko payed the rent. Bought the food. Gave Adam a few dollars to buy records, booze, drugs when he was still using them. But he never let him hold on to the cash.

"If I gave you your pay you'd waste it on smack," he told Adam.

Adam had to admit that he was probably right. He never put up much of a fight.

At night, after the set was over, after the men had finished 'listening to records' with Adam, Mirko would come home. He brought a record every day. Something recorded live in Bangkok or Vienna. Somewhere far away.

Adam sat amidst the trappings of a junkie: spoon, needle, belt. He listened to Chet Baker and hummed quietly.

"Adam," said Mirko, "you are a goddamn mess."

Adam smiled through his humming. He was shirtless. His chest concave. His pants unbuttoned exposing a patch of hair at the threshold between his torso and his pelvis.

Mirko sat down beside him and raised the volume a notch.

"How much longer will it take to pay for the surgery," Adam whispered.

This time Mirko did not give the standard response. He looked deeply into Adam's closed eyes. "Is it what you want?

Really? I mean you're sure beyond any doubt that you'd rather be a woman than a beautiful, beautiful boy?" He ran a soft hand through Adam's greasy hair.

Adam didn't open his eyes. He just smiled broadly and nodded. "It's all I'm sure about."

But another year went by, and then another. The men kept coming. The drugs kept flowing. He sang every night. He grew thinner. His teeth and hair seemed to lose something of their hue. His little record collection had become thousands.

"Adam, meet my friend Karl. Karl loved your set. Why don't you take him upstairs and listen to some of your records?"

Adam led the man up the stairs into the little apartment above the bar. He headed for the record player, but the man grabbed his arm before he could get there.

"Wait just a minute, hon," said Adam.

The man smiled widely. Something about his teeth reminded him of that night so long ago in Denver. The night Kim had killed the rapist. The night everything decided to shred itself all to bits once and for all.

"I'm asking you nicely to be patient," said Adam, "while I put on this record."

The man clung to his arm, his nails threatening to cross the threshold of his skin, leaving what was meant to stay inside exposed. His jaw muscle twitched as he tightened his grip and beads of bright red blood gathered around the man's manicured nails.

"You don't have to," said Adam.

The man squeezed even tighter, exposing elongated canine incisors. He threw Adam down on the bed and hissed like a snake. His face pressed against the Lyre pendant on his necklace. The shopkeeper had told them that it represented Milton's

Il Pensoroso, the poet of the intellect who cannot quite inhabit the revelries of the body. The edge of it dug into his cheek. He wondered if Neal Cassidy had ever been in this position. He wondered where Kim was. If his military career was all he had hoped it would be. He wondered what he looked like without that long, pink hair. He wondered if Bill, the Coloradan with wild eyes, was the only man he had ever had to kill.

He did not remember much of what happened after that, but when Mirko came home, a copy of Chet Baker live in Madrid extended before him, Karl sat, castrated and lifeless in a chair in front of the stereo, the broken neck of a guitar protruding from his chest. Adam, again surrounded by the trappings of his habit, leaned back, a serene expression riding over his lips. Madrid, he thought, sounds like a nice place to live.

The ringing stopped.

"You've reached Tommy and Missy. Leave a message and we'll get back to you as soon as we can."

"Tommy, it's Sheila. Sue is dead. I don't know if you care or not, but I, for one, would like to see you. You know where to find me."

Carefully, she placed the receiver back onto its saddle. She took as deep a breath as the humid air allowed. She ran her finger over the table's plastic paisley top. She wondered if Tommy would listen to the message. If he would call her back. If he even cared anymore.

She heard the water running from the bathroom where Mickey was showering. What would she have become if he hadn't appeared that night in Spain, the night he literally fell into her life with a drunken slip on the staircase of the bar where she was singing. What would he have become. Suddenly, she was aware that she heard the television in the background.

The firm, artificial depth of a newscaster spoke of Tulsa. She stood and walked towards the set. People were gathering by the hundreds at the Stamford Museum of Art. There was a painting there that was changing, adapting. She heard the name Jared Rowland and knew exactly what it meant.

"Sheila," said Mickey.

She switched off the set and turned towards him. He was wet, with a dulled-from-age white towel wrapped around his waste.

"I'm late," he said through a smile.

"What else is new." She poked at his ribs with a long green acrylic nail.

8

I

The grand hall of Union Station feels like the lobby leading to a time machine. Amtrak should be embarrassed to run its trains, late and putrid, into such a temple. I cross the hall for the bus portals. I find the Megabus's dock and then the bus labeled for St. Louis. It is going to be a full bus. Soldiers with green duffles thrown over-shoulder stand huddled and austere. They look tired. A short three-tone jingle plays before announcements on the loudspeaker, and each time I see a burst of orange and blue loft across the vaulted ceilings. I wonder if the soldiers are coming form Iraq, going to Afghanistan, or maybe just heading to some Southern base where they will practice dentistry. They are short and tired. In my mind they should be tall and vital. An old woman picks at her tooth with a plastic toothpick in the shape of a sword. Her hair is bluish and permed.

The Megabus is a double-decker. I want to be up top so that I can watch the plains unfold across Southern Illinois and think about nothing. Not Sue. Not Missy. Not Dad. Not

Mom. Not Adam. Not Eve. Not the band. Not the college degree I never finished. Not the war I drunkenly decided the night before I should have gone to fight. Nothing but the empty plains and their unfathomable history. Land is a mantra. A brain can only generate silence when it is confronted with horizons bending towards their endless spherical destinations.

I climb the stairs to level two and find a seat near the back. The old woman with the toothpick is heading my way. She looks like a dictator's wife. She takes the seat beside me without looking in my direction. The toothpick, shaped like a sword, protrudes from between her teeth. She takes it out, folds it into a plastic bag, and deposits it in her purse which she then stows between her feet.

She looks at me like an analysts, eyes squinted, mouth slightly ajar. After a moment she nods and looks forward again, apparently having decided that I meet her approval.

I nod in return.

I awake next to the soldier. His head has fallen on my shoulder. He is a prodigious drooler. I nudge him a bit and he shifts towards the other side. The old woman is in a seat by herself towards the back. I do not know when she moved.

I look at my phone to see if Missy has texted. Nothing. I see the moon outside of the bus. Today is nearly full. It must be waxing.

I try to adjust my shoulder, disturbing the soldier's head from its position nestled against me. He rustles in his place, licks his lips and opens his eyes catching a glimpse of the moon in the early evening sky.

"Beautiful," he says.

I think of how Missy might respond.

"Harvest moon," he says.

"Almost," I say though I have no idea why. I do not know the difference between a harvest moon and Warren Moon.

"I haven't seen one like that in a while."

"You've been away?"

"Yeah." He lets it linger. "Not Iraq or nothing, but overseas."

"Oh?"

"Spain," he says. "Cadiz. Sun never goes down over there, so you never have to worry about the moon."

"Never?"

"It gets dark late."

"You going back?"

"Hope so."

"What about Iraq?"

"Hope not."

That ends that portion of the conversation. The only subject everyone wants to know about is the one subject no soldier wants to talk about.

"What are you doing out this way?"

"Going home. Catching up with the family."

"You have a big family?" Stupid question. The phrase 'thank you for your service' flits through my mind over and over again.

He smiles. "Big enough. You?"

"Not really. A brother." I cannot bring myself to say sister. "He lives in St. Louis. That's why I'm going." I try to think of something—anything—to say, but I cannot and he shuts his eyes again.

It is completely dark outside of the windows now. When I try to look out I just see back in.

The bus pulls in at midnight.

The soldier wakes up slowly, at first it seems like he might not know where he is.

"We're here," I tell him.

"Home sweet home," he says through a yawn. "You got a ride?"

"Nah," I say. "I'm heading to meet my brother at his work."

"Where's that?"

"The Nile. Jazz club down by the river."

"I know it," he says with a smile that indicates he knows it well. "Let me come along. I'll pick up the cab. You get the first round."

I nod.

"My mom's place is down there. She works the river boats and won't be off until late. Rather get a drink than sit by myself watching the news until I wish I was in Iraq."

I nod again. "Deal." Eve will be singing until at least 2 anyway. I could use the company.

"Mickey," he says extending a hand.

"Tommy," I say extending one in his direction.

"Like the Rock Opera?"

"I guess."

"Cool. I love the Who."

I'm more a T-Rex, or Roxie Music kind of guy, but I don't want to make waves. "Me too."

When we step off of the bus, I notice how short he is again. He has a short man's confidence. His chest juts out, the horizontal push attempting to make up for the vertical limitation. His hair is a little too long for a soldier's, but just slightly. His eyes light up with his first breath of St. Louis air. I get the impression that he has seen a lot of nights out in this town.

He wants to stop at his apartment before we go to the bar. He wants to change out of his soldier duds and into something comfortable.

"Take us to the riverfront. You know Judy's?" He asks the cabbie.

"Yessir," says the cabbie.

The seats are leather. There is no air-conditioning. My ass is itchy with sweat. The windows are rolled down, but the humid St. Louis air almost makes it worse, like standing in front of a blow dryer.

Mickey's house is right by the river. We exit the cab on a cobblestone road that smells like the Mississippi. The first floor of the building houses a bar called Judy's. We go up the stairs of the three-flat to his place on the top floor. He pushes keys into what an inordinate number of locks. "St. Louis," is all he says in way of explanation.

The walls are painted a deep red. The carpet is covered in intricate Celtic patterns. There are multiple suits of armor leaning against the walls. Swords and shields are mounted around the apartment. The coffee table is a massive Chestnut tablet with more celtic patterns gracing the intricate, carved legs. The couch is a red velvet material with bent wooden feet. There is a harp in the corner of the room. I realize that I have never seen a harp in person before. The only thing that seems to steal from the eerie medieval vibe is a 46 inch plasma screen mounted on the wall.

Mickey notices me staring. "Trippy, right?" he says.

"Jesus," is all I can respond.

The windows should look out over the river, but they are all mirrored to reflect back into the house. There are keyed locks on every door and window.

"My mom's a bit of a collector," he offers in way of explanation.

I guess.

He flips on the plasma screen and heads back to what I presume is his room.

CNN. A bridge has collapsed up the Mississippi. 16 cars were swept into the river. I wonder if they will make it as far South as St. Louis. Detroit is in trouble. Lay-offs at all the major car factories. The painting in Tulsa is drawing ever larger crowds. A team of scientists is investigating the slowly changing patterns to no avail. The latest theory is that it's some sort of nanotech.

When he comes back he is a different person. Well-fit black jeans ride low on his waist. A plain white T-shirt reveals arms covered in tattoos. A cardinals cap, soft with age sits where his army cap had.

"Ready?"

I nod.

The Nile is only a couple blocks away. We go out of our way to walk along the river. I look out into the middle trying to spot a car floating down from the collapsed bridge in Minneapolis. How far away is Minneapolis? How fast does the river flow? How long would it take for them to get here? Would they be fished out somewhere upstream?

The moon reflects off of the river and illuminates the string of stagnant riverboats that take advantage of the more limber maritime regulations on gambling. I think of Mark Twain captaining one of these riverboats. I think of Mark Twain and his character's Huck and Jim all riding the riverboat together, but this time fighting the tide to the North instead of just floating towards the South, being passed by a string of floating cars, their passengers struggling for air as they head towards the gulf. But not just 16 cars, hundreds. Cars pumped straight from the factories into the river, automotive workers with massive oars steering them South for no apparent reason.

The Nile doesn't have any windows, and the solid black door is closed. Mickey knocks and a giant of a man in a tuxedo opens the door. He looks at me, then at Mickey, then gives a nod.

"How's the old lady, Mick?"

"Same as ever, Buddah" he says to the hulking brow that hovers over this massive body.

I hear Eve singing as soon as we open the door. Her voice is like a layered chocolate cake: rich, sweet, overwhelming. It is the sound that let me sleep when we first left Oklahoma. It is the sound that made the dark contents of closets and the gaping space beneath my mattress bearable when I was a kid. He would sing me to sleep every night, nails running gently down my spine. He would sing Etta James, Ella Fitzgerald, Nina Simone, or maybe Chet Baker, or Bob Dylan.

It is Edith Piaf as we enter the Nile. I try to ignore the cold blues and grays that bank off the walls and back towards the stage, filling the space with heavy clouds of color. She sings L'Etranger. I close my eyes for a moment to keep the moody palette at bay. Another man, bearded and bear-ish, but slightly smaller than Buddah, leads us to a table behind a red velvet cord. An ice bucket and a bottle of champagne are brought out without us placing an order. The waitress who places them next to our table is thin and serious. She has the fingers of a piano player and the expression of a nun. I am scared as I recall our arrangement that Mickey would pay the taxi and I would pay the first round.

"Mickey, I don't..."

"Shhhh..." he says, pointing to my sister, then to the bucket, then waving a finger in a way that indicates payment does not matter. She hits a high note and a bright blue bolt shoots for the ceiling.

"So that's your sis?"

I think I remember telling him it was my brother I was coming to see. But, now I am doubting myself. "Yeah."

"Small fucking world."

"You know her?"

"You could say that."

"Well..."

"We're acquainted," he says smiling.

The room is completely wooden. The floors, walls, bar, booths, all made from the same aged and polished Oak. It reminds me a little of the diner from the night before. I wonder if Al Capone ever spent time in St. Louis. The only parts of the room that differ from the polished brown are the deep black shine of the piano, and the crystalline shimmer of the many-colored bottles behind the bar, and the mirror they rest in front of. The bartender is in a tuxedo, as are the waiters and the pianist. Eve, who was tall as a man, is a giant of a woman. She is wearing a long black-sequinned dress, towering above the crowd from her perch on the bar. The microphone chord hangs down from her wrist and traces a path back to the stage. She has not looked in our direction once since we arrived.

The crowd pays attention, which in the world of jazz is the highest compliment there is. The fear of a jazz musician is to fade into the background, to become white noise. It is like forcing a classically trained painter to hang billboards. This crowd has their eyes locked on the imposing figure with its mysterious, nuanced voice. Her voice has a depth that is decidedly feminine. Her neckline is smooth and womanly, the curvature of her body, always awkward as a boy, suits her perfectly now. Her hair is dark and natural. It falls over her face, parts above the eyes and hugs her chin. She wore it shaggy as a boy.

There are a couple of Japanese business men getting drunk at a far booth. They sway to the music between shots of Johnny Walker White Label. Mickey pours us each a glass from the bottle of champagne and we toast. I do not want to drink, but it feels rude not to.

When Eve's set is finished she walks towards us. She slides into the booth next to me and pours herself a glass.

"So you found him," she says looking at Mickey.

He looks at me and shrugs.

I am deeply confused.

"Sorry to send you an escort, Tommy, but you can never be too careful."

"Careful?"

"I'll explain later," she says before taking down a glass in one gulp. "First," she puts a finger on my shoulder and stares straight into my eyes.

I evade her gaze, looking instead at Tommy. "Are you even a soldier?" I ask.

"Was." He looks at my sister and I can tell now that they are lovers. I wonder if he knows. He must know.

"And your mom...?"

"Is indeed working the river boats, so to speak."

"So to speak..."

"She runs a couple, you could say."

"You could say," I repeat him.

"You could say that, yes."

I feel dizzy. I drink. It has been a strange couple of days. Mickey lights a cigarette and offers me one. I do not smoke. Something Eve taught me. If you want to have a singing voice that lasts, never smoke.

"How do you feel about a duet?" Eve asks me.

I stare at her. "Maybe later." I grab her hand. "What the hell is going on?"

"I have to get back up there, Tommy." She pulls her hand away. "Mickey will take care of you." She walks back to the stage to the muted applause of everyone in the room but me.

As the piano begins playing "Lilac Wine," Eve walks slowly to the stage and lets the first syllables sneak past her lips. Mickey watches her move like a cat focussed on a moth. He pours the end of the champagne into his glass, then the contents of the glass into his mouth. "She's gonna be a while. You wanna take a walk?" he asks.

I want to know what the hell is going on. I give him an impatient look which he seems to understand.

"C-c'mon," he says as he stands and heads towards the door.

We pass the big bear near the bar and the big Buddha at the door. The words "Like my love" flow from Eve's diaphragm filling the the room with a thick blanket of violet sound that dissipates from my field of vision like a clearing fog as the door slams shut behind us.

The air, even past midnight, is unbearably heavy with humidity. We walk towards the river. I have given up on spotting any of the cars from up North. I see the arch in the distance, like a monotone rainbow.

"What the fuck, Mickey?"

He is looking across to the faint glow of East St. Louis. "I think it's best to let Eve explain."

"Seeing as she's not here, why don't you throw me a bone."

"Honestly, all I know is that it's about your stepmom."

"What's about her?"

"Listen. A couple days ago Eve gets a call. She's upset, but not too upset, you know? I mean, Eve wasn't too close to the family, as I gather you aren't either."

How observant.

"But a few hours later, a letter shows up in the mailbox."

"And...?"

"And... It's from Sue."

"And...?"

"And... you need to hear the rest from Eve."

"What did it say? What was it about?"

"Listen, Tommy, all I know is that Eve got a letter, flipped out and put me on a bus to Chicago to find you."

I believe him for some reason. "How the hell did you find me?"

He pulls a picture of me from his wallet. My address is written on the back. "I got lucky. You were leaving your house right when I showed up. I followed you to the pawn shop, then right back to the bus station where I came from."

"Why didn't you tell me who you were?"

"I don't know. I didn't want to freak you out."

"This is how you go about not freaking someone out?"

"I see your point."

I take as deep a breath as the thick air allows. "So, you were really a soldier?"

"It's a long story, that."

There is a small barge moving slowly down the center of the river. "We don't seem to be in a hurry."

"True." He pulls out a cigarette, lights it with a match and throws the match into the river. "I had some problems as a kid, you could say. Fell in with the wrong crowd, y-ya know?" There is a gush of shouting from one of the riverboats. Someone must have won big. "I was selling drugs. Doing some. Stealing. I did just about anything for money." He opens his eyes wide and looks straight at me, challenging me to push his statement to its logical conclusion.

I understand.

"So the day came, as it always does if you go that path, that I was standing in front of a judge. Same old choices for a kid like me, jail or army." He throws a cigarette into the river and lights another one. "I was never in Iraq or Afghanistan. I did communications. I was stationed in Germany, near Dortmund. It was a pretty sweet gig, really. We got to go to the bars once in a while. The countryside was beautiful. I wasn't in a war zone."

"So why leave?"

"They decided I should head for a war zone. I felt differently. I hopped a train to Spain. Holed up in a cheap hostel in Cadiz. I didn't have much cash, so it wasn't long before I was up to the same old tricks. Selling what I had to sell." He held his arms out to his sides and looked himself up and down. "One night about 3 am I'm standing in a plaza in Cadiz, Plaza San Francisco, waiting on some horny middle-aged husband to come by so that by the time the sun comes up I can afford some breakfast. I hear this voice coming out of a bar. It's Ella Fitzgerald's 'You Won't be Satisfied until you Break my Heart.'" He hums a few bars with his eyes closed. I can't explain it, I'm just drawn in."

I try to think if I've ever known a prostitute before.

"I wander towards the bar. I'm thinking I might try and sneak in for a song or two. I'm from St. Louis after all. I love me some blues, jazz, big band. My mom's a freak for the old stuff. I grew up with it. So, I stroll in. It's one of those European bars that's in a basement cave. You go down a twisting stone stairway to get in. I sit at the bar and order a drink. I figure I can run when I finish, so I have a few even though I'm broke. Her voice feels like home, you know. I just get lost like I haven't in years. I'm downing pitchers of Sangria and bobbing to the tunes. Dinah Washington, Ella, Etta, she's running through the classics, and I don't know if I want to laugh or cry, and if I cried I wouldn't have known if it was from happiness or sadness, if I laughed if it was from joy or madness, you know? Lost. That music brought me home in a way I hadn't been home since I was five, laying on a carpet in my mom's living room while she played records. Then she caught my eye. I swear she was singing to me, right? She even gave me a little wink. After an hour or so, and a few pitchers, her set ends. I'm the only customer left in the bar which was close to empty in the first place. I'm lit, and I have zero cash, remember. She walks off the stage. The bartender tells me what I owe, and I run, only, I'm so drunk I trip after a couple steps. Crack. I just remember a flash. I was out."

"And then...?"

He looks out at the moon over the river and adjusts his cardinals cap. I wonder where Missy might be. "And then... I don't really know. I woke up in your sisters hotel with a nasty headache. She sang at that bar for a month. I stayed in her hotel. After a month she worked a cruise ship. I stowed away in her room. We went everywhere, man. Six months. She eventually got me a job working a craps table in the ship's casino. They didn't want paperwork. They were used to shady fuckers."

"And now?"

"And now I avoid the police very carefully, so as not to spend a very long time in the brig."

9

They

She looked at his closed eyes as he slept. His eyelids bounced as his pupils slid back and forth beneath them, the engine of some dream she couldn't access. She could never access his dreams, not even when they were awake and she asked him. He had all the money in the world. She couldn't understand why instead of retiring to some Mediterranean or Caribbean paradise, they festered in Oklahoma City trying to attain ever-increasing influence. For what? What was left to influence? She loved Will, but Karen Jenkins hated Oklahoma. It was backwards in all the wrong ways. Sure it was clean, quiet, respectful in its attempts to achieve some nostalgic sense of gentility, but that very place that it aimed to imitate never existed, and what pieces of it had existed were largely built upon oppression. Oklahoma was Indian land where the Cherokee had been slave holders over the African population, until the Irish, Italian, Polish and Czech to name a few pushed out the Indians and created their own systems of treading on whomsoever they were permitted to tread. And, their current sense of the world was based almost entirely on a dismissal of reality. Global warming was just the "scientists" trying to subvert the Capitalist order and empower some cabal of Leninist environmentalists. Their embrace of the "right to work" basically meant denying the right to wages that were inline with neighbouring states. And the guns! What was it with these rednecks and their god damned guns? As if anyone wanted to steal their broken down firebirds and collections of crystals.

The people were large and the most booming business, outside of fracking, seemed to be private hospitals that leached off of the rampant substance abuse, over-eating and complete abandon of exercise. And, about that fracking... It had produced thousands of earthquakes where there had been practically none, and yet again science was met with flat out denial by the very people who stood to lose the most through their proliferation. Earthquakes were like tornados: unaccountable acts of God more likely to have been visited as a response to homosexuality than because of some material reaction of the Earth against having pressurized water pounded into the mantle, putting the ground beneath our feet on roller skates.

Then there were the churches... They were unbearable with names like "Tough" and "Bolts." Their signs pandered to the most profound irrationalities on a daily basis. "Jesus stands for safe borders." "God wants you to keep your home safe at any cost." Karen grew up in the Catholic Church, which down here basically meant she was a Jihadist. Every Sunday she went to St. Thomas's in downtown Tulsa with her mother, her father, her brother and her grandmother and listened to the sermon as she fumbled through the endless routine of sitting, standing, and humming along pretending to remember the script. As an adult, she acted as though she had never really internalized it, and it is true that she had largely thrown it off over the years as is the custom with Catholics. But, briefly, as a little girl, it had all been very real to her.

She stared up at the bearded, long-haired, white bodied man, malnourished and bleeding from his torso and she thought he looked like some of the men in her neighbourhood, the ones who hung around smoking cigarettes near the veterans hall. He did not look like her father. That was clear. Her father had dark brown skin, and he was portly. Always clean-shaven and well-fed.

The priest at their church was a thin, mixed-race man who spoke in crisp, bland sentences at the alter, but came to life after mass, particularly with the black congregants, who he seemed to feel a particular responsibility to bring into the fold.

It had not been on purpose, really. At least she did not think it had. Her father had friends over every Sunday after church. They drank whiskey, listened to records, ate barbecue. One of her father's friends, an English professor at Tulsa University, had butted into a conversation about Robert Johnson and the myth that he had sold his soul to the devil.

"That story has a long tradition behind it," he said. "Nothing new for Mr. Johnson I'm afraid." He stubbed out his cigar. "The crossroads has goes way back, Greece, the bible, Faust…"

"So what?" asked another of her father's friends.

"Well, so it was just good marketing. Johnson took a story that he knew had a proven track record, and he made it his."

Karen was not convinced. If the story had been told over and over and over, well, maybe that meant that it *was* true, that it had to be in one way or another, and that somehow people had been selling their souls for a very long time.

Her soul, she imagined, could not be worth very much. Fortunately, what she wanted more than anything in the world was not that lofty: The violin solo in the youth orchestra. She did not remember a particular moment when she offered her soul. It was more a thought that picked and picked at the edges of her consciousness until it was a full blown obsession. She reminded herself over and over again that she must not under any circumstances allow her soul to be sold. She prayed incessantly under her breath when she was out of sight of her classmates or family. As she practiced the violin she let the words of the Hail Mary flow forth with the movements of the bow. She barely slept as she knew she must maintain vigilance against the unspoken offer to purchase her most valuable possession.

And then, the orchestras director made her the offer. The solo, he said, was hers if she wanted it. Then she knew that it was happening. She could not say no, but saying yes was tantamount to admitting that the transaction was complete.

She collapsed into a thirteen-year-old neurotic disaster, unable to focus on school, unable to practice her solo, unable to admit to anyone that she was no longer a human being, but merely a soulless vessel traversing the Earth until her days would unceremoniously come to an end.

Because she was unable to practice, the solo was a disaster, a complete and total embarrassment, which only made the injury of the lost soul that much more intense. She had sold her most prized possession and had not, like Robert Johnson, become a virtuoso. She had not bargained to be the greatest living violinist, or even a good one, not even to play the solo successfully! She had merely asked to be given the solo. It was the last time that she played the violin.

The following Sunday she asked her mother if she could confess. She had only done so once before, at her confirmation.

"Of course, baby!" Said her mother, scarcely concealing her excitement.

Her father looked on proudly as if she was making the first mature decision of what was bound to be a long, upstanding life.

Inside the confessional it was dark, and smelled sweet and smokey.

"Forgive me father for I have sinned," she said, remembering her instruction from the course a year earlier. The phrase felt grand in an unnatural way, especially spoken to this man who had been so kind to them, so open.

"What is it my child?"

My child she thought. How strange! What was it about this room that converted the relationship of this man, this family friend who performed for them each Sunday, into that of father and daughter? Her eyes, red and throbbing, let loose the slow drip of all her corralled frustration. The months of sleeplessness and compulsion poured down her cheeks in warm, comforting stream or mucous and salty tears. "I… sold my soul."

After a brief moment of silence, the priest let out a single syllable of explosive laughter. "Well… How? Why, I mean, can you possibly think that?"

"I wanted the solo in the orchestra, and, I don't know how it happened, it just did…"

"No," he said with an assured force. "You did not."

"I…"

"Your soul my dear, is not some saleable good. It is not a material possession that you have the capacity to trade away. It can be lost, dear, don't get me wrong. But, it takes time to lose one's soul. It happens little by little and no one hands you a check. And you, darling, you have nothing to worry about."

She thought about that moment all of the time. As she looked into the eyes of her Will, she wondered exactly when and where they had lost course, exactly when and where they had forgotten why it was they did what they did. She wondered if she had finally, thirty years later, sold off what she had managed to salvage as a little girl.

10

I

The boat is still bathed in light after 2 am. Loud chatter spills from the casino. The cacophony of voices blends into the byzantine array of lights and patterns. To me, it all looks like a paisley cornfield that I will have to wade through. People's faces, shrouded in indifference as they feed machines like sentient robots, pop up like individual stalks in the sea of corn. The bright lights and clanking metallic sounds makes me feel like the projectile in a pinball machine. The places we choose to occupy end up occupying us. A dense cloud of smoke hovers above the heads of seated gamblers. The waiters struggle to keep the ashtrays from overflowing. There is no music other than the ceaseless orchestra of coins falling, levers pulling, bells ringing, and people groaning in frustration and ecstasy.

Mickey leads me past security, down a long hallway lined with electric fixtures that are designed to look like candle-holders. We approach a door marked with the number 47. A sign to the right of the door reads, *Mme. Trouché.*

"Mom," says Mickey as he pushes the door open.

"Mik," says a short, dense figure with a jet black bob. Her face is mostly jowls like a basset hound with the bloodshot eyes to match. "Have you come to play, or to molest your dear mother as she tries to accomplish all of the many objectives that she..." she looks up and notices that her son is not alone. "...You have brought me something fresh, I see." She extends a small well-manicured hand. "Charmed."

"Hello miss Trouche," I say. I pronounce it 'troosh'.

"Trouché," she corrects me with the subtlety of a Southern Aristocrat. "I've been trying to get them to add the accent to the sign outside for years. And it's Madame around here. I have to keep the order somehow and find confusing the underlings with an heir of the foreign goes some distance to doing so."

I nod.

"So, you must be the long lost brother of our siren."

"I haven't been so long lost, or lost at all really. Just in Chicago."

"Oh, dear me, never has a city been more lost than Chicago. This is the midwest, my dear boy, and Chicago is pretending to thrive. Look about you, when all your friends are derelicts and you are rich, you might just be a dealer in something unsavory. Detroit, St. Louis, Cleveland, Milwaukee, who has been leading them astray? Chicago, I say, is the most likely candidate. North or South?"

"North."

"For god's sakes don't tell me you're a Cubs fan. There is nothing more pathetic than a Cub's fan."

"Actually, I don't really like baseball." Hillbilly Cricket, I think.

"I stand corrected. Absolutely un-American, this one," she says looking at Mickey, "and this from a woman who calls herself Madame." She looks me over with the eyes of a disapproving great-Aunt. "I was sorry to hear about your Step-mother, what was her name, Sue?"

"Yes, and thank you. We weren't close."

"Nonetheless, these are road marks. Births, deaths, they remind us that time is the material of life. Close or otherwise the death of family—and the partner of your father is certainly that—matters. Death stops the daydreams of its onlookers and forces them to recognize the air they breathe is made of something more than their own convoluted egos."

There's a knock at the door.

"Enter if you pleeeeeze," says Mme. Trouché.

Buddha opens the door and lets Eve pass. She is wearing sunglasses and a shawl. She could use a shave. Buddha bows his head and retires to a corner. Eve takes off her glasses to reveal grey-green eyes.

Eve smiles at me. It's the smile I have always known. It could convince a nun to go on a coke binge. "Tommy," she says. "I can't believe you're here."

Neither can I for that matter.

Mme. Trouché points towards the door. "We should leave you two."

Buddha and Mickey take her advice, and shuffle out into the hallway. Mme. Trouché follows suit, shutting the door behind her.

Eve has no problem maintaining eye contact. I wish I could say the same for myself. I survey the room. There is none of the medieval pageantry of the apartment from earlier. Her desk is a dark, solid wood. The walls are painted a purple so light it is almost white. The floor is polished concrete.

She reaches a hand halfway to my shoulder. "It's been too long, kiddo."

I nod.

"We should get together under normal circumstances sometime."

"I'm not sure I know what normal circumstances are." These last couple days feel like they are happening around me rather than a series of events the unfolding of which I am a part of. I feel more like a spectator than a participant.

"So, I imagine Mickey told you about the letter." She squints just with her left eye. She has always done that.

I nod.

She reaches into her purse, pulls out an envelope and hands it to me.

I hold the envelope, ripped open along the top edge, in my hand.

"Well, are you gonna read it?"

"Now?"

"Now. And ignore the Adam. Sue refused to… well, you know."

I nod.

> *Dear Adam,*
>
> *I often wonder if you will miss me when I'm gone. I can tell you now that if missing is possible from wherever I am, that I am missing you and your sister both. You probably don't believe that, but it is true. The time for reconciliations is unfortunately past, and now all that remains to be said about my time is that it is short, so I will try to keep this sweet and to the point.*
>
> *This all goes back farther than you or I and involves your family in ways you wouldn't begin to imagine. I wouldn't have imagined it, not until a few months ago when I found the correspondences that are likely to seal my fate. Correspondences your mother had kept for years.*

Mulroney Flanders, my boss, as you know, is a powerful man. Over the past years his little newspaper's reach has grown from Tulsa all across the nation. Now he owns television stations, magazines and newspapers from coast to coast, and he is buying beyond our shores. His father owned the Tulsa Tribune, and his father before him. Misinformation has been a family legacy. The Flanders' feed on ignorance, chaos, division. It's their lifeblood. I'm sorry to have aided them in the distribution of lies for so many years. Work is sparse in the reporting field, and a lot of us sacrifice standards to keep jobs. I know it is not a good excuse, but maybe it is a valid explanation of why the world you inherit confronts a crisis of information in an age that should make our work more precise. But, this is not meant to be my last confession, and I digress...

The world being the world, and more importantly, Tulsa being Tulsa, that legacy of misinformation has been paid for by close connections to oil. The Flanders, and the media empire they are building subside on agreements with the local money and political power, and in this town, hell, in this state, and more to the point, on this planet, that money and power comes from petroleum.

We have to go back 90 years. In 1921 some of the worst racial violence this country had seen since the civil war exploded in Tulsa. The Tulsa Tribune reported the story that apparently ignited the spark. No record of that story remains. Within days of the event itself all copies had been destroyed. Many, many readers, however, attest that it existed. It was a call to the lynching of a young man who was accused of rape. Even the Tulsa

Sheriff, not a man known for his sensitivity, said the charge was thin.

The money behind the Tulsa Tribune largely came from Willard Stamford, the tycoon who first began Stamford Oil. He was no tycoon then, but an upstart whose biggest challenger was an older man, a black man named Eldridge Fairmont who owned half of Tulsa. Stamford was Flanders' best friend. Willard Stamford III, as you may be aware is a three-term congressmen who is in the midst of a campaign to become Governor of Oklahoma. He has transferred his shares in Stamford oil, a company that is likely to be refining the lion's share of iraqi crude, to his children.

The violence that issued from the riots destroyed Greenwood, which was the most affluent black neighborhood not only in Tulsa, but in the country at the time. Eldridge Faimont, and most of the residents of Greenwood lost everything. Most fled to Northern cities to begin again. Stamford lost his only real competition, and it was only then that his little Oklahoma operation began its march to national and later global dominance.

The event itself has been ignored in American History, in part thanks to the efforts of the Tulsa Tribune. Those who remember it, remember it as the explosion of a powder keg, a random outbreak of violence that had been resting under the surface. It should be remembered as the systematic destruction of a thriving black community by white citizens aided by the national guard. The black neighborhoods were blocked off making escape impossible as the government provided white militias with planes that were used to fire bomb the stranded people from above.

Your mother, as you know, was writing her dissertation about your grandfather, the artist Jared Rowland. Jared was the son of Dick Rowland, the young man who the mob sought to lynch. Jared's mother, your great grandmother, was pregnant with him during the riots. Jared's work sought to memorialize the events of 1921. In the course of her writing, your mother found documents that proved a conspiracy between Willard Stamford I and Muroney Flanders. The riots were designed to destroy Fairmont and make room for Stamford. As you can imagine, this information, which incriminates the patriarchs of two wealthy families, would be a serious indictment of the legitimacy of immense fortunes. Your mother was killed, 80 years after the fact, because she knew this. Also, Tommy, I know this makes no sense, but your mother was convinced that Mulroney Flanders is still alive. I have also become convinced. I can't explain it, but I have seen him… I have seen him in my sleep, but it is more than just a dream. He is dangerous, Tommy. He has to be stopped. You have to stop him.

I have enclosed letters that will help you understand how you are involved. I wish that I could be of more help, but I fear this is the end of my participation in this investigation. Break it wide open for me.

All my love,

Sue

I don't know what to think. I am no detective. No journalist. "What now?" is all I can think to say, and I say it more to myself than to Eve.

"What now?" Eve repeats more to the room than to me or even herself.

"Did you tell someone?"

"Like who?"

"Like who? Like the police?"

"Sue was a reporter. She was afraid to go to the police."

I scratch hard at the crevice on the inside of my elbow. I need a shower. I have not showered in altogether too long.

"What the hell, Eve?"

She looks towards the corner of the room and says nothing.

"She mentioned letters. Where are they?"

Eve smiles. "Sue left them in a locker at the bus station."

I chuckle. "That's Sue."

"Did you read them?"

"Not yet."

"And..."

"And, I don't know..."

There's a knock.

"Sorry kids, I'm gonna need my office for a few," shouts Madame Trouché through the thick wooden door.

"Does she know?" I ask Eve.

She nods.

Madame Trouché walks in. Her jowls jiggle as she moves towards her desk. "So we're all up to date," she asks me without looking.

"I guess..." I answer.

"How, you must be asking yourself, as I know that I would be should the circumstances find themselves in a state of reversal, can this beautiful southern belle of a woman, the one, the only, Mademe Trouché, be inculcated into this mess?"

"Well, I hadn't..."

"Allow me to put your anxious mind at ease then, boy."

I nod.

"I'm a lover of truth and fine publications, and as such a natural enemy to the supposedly late great Mulroney Flanders. His drivel is working hard to destroy generations of hard work deployed in the interest of creating a media that was free to speak its truth and equipped to do so to the best of its ability. As to Stamford, I just don't like him. Sonnofabitch goes on TV claiming the bible knows more about the current state of the atmosphere than a scientist. He's a sycophant. A true believer in whatever ideological sludge they happen to be drumming up because that sludge more often than not is aiming at drumming up the literal sludge that makes him a rich man. I am a deeply Christian woman, and I go to the bible for many things, but when it comes to measuring CO2 in the air I breathe I'll go for more recent publications. It's an existential matter, isn't it? The man lacks sense, and if it ain't sense he lacks, it's ethics, either way, he is unfit. Those reasons would be enough to help you. But, I have yet another, more immediate."

She slaps a paper down onto the desk in front of her. It's a copy of the St. Louis dispatch. The headline reads "Gambling Boats Immoral?"

"The answer they arrive at is a decided yes. Mr. Flanders recently bought this paper and they've been on my ass since day one. Any chance to take a shot at that waste of skin is a welcome one. You just tell me what you need."

Take a shot at? What we need? What the hell could we possibly need? I'm on my way to a funeral. I stopped to see my brother. That's the end of it, no?

"I'll tell you this much, if I know them, they already know you're here gunn'n for 'em. They sure as hell know 'bout that letter."

How? How could they possibly? Gunn'n for 'em? For who?

There's a knock at the door. Buddha looks cautious. I notice for the first time how inhumanly deep the ridge of his brow is. This is the first time I've understood the descriptor Cro-Magnon. He puts a bulky mitt on the knob. "Yes." His voice is surprisingly soft.

"Madame Trouché has visitors in the lobby," comes a voice that could belong to another century's butler.

"What do they look like?" asks Buddha.

"Blue uniforms and pentagonal hats," comes the response.

"I planned to make a dramatic departure this evening. You all, I imagine, did not. Alas, the unexpected spices up yet another evening here at the Queen Mary. Buddha, show them out the back way."

I fear what the back way out of a boat may be.

Buddha pulls a book shelf away from the wall and reveals a narrow passageway. I wonder how Buddha is going to fit through it, but he does so with little effort. He must have the collapsable skeleton of a rat. He lights a flashlight and leads us through the narrow space. After a few minutes I hear casino noises on both sides. Eve puts her hand on my shoulder and squeezes. The best kind of shudder runs down my back.

"You okay, kid?" she asks.

"Okay considering." Considering that I'm apparently escaping the police by sliding through a secret tunnel in a riverboat casino.

Mickey is in front of me. His boots grind dirt against the bare wood floor.

We come to a door at the end of the passage and Buddha puts a finger to his lips. "Shhhh," he says, before he cuts the flashlight. When he opens the door the light from the full moon streams in. We are just a foot or so above the water level.

He pulls a yellow square from where it is mounted against the wall and steps outside.

There is a sharp sound like a gas hose has been cut and the little yellow square becomes a big yellow raft, which he tosses into the water and holds tightly in place with his foot. Mickey grabs two ores from inside and we all, all except Buddha that is, jump into the raft.

That disarming soft voice again, "You know what to do?"

"I know what to do," says Mickey.

I wish I could say the same.

11

I

When I rock, I rock. It was a good show. I do not say that about many of my own shows. That one was special. New Year's Eve, 1999. I don't think I believed the world was set to end, but I sure wasn't as convinced as I let on by rolling my eyes at everyone who mentioned it. There was a low-grade anxiety constantly with me that night. An adrenaline that wasn't totally native to the New Year's festivities. That was my first year out of high school. I knew nothing. I didn't yet know that there would be someone saying that every year was the end of the world. I hadn't, obviously, lived through September of 2001 and its endless aftermath. I hadn't heard of the Aztec predictions, or the crazy minister from California. Global Warming was a threat, but not so much a fact of life being blamed for the expanding power of hurricanes, the growing number of tornadoes, the increased devastation of tsunamis, the absurd proliferation of Earthquakes taking people out in numbers that had been reserved for medieval plagues. None of that was part of my world yet. Well, there was Heaven's Gate, Plano,

TX, Oklahoma City, Columbine. Those almost seem quaint now. I know that must be an optical allusion, an equation that does not take into account time as it exists from my particular perspective, maturity, etc... But, still, in a pre-global world, whatever the hell that doublespeak means, crises were also more local. A terrorist was just that, a terrorist who required an investigation, not an impetus to restrict the global flow of people and the civil rights of citizens across the world. Messed up kids were messed up kids, who we all knew had been failed, but also taught us something about how we could NEVER, NEVER, fail like that again. Now they are forces of nature, enemies that cannot be deterred and so must be met with full force at all times. Now my consciousness is so overflowing with threats, that I do not even take the serious ones seriously. But in 1999 I still hadn't lost the ability to fear the end. The music made the fear go away. My favorite teacher in high school religion class taught us a little Nietzsche. The Birth of Tragedy. I found the bacchanalian flow and rode it to forgetfulness. Not a forgetfulness of the world, but of my mind's insistence that it was the world. I wanted to ride the undercurrent which is impossible to do without forgetting yourself. The undercurrent does not care about your self. It cares about selves in relation. That is what music is when it is done right. Selves in relation. It helped that I could see the way the music traversed the room, waves and bursts of color flowing and pulsing through the crowd. I could see the music like a sea swashing over the dance floor, pounding against the walls of the club as if they were the Cliffs of Dover and reverberating like back across the room. It was physical as it touched each audience member, brought them into a shared emotional space. This was the undercurrent, the recognition that the limits of the body were just an illusion. We were all connected, physically connected, by the waves that traversed space as if there were telephone wires from one person to the next, connecting them though their eyes and ears, through their noses and skin. I could see the crowd swimming in the music. We were all one organism. I read later that Nietzsche did not like that work as he got older. Well, I still like it. Though, I understand growing out of the ability to live it. I am barely 30 now and I know it has become harder to be an undulation in front of a crowd. I approach music more academically now. I understand the physical reactions, the vibrations of strings, the effects of different tones in creating tension and allowing fulfilment, the architecture of experience. Most artists lose their magic as they increase their proficiency. Not all of them though. Some of them can keep the childish energy in their work even as they develop their mastery. An artist needs to heighten perceptions and talents without losing sight of the reasons that led to creation in the first place. It is a balance between structure and whatever swarming, chaotic stew that structure emerges from. You immerse yourself in a world even as you acknowledge that the world is a construction, a composition, a piece of music, lovingly manipulated from the strange alienated perspective that each of us, each member of the orchestra, calls home. We are all inside and outside, endlessly forgetting which we prefer, which we should cling to, which we should shun, which gives us power, and which draws the power from us. We are protectionists, and we are interventionists. We hide our poems in drawers, and we paint masterpieces that end wars. We write songs that lay bare the tenor of a lonely soul as they pour over airwaves in dozens of nations, and we sing in the shower about the toast we just ate for breakfast. We smile at the stick figure our significant other drew on our ribcage, and we buy up art sight unseen to be catalogued and stored in some warehouse. We draw a smiley face on the frosted window of a second hand Pontiac. We learn to play the guitar and sing like Thurston Moore. Some of us croon. Some of us growl. Some of us whine. Some of us belt. Some of us try to abstain, though we cannot help the little breathes that escape from our nostrils and alter the tune even against our will.

So, it's New Year's eve, 1999. I was afraid, but I was afraid with everyone. It was fun. We were vulnerable together and I had the privilege of being the vessel through which the undercurrent flowed allowing us all to turn an irrational fear into a source of energy. It was a party.

The old man, well, I did not give him the time I should have. Missy went out of her way to do something that, in retrospect, was totally amazing, and all I could think at the time was that she was interfering with my life, with my family, with my party...

She brought him backstage after the show. It is hard to swallow the energy from performing so quickly. You need time.

"Tommy," she said. "This," she began with a proud smile. "This," she ushered the old man in the fedora towards me, "... is Jared Rowland's best friend in the world Donnan O'Dea."

"Jared Rowland, whoa," I said. I had never met my grandfather. To me he was just some artist my mom had dedicated her life to. Just some painter whose prints had filled our house. Dark bodies crouching under cover of night. Fire filled streets. Planes flying over crisp brown fields. He painted the images that colonized my mother's mind. That drove her slowly mad. It was only slow in retrospect. It had seemed fast when it happened. From one day to the next the tolerably dysfunctional took a deep dive towards the raving mad.

"Pleasure t' make yer 'quaintance, Tommy." He held out his hand.

"And yours. You knew my mom, my..." I felt my anger as if it was someone else's. .

He nodded his head. "I knew your mom well."

I could not say that was welcome news. "And what brings you here?"

He nodded towards Missy. "There's something I'd like to talk to you about."

I was grateful. In some deeply inaccessible region of a self long lost, I really was grateful. But, I was also scared of letting that self resurface. Self-absorption as self-defense. 19 and at a party. There is no good excuse. I just was not ready. I was not ready to hear her name. To think about her. To think about the bullshit project she poured her last years into.

"Well, Donnan, how about a beer first?"

He nodded ascent.

I grabbed two beers, opened his and then my own. He took a sip and I put mine all the way back.

"He turns one hundred in a couple of hours," said Missy.

"Happy birthday, Donnan," I grabbed another bottle and opened it. "Here's to you." I put the bottle down in a couple of gulps.

Missy bit her bottom lip and stared at me

Donnan touched the brim of his hat. "Maybe you're not in the mood to talk tonight, Tommy."

"Donnan, I am always in the mood to talk." I lifted my glass and he lifted his. "Cheers."

"Cheers, lad."

"But tonight, maybe we can skip the remembrances and just celebrate your birthday and the world's continued march forward. Tomorrow is for everything grave."

I would not have discussed it the next day or any other. I was angry at my family. I am not even sure I knew that then, though. Anyway, there would be no tomorrow for Donnan. He would not live to see 100. But he left me a case filled with letters. Letters that I waited too long to open. The first was from him.

Dear Tommy,

The thing about being called psychic is that you always suspect it's not quite right. Psychic implies some sort of knowledge. I've never felt very knowledgable. I barely remember my name most days. If you're anything like your grandfather you know what it's like to see the world differently. I imagine you are like him. Genes like that don't subside easily.

I was 19 when I wrote my first and only book. 1919. Just after the first war. Before the riots. 2 years before I met your great grandfather Dick, and nearly 20 years before I became friends with your grandfather Jared in yet another war. I had always written, but I had never made it more than a dozen pages or so, and even in those short sprints I had a hard time keeping focus. It was not until after the war that I started to put together longer stories. Something about war turns a sprinter into a marathoner. At least, it did me. I suppose it could just as easily be parenthood, divorce, the death of someone near you. Experiences with mortality (and the birth of a child or the end of a relationship are experiences with mortality) tend to knock you into some deeper flow where you can somehow sense the river beyond the tributaries, the ocean beyond the river, the cloud above the ocean, the mountains beneath the clouds.

Still, I don't remember the writing of the book. I remember sitting down to write, and doing so frequently. I remember long mornings in a dark closet at the boarding house where I stayed. The closet was the only place a man could write without having others see. In Oklahoma in those days, a man didn't want to be seen writing. Probably, he still doesn't in some circles. It was a strange little house in Ardmore, Oklahoma. There was room for about ten of us, plus Ms. Cooley who cooked tolerable food and made the space tolerably clean. I had a great big window with no shade in my room. Every morning the sun dripped through the window little by little until the place was a giant reservoir of the yellowest light in the world. I've never been able to write in the light. I need a dark space that makes it impossible to see the difference between me and the world. A place where imagination pours into its surroundings. The only choice was the closet. It was a big closet. Big enough to accommodate an old student's desk and a little metal framed chair with a warped wooden seat. The only light in the room came through a little sliver of an opening at the base of the door. I sat there morning after morning for what seemed like an eternity, but couldn't have been more than nine months give or take. Still, that quiet dark feels like the place I've spent most my life, or sought to anyway. There was a little chain that hung from a lightbulb above my head. I never pulled it. Never had any use for the light. The floor was a continuation of the hardwood in the rest of the room. If I try I can still feel the grain of that wood against my toes. Like a tongue depressor at the doctor's office, it sends shivers down my spine just thinking of rubbing the rough bare skin of my big toe against the ridges of that worn wood. The boards were loose and fidgety underneath me as I wrote. I always used that uncertainty as a metaphor. The ground underneath us is unsteady. The Earth not so solid as it seems. Knowing that is what makes creativity possible. People who are not creative, or those who see themselves that way, anyway, are just people who cannot see that all reality, the condition it's in, the brief and unique organization of atoms that currently allows for the present, is just a coincidence, and no less holy for being so. God, if you need terms like that, is the glue that keeps it all from blowing out into the deep meaningless sea. God, if it's anything, is a story that makes all of that mess, into all of this life.

The point is, I remember the closet, but I don't remember the words. Not from the writing of them anyway. After months and months of mornings in that closet, they were just there. I sent them to a publisher. He published the work, and it disappeared before anyone knew it existed. I never wrote again. I started making sculptures, works that lent themselves to less literal interpretation. I barely thought of it again myself. I was too busy working. Traveling the country doing the work that kept food in my stomach: unionizing the autoworkers.

A couple of years passed before I suspected anything. I was 21. It was a brief glimpse. An awareness at the edge of awareness as I was losing consciousness on the front porch of your great grandfather. It all just felt so familiar. Not dejavu. Something more real. I didn't have the sense that I'd been there, but the actual memory. When Dick answered the door that night, just a few nights before Greenwood burned to the ground, I already remembered meeting his unborn son 20 years later. I already remembered meeting you so many decades after that. I already remembered the mob coming for him later that night, and the bombs that would fall in the coming days as I hid in his closet, recovering from my wounds. Dick had no reason to take me in, but he did. And I knew that he would. I had written it two years before. I know this is all impossible. I doubt it even now, and it's beyond doubt.

I suppose I should tell you the story of how I ended up on your great grandfather's porch. I had been trying to unionise some workers at a little plant in the Port of Catoosa. The anti-union folks had the numbers, and they were a violent bunch. The right to low wages has been a thing long clung to by the workers of Oklahoma. Best way to compete with the socialists is to be less educated, work longer hours, and get paid less for your sacrifices. In those days there were not a lot of friendly faces in those parts. Suppose there still aren't. Strange that all of the talk was about the material process of history. The conversion of goods, resources, the earth itself, into riches and power. Well, the future is material, too. It's just material that we have yet to see shaped. That doesn't mean it hasn't been shaped, just that we haven't seen it. I considered my job to be that of a sculptor, taking the material of the present, the workforce, and trying to shape it into a better future. They got me for agitating, labeled me a communist and sent me to court. I was convicted that very day, but before I could even get to jail the police car was stopped. About a hundred men in white robes gathered around me. Some of them had yet to put on their triangular white head coverings, and I could see plain enough that the judge, the police and half the jury were right there in the middle of the road. They had a rope, and I thought for sure that I was going to be lynched. There had been a rash of lynchings in the state. Mostly black men, but there were also communists, socialists, Catholics. When it came to who they were lynching, they were surprisingly open-minded. They went through what struck me as a rather absurd ceremony. It was disappointing, I remember, that my would-be-murderers didn't have a more coherent sense of themselves. I felt like if I was bound to be sacrificed, I would at least have liked it to be by a group with purpose. This felt like I'd just been rounded up by some group of bully's and brought to their treehouse. The rules, and the protocol, it seemed, were being improvised. The incompetent are capable of anything.

Half the group aimed to lynch me, but the other half, led by who I believe was the judge from the courthouse, prevailed. I was whipped until my back was raw, laid out on the ground, the wound was scalded with hot tar and covered in feathers.

Then I was kicked down the road. The shout I recall hearing as I ran away was, "If you make it out of town alive, don't come back. You won't be so lucky twice."

Lucky.

Strange to think there was a perspective from which this was a day in which I had been lucky.

Something happened as I ran. Something that I've never shared. The world grew dark as if I had lost consciousness. I felt myself appear suddenly in a completely dark space. There was a man at the other side of it all. An old man, floating in a blue sphere, his arms crossed over his chest, untrimmed nails yellowing on his fingertips. He leered at me for I could not say how long. His sight went right through me. I could feel him moving closer, though to my eyes he stayed at the same distance. He spoke, but his mouth didn't move. The words were just there in my head with no notice. "Donnan," he said, "you will help us find him." I blinked and I was on Dick's porch. I don't know how to explain it Tommy, but I knew even then it was you they wanted me to find. I just had to wait 80 years.

Every time I pick up my book it has a new chapter. It's a curse to know what's going to happen next. But, I look. I can't help myself. They are all words I supposedly wrote. The most recent chapter has been the hardest to read. The chapter that ought to pretty much end my role in all of this, and begin yours.

Your friend,

Donnan

12

I

She was lost in her work. Her work was who she was. I envy her in some ways. I want to be consumed the way she was. I do not want to drink, though it happens, or do drugs, though it happens, or be consumed by the pursuit of sex, though it happens... I want hours that evaporate from reality into notes like lost moments of some kid with carpet indentations across her elbows from hours hovering over toys that are more real than most anything that will come later in life, you know? I want my mind to dissolve into activity. I want to know that whatever I do, though it may not be important, has really been done. The only worthwhile work is work that consumes. It is impossible to do evil once you have lost yourself. Though, I hate her for having been so lost. Maybe it was evil after all. Maybe losing yourself is exactly what evil is. Maybe she should have been more concerned with being there, with being a mother.

I have always told myself that my mother was selfish, but maybe she was actually selfless. Maybe she was so consumed by the abstraction of her work that her world, her self, her physical plane, just couldn't matter as much as the immaterial pursuit. But, what's more selfish than being consumed by abstractions of your own creation? Is it better to live in airy, ephemeral ideas or in crude, uneven bodies? This is the droning subconscious plea that I ignore as I sit for hours with my fingers wrapped around the neck of a guitar: Can one work, I mean really *work* and still be present in the most profound sense of the word? Can one *be* if they do not work in that way. Maybe it is some long forgotten inner puritan, but at some level I know that to work is to be. And yet, that is exactly the attitude that tore my mother to bits. Maybe I'm not a puritan, but a capitalist, a communist, a maoist, a humanist, a methodist, an anarchist, a cabalist, a flautist. Maybe it does not make one grain of fucking difference, because maybe, just maybe, the whole thing boils down to a big fat I think therefore I ain't. Maybe the flute choses me. Maybe the flute uses the hands and wits of humanity to become, and then co-opts our breath and creativity to create its music. Maybe that is the single greatest misconception of humankind. Maybe my mom knew that, and maybe I hate her for it.

I remember little things.

We were driving in her '82 Escort down Western Avenue. I remember looking out the window. Seeing Lane Tech high school and thinking that in another country it might have been a palace, or maybe a prison. She spoke to me like I was an adult with deficiencies rather than a child. She spoke to everyone that way. It did not matter who she was speaking to, because she spoke for herself, not for whoever was listening.

"We've forgotten the most obvious things." That was a mantra for her. It sat near the beginning of most her ramblings. "It's not how much you weigh, but how you feel. Watch what you eat, not what you weigh, ya know?"

I nodded, as I tended to as an eight year old swimming in the deep end.

"That's a metaphor for all the rest of it. Attention to quality of experience, not appearance. We have that backwards in our world."

I offered another nod.

"We forget that human thought is just one incarnation of a heterogeneous mental reality—one incantation of a many-pronged song, not even a verse unto itself, but a tenor in a chorus that strikes one note in one verse of a thousand hour opera in a universe filled with thousand hour operas.

"I don't need Lacan or Derrida to tell me that words and their meaning are abstractly related. I just need to remember sitting in front of your crib and saying *Tommy Tommy Tommy* over and over. Drilling your identity into you. Forging a false connection between you and this word. *TOMMY*."

I remembered standing in front of the mirror myself and repeating my name. Feeling that strange distance between the sound and what I felt to be the me beyond it.

"I don't need Marx to tell me that my time is not fairly connected to the profit it generates for my family. I just need to drive by the bosses house one lunch hour while he's playing eighteen holes of golf on the course that's his back yard.

"I don't need Heidegger to tell me the world is not the Earth. I just need to remember the difference between finger painting a tornado and having one tear the roof from my house.

"I still need someone to explain to me what the hell Einstein was getting on about."

I was in full agreement at least on the last point. All I knew about Einstein was that I desperately wanted to have the hair that graced his head on the poster in my mother's office. I spent hours with a brush and a blow dryer trying to duplicate the effect to no avail. I think my obsession with Einstein's hair is what first led me to rock and roll. I always wanted genius hair. I would have followed it anywhere.

"And Bob Marley. And Gandhi. And Keats..." I only knew the middle one. He seemed harmless and stern like the man who sold candy at the bodega on the corner. Gandhi was bald, so I was less intrigued by him "...Oh, Keats. It's the negative capability, to have, to hold, to dispossess, to liberate, to embrace, to despise and be baffled by and want all of these contradictory realities in the same instant and by doing so, to confound the mind and see beyond the one simple formula we like to refer to as 'intelligence'. And they go on about finding artificial intelligence. Ha! It's all artificial. Every last drop.

"Anyway, you know it's not in the forces of opposites that we find strength, right?"

I probably nodded in agreement.

"That's just where we find friction. Strength? We find that in encompassing those opposed forces. In recognizing how they both, mortally opposed, contribute to the same holy whole. The inexplicable 'one'.

"It's not dialectics. Mommy's not into dialectics."

"OK."

"Call it the forest *and* the trees if you like."

"OK."

"Call it murals *and* postcards."

A nod sufficed.

"Call it atoms *and* universes."

"I will."

"Call it pointless to define."

"Pointless?"

"The Universe is a koan, kiddo. It exists, in one way or another, to defy your every effort to define it, to speak it, to exploit it. No matter how hard you try to escape this one simple reality, you will always be the implement of far greater movements.

"Call it God. Call it Nature. Call it Brahma. Samsara. Moksha. Nirvana. Call it Betty for all I care. The point is we're all chasing our tails no matter how strongly we think otherwise. Sad sacks, us." she smiled at the sense of conspiracy she had created, "But, we're lucky, too. Lucky to be whirling ecstatically around, necks bent towards tailbones chasing our invisible appendages."

I thought of our Beagle, Bailey, who had an affinity for tail chasing, but didn't strike me as a philosopher.

It was comforting, in one way or another, to have a mother who was so involved in understanding the world. It made reality feel like a plate of spaghetti that had been all chopped up into nice little bites. It still looked like a disaster, but there was no need to worry about getting noodles caught in your tines. She threw around the names of French philosophers like kids at my school threw around the names that filled out the Bulls' roster. Horace Grant: Lyotard, Steve Kerr: Rousseau, B. J. Armstrong: Descartes, Bill Cartwright: Foucault, Dennis Rodman: Baudrillard. She expected the people she spoke with to be as familiar with them as she was. One of her biggest flaws, as far as I was concerned was that she was quick to recognize other peoples intellectual blind spots. This tendency combined fatally with an equally powerful one to condemn whole terrains of knowledge in which she was less than expert: Economics, for instance, was a 'charlatan's profession'. She was two years into her doctorate by then. Social linguistics at the University of Chicago. She was studying the way that news shaped reality. She was focussed in particular on how racism in the Southern states had been perpetuated through media validation. That was not to say, she was quick to remind, that it did not exist in the Northern states as well. She had just chosen to focus on the place she grew up. Her dissertation was focussed on the Tulsa race riots of 1921, and the media culture that, according to her, allowed for them. I did not realize at the time how personal the topic was.

She dressed in a slightly feminized version of the classic male professorial getup. She tended towards plaids, tweeds, the occasional poorly fitted denim. Her haircuts were irregular both in regards to the intervals at which she got them and the relative lengths of follicles which pushed outward at random in alternating greys and blacks. Her glasses, a little too square in their translucent red frames, always sat low on her nose and made it a matter of course that she looked down at you over them as she spoke. She was pretty, though. She had a thin, farm-born, toughness that was singularly attractive. At least that is how I remember her.

And there was depression that came in violent spurts. Adam brought it out in her more than I did, but I was her touchstone. She came to me when she needed to feel like there was ground under her feet. The only thing worse than being the source of a depressive's ire is being the place they go to lick their wounds. Real abuse is reserved for the ones we trust.

Adam had come home with one of his high school girlfriends. No, it was boyfriends by then, which honestly I think mom preferred. Having a gay son seemed to cement whatever liberal academic identity she was gunning for. No, it was definitely a boy. I remember him now. Kim. An Asian kid with shoulder length hair parted down the middle and dyed pink. He had enlisted in the Marines and Adam was going to drive him to boot camp in San Diego. Adam was barely eighteen, but he had been out of school for years. He had dropped out in his sophomore year and taken a job as an assistant in a frame shop. Kim worked in a coffee shop on Belmont Avenue where Adam spent his evenings and weekends chugging down free bottomless coffees, and singing along to Kim's piano on Saturday nights.

"You're not taking my goddamned car to San Diego, Adam," had been mom's initial response to their request.

Kim, who was tall, slender and unmistakably feminine, rolled his eyes as he tossed one of the legions of pink hair flanking his face over an ear. I noticed the deep green paint on his elongated nails as he made the gesture.

"And Kim, what the hell are you thinking?" She asked. "There's a war going on and you sign up for the Marines? Are you a fucking dunce?"

It was Iraq part one. Bush part one. The strange sequel, and its bizarre affront to democracy, sincerity, security, were still unimaginable. Jeb was still the second most renowned Bush.

Kim spun his hair around the green-tipped finger as he gazed out the living room window.

"Don't talk to him like that," Adam said.

"I'll talk to him how I see fit, Adam." She turned her gaze back on Kim. "What, kid, tell me what in the hell are you thinking?"

I thought of the Kim I had come to know. The Kim who brought me to Sox games with Adam. The Kim who screamed the lyrics to The Humpty Dance—"I gotta big nose, big like a pickle"—out the window of Mom's Escort as we passed the Sears Tower on the Dan Ryan. I tried to imagine him holding a machine gun, dressed in fatigues, his hair trimmed short, sweating in some far off desert.

"We're taking the car, or we're hitching. Your choice."

"Don't the *Marines* pay your way to training camp?" She said the word Marines as if it were a venereal disease.

"They pay his," said Adam. "But we want to go together."

"Well you can't, alright. You just flat out can't. Not in my car." Her voice rose and took on a familiar sharpness. A sharpness that usually preceded screams which turned to strange vibrating howls that blared from under torrents of tears. It was the only time her armor of rationality, or at least intellect, showed chinks. The irrationality of the screams terrified me like being caught in a cyclone.

When her facade was shaken, its greatest threat was the even temper of whoever happened to be her opponent. She couldn't handle being one-upped at her own game. Adam had mastered this bit. "Well, mom, I'm sorry to hear that. We'll just go stand on the side of the Kennedy and try to hail a ride," he said like a teacher trying to appease an intransigent kindergartener.

"You little son of a bitch," she said.

Adam offered the obvious, "You said it, not me."

Kim's eyes widened, but he would not allow his mouth to smile along with them.

Her volume shot to the top of its range. "You just fucking hate me, don't you you little shit? You really fucking hate me."

Adam baited her further with his faux tranquility. "No mom, I don't, but sometimes we have to think about our own needs. Do what's right for ourselves." He added a little hallmark to that final bit by reaching out for her hand.

"You punk. You little..." she struggled for words, and it was not finding them that really pissed her off, sending her into a fit that would only make her inner progressive hate her all the more when the storm had been weathered. "You little fucking faggot!"

Adam had won. That was clear to everyone, and while the damage was done why not fire off the remaining shells.

"Why don't you just go fuck each other in the ass. Or better yet find someone on the highway who likes little boys. Are you into that, too, Kim? I know Adam likes to take it from old men. Don't you Adam? Don't you? Why don't you tell Kim how you like old men to fuck you in the ass."

The last dagger came from Adam, and was no more than a calm nod that clearly indicated to everyone that she had just proven the point he needed to be proven.

"I won't be coming back," he said as he turned towards the door.

"I'll fucking kill myself you little shit. How would you like that. How would you like it if I slit my fucking wrists and you never have to see me again in your whole fucking life?"

"I wouldn't like that at all, mom." That jazzy resonance was already there in his voice, in his cadence, toying with the emotions of those held captive. Even then we were his audience.

The wailing began. It was like a calliope announcing the arrival of some circus. She grabbed a knife from the kitchen door and pulled me into her bedroom. Screaming words in wails that shattered into a thousand pieces, "I'm gonna do it you little bastard. I'm gonna..."

The door slammed. I was curled on the bed. I remember my position—rolly polly like—but I do not remember how I felt. I do not remember crying. I recall it all like I was just an observer. Like someone who was laying on the side of the road waiting for an ambulance after being struck down by an Oldsmobile.

The wails subsided.

"I would never," she said. "I would never, ever, ever do anything to hurt myself." She still clutched the knife as she came to hug me. "You know that, right?"

Adam never came back to our house.

He came back to Chicago. He worked as a Bell Hop at a downtown hotel, and then as a singer in the lobby of the same hotel, and then as a singer in the little bar across the street, and then a bigger bar, and then a club, and then a bigger club, and then he was gone. His voice was the only thing that could put me to sleep as a kid. I could have imagined that he would eventually record an album that would put him on the circuit. I never imagined that he would do it as a woman.

13

Him

The river's current is much stronger than it seems from the shore. Our raft moves fast and is tossed from one side to the other like a suitcase in the hands of an inebriated baggage handler. Mickey seems confident with the oar and Eve is cool as always, so I decide not to pretend not to panic.

"Where do we go now?"

Eve does not look at me. "Back."

Back, I think. Great.

The raft struggles towards the bank and Mickey asks me to take an oar and try to help him stop us against the cement river walls. I jut the oar towards a crack in the cement and we slow, I jut it against another and we slow further. I am beginning to feel like a kid on a merry-go-round. Mickey juts the other oar in the same way and finally we are going slowly enough to stop ourselves.

"Get out," Mickey says, "and hold us steady with the oar."

I pull myself onto the bank and hold the boat still so that Mickey and Eve can get out.

"Drop the oar!" Comes a voice from behind.

Shit.

I hear a click that is familiar from a thousand movies.

Shit.

"Drop it."

I know they will float away if I do. Mickey's oar is already on the bank. I try to drop the oar into the boat, but it bounces out. I watch as Mickey and Eve drift back into the river, oarless.

"Nice aim, shithead." I recognize the high-pitched screech of a voice. "Let's go."

I go in the direction I am pushed. Which is towards a black car. My vision goes dark and I feel a soft fabric against my face. I hear the car door open and inhale the smell of new car. Pristine leather.

"Where..."

"Shhh," the high pitched voice says in a way that is eerie and comforting all at once. "Soon enough."

Soon enough, what? Some things I want to know now. Some things I never want to know.

The ride is not long, or maybe it is, but it does not seem so. I am singing "It's All Over Now Baby Blue" in my head. I get through the song 3 times, but I am not sure if I was singing fast or slow, or even taking long breaks. I wonder how Bob Dylan would have handled a moment like this. I imagine him sitting next to me. Not the current Dylan, but the "Don't Look Back" version. The cocky kid who went to teach England a thing or two about poetry, and the media a thing or two about what they could and could not know.

Bob sits next to me, a stoned confidence exudes from his hairy upper lip. Imaginary friends are the only ones you can see when you have a black velvet bag over your head.

"What the fuck are these ape-sized assholes doing to you, man?" He asked me.

I shrug. Not a lot I can say about it.

"Man, I wouldn't let some Cro-Magnon criminal fuck, interfere with my day like that. I'd tell that fucker, hey man, you know what kind of world we live in, you know all the BULLSHIT we all have to step on every time we wanna step out for a short stack of pancakes and a mug of hot joe, you know that world, that shit on ignoramuses like you, bully's, man, who just take what they want, push the small of stature, folks like us, out the way and take it, well guess what big fella, guess the fuck what, Bob Dylan can use his fists, yeah, that's right, I may be little and fuzzy and talk funny, but I can throw the fuck down motherfucker." He flexes and looks at the reflection of his own bicep in the mirror. "And then, and only then, after he'd heard why his unjust derrière was about to be stomped, would I open that car door and roll that bastard out onto the side of the road, take hold of the wheel, steer this rolling steel Goliath towards the nearest off ramp, and stomp some motherfuck'n bosses, too. That's right, man."

I look down at my hands, which are tied together, and which, because of the sack over my head, obviously I cannot see.

"Ah, man, you gonna always find some BULLSHIT excuse, ain't ya man, well, shit, then I can't help ya. Nope, this ain't on ol' Bob if you're gonna just play that whole my-hands-are-tied card. Hell no."

I am tired of Bob.

"Plus, why don't you sing something a little tougher, dammit, you be all, like, 'it's all over now baby blue'n before you even tried to save yer damn self, and that defeatism shit'll eat you alive, Tommy, eat you right on up before you take another breath, but, on the other hand, if you was to sing along to some, like, 'Hurricane,' or some 'Subterranean Homesick

Blues,' or some tougher shit which I also, by the way, wrote, but that is not totally defeatist, but instead a rock solid ass-kicking tune, then maybe, just maybe you could fight your tired little weak ass out of this situation, yeah?"

I started to hum Hurricane.

"Are you humming?" asks Buddha. "I've had some weird assholes in the back of this car, but you son..."

I stop humming. Bob is gone.

I hear a train in the distance when we step out of the car. I don't think I have ever experienced darkness in this way. I remember as a kid I would wrap myself like a caterpillar inside of stage curtains. Long black velvet tubes reaching from the base of the stage towards the tracks along the ceiling that guided their opening and closing. I would stand at one end and spin and spin and spin until the curtain was wrapped around me like an enchilada shell, the fabric tight against my body, holding my breath near to my skin. It was dark inside, but not as dark as it is right now. I always made sure that a little light could come in near my feet. With a little light you can remember who you are, what your hands look like, how far your feet are from your eyes. With no light there is also no memory. No context. No distance. I am beginning to wonder who it is in this hood. I think of the photos from Abu Grahib. Did those prisoners remember who they were as they stood hooded and attached to electrodes? Was it possible for them to remember why they were there? Was there a reason? Did it matter as they disappeared into the darkness and became subject to those soldiers', those kid's, cruelest instincts? I thought, too, of the smiling faces of the soldiers who had become their tormentors and wondered if they were not just as lost despite the light that lit their sins. Maybe, in the end, it is better to be the one in the dark.

"You know why we're here." A deeper voice now, raspy and playful. It's a voice that must be attached to a smiling head, though the smile is likely of the cocky, taunting, unstable variety. The man is standing close, I think. I smell aftershave.

I do not know why we are here. I shake my head. I am not sure if they can tell I am shaking my head, so I exaggerate.

There is laughter. I hear at least three people, I think. Buddha's high-pitched laughter, the aftershave man's rasp, and another that is distinctly feminine. The feminine laugh is the shortest and least convincing. Maybe she is not taking such joy in my torment as the others.

"I want the letters. I want the journal. I want every bit of evidence that you have implicating my employer's family." There is a knocking of one solid object against another that I perceive as a threat.

"I... I... don't..." My brain feels like a television searching for a satellite signal even before the sharp pain registers n my temple.

"I... I..." the raspy voice taunts. "I'm not interested in don't, only in do, so let's try and make sure all of our responses are phrased in the positive. Can we accommodate?"

There seemed to be little leeway in my potential response. I nodded, still unsure if the world outside of the black velvet bag could decipher my movements. I felt something itchy on my cheek. Blood.

"Where are the letters?"

I don't know is out of the question. I try to rush to some sort of acceptable response.

I am too slow. I feel a blow to the back of my knee and then my kneecap hits the pavement, followed quickly by my face. My hands, tied behind me, struggle against the rope to free themselves. I hear that familiar click and a hard round implement pushes against the back of my skull.

I am a bug.

I am too be squished by the boot of what is to me only a voice.

My life does not flash before my eyes, but there is a clarity, this moment is all that is left. It is too valuable to be wasted on fear or recollection. I know the buzz, the static, the white fuzzy empty that is all being. I am at ease in this moment because choice has been eliminated. I am fully without will, and so there is no reason for anxiety. No reason for panic. A life full of speculation that I may be destined for something greater becomes a bad joke that ends with a vulgar blast, and to be honest, it is a relief.

"Wait a minute, Buddha," says the female voice.

The rasp comes next, "Someone playing guardian angel?"

The woman again: "No, but I think it's less than prudent to take out the only person who may be able to stop the disintegration. Especially when he's the only one know where we can find what we need before he has told us anything."

The disintegration?

The rasp: "Ah, but we still have big sis and her little lover."

Now Buddha's high pitch, "floating towards Memphis on a raft with no oar."

There is a silence in which it is apparent that everyone is waiting for the result of the raspy one's consideration.

Another click. This one, I hope, means the opposite of what the last meant. The pressure against the back of my skull lightens.

"Your angel has a point," comes the rasp. "But, we knew that already, didn't we."

I breathe what may be my first breath in over a minute. It is breath thick with the staleness that fills the black velvet bag that has become my world. I try to touch the bag from the outside, but my hand seems to reach and reach but find nothing solid. There is nothing where my head should be, nothing above or below or behind. The complete disorientation creates a sense of panic."

I hear the three of them laughing as I fumble in search of my head.

"I don't know anything. That's the truth."

"The truth, my little friend, is something that my boss is in the business of making, so if you try telling anyone anything about this, I imagine we can manufacture a world in which you never existed, and I don't imagine anyone will care too much," the raspy one says.

The woman, my guardian angel, speaks next, "We need those letters, and that journal. You'll find it for us. Tomorrow. And we'll find you."

"What the fuck," I say more to myself than to anyone else.

"Let's just say the letters hold up a mirror to the ancestors of some very powerful people who don't like to see their own reflections."

I feel a tooth snap before I can even register being kicked in the mouth.

There is pressure on my wrists, and then my hands are free.

Buddha, now: "You will count one thousand before you stand."

One, two, three, four, five, six, seven, eight, nine, ten, eleven, the foosteps move away in the direction towards my left, I think, twelve, thirteen, fourteen, fifteen, sixteen, I hear something big and metallic moving, possibly a door, seventeen, eighteen, nineteen, twenty, twenty-one, twenty-two, twenty-three, twenty-four, twenty-five, twenty-six, the same sound of grinding metal, twenty-seven, twenty-eight, twenty-nine, thirty, thrity-one, thirty-two, thirty-three, thirty-four, thirty-five, thirty-six, thirty-seven, thirty-eight, thirty-nine, forty, I hear voices in consultation, but I can't make out what they are saying, forty-one, forty-two, forty-three, forty-four, forty-five, forty-six, forty-seven, a car door slams, forty-eight, forty-nine, fifty, fifty-one, fifty-two, fifty-three, fifty-four, fifty-five, fifty-six, fifty-seven, fifty-eight, fifty-nine, sixty, an engine ignites, then another that sounds like a motorcycle, sixty-one, sixty-two, sixty-three, sixty-four, sixty-five, sixty-six, sixty-seven, sixty-eight, I pull at the bottom of the velvet bag on my head to loosen the rope, moist and sticky with blood, that has tightened it around my neck, sixty-nine, seventy, seventy-one, seventy-two, seventy-three, seventy-four, seventy-five, seventy-six, seventy-seven, seventy-eight, I get the back high enough to expose one eye, but it is still too dark in the room to see anything, seventy-nine, eighty, eighty-one, eighty-two, I pull the bag off entirely, eighty-three, eighty-four, eighty-five, I am still counting as I realize the motors have faded off into the distance and there is nothing but silence and darkness here, eighty-six, eighty-seven, eighty-eight, the room feels vast and empty. I stop counting. My eyesight begins to adjust and I realize that I am in a warehouse of some sort. I am alone, I think. I stop counting.

My ribs throb, my face and mouth are on fire. I think a tooth is cracked. I walk towards where I think the loud metallic sound came from hoping that it is a door. Light streams through a slight crack and illuminates giant spools of something. I walk towards them. Paper. Newspaper.

"I thought I said count to one-thousand," comes the voice of Buddha followed by a serpentine hiss. I catch the briefest glimpse of the inhuman rage on his face, sharp, overgrown canines protruding from beneath his upper lip. He rushes in my direction at an inhuman speed.

CRACK!

PART 2

1

Me

Stories have roots that reach into the mineral rich soils of our pasts. Tendrils reaching in every direction to connect, offer a base for growth, grasp the earth firmly so as not to spiral out of gravity's grip. They sprout, blossom, bloom, reach towards the Sun; whither, dry, die, and fertilize the soil all over again.

I can't think of those tendrils, entrenched in the ground on which we walk, without thinking of other forms that they resemble: synapses, spanning across the grey terrain of brains, creating the landscape of ideas, empathizing, judging, grasping and adapting all that might have trespassed upon the paths before, mechanizing for power, relenting to love. The very tendrils questioning their own existence before the chasm of the material world that they perceive, that they are of, but to which they never fully comprehend themselves in relation. They exist in contradiction, in language, in signs and electrical impulses that allude, somehow, to so much more.

And, then I think of rivers. Slinking arms and wrists laid lazily across the Earth until bursting into withered skeletal hands: fingers pointing towards major bodies of water that allow us, each and every one of us, to live.

I think of a family tree… All the coincidences of time, location, attraction, necessity… Seeds are planted, they grow. Stories bloom across generations. Your great great grandmother missed a train outside of Prague, Dublin, Jakarta, and met a man in a cafe outside the station. They meandered through an afternoon, an evening, a week, a month, a bed, a series of ovulations that finally bore fruit. A lifetime passes, and things happen. History happens. Politics happen. Pandemics happen. Depressions happen. Wars, and birthdays, and friendships, and powerful moments before works of art, and conversations that change the course of one's mind, and glasses of water and cups of tea, and step after step after step across the face of the planet… It all happens. Somehow all of this emerges.

Your ancestors were captured, traded, violated. Or maybe they were nurtured, loved even. And, these branches, withered like fingers, they reached across generations, pointed towards the oceans they had crossed like ivy spreading over the facade of a brick building, flowed across landscapes to escape religious persecution, slavery, their own sordid pasts, reached into the soil and planted, harvested and nourished their bodies, minds, and plots of land until one day all of the seemingly infinite complexity had led to this instance: A man gets on an elevator and so many lives, so many generations, change direction. By accident.

2

Us

"She knew about Flanders?" Kane stamped a foot against the concrete in the dark and the sound reverberated through the warehouse.

Tommy felt the tip of the pistol between two ribs. "Who?"

"Your mother?"

"Seems that way, Doc." Tommy held a finger in front of his face in the dark. He could dimly make out the outline. His eyes had begun to adjust.

"Do you believe in them?" Kane asked.

"Believe in who?"

"In them. In what they are." Kane seemed authentically curious.

"Does it matter if I believe in them?

Kane laughed. "I've seen them feed. It's strange. It's not so terrifying that they are predators… I've watched a lion eat. That doesn't scare me. It's that we are prey. We're not safely outside the lion's cage watching. Nature's not something over there. No, we're right here in the middle of it. Just food.

Sustenance for another body. And, we pretend they don't exist. So, no, Tommy, to answer your question, it doesn't matter if you believe in them."

"I do."

Kane lets a few seconds fill with emptiness. "They're not so different from us."

"We all have to eat, right?" Tommy says.

Kane laughs. "We do indeed."

"I mean, if I were a chicken my outlook on humanity would be pretty grim."

Kane closes his eyes tightly. "Every organism does what it is programmed to do."

"That's all there is to it?" Tommy asks.

"That's all there is to it," Kane answers.

"So, why tell you the story? What's the difference?"

"Stories are organisms too. They consume. They are consumed."

The muscles around Tommy's eyes contract. "Are the words starting to paint you the picture?"

"Starting to," said Kane.

"I'm thrilled." Tommy spits at Kane's feet.

Kane smiles. "What's it like, Tommy?"

"What's what like?"

"To hear colors? To see sounds?" There seemed to be a real curiosity in his voice.

Tommy thought for a moment. "What's it like not to?"

3

Him

Shreveport was even muggier than Oklahoma City. He walked into the nervous bustle that had conquested the typical tranquility of Stamford's Gulf headquarters. The building was a four-story, beige square at the far end of a parking lot. Around it lumbered the urban simulacrum of the refinery. From the highway at night it could be mistaken for a major city instead of the outpost of an outpost that it really was. The air around Stamford's Shreveport operation was thick with the singular smell of grease. The people that scuttled around the parking lot and refinery grounds fell into two categories, those with dirty hands, and those in suits. Dr. Kane felt a tinge of guilt at being counted with the suited. He missed his days in the field. His days as an assistant professor with Oklahoma State University assessing the cycle of prairie fires. Days when his hands were dirty with the remnants of scorched plant life.

The people inside the square beige building were of one type: Suited.

"Eli," said Karen barely looking up from her notes.

How tired she looked, thought Kane.

"We're going to need you to work quick on this one." She handed him a file which told him what he was going to tell them. He knew it by heart without looking. No substantial long term damage. Unreliable numbers as to the level of the spill, grossly overestimated by the EPA and their auxiliaries, evidence that microbes native to the gulf had already begun the work of depleting the contents of the spill, and finally a gleeful affirmation of the elasticity of nature and a guarantee that the gulf would make a full and fast recovery almost without human aide, though, to put minds at ease, more specifically, to put the minds of voters at ease, Stamford would be more than willing to supply whatever funds necessary for the cleanup. In reality, Kane knew, that money would only be supplied until the spill fell out of the news cycle. Stamford had been hit with a huge penalty after the Alaska ordeal and only kept up payments until public thirst for the issue declined, then it was back to never-ending legal motions to stall any financial obligation. The Alaskan ecosystem was still a science experiment gone horribly awry.

"Okay, so I know what I'm going to tell you, now give the me the truth."

"Truth," said Karen as if she had spoken the name of some long standing rival, "is that this one's bad."

He remembered how vibrant she was when they had met years ago in Boston at the audition for the community theater. How many years had it been? "How bad."

"It's not quite Chernobyl in the gulf, but there's no foreseeable closing of the well, and it's gushing into the water real damned fast. No reliable numbers—and we'd like to keep it that way—but it's a lot of fucking oil, Kane." He hated it when people he had been speaking to used his name at gratuitous intervals. That was something he did when he aimed to intimidate.

"Well, Karen," he hoped to adjust their behavior through mirroring. "I promise I won't give you any data that might be useful, Karen." It had been a Shakespeare play. *A Midsummer Nights Dream.* He had done sets and she played Titania, the queen of the forest. She was good. He wondered if she even remembered that person. She still haunted his dreams.

"Thanks, Eli."

Not so much as a plant in all of the office. Guilt? Like hanging pictures of the executed in a prison corridor.

"So, get to work. The helicopter will take you wherever you need to go. I imagine you'll at least want to to go to the coast to keep up appearances."

Appearances?

Eli surveyed the gulf from a helicopter. The damage was immense. A thick black surface, the size of an overgrown tropical storm, coated the water. The fish that cannot find their way clear would be done for, but most of them would probably be able to escape. The industry in the area would be temporarily destroyed, and the long term quality of any seafood products would be severely damaged. With enough time, though, it would recover. The problem for his employers, he knew, is not enough time for recovery, but enough time before election season. Enough time for this to get out of the news cycle before the trials begin and the real consequences, the financial consequences, could be averted.

No. There were no consequences beyond the human. Just reality. And what did that even mean outside of a human context? A plant just died and disintegrated and, with the right circumstances and enough time, became petroleum. It did not understand vast theories of reincarnation, or even capture the irony in drowning in the remnants of its own dead relatives. A plant just did what substance should: submitted to the natural order for better or worse. Humans were a very different kind of substance, one that insisted on bending the natural order. Always trying to improve, but in the end just creating disaster after disaster. Humans took this beautiful innate ability to ponder and produce, and somehow they distorted it, made it destructive, turned all of their creative powers towards abstracts like money and power and ignored the more concrete goods of abundance and community. Tragedy was probably also something that was only meaningful in the human context, but waste of this precious gift, this waste of the random result of millions of years of the mysterious transition from the physical to the biological to the intelligent, was surely tragic.

This was it, he thought, this was the sign that he had been waiting for. The end game was more or less at hand. This disaster was the call to action. If Stamford pushed through with the pipeline, and they began processing crude from the vast tar sands of Alberta, rather than taking the obvious necessary steps towards a massive transition to wind, solar, wave, hell, best of all, capturing the massive energy produced by the Earth's own physical dynamism, tectonics, even orbit and rotation, there would be short days for the contemplation of environments. There would be no need for contemplation at all. No one to contemplate. Life would continue. Just not the human brand of it. Possibly not the mammalian. *They* would be fine though. The creatures were more resilient. More resourceful. He wondered for the first time if Karen was one of them.

The stain floating over the gulf was a stain on the human brand. It was a communication of incompetence, of indifference, of cruelty. He wondered at the strange biology of communication. The tens of thousands of years that went into producing the crude, the thousands that went into the theoretical and physical development of the mental faculties to produce the equipment that so suddenly failed, flooding the gulf waters with oil, and now, his eyes take in light which reflect a circumstance, his own almost unbelievably unique series of synapses effect and are effected by the information as it decoded from the image in a process that has evolved over millions of years, and all of this results in his knowing a thing: that humanity had to end.

4

I

I wake with a jackhammer in my brain under sunshine that hits me like one of those giraffe-necked lights at the dentist. There is, I then notice, actually a jackhammer sounding nearby. It is not just my head. It is cold despite the sun. I am being poked by something. The butt end of a flashlight.

"You alright, kid?"

A cop.

"What?"

"You alright?"

Flashback to a hundred interactions with Chicago cops. They pull me from a group of white friends and throw me against a wall. They arrest me, and only me, for underage drinking at a party full of white classmates. A week later, they let me go when they bust up a group of darker-skinned friends. I'm an enigma for police. Too dark to be white. Too light to be black. The style and manners of the son of a professor. They never know whether to coddle or to brutalize me. I nod as best I can. I try to smile, but it hurts, plus exposing a cracked tooth will probably not convince the officer that I am alright."

"You know where you are?"

"St. Louis."

"Close enough," he says. "You're on the Illinois side, East St. Louis."

I nod.

"Must've been some drunk you put on last night." He offers me a hand which I accept. "Casinos?"

I nod as he pulls me to my feet. "Yeah."

"I ought ta run you in for sleep'n on the side of the road."

"No, please, it's not necessary," I mumble.

He pauses, eyeing me for clues as to whether or not there is more to the story. I hope he does not ask, because while I know there is more, I would not know where to begin explaining. His eyes are running all over me. Am I a black kid, a criminal who needs to be beaten and booked? Am I a white kid who just had a little too much fun? I can see him making the calculation, his hand hovering somewhere between pocket and holster. My olive skin is just a little too dark for me to be totally innocent, but then those blue eyes…

"You from around here?"

"My bro...sister is. I'm visiting." And the hair… It's curly, but I could just be Jewish.

Suspicion successfully increased.

"From Chicago."

He nods as if Chicago somehow explains everything.

"You get along, but I don't wanna see you again, ya hear?"

"Of course. Thank you occifer," I slur through my broken tooth.

"Find yourself a bathroom and get cleaned up before you bump into a less friendly arbiter of the law."

I close my mouth tightly and nod.

He points to a gas station called the Fill 'n Chill across the street. "Tell'm officer Ramsey said you could use the john."

The kid at the counter seems accustomed to these types of visits. "Ramsey send ya?" He is twenty-five tops. He is reading a dog-eared copy of Machiavelli's and wearing a NASCAR hat. Mutton-chops cover what might be premature jowls.

"Yeah."

He hands me a big wooden paddle with a tiny key attached. I think of Eve and Mickey. I hope they are on dry land, preferably in the state of Missouri, though I guess I was proof that Illinois would suffice.

"The hell happened to ya?" The kid stares at me over his ragged copy of The Prince.

"Bicycle accident," I explain.

He measured my response and came up doubtful. "Here." He throws me an old, more or less clean towel from behind the counter.

"Thanks," I say.

I carry the giant paddle and the towel around to the back of the gas station. There is a tow truck parked on the loose gravel lot and a couple of old black men smoking long cigarettes. They stare at me, cigarettes dangling from lower lips as I try to balance the oar long enough to fit the key in the doorknob. I get the feeling I could just push the brittle old door open. The whole lot smells like a river of gas covered with a blanket of unsettled dust.

The cracked mirror inside the bathroom reveals the damage. It could be worse. I cracked an incisor, have a split lip and a relatively low-grade shiner. I had been bleeding from the cheek, but it is a small wound. I worry about a rib, but it is hard to tell if it is a bruise or a break. Either way, tolerable for now.

I put water on the towel and wipe my face and body. I turn my shirt inside out, which only helps slightly. The dried blood is abrasive and sticky and irritates my chest.

The two old black men are still smoking, but now the cigarettes are stubs. The license plate of the tow-truck says SVD2L8.

I hand the oar to the kid at the counter.

"Where's yer bike at?"

"My what?" Right. "Oh, I, uh, it was junked. Hit by a semi."

"You got hit by a frigg'n semi?"

"No, just the bike. I fell, it got hit by a semi." Believable enough?

"Hmmmm..."

Maybe not. What the fuck did he care?

"Where you headed?"

"Back to town, I guess."

"Which town would that be?"

"St. Louis... Missouri. Can you tell me how to get there?"

"By bus?"

I have no cash, so I shake my head.

"Well you ain't driving, and whatever bike you might of had is out of the question I guess."

I nod.

"The bridge is just at the end of this road."

"Great." I start out the door.

"But you ain't gonna be able to walk over it, unless you want a lot more damage done to ya than ya already got." He is looking at his book now rather than me.

I linger in the doorway awaiting some additional advice.

"Go around back and talk to Gus." He looks up from his book and scratches a mutton-chop. "Fella linger'n 'round the tow truck. He heads into the city pretty regular and he might take ya 'long."

Gus is working on a new cigarette. He eyes me as I walk towards him. Too black for the cop, too white for the tow truck driver.

"Can I help you?"

"I need a ride into the city. The boy at the counter said you might be of some help."

"Did he now? Well, one thing 'bout that boy is..." he takes along drag "...he a fuck'n idiot."

I smile exposing my cracked tooth.

"The hell happened to you?"

"Bike accident." Consistency in lying is important.

"Bike accident? The hell you doing on a bike at 5 am?"

I have no answer that will not lead to more questions, and I really do not feel like fleshing this lie out. "I need to get to the city."

He nods. "I need another six inches on my frankfurter, but looks like we both outta luck."

"I'm no trouble."

He has a trucker cap, the kind with the flat bill and the net back. It says COOL on the front. His plaid shirt is tucked tight into crisp dark jeans that cover tan boots. He is clean-shaven on his neck and cheeks, but has a full white mustache. "I can see that you ain't." He flicks his butt to the far end of the lot. "A'ight. C'mon then."

I jump up into the cab. There is a small copy of The Prayer of Serenity laminated and displayed on the dash. I read it. *God grant me the serenity to accept the things I cannot change; the courage to change the things I can; and wisdom to know the difference.*

I recited that prayer at Sue and my father's wedding. I was 6. It is a bad sign if you know that prayer by heart at 6. It means you have spent a lot of time around addicts. I started on AA meetings, or what they called ala-tot, at 5. My mom and dad were both big drinkers. Dad quit first, when he met Sue. It took mom a few years, but even while she was still drinking she put me in the meetings. She knew it was hard.

Gus notices me looking at the prayer. I notice his hands, big and well-formed shaking on the wheel.

"That there pulled me through a lot a tuff'ns."

He hits play on his truck's tape deck.

"Schubert?"

"What you 'spect, The Platters?"

"Well..."

He laughs. "'nother day you mighta been right. Today, though, today's a Schubert day. Ain't noth'n like cross'n the Missipi to Schubert to let you ponder on that grand ol' sweep of history." He sweeps his hand across the horizon as if he were calling it all into being.

As we approach the Mississippi, the arch reflects the Sun's light onto the river. The water shimmering under the light mimics the unsteady fluidity of the piano. A barrage of blue and gold flows out across the water's surface, and before I comment on the way they leap up froth choppy waters, and I remind myself that only I can see it.

"This fella was born when this here was barely a country, and Austria was still an Empire. Not like now. River under the sun always looks the same, though."

If only he knew.

He looked out the window, over the river that shimmered under the morning sun. "I studied in Austria. Piano. Vienna."

"Were you professional?"

He holds out his shaking hand. "Was."

"What is it?"

"Nervous thing. But this here ain't so bad. Not only will it do in a pinch, but it has done," he looks around the truck's cab.

He sees me eyeing the prayer again.

"I ain't no drunk."

"Oh, I, uh..."

"There's lots of reasons to lose, and lot's of reasons to need to come to grips with that which can't be changed. Hell, half of time can't be changed."

"What do you mean?"

"The past, boy. The way I figure it half of time is in the past and the other half is in the future. Don't matter how you count it. Could be a million years back an' only five to come. Still half an' half as far I'm concerned. Can't change the one half, might could change the other. That there's the only wisdom you need an' the only difference that matters."

He pulls off the highway near the Cardinal's stadium. "Where you need to be?'

"I, uh, I guess here is fine. Near the river."

"Near the river, the boy says." He pulls the truck to the side. "In that case..." He offers a shaky hand. "Been ever so brief a pleasure to make yer 'quaintence."

"Likewise."

5

Her

"It's Eve," she had said it a thousand times. Nudged friends and family smoothly at first, then more coarsely, like sanding the varnish from a desk in reverse. They took it as a death. It was a death. She had to kill Adam. Not because she hated him. She did not hate him. She loved him. He had been there for her, even supported her through the transition. If anything, Adam had committed a sort of compassionate suicide because he knew if he did not, he would have smothered Eve, and he loved her too much to let that happen. The question she had asked herself over and over again was, *why couldn't they coexist?* She suspected the answer had more to do with the world looking in than with the world looking out. If just being Eve was too hard for the people who saw her, how could they possibly see Adam and Eve all at once? The world forced her to choose, and if the choice was imposed it would be an easy decision.

6

I am alone by the river. I had not thought this far ahead. I have not even thought back as a matter of fact. I should probably be running, but I have to find out what happened to Eve and Mickey, what was in those letters and if I was going to need to protect the letters or myself.

I cannot go back to the riverboat. I cannot trust Madame Trouché, not after what I saw, or heard, from Buddha. Maybe she doesn't know, but maybe she does.

I can't run, because I have no idea who is after me and how good they may be at finding me. My only option now is to find Eve and Mickey, and failing that, hide for as long as it takes for this to go away.

I walk down Broadway back towards The Nile, mostly because it is the only place I know. Downtown St. Louis is dead quiet at 7 in the morning. The only sounds come from the highway interchanges that cross each other after Eads bridge. I wonder if it is Saturday. I think it is Wednesday, but I am pretty unclear on that at this point. Could be Saturday. It feels like downtown on a Saturday. Maybe St. Louis is just a quiet town. The morning coolness is already giving over to what will undoubtedly be another day of relentless and sweltering humidity. Sweat stings the wound on my cheek.

When I get to The Nile, the door is locked, but the shutter is up. I knock. The sound of big feet slapping concrete approaches from behind the door. I hope that Buddha is not working. There is a loud jangling of keys, the sound of metal grinding against metal, and the door is pulled open from inside. The second ape of a bouncer from the night before is there.

"Ah ha. Wondr'n when you might pop in," he says. He is immense like Buddha, but soft and hairy, like a brown bear. He gives an impression of a creature whose demeanor might fall anywhere between Paddington and the beasts who devoured the Grizzly Man. I do not know if this is a good thing or a bad thing.

"Come on..." he gestures with his head towards the inside.

I look past him, but delay.

"Come in. You're safe here."

I am not convinced, but what choice is there? I head in. The bar is still dark, and smells of stale beer from the night before. A gaunt elderly man is mopping at the far end of the room. His expression reminds me of Gilligan after arriving at the existential certitude that the island was inescapable. He moves the mop slowly as if in protest.

Madame Trouché is seated at a booth in the back corner. She is wearing a hat that sends a Saturn-esque orbit out around her head. Her glasses are dark and bulbous like a bee's eyes.

"Tommy, boy, how do you this warm Summer morn?"

I open my eyes wide in response.

"Right. I s'pose I owe you an apology."

I nod.

"Well, I trusted the wrong man. It isn't the first time, but it's not a frequent miscalculation either. As to apologies, well, I *am* very sorry. I don't say that often, so you can take it to heart."

"Eve? Mickey?"

"No word, yet, I'm afraid. Mickey is an industrious young man, however, and Eve is fairly capable, herself. They'll show up."

I wish her reassurances were reassuring.

"You, in the meantime. What is to be done with you?"

I don't know.

"I suppose you can hold up in fortress Trouché."

"They said they want the letters by tomorrow."

"Well, do you have the letters?"

I do not. She knows this.

She reaches into her silver sequinned hand bag, the kind with the snap at the top, and pulls out a key with a rounded orange plastic top.

"I suppose you'll be needing this, then." She throws the key towards me and I just barely react in time to catch it before it slips between my fingers. "Monk, you'll go with him."

My face must betray my grave doubts about the quality of her help.

"Monk is not Buddha. Buddha had only been with us 6 months. Monk, well, I raised Monk from a scrawny teen."

I find it impossible to imagine Monk as a scrawny teen. I imagine him as a roid-ridden toddler.

Still, I do not trust her.

"Bring him to the house after you've picked up the letters. I'll send notification the moment I hear word from Eve or Mickey." She reaches into her purse. "Here." It's a hundred dollar bill.

I take it.

"Locate some less bloody attire, and maybe some victuals to nourish that abused body."

I am not sure if she refers to the effects of the beating, or my personal habits in general.

Madame Trouché hobbles to the door. When she opens it light streams in as if it is a portal to some brighter universe. She disappears into the light.

Monk looks at me. For a minute I am unsure if he is going to help me or kill me. "So what's for lunch?"

"Something vegetarian," I say almost without thinking.

"Are you a vegetarian?"

"I try." Missy is a vegetarian. She hates it when I eat meat. "And often fail. I'm not great with staving off a craving"

"I know the feeling," says Monk.

The disillusioned Gilligan sweeping the floor looks up from his dustpan. "Hitler was a vegetarian. Einstein, too. How's that for relative?" He expels a sharp laugh that unsettles the dirt he'd collected in the pan. "Goddammit." He starts sweeping the mess all over again.

Monk drives a Subaru Outback. I had expected a black SUV with tinted windows.

"What?" he asks when he sees me staring at his car. "Did you expect something more intimidating?"

"Well..."

"There's nothing more intimidating than power where you least expect it."

We stop at a falafel joint near the train station. Monk runs in and brings back two pitas stuffed with humous, falafel, tabouli and tahini. He looks at his with considerable suspicion. I look at mine with the realization that I have developed a mighty appetite. I need to call Missy.

I take a big bite and realize my tooth is worse than I thought. It wriggles a bit in its socket. Otherwise the falafel is a bread covered packet of much needed nourishment, and delicious to boot. Every bite is masochistic, the flavor worth the pain.

Monk chews in big circular motions like a horse. Halfway through the first cycle he is nodding. "Mmmm hmmm.... Mmmm hmmm... That's not half bad."

"Even the most dedicated carnivore can take respite in the occasional falafel."

"I'm no carnivore," says Monk wiping hummus from his beard. "I've been veggie since before you were born."

"Why the surprised puss directed at the falafel, then?"

"Just never tried theirs. I always eat at Aladdin's across town."

We eat our meal sitting in the parking lot. The Subaru was an oven.

"How 'bout some AC?" I try not to sound too desperate.

"Not on my watch, kiddo."

Monk goes into the train station first. I sit in the car, boiling. I look around for anything suspicious. A homeless man is tottering on a bench. If he is undercover, he is deep undercover. A couple of women, one in blue jeans and a black blazer with the sleeves rolled up, the other in a short forest green summer dress, stand talking near a sign that advertises Burger King's latest attack on the coronary system. A glass high rise across the street houses the St. Louis Daily News.

Monk startles me when he opens the passenger door. "All clear. Come on."

I walk behind him towards the station. It is small inside. Not like Chicago. I see the lockers at the other end of the main hall. Monk lifts a big bushy eyebrow towards them and indicates that he will stay near the door to keep watch over me and the entrance at once. I step up to the lockers which are painted a light shade of blue and look for h47. I find it at the end of the second row. The key slides in and turns easily. There is a plastic bag filled with envelopes and an old leather journal. I had been expecting a black leather case, or a duffle bag in the interest of discretion, but this, this is seriously discrete. I pull the bag from the locker and head back towards Monk. He holds the door for me as we exit. I pretend the plastic sack is a leather case handcuffed to my wrist. I pretend that I am a gangster from some movie, played by Bogart maybe, heading to my limo with my bodyguard and a case full of ill-gotten money. Then we get outside and I see the St. Louis Daily News again, and I remember that I am carrying letters that have nothing to do with me, yet may get me killed. I remember that my bodyguard is a man named Monk who is a vegetarian, drives a Subaru and is possibly a creature of the night. I remember that I am way out of my league here.

I look up at the window and see a couple of faces looking out. This is the breeding grounds of paranoia. The places where you suspect but cannot know. I remember reading that Hemingway's friends all thought he was paranoid in his last years. He thought he was being followed by the FBI. On a trip with a friend he pointed to a couple of men eating in a diner and said they were agents. He was put through electroshock twice because of his paranoia and depression. When the files were finally opened up it turned out to be true. He was being followed by Hoover's G men. Sometimes paranoia is rational, in which case I suppose it is not paranoia at all. One of the guys in the window takes a bite of a sandwich.

Monk brings me upstairs into the Trouché residence. The vacant human forms that are the suits of armor give me a constant reason to feel freaked out. They are worse than ghosts, because you can see them. The red wallpaper, spotted with gold leafing, the burgundy carpets, and the mirrored windows all add up to a psychotic effect.

"You all set," Monk says with a smile that indicates he can read my mind.

"Uh, I guess."

"You'll be well protected," he says flicking the nail of his index finger against the blade of one of the suit's swords. The sound reverberates for a solid five seconds as he turns and shuts the door. "They've been fighting the for years."

At least four locks are closed form outside. I look for somewhere to open my plastic bag, preferably a room that is free of medieval relics. I try several that lead to more of the same, but finally I find a door at the back of the hall that reveals something different. A white-walled room with Clash and Wu Tang posters, a record player with stacks of records and a bed. The window is not even mirrored. This must be Mickey's room.

I look through the records. I throw on the Smiths and plop down on the bed, the letters opened in front of me.

7

Letters

May 18, 1951

Dear Donnan,

I was 17 when my company left this country for the first and only time. I had barely been away from the nuns a year when I signed up with the Abraham Lincoln Brigade. It was the Spring of 1938 and Spain was in the midst of civil war. Must have been a little over a month later that we met, more than 25 years ago now. I still don't know how you found me. Most of the American soldiers, the white ones anyway, wouldn't speak to a man of my hue, even though we were all volunteering to die for liberty in the abstract. I suppose they didn't have a lot of love to spare for your kind either, except for those who descended from the same tribe, and wanted to know more about the Ireland their ancestors left behind. Spain was hotter than Oklahoma. You and I never got around to talking about the weather. We passed time discussing the painters and writers that made us come to create, but not much time at all dedicated to telling about the places that created us. Then, you had already spent as more years in Oklahoma than I had on the planet. So, what could I possibly have told you? Still, I would have loved to know more about your life in Ireland.

Speaking of homes, how've you found your new one? Chicago! You know my father was there after the first war working as an artist and musician. I would love to meet you there one day not too far from now. Maybe we can share a studio. Relive the past in even stranger detail.

I've been painting a lot since I came home. I wake before dawn and use my brush to say my prayers until lunch time. I have given up on the church since Spain. Something about a culture so brimming with religion makes the whole things seem implausible. I grew up with the Catholics in the orphanage, but their beliefs never fully penetrated my consciousness. The paintings are coming out dark. The brush seem to lay its paint heavy no matter what I aim to do. Thick outlines surround the knuckles and elbows of my subjects. I have become obsessed with joints. The strange continuity of the places where one body part transitions into the next. How does anything become anything else? How do the fingers become the hand, the hand the wrist, the wrist the forearm, the forearm the elbow… How do I end where the space between our bodies begins, and how does that space become you? The whole world is an endless connection of continuities that keep us connected, but of course they also keep us apart.

Well, dear brother Donnan, I would very much like to find myself in your company again.

May your path be lit.

Jared Rowland

March 23, 1941

Dear Donnan,

Have I told you I have been taking instruction from a German here in Tulsa? I know, I know. A German? He suffered in the war that came after ours, and finds himself here consequently, though he has elaborated in no great detail. He is only a few years older than me, but far more accomplished. He is a well known painter in his home. His name is Martin Bergman Perhaps you have heard of him? He's obsessed with locating the essence of an object and slapping it right down on the canvas. Every last damned thing, he shouts, has an essence, not an ideal form mind you, but some deep rooted type of being that it is the duty of art to access. It is a relief not to simply recreate the impression of the physicality of an object's appearance. He aims to allow the image to get at something fundamental, something behind the object, to release the forms.

To a man whose grandparents were slaves, liberation from form is a particularly appealing prospect. Art that speaks past physical limitations to the currents that inform them has always been a goal of mine.

I was rejected, as you well know, from every art academy in the middle of the country before the war, so I consider it a blessing to have found, not only a mentor, but one of such broad principles. Things seem to be looking up.

I go to his home everyday at 6am, and we work side by side until around noon. His home is in West Tulsa on a large track of land. There's an old barn behind the house in what seems to be an abandon pipe yard. I assume that because there is an abundance of pipe about and no good reason as to why. The wood on the sides of the barn is aged and water-logged. I imagine it has a healthy infestation of some kind as well. Inside it's nice enough. Space to work is all I need, and there is plenty of that. We set up our canvases along the far wall and leave the side barn door open so the sun can shine in on us as we work. He seldom stops to see what I am doing, and he seldom draws my attention to what he is doing. At noon, though, just before lunch, he stands in front of my canvas for a long stretch inhaling as if he's trying to breathe in the fumes from the paint.

I painted some shoes the other day and he said that he could taste the sweat form the fields that stained their insides. These shoes were marked by their use, he said. They had become "an emblem of a life force spent in the aid of feeding fellow humans." Bergman has the voice of an elderly German even though he is still a young man. "Der vas sacrivize in dos shoos," he said. Half the time I think he's madder than a box of frogs, to steal a favourite phrase of yours. Nonetheless, I was relieved to find that I had done more than to reproduce some sweaty old footwear, which, in all honesty, is all I meant to do.

It will always befuddle me that the brush can extend its voice farther than I ever intended to extend my own.

I told him that my only goal had been to try to give them life.

"Life!" he shouted. "Life is a matter of biology. Life is easily calculable! What you should aim for is much greater than life. Aim for meaning! Aim for the body!"

How, I asked him, nearly shouting myself now, is the body greater than the life that fills it?

He laughed a good hearty laugh at my question. "How can anything, any substance, ever be greater than the container that holds it?"

We spent the rest of the afternoon, a time usually reserved for personal affairs, painting a rusty old gas can that he found rotting away on his lawn.

At first I was sure he was just another crazy kraut. Little by little though, I'm coming to understand what he means. I am beginning to see that meaning is indeed a substantive affair. I told you before that I'd given up the church. I see now that it was in part the church that led me to see meaning as something that exceeds the physical. The whole basis of my beliefs has been that old transcendence. When you think of it, nothing could mean more for an artist than to recognize that there is no beyond. It is all right here in the body, all right here in the paint. All right here in an embrace.

Well, Donnan, that is me for now. Please tell me how things are developing for you in the Windy City.

Your dear friend,

Jared Rowland

Dear Donnan,

I have an exhibit! At least, they promised me one. It will be at the Stamford, which is a museum built to look like an old Italian Villa. I imagine it to be similar to some of the places we held up in Spain, but I have not been there yet to tell you the truth.

Bergman is constantly telling me that what separates a human being from any other kind of being is that they are compelled to understand and explore their own consciousness. He says essences are so important because we don't relate to them so plainly as other animals, and so it becomes our central purpose to find them. The funny thing, he says, is the essence doesn't even exist until you create that distance. 'Care' according to the kraut 'is da human ability dat makes us distinct.'

The point is, if you are going to paint something right, to paint it full and display its innards, first you have to care. So, what do I care about? I thought about Spain. I did care, and do, about that country. That's what brought us there. The freedom of others is a worthy concern, because none of us are free until we all are. I will fight for freedom wherever the fight finds me, but I want to paint what is close to home. Besides, Picasso just about covered that Spain ground. I keep thinking about those Goya paintings we saw in Madrid. The two that show the Spanish resistance to Napoleon's army. The futility of resistance and the strength of futility. The man in the plaza with his hands up facing the firing squad. The death that comes before freedom. I think of my father. I told you the story.

What better place to paint the essence of America than right here in Greenwood. It's a neighborhood that seen more than its fair share of history, even if that history disappeared from everyone's consciousness.

Your friend,

Jared Rowland

Dear Donnan,

Bergman's been brewing his own beer, a German lager he says, in the barn where we work. The other night he invited me to join him for a few. I had just finished the first of my paintings for the exhibition—another story entirely—and he wanted to celebrate. A few turned into a dozen as you're well aware can happen (I remember plenty of long gone evenings with you in Valencia).

"Alcohol is a benevolent dictator. It imprisons da soul even as it gives you everything you think you vant and need," Bergman says. "But, ultimately none of us is without some leader to which we bow." I assume he is right, but I could not name mine. Art? I think that art is a means more than an end. Art cannot be the dictator, it can only increase or decrease a dictator's power. Religion? Yes, religion can be a dictator, but I've already sidestepped that one to the extent I am able. Booze without a doubt, but I really do not partake like I used to. Maybe I am masterless at last!

I've begun the paintings for my exhibition and even finished the first. It is an exposition of scenes from Greenwood during the riots of 1921. I have been doing research for the project. I am approaching it like an excavator. I want to get into the time, the moment, find the 'essence' and root out this piece of history, this moment that I believe will drive people to care about something that has been wiped from their consciousness. I know people would care if they knew, but most importantly, this is the way that I can take what I care about and use it to shape the world just a bit. Maybe.

I am collecting all the articles, photos and first hand accounts that I can for now. There is not much information. And a few strange inconsistencies. I will tell you more as I learn more.

As always, I wish you were here,

Jared Rowland

Dear Donnan,

I'm glad to hear that you have found work. I know that being a garbage man is not exactly a dream come true, but I also know that someone as industrious as you will find plenty of treasures in the trash of others. Maybe it will even play a role in your work. Of course it will! How could spending your days in the castoffs of your fellow citizens not inform your vision of the world.

I have been digging through another type of society's castoffs as you know. The paper that one generation leaves the next as a ghostly record of its own time on Earth. I have been spending days flipping through old documents and photos in Tulsa's archives, and even gone to the papers to see peruse their old editions. As I told you before I want to immerse myself in the event. I want to hold it like a grapefruit that I can juice until I smell the citrus and taste the pulp.

The other day I was in the Tulsa Democrat's offices, looking through the papers from the days and months before the riots. The man who works the counter knows me well by now, though I don't think he knows the nature of my work. He is a strange creature: Tall and gangly, soft in the eyes but with an itch to be a cowboy. I asked him if they printed multiple editions of the paper back in the early twenties. He said that they did, under special circumstances, make the occasional change, he thought. The reason I was interested was because everyone that I have spoken to in the black community remembers a very specific article on the day before the riots that called for a lynch mob of whites to storm the sheriff's office and kill a man who was being held on charges of rape against a white woman. That man, as you know, would be my father. The thing is, not a single copy of the paper I have found has any such article. I can't imagine that dozens of people are inventing the same memory, though I suppose stranger things have happened.

I'm thinking of being more direct with the soft-eyed, would-be cowboy to see if he may be of some greater help. Here's hoping, anyway. I've made progress on a couple more paintings for the exhibition as well, but the deeper I get, the more I realize that I need to know before I can truly render these events on canvas.

Yours as ever,

Jared Rowland

Dear Donnan,

It looks as though I have found the leader to whom I bow, the prime mover of my little system. He owns a newspaper here in town, the very one which I noticed the article to have disappeared from.

A couple of days ago I did indeed confront the cowboy with my project. He feigned interest. "Well all be," he said, "Now that sounds like a project I might be able to help with." He disappeared past the door behind his desk. He must have been gone fifteen minutes. When he came back he wasn't alone, but accompanied by a tall, balding, jowly old man whose skin was covered in liver spots.

"Son," said the old man, "Now, Clint here tells me you're looking into an article from '21." Clint. Of course his name was Clint. "Yes, sir," I told him. He nodded. A grin that could safely be described as shit-eating covered his face. "Uh huh," he said. "Well let me just go 'head and be real clear right out front here that the article you're looking for don't exist. Never has. You ain't the first to wish it did, but let's just put that right on to rest." I asked why so many people remember it if it never existed. His smile dimmed a few shades. "Mass hysteria, I guess. Sometimes when bad things happen, people just wanna be sure there's a reason, but I can assure you that this, this here, this ain't got no rhyme or reason, not one that can be located here in our archives, anyway. Now you run along there boy, and do something a little more productive with your time." There is not much I hate more in this world than being called boy with that particular tone. The whole while Clint stood behind the man looking like he might feel a bit guilty.

"Well, sir," I said to the man in my best 'boy' voice, "if you say they ain't nuth'n, then they ain't nuth'n, but I may just sit here 'n look 'round all the same if ya don' min'."

"Well," he says, "we can't have people digg'n 'round in our files try'n to find things that make the paper look bad. You understand."

I began to tell him that I did not understand and why, but when the good ol' boy security guard stood up from his little rocking chair and pushed me towards the door, I decided this was a battle best abandoned in the short term.

yours,

Jared Rowland

Dear Donnan,

I had a surprise this week.

I went back to the offices of the Tulsa Democrat, and not surprisingly, I was turned away. The security guard stood as soon as he noticed me and shook his head. I was in no mood to battle with that big fella, so I let the door close in front of me before I had even opened it fully.

I stood outside and kicked at the dirt in the parking lot, pondering my next step, when that soft-eyed cowboy kid showed up from around the side of the building. "Hey you, hey fella'," he whispered. I headed towards him. "I'm sorry 'bout the other day," he says. "I's jus' doin muh job." I told him that I understood. Well, then he pulls out an old yellow envelope and hands it to me. "I hope that finds itself uh use," he said, before he disappeared back behind the building. I guess that shit-eating grin was just hiding his shame.

It was the article, Donnan, the one that had disappeared from every copy of the paper left behind. The article that called for that boy to be lynched, and likely led to the riots. The headline read "To Lynch Negro Tonight" and was written by none other than Mulroney Flanders, the papers owner, himself. It didn't use words like 'suspected' or 'accused', but said flat out that this boy had raped that white girl, and that he would be lynched for it.

I have painted it into my works. Almost like a collage, the headline floats above the scene, above the clouds where the by-planes drop bombs onto the neighborhood. It's almost pastoral, the way those June clouds hang up there in the clear blue Oklahoma Summer sky. It seems infinite that sky, like it just flows straight into the heavens. I reference Goya in the foreground. The destruction of a world, the destruction of the possibility of a South that thrived on an equal footing, instead of one that's wallowed in an unbalanced poverty. Black Wall street becomes just another slum, and here's the headline that let it happen. The headline that managed to then disappear from the face of the Earth.

Well, not quite.

Yours,

Jared Rowland

Dear Donnan,

It would appear I have yet another master, though, I can't name him.

The Stamford Museum cancelled my exhibition upon seeing the first of my paintings. Someone in the organization didn't like the topic very much. Bergman went in a fury to the director, who is a good friend from the academy in Paris where they both studied long before the war. The director said this came from the top. Not from the top of the museum people, but from the top of the Stamford Corporation, the company that funds the museum.

Apparently my name rang a few bells, and a glimpse at the work confirmed what was suspected.

As always,

Jared Rowland

8

They

Will paced his office. It was late. The plaza underneath his window was dark, and the window itself had become reflective, hiding the world beyond its surface and illuminating his office in reverse. He saw himself in the mirror-image of his office. Pacing. More or less fit for a middle-aged man. A bit of a paunch emerging, hair just barely beginning its slow retreat. He had taken off his tie and jacket and rolled up the sleeves of his white dress shirt. His degrees, from Duke and then Harvard, hung in frames that he could see over his shoulder. Willard Stamford III. That III might have been a point of pride, but instead it was a constant source of doubt. Had he earned anything in life, or was every last blessing a result of nothing more than having been born who he was? He looked to the other wall at pictures of his two children, a boy and a girl, and their mother. Their mother was no longer really his wife. Legally, yes. They remained married for the kids, they said, but really it was for the position. For him, it was better politics, better optics. The boy's name was Willard as well. Willard

IV. Why, he wondered, had he done that? He had hated the boundaries drawn by his name. So had his father for that matter. His father who had never done anything of value. He collected: maps, rare books that he never read, art, antiques, women… But, what was he? What was his calling? What was his passion? Those were questions that were never answered. Never even asked.

It was his grandfather who raised him. He practically lived in the mansion in Riverview, Tulsa. He had rarely spent more than a month at the house in Boston where his father had taken up residence.

In the Summer's his grandfather would bring him to their home in Iowa. They would fish and hunt for a week, and then Will would be put to work. He was sent to detassel corn. Detasseling was strange work that involved helping two different strains of corn to cross-pollinate. It was difficult work that left his hands raw and covered in minuscule cuts from the husks. He pulled off the immature pollinators from the tops of the stalks, allowing the corn to be fertilised by its neighbors of a different genetic strain. It was an oddly intimate act. Sexual even. The other's that worked alongside him had no idea that he was the grandson of the man who owned the company. At least, Will did not think they knew. If they did, they never let on. During the weeks of detasseling, he slept in the workers quarters most nights, ate with the workers, listened to their stories. But, in the first week, as they hunted and fished, he stayed with his grandfather in the family estate. The senior Stamford came alive in the flat, wooded land around their home in Iowa.

At night, his grandfather would hold forth about the Soviets and the risk they posed to the United States. "It's dehumanizing," he would say, "to separate a person from the fruits of his labor." His blood pressure rose with the topic, and the topic was a frequent one. His face would redden, and his fist would pound with increasing force as he delved deeper into describing his nemesis. "They followed me everywhere I went," he said. "I was there to help them for chrissakes! To make sure they could produce the damned oil that kept the state afloat!" He sipped his whiskey as he reminisced about his time in the Soviet Union helping the state run oil company set up drilling operations. He had exactly one whiskey every evening. "Their people can't travel, can you believe such a thing, Will? They won't let their own people leave the country, because to do so would be to let them taste freedom. I'll tell you boy, they want to have their way over here, too. We have to be vigilant, to guard against slipping into the grips of their ideas! It's a canver, Will. A cancer!" He slammed his glass down, spilling a bit of whiskey over the edge. "That, boy, is the battle of this century. We have to keep our country free. We have to keep Fascism and Communism both out of this country. We have to keep this country free."

Will nodded. Secretly, he had sympathies for that far away place. Not for the government, but for the project, for the people who had been willing to try this bold experiment. It was noble to be so optimistic, he thought, to assume that people could find a way to organize the materials of the world fairly, to assume that everyone could dedicate themselves to their calling. He also saw the folly of such thought. Groups needed leaders, and leaders wanted rewards. He had learned that by watching the captain of his school's football team and the way that everyone seemed to bow down to him, including the girls in his class. He had learned that by watching his grandfather. And the truth was, his grandfather *was* smarter than most of the people around him. He *was* someone who created for others. He employed thousands of people, many of whom hated him. He had seen people who thought they could do what his grandfather did, to shoulder the burden of this massive company, to bring it all forward. It was easy, at some level, for people to criticize from outside, but most of those who did had very little idea of what it took.

Then, maybe there were simply two conversations that just spoke past each other. Maybe the Communist ideal, at least at its base, was really focussed on something entirely different than what the Capitalist ideal sought, and attempting to make them enemies, or place them at odds, was like trying to decide between you heart and your lungs. Maybe, the ideologues on both sides aimed to shout so loud that no one might ever realize that they only possessed half the truth, and that they were desperately insecure, and so needed to cling as tightly as possible to any bit of truth they could claim for there own and exploit for power. His goal, the thing that would later motivate him to study law and enter politics, was to bridge those two conversations. But, he would find that while individuals from both sides could be understanding, even flexible in their thinking, the networks that they built in support of their ideals were relentless. Somehow humanity had managed to relinquish the greatest gift that it had been given, the ability to deliberate and to chart its own course.

Sometimes during those Summers, his uncle Mulroney would visit. He was a strange man. Lank, and dark, he only appeared for long conversations around the dinner table. The rest of the time he hid away in his room. He was not interested in politics the way Grandpa Willard was. He spoke about history as if decades and centuries happened in the span of a breath.

"You can't aim to control the little movements, Willard," Will remembered him saying one night while sipping a glass of red wine around their long oak dining table. "Who cares if they call themselves communists, or fascists, or Catholics, or Protestants. Those are little movements with little goals which will inevitably fail. They're ideologies, like strains of influenza attacking a healthy immune system." Will could see his grandfather's growing frustration. "They split people into competing teams and allow them to kick a ball back and forth somewhere near center field. Ideologies are meaningless accept for as means to an ends."

"What ends, Mulroney?"

"Gaining power. Influencing behavior, thought, creating the sense of an enemy."

Willard laughed. "And what's wrong with power?"

He looked straight into Willard's eyes over the rim of his wine glass. "There's no such thing."

"Then what is there, Mul?" Willard always called him that when he was frustrated.

"Pleasure. The unfolding moment. Progress towards the recognition that we are all one organism."

Willard dismissed the comment with a wave of his hand. "This coming from the media magnate."

Flanders rolled his eyes and offered a coy, defeated smile. "The illusion of power can be a sort of interim pleasure."

There were sounds that night. Will remembered a knocking that began in the distance, just loud enough to keep him awake. He pulled the covers tight against his chin, and felt his breath grow short and tight. The sounds of floorboards contracting under footsteps stretched throughout the old house as the knocking moved closer and closer to his room. The darkness of the farm was near total, and Will's consciousness was completely absorbed in the encroaching sounds. From deep within the blackness of night, it was almost as if sight had never existed, and the world was made entirely of creaks and knocks, the scent of raw pine, and the tense pulses running through his neck and shoulders. He tried to distract himself by thinking of the work of detasseling. In his mind he roamed a field of tall corn stalks, pulling the tassels off of the tops of the corn, preparing it for fertilisation. Each plant was both male and female. Will's job was to partially degender the plants to ensure that they would only breed with their selected mates, creating a hybrid corn as opposed to one that bred with its own variety. He pretended to be a god out there in the field, separating the wholeness of the corn plant into its gendered parts, aiding in the creation of a new species. Bit by bit his mind drifted to girls in his church back in Oklahoma. He thought of many of them lined up in a row. He thought of them bound with him into one corn stalk. A single being. The thought of the union squeezed out the sound of the knocking in the distance and the creaking that seemed to grow nearer and nearer. His hand moved in the darkness under the blankets and the sensation melded almost indistinguishably to his imagination, became the whole of his experience. Himself and the girl wrapped into the sheath of the corn cob, the tassel dangling down above their head. Just as he gasped as silently as he could he heard a sound from the field, an animal crying out briefly in pain. The knocking stopped. He was completely absorbed by the dark and the quiet. All he sensed was the ecstatic beating of his own heart.

9

I

Donnan. It has been nearly a decade, but here he is. His words at least. I have to call Missy. I go to the phone in the living room that is on a hand carved wooden table with animal-esque feet. There is a shield mounted on the wall just above it. The pattern on the shield shows a man with wings flying above a village. A woman beneath the flying man steadies an arrow pointed in his direction. There they both are, trapped in that gesture in the shield's image.

I dial her number with a heavy index finger. I hope she will answer.

It rings three times before she answers.

"Yeah, Missy here."

"Missy," I say.

"Tommy," she says in a way that gives me no idea if she is excited or angry to hear from me.

"Listen."

"No. You listen. Where the fuck are you?"

"Where am I?" I ask.

"Yeah, where are you?"

"St. Louis," I say. "Visiting my brother."

"Eve?"

"Right."

She is silent for a moment. Then a frustrated exhale. "I went to the house last night. You weren't there. I've been calling you for two days. Nothing."

"I lost my phone. I'm... It's a long story."

"How do you just disappear like that?"

"What do you mean? You're the one who was gone when I woke up. You're the one that packed your shit and, as you say, disappeared."

"I was pissed. I didn't think you were going to leave town. I thought we would at least have a chance to talk. You scared the shit out of me."

"Listen. I need to know something."

She exhales another exaggerated breath. "What?"

"You remember the old man? The one from the New Year's Eve show. Donnan O'Dea."

"Dredging up old fights are we?"

"No, I just… Listen, I need to know how you found him."

"Why?"

"I promise I will explain later, just tell me what you can."

"Okay, well, It was a coincidence, really. First I had wanted to take Prof. Cameron's class on Annie Leibowitz, remember? You said Leibowitz was, like, totally vain, empty, promotional bullshit, a great photographer wasting her talent on Rolling Stone covers and all that kind of self-righteous baloney, as I recall."

I did recall. She was making the rich and beautiful more rich and beautiful, rather than exposing the labor, industry, war and exploitation that let the rich be so rich, etc... etc...

etc... I had said something pompous like that. I love Annie Leibowitz...

"You told me I should take Prof. Lynch's class on Diane Arbus instead. I listened. I took the Arbus class, but la-a-a-a-a-me. Could not get into it. I got it and all. I saw what was cool about her photos and the importance of exposing these strange corners of life in a 1950's world that was so obsessed with appearing wholesome and defining wholesome as normal and normal as white, tall, healthy, middle-class, etc.. etc... etc.., and all that bullshit. But, I couldn't help feel like Arbus was a voyeur, a ring master who, sure, maybe fell in love with the circus freaks, or whatever, but still made money off of the rest of the world's morbid curiosity."

"Missy?"

"Wha?"

"Can we leave the dissertation for later?"

"So, anyway, I dropped the class and shifted into the only one left open for Freshman: Pre-war American expressionism. It wasn't a photo class, but it filled a requirement."

"And?"

"And there was a whole unit on this German immigrant, Martin Bergman. A few paintings by one of his pro-te-jaaaaaays, Jared Rowland, had made their way into the class. I didn't connect the dots right away. No one big, right? Rowland, sure, that was your mom's maiden name, but there must be tons of Rowlands in the world, right?

"Then one day an old, old, old friend of the professor's, a novelist, or a sculptor, or a garbage man, or something I think, came to speak, and he happened to also be an old, old, old dear friend of Jared Rowland. He only talked about the paintings, never the man. Rowland wasn't a well-known artist. There were no biographies, no web pages. He just happened to have been a friend of this man who was a student of Martin Bergmen.

"It was like a week after that I asked you your Grandpa's name. And you were all," she imitates a dopey voice meant to be mine, '*Uh, Jared, I think, why?*'" She pauses, inhales slowly and exhales all at once. "Jared. I knew your family had moved from Tulsa, the home of Bergman, to Chicago. Could it have been him, I ask myself? I asked you about him, and you said something like," again the dopey voice " '*I never met him, you know that. All I know is his name. My Grandpa died before I was born. She barely knew him, but his name was Jared So...*' So I say, 'you must have seen pictures, right? Something?' And you say…" Again dopey me: " '*Do you have pictures of your great grandfather*?' At which point I reminded you 'Well, dickface, I'm adopted, so I don't even have pictures of, like, my parents, but my adopted parents, yeah, they have photos of my grand-parent era folk. And you said '*Hmmm, well, I sort of remember photos of grandpa Jared being around when we were little, but nothing sticks, ya know. Like I say, he died before I was born, so...* And I asked. 'What did he do? Like, for a living?' And brilliant, sensitive you once again sounded off with one of your charming responses…" Super dopey now, " '*Missy, what's with the sudden interest in my distant relatives?*' But I just knew it. It had to be him. And now his best friend, the old man from the art class, was here to meet you. That night, the night of the concert, I spotted Donnan from the stage. I thought, this, this was a great New Year's present. I just knew you would be totally psyched. Your grandfather's best friend."

"And I was an asshole."

"And you were a great big asshole."

"Never too late to say sorry?"

"Sometimes it is actually too late to say you're sorry."

"This time?"

"This time... We'll have to wait and see."

"Wait and see," I repeat.

I hear her finger tapping on some surface. "So, what the hell is going on?"

"Honestly, I don't know." I do not want to worry her, and besides, I do not really know. "I'm on my way to the funeral. A lot of family shit is coming up, and, I, I guess I just missed you..."

"But, why Donnan?"

"Oh, I, uh, found some old letters from my grandpa addressed to him, and, I, uh, just started thinking about what a kind thing you did by bringing him there and how horrible it was of me to act the way I did."

"It was horrible."

"Do you forgive me?"

"Douche, I forgave you for that a long time ago, what I am busy not forgiving you for at present is your total lack of will to do anything with yourself."

"I..."

"Shhhh..." she says. "I love you, Tommy."

"I..."

"Shhhh..." she says. "I reaaaallllly looooove you."

"I..."

"shhhh..." she says. "But, I need to know that we are heading somewhere."

"I love you, too."

She lets a few seconds breathe. "Are you okay?"

"I honestly don't know."

"Do you want me to come to the funeral?"

"No. I'll be home in a few days, I hope."

"You hope?"

"Things are weird here. I'll be back as soon as I can."

"Okay?"

"I have to go, okay?"

"Okay?"

I move to lower the receiver.

"Wait!"

"Yeah?"

"Do you want the journal?"

"What journal?"

"The journal that Donnan gave you."

The journal that Donnan gave me.

"I have it here. Wait."

I hear a rustling as she sets the receiver down and moves through the room.

"Got it," she says. "I'll read you a bit?" she asks.

"No, that's…"

"I'll read you a bit."

She makes a noise, a *bleep bloop bloop*, as if she's a computer choosing at random. "…and here we go…"

She begins to read:

"I picture my father sitting alone in that cell. The lights of the prison have dimmed for the evening. The Sheriff and his men speak in hushed voices down the hall from where he sits. The bars are cold against my father's fingertips. That cold is a mixed blessing. On the one hand, it means he is alive. As long as he can feel he will revel in feeling. Cold metal has never felt so warm and welcome. On the other hand, every moment is a reminder that there may not be many more. He can hear—in my imagination he can, anyway—the rumbling in the crowd outside of the prison. He knows this type of crowd all too well. Crowds like this justify in the aggregate what no individual should be able to justify. One man's rage is passed to the next and amplified through its acceptance. The rage cycles through the crowd and if it is unimpeded, it manifests itself as that most historically powerful and ethically ambivalent beast: the mob. My father sat in his cell, his fingers pressed against the cold iron in that dimly lit cube and he listened as the beast outside gathered force. He didn't know, he couldn't have, that there were actually two crowds gathering, collecting what they saw as their own righteous indignation, two beasts milling about, preparing to punish the streets of Tulsa, Oklahoma.

I wonder if he saw the world as I do? I wonder if colors came complete with soundtracks and personalities? Maybe for him it was something else. Maybe smells induced hallucinations. Maybe sounds were colorful. What color was rage? Was it green like envy? Black like the night? Red like blood? What color lofted from that crowd into my father's cell to keep him company as he waited for all that gathering irrationality to exceed its capacity for containment, to release itself, an explosion of violence onto his body. What color would the sound of that be?

I wonder where my mother was that night? Did she sit comfortably in her father's mansion? Did she know what was happening on Tulsa's North side? Was she running through the streets looking for some way, any way, to help him? Did she know what was happening? Did she know that I was already wading around in her belly?

I don't have much of an image left of her. Blond. Light-skinned. White. I remember her smile as having been broken in the middle, only half of the surface of her lips either willing to or capable of lifting, mocking the sadness that always occupied the other side. I don't remember when she gave me up, or how. I don't remember how I passed from her arms into those of the nuns.

Greenwood was supposed to have been the beginning of something. A promised land. And there he was, locked in a cell as the aroma of the embers of his dreams meandered through the city streets and into his empty little cell. Gun shots cracked the air like nuclear crickets. I imagine a certain serenity amidst all the destruction, a certain relief that came along with the final expression of all those mounting tensions. They all knew, the residents of Greenwood, that it was too good to be true. They all suspected that one day the rug they'd spent lifetimes weaving would be yanked out from under them. And, now they'd been proven right.

I wonder if my father fretted over his theater. His precious Orpheum. Up in smoke like a dream inspired by its namesake. He'd spent as many evenings as he could afford to sitting there, staring at the screen like a conscious voyeur of his own dreams. The actors were hardly ever black, and never both black and dignified, but that didn't stop him from being absorbed into their worlds.

I imagine my father in that cell listening as the shots cracked out at irregular intervals. Not a war zone, or even a fireworks display, but something more disturbing for its sparsity. People were taking measure. Conserving ammunition. Making sure that each shell had the best odds of inflicting fatality. I imagine the smoke wafting up from Greenwood Avenue, and I wonder if my father suspected that the garage beneath his rented room had been lit ablaze. I wonder if he suspected that the wood around his precious Orpheum was growing rapidly more brittle and crisp. The celluloid turning to jelly inside its metal shells: growing more gooey and gelatinous than the initial ideas of the director. I wonder if he slept that night as Tulsa's more bitter and militant white men advanced and retreated on the neighborhood. I imagine a vile-breathed guard whispering updates with pleasure as block after block went up in flames. I wonder whether when he heard the news that the national guard was moving in he thought it was good news, or if he already suspected they were coming to subdue rather than restore. The bombs that fell from the air wouldn't have made noise, but the rate of the burn increased, and the smell of promise in flames would have intensified.

And mom.

I have one picture of each of them. I keep them in a box with four letters. Three from my father in Chicago. One from my mother who never left Tulsa. All four addressed to orphanage. They were both dead by the time I was solidly adolescent. Hunted. Haunted. Powerless in the face of the moments that made them.

Then there was that other woman. The elevator operator who accused him of assault.

The woman came from Kansas City. She had a history of litigation. She'd been a plaintiff. A defendant. Narrowly avoided jail a time or two. No one looked into her much when she said the shoe shine boy tried to rape her. The tension had been building. Tulsa was a national center for racist movements. There'd been lynchings all across the South. Greenwood was a harbinger of exactly what they feared: that segregation might actually allow for something to thrive in isolation, and that all their preconceptions about superiority would be proved impotent. They didn't want to share their theaters with blacks, but they didn't want them to have their own either. They didn't want to share their lunch counter, but whatever counter they used better damned well be an inferior one. Perhaps more to the point, they sure as hell didn't want blacks forming their own media, creating their own oil empires, occupying their own feasible economies. The accusation, true or otherwise, gave them just what they needed: a trigger.

I guess no one will ever really know what happened in that elevator other than she and my father. But, I think I have a pretty good idea."

There's silence on both ends of the line.

She exhales, "Jesus."

"Jesus," I confirm.

10

I

A knock at the door wakes me up. I was sleeping in a pile of letters and brittle envelopes. I creep out of the room and down the red-walled hallway towards the front door, my already elevated pulse raising even higher as I pass the empty suits of armor. Whoever it is knocks again. Harder. Empty Suits, I think, they are just empty suits.

"Who is it," I squeak.

"Madame Trouché," answers the voice of Monk.

I unbolt the door from the inside and Monk pushes it open.

Exhale.

"Good morning, Sunshine," says Madame Trouché.

Morning. Shit. That means I will have to meet the warehouse people again today.

"Have you heard from Eve or Mickey?" I ask.

"They washed up about twenty miles South, it would seem. They're fine. I sent a driver to pick them up an hour ago. Down the river without a paddle." She chuckles to herself. "So, you have, I imagine, been engaged in a smidge of reading?"

I nod.

"And?"

"And, I don't get it."

"Don't get what?"

"Why do these people care about some old letters from my grandfather to his friend?"

"They implicate people in the fomentation of some of this country's most inflamed racial violence since the civil war. And, well..."

"90 years ago. The grandfather of the guy who owns the paper now. I don't see it."

"Tommy, there's more inbreeding between the Flanders and the Stamfords than you might find at the Hapsburg's poodle farm. Your grandfather found evidence that the two together conspired to instigate a riot that destroyed the African American community in Tulsa, and consequently much African American wealth nationwide, and in so doing destroyed the Stamford's competition. Sue's letter told you that much."

"But I don't see the evidence in my grandfather's letters. Sure, he was shut out of the Stamford Museum and the Tulsa Democrat, sure he mentions this headline, but, conspiracy? Of enough note to go around killing people 90 years after the riots, 50 years after my grandfather's snooping about?"

"The evidence, Tommy, is there. It may not be enough to destroy media empires, or to bring down oil dynasties, but it could sure make things difficult for someone who is running for Governor at a time when energy policy is being completely upended." She reaches for the remote and turns on the giant wall-mounted flat screen.

The header reads, "Oil to Foil?"

The newscasters voice is deep and mechanical:

"Oklahoma senatorial candidate Will Stamford's campaign hits a bump today as an offshore rig owned by the company that bares his grandfather's name exploded leaving three dead and unknown quantities of oil pumping into the gulf. Stamford holds no official position with the company, though he has served on their board in the past and holds significant shares in Stamford Corporation. In his public comments he expressed deep regret for the incident, urged a full investigation and reiterated that he os not currently employed by the company. A representative for the senator said he would make more complete statements before the day is out. We now move to Shreveport, where we are joined by an Oklahoma State University scientist who has conducted significant research into the effects of oil spills on ecosystems. Dr. Eli Kane, thank you for joining us."

Madame Trouché hits the power button and the TV goes black after a miniature supernova.

"He's on the ropes here, kid," says Monk. "Yesterday might have been aimed to scare, but now, now they can't afford another scandal."

"So what can we do? Go public? I'll bring the letters to the paper."

Madame Trouché looks at me as if I've just taken my first steps. "If you can find one that Flanders doesn't own, go for it. Otherwise, it's capture and kill."

"The police?

Now it's Monk's turn to make me feel naive. "They're worse than the papers."

"So?"

"So, we need to be sure we have the headshot, and then we present our case publicly."

"The headshot?"

"We need to be able to prove, not only that the grandparents were rotten, which won't shock anyone too greatly, but that this generation right here is actively trying to cover it up. We need to show that this generation is just as bad as those that came before it."

There is a knock at the door. Monk looks to Madame Trouché who nods assent. Monk opens one lock, then the next, then the next. The door swings wide and reveals Buddha with a wide smirk.

"Morning, Judas," says Madame Trouché.

"Boss," he replies.

Monk and Buddha stand face to face inches apart, each with their eyes locked onto those of the other.

"How can we be of service," says Monk through clenched teeth.

"I'll be taking Tommy off your hands," he says in that high-pitched voice.

"Will you?" asks Monk.

"Yes," comes the voice of Madame Trouché, "he will."

I am uncomfortable with this development.

"Tommy needs to know what it is they want with him," she continues.

Tommy would really like to have his opinion consulted here.

"Tommy, can you handle this?"

"Handle?" I say. I am fairly sure of two things: I cannot handle this, and I do not have any choice in the matter.

Buddha puts the bag back on my head when we are outside. "You starting to like the feel of velvet?" he asks. "Careful there. Maybe you're catching the family disease." He tightens the cord of the bag, pushes me into a car and slams the door.

The ride is not long. There is nothing on the radio, and Buddha says nothing. The entire universe is the black inside that bag. It is immense. It occurs to me that something can be so big as to feel claustrophobic. Or maybe it is not claustrophobia, but something more like the sensation of swimming in the middle of a lake at midnight when the shore is invisible. It is not that the borders are too close, but that they are not anywhere on the horizon. They are infinite so you cannot exist inside of them. You might disappear in a darkness like that. I might disappear in this bag. I touch my fingers together. Still here. I wish I could disappear. Just for a minute.

Buddha, I assume, opens the door. A hand finds my shoulder and my feet find the ground which is paved. It is not the gravel of the warehouse. We start walking briskly. I hear a sliding door.

"Good morning, sir," comes a strange voice brimming with all the rich generic quality of an underling. "I'll bring coffee when you're ready."

The air is cold inside the building. We stop for no apparent reason. I hear a ding. The elevator? We enter. I cannot decide if we are going up or down. I assume up, but it is not clear. You would think there would be a sensation for that, but apparently, as we are pretty much ground dwellers, that was not on the list of evolutionary specs.

The elevator door opens. I am pushed out into an ice cold room. The bag is pulled off and footsteps retreat while I wait for my eyes to adjust to the light, but they do not adjust. I cannot decide if it is dark or I am going blind or if the bag is still on my head. My hands are free. I push a finger to my eyelid. Nothing. No bag. No blindfold. No eye. No head. No hand. Something comes into focus in the far corner of the room. It is a blue hue. I put my finger between the source of light and my line of vision, but there is no interruption in the hue. I move my finger close to my face. Still nothing. Still no change in the blue hue that continues to come into focus. A shudder runs through me, but I move closer to the hue because I do not feel like there is any other choice. A figure slowly comes into focus: long and skinny, a deep blue body at the center of a lighter blue hue. What seem to be strings or wires reach from the bottom of its feet and into the floor. As I move closer they look like a system of arteries. No, roots. They are roots. The figure's bald head moves slowly. The eyes are closed.

"Welcome home, Tommy," comes a soft voice.

"Home?" In this darkness I am not sure if I am speaking or thinking.

"In a manner of speaking." The mouth does not move as it speaks.

"It's cold."

"It has to be."

It has to be. Cryptic. Great. The blue orb in the empty darkness is also speaking cryptically.

"Where are we?"

He does not answer. The mouth on the body is not moving. I wonder if it is this body speaking to me. He gestures towards a giant canvas before him.

That clears it right up.

"You're wondering what this is all about?"

"Mmm hmmm, yeah, that would be a fair characterization of my position."

"It is about the size and shape of the world we live in. Who draws the lines. Who uses the resources. Who controls the future. The past. Who speaks, and who is forced to relinquish the right to speech. It is about the very nature of progress. How we get to the next step in our evolution."

"Who are you?"

"I don't have much use for names. I'm not interested in the identities of individuals, least of all my own."

"What are you interested in?"

"Gardens."

Ah ha, now I see... Perhaps best to get to the point. "Why am I here?"

"Unfortunate genetics." The voice chuckled. Grand. A sense of humor to boot. "Your grandfather was the student of a great painter, a great philosopher of art."

"Bergman?"

"Your grandfather was a greater painter still than Bergman."

"I barely remember his paintings. Until now. The news..."

"No one does. I've made sure of that."

"Why?"

"They tell too much. And so do I."

"What do you want from me?"

"I want you to give me the journals, the letters. I want you to see your grandfather's paintings. I want you to help me create a new Earth for new beings, I want you to help me create the future as it is destined to unravel."

Seems reasonable. "I don't have the journal. I only have some letters. And a new Earth seems a little over my head."

"You will find them. We will find you."

The room is dark again. I am alone. My head pounding. I push my hand out in front of me and hit a solid surface near my face. I try to shout, but something muffles my voice. I stick my tongue out and touch a velvet surface. The bag is still on my head. I am jolted up and come crashing down onto something hard and metallic against a rib. The sound of screeching breaks and the smell of burning tires surrounds me. A door opens and a few seconds later a latch near my head. I can smell fresh air. Someone grabs me by the armpits and yanks me from what I assume is the trunk of a car. I am thrown to the ground.

"Tommy," I hear. It is Eve's voice.

The bag is ripped from my head.

Eve is badly beaten. An eye swollen closed. Her hair cut short and jagged like it had been done with a knife. She is at least two days unshaven.

"Eve," I say. "Are you..."

"I'm fine," she says.

"Shut your fucking mouths," says the shrill Buddha.

We are in a forest. If the moon was not full the night before, now it is. Light spreads across the forest floor like the whole hemisphere is just a 3 meter diameter of cement under a street lamp.

I see Mickey tied to a tree. He is bleeding from too many places to list.

There is a gun on the ground between Eve and Mickey. Buddha gestures to it, then looks at me.

"Pick it up," he says. "Come on."

I hesitate, but see my choices are limited.

"Come on Tommy, pick up the gun."

I pick it up.

"Your Tranny sis, or her little soldier lover boy. Tough choice shit brains."

I do not understand.

"Pick one and pull the trigger, or I do them both." He aims his gun at Eve. "Sis first."

Mickey looks at me and nods with the little energy he has. I raise the pistol. Aim it at his head. He nods. Eve mouths 'no'. I'm sure I cannot do this. Tommy nods. Eve begins to cry, repeating 'no.no.no'. I cannot do this.

"He's dead anyway," says Buddha. "Your doing him a favor."

Mickey nods.

I squeeze the trigger a little and release it. I cannot pull it any further. I aim to the right of his head.

"Nope," says Buddha and he pushed the barrel of the pistol back to the left. "Pull the fucking trigger or I'll pull mine," he says with his barrel still aimed at Eve.

My pulse is raging in my eardrums like a sprinter on a gravel track.

"PULL IT!" Yells Mickey.

I do.

CLICK.

There is no bang.

I am confused. Like someone told me that a glass of water was vodka.

Buddha laughs.

I inhale.

Laugh.

Fall.

PART 3

1

Me

So, why the man in the blue orb? How else to illustrate the cultural miasma that we're all drifting through: the stories that stay, the monsters that remind us about the edges of the human. The beasts won't die, and that reminds us of how long wounds take to heal, of how long memory takes to disintegrate, of how long it takes to rewrite the stories written in the bodies that populate the Earth. Or, maybe it was to show the persistence of nature's habits: the lingering prejudices of the reptilian brain, the desires that have long outlived any efficacy. Some traditions are malignant. We obstinately maintain irrational beliefs, superstitions about difference, fears based on handed-down stories, distance maintained by the most feeble lies: the smell of a recipe, the divergence of a pronunciation. We are stratified by malignant narratives… and so, I wanted my monster surrounded by that same sort of ectoplasm. I wanted the malignancy to be visceral. Or, that's my best guess anyway. There is an unholy lasting power to bigotry and ignorance. They feed on us. They travel through the population like a virus. They don't die a natural death with the passing generations. They infiltrate our culture, distort our inability to read the people in our midst without layering a million stories upon their bodies, mutations that attach themselves to the DNA we pass along in the forms of writing, gesture, casual commentary to those who are nearby. They cross continents at the click of a button, just like our more noble adaptations, leaving us to wonder in yet a new genre, what is more powerful, the malignant or the benign?

2

Us

Eli's eyes were vacant as they drifted over the old man's body.

"You look tired," said Tommy.

Eli snapped back into something resembling reality. "Tired…"

"Who was he to you?" Tommy asked Kane, staring at the body which seemed to be ageing before their eyes.

"My boss, I guess. All of our bosses, in a way," Kane stood and took a few steps towards the metal tube, the blue glow having faded almost entirely. "Have you heard of Morpheus?"

"A God?"

"A God who could slip in and out of the dreams of humans, changing shape, distorting reality, painting a picture that became the world that we all occupy…" Kane stood directly over him now. "Dracula was a version of Morpheus. A creature that haunted our dreams, played into our desires, showed the hungry a world filled with pleasures, a world that blurred the line between ecstasy and annihilation…"

"And, this guy, Flanders…"

"He owns the papers. He owns the networks. He owns the narratives. He tells us what to fear. What to buy. What to want. Who to want. He owns us."

3

They

They met at Harvard. They were in a constitutional law class together in their third year of law school. Karen knew of the Oklahoma magnates son, Willard Stamford. She avoided his type, though whether she did so from righteous spite or lack of self-confidence she was not certain. Will had noticed her. She was always ready with an answer, and it was always an answer that surprised his own conservative upbringing and challenged his understanding of the constitution. How could a document be a living thing? How could paper, breathless, bloodless paper, adapt, evolve? He did not want a politics of stagnation. In his interior world, he could admit that the P word, progress, was inevitable, desirable, necessary, but how much, at what rate, and by whose guidance?

He caught her eye one afternoon crossing campus and the two came together by force of some invisible magnetism.

"You're…" he fumbled.

"Karen," she said, extending, or partially extending, a hand.

He crossed the distance left by the effort with his hand to grasp hers.

"I've seen you in," he said.

She nodded in agreement to an obvious observation.

"In class, I mean. You make me think," he said, blushing.

She looked at him slant.

"I mean…" he fumbled for words.

"I'm glad," she said, and then smiled. "Someone had to eventually."

He grinned at the jibe.

"That was rude," she offered.

"No. Funny. And, to be frank, true," he said.

"So, what do I make you think about, Will?"

She knew his name. "Change mostly," he said. "The mechanisms for change, for moderating change so that it happens at tolerable rates."

She laughed. "Tolerable rates?"

"How to prevent stagnation, I guess. But, still to respect the spirit of a document."

"There's no such thing as stagnation, Will," she said. "Just because somebody wrote something down doesn't mean the world is suddenly less dynamic. It's evolution."

"Wrote something down? That's a sort of flip way to talk about the constitution," he said.

"I revere writing. It gives us the material for the real work."

"And what's that?" he asked.

"Interpreting."

He blinked and kept his eyes closed for a second longer than was natural. "Can we maybe get a coffee?" he asked.

"How should I interpret that question?" She asked.

"However you want."

They became friends, or more aptly, sparring partners, and when Willard Stamford went into politics, the first call he made was to Karen.

4

I

I wake up in a chair at a truck stop. There is a man sitting across from me with glimmering Manson eyes trained on me. He smiles a little as I yawn and try to look casual. I notice his shoulder is bobbing regularly like the part at the top of an oil rig. I follow the arm down and see that his hand is inside his fly. I move slowly so as not to startle him. He quickens his pace. Lets out a little moan as I move towards the door.

It is hot oustide. It smells like gas and sounds like the highway.

"Excuse me," I say to a passing trucker who appears to be Middle Eastern. "Where are we?"

"Lebanon," he says.

Lebanon?

My face must look confused. "Missouri. Lebanon, Missouri. 'bout 2 hours from Joplin." He keeps walking across the parking lot.

Joplin?

"Wait, excuse me…" I run behind him. "Just a minute, sir."

He turns. "Sir? Well this ought ta be good." His accent puts him clearly in the Texan.

"Are you by any chance heading towards Tulsa?"

His name is Riyad. He was born in Saudi Arabia, but his family moved to Texas when he was still an infant. He does not speak Arabic. I learn these things quickly.

I think of the gun, and I wonder if Mickey and Eve are alive, if they know where I am, if they blame me for pulling the trigger. I wonder if I blame me? I tell myself I knew the gun was unloaded, and that even after Buddha had redirected the barrel, I still aimed wide. I tell myself these things, but I am not sure of them. I tell myself that I only squeezed the trigger because I was surprised, but I am not sure of that either. I am not sure of anything.

I think of how lucky I am that Riyad has no idea what I am thinking.

I smile in his direction, not having heard the last few phrases of his life story. Something about a ranch in Lubock, a grandma who makes a Saudi version of apple pie with a honey sweeter than any you can find in the states. Sweet as a spoonful of Skittles, he says. Apples are from the Middle East, he says. I wonder if that is true. I think of the phrase, 'American as apple pie', and wonder if it is a misnomer. I remember a story of how apple seeds traveled from their original homeland into the world at large in bear shit. That is a tale of migration. The apples that came further down the germinal line from those seeds must have never heard the end of it.

"How'd you come across that shiner?" he asks.

"The what, the shiner?" The glass on the front of his rig is so spotless it almost seems transparent beneath the reflected sun.

"Yeah, how'd ya bust yer eye?" He points to his own eye underneath his sunglasses as he speaks.

"Cardinals game. Ball hit me right in the face." I mime a ball flying through the stadium and landing on my eye socket.

"Shit," he says. He pulls off his Ray Bans and looks close at it close. "Looks fresh."

"Yeah. Yesterday."

"Yesterday?" He counts something on his fingers. "Nope. Cardinals were in Minneapolis yesterday. Matter of fact, they've been out of town all week."

"Right."

"Yup. You wanna start shoot'n straight now, cowboy?"

I do not. I cannot. I wish he had chosen a word other than shoot. I cover my face with my hands.

I think I might be crying. My fingers are wet. Yes, I am crying. First time in years. Since my mother's funeral. I picture her laying there in her casket, arms by her sides, the blue of her face shoddily covered in a pasty white cream. My father, despite the fact that they had been divorced for years, stood in the front of the casket, greeting mourners with a barely lucid grin, his hair unwashed, uncombed, his cheeks sunken. It was his fault.

"Bar fight?"

"Excuse me?"

"Was it a bar fight?"

"No," I say.

"You were drunk, though, right?"

Easier this way. "Yeah. I just got drunk, passed out, and woke up with this little artifact of my time in St. Louie."

"Been there boy. Been there." He pulls down the visor in front of him. The prayer of serenity. Again. Shit. Is this a trucker thing? "That there helped me through it."

"Yeah?"

"You betcha." He pulls out a card that has his phone number on it. "Anytime you feel like getting well, you let me know."

"Thanks, Riyad." I mean it, I think. It feels good to be cared for, even if it is by a stranger and under false pretence.

"You just cry it on out there kid," he puts a hand on my shoulder and squeezes. I feel a rush of blood to my shoulders, and my tear ducts open up.

"There's a bed in back. Why don't you have yerself a nap."

I go to the bed and cry myself to sleep like I can't remember doing since I was a baby.

The man and Sue are together in the garden. He is brushes his fingertips across the small purple berries of a plant. Sue is on her knees tending to the dirt with a spade.

"They let us live, you know," says Sue. "They let us breathe. Thy let us eat. They help us heal. They help us escape into little glimpses of other worlds." She pushes three seeds deep into a hole that she made with the spade, covers it and packs dirt over the top.

Sprouts spring forth from the hole immediately and begin to reach up towards where the man is standing. It is you. He, I mean, is you. The man in the dream. I did not know that then. When they are at his height he—you—looks at the purple berries that have formed under the foliage on the branches.

"Belladonna," the man says. "Medieval women put extract from the berries in their eyes to dilate their pupils. It was considered beautiful in those days." He pulls a berry from the branch and rubs it between two fingers. "In the States we tend to call it Deadly Nightshade. Close relation to the potato. Very psychoactive." He eats one of the berries. "But more than a little would likely just kill a person."

I try to say Sue's name. I want to ask her where she is. Where we are. I open my mouth, but no words. I feel paralyzed and I become conscious of my body back in the cab of the truck, cruising down the highway between Lebanon and Joplin.

"It was a common tool in the kit of medieval witches, too. These days it's just another weed," you said to me.

Sue looks at me and smiles an it's-all-going-to-be-alright-smile.

I remember in that place between wakefulness and sleep that I am on the way to her funeral, and that it is not in fact all alright.

I become conscious of Lynrd Skynrd playing in the truck and slowly regain mobility as Riyad thrashes about to "Saturday Night Special."

The truck pulls to a grinding halt at a truck stop in Joplin. There is a meeting going on, he says, and he wants me to meet some people who might be able to help me. I step out of the truck into the mid-afternoon sun. It smells like gas and fried food.

The chapel is a trailer without a rig. It has been painted white, and the wheels have been replaced by cinder blocks and a two-by-four scaffolding. There is a small wooden staircase built to lead to a door that has been built into the middle of one of the long sides. A cross, red, hangs above the door. Written above the cross is the passage, *their foot shall slide in due time*, Deuteronomy 32:35.

Inside are 8 rows of wooden chairs, no two alike, about half of them occupied. A podium stands at the front with a man, kind-faced and jowly, behind it. At the back is a small table with a pot of coffee and mounds of disorganized literature.

The man behind the podium looks as though he was ready to begin as we opened the door, but he has decided to wait for us to settle. He nods in the direction of Riyad and I can tell that they are familiar with one another. His hair is tall and white, brushed back into a pompadour that perches over sharp eyes and soft cheeks. He has the softened intensity of a retired military man who has had his first heart attack and wants to be sure not to squander what remains of his time.

"Pastor John," says Riyad.

The man, Pastor John, clears his throat as we sit in two too-small wooden chairs. I am afraid that mine may snap underneath me. He begins to deliver a sermon: "Destruction is always at hand. Destruction is always unexpected. Destruction is often the fault of none other than the destroyed. These are lessons that were taught to some of our first settlers by the great John Edwards as is emblemized by the passage that adorns the mast of this humble chapel. *Their foot shall slide in due time.* These are lessons that continue to be of value in this cousin of that New World that we inhabit today. Little has changed my friends. That garden of innocence has been converted into an Empire unlike any in history. Those bodies deemed 'savage' by the early arrivals converted and displaced, the nature that stood has been put to work in the aid of consumption, all that was threatening sterilized, and yet imperfect we remain in this most domesticated world.

"Most of you are here for addictions. Well, my friends you are not alone. This is a world of addicts, your addictions just happened not to be the most popular, the most acceptable. Breathe that air out in the parking lot if you want to know addiction at its most vile, most invisible. Smell the fumes that loft from those pumps that send our rigs around the country in the name of commerce. That there's addiction my friends. *Their foot shall slide in due time.*

"We are imperfect all. Destruction is at hand. And to see THAT as beauty, now, my friends, that is faith. Destruction is beauty because God can do no wrong. And now this next bit involves something of a balancing act, because, while seeing destruction in God's plan as beautiful may be right, seeking it out in yourself is not. You are not God, and destruction that you bring about is not beautiful. Destruction at your own hand is nothing more than blindness. God gave you eyes, not so that you could tear them out, but so that you could see.

"Every drink you poor down that gullet, every pill you pop in your tired face, every needle, every line, now that is nothing but you tearing out your own eyes. And I would take it further. Destruction at your own hand, may be common, but it is not inevitable. I say to you my friends, if destruction comes, then I will be there to meet it and I will even say, why, my lord, this destruction is a beautiful thing. BUT, I will not invite it, and I will not bring it about, and I will, indeed, fight it at every step until it's arrival.

"Preservation. I will preserve myself until the moment of destructions imminence, at which time my embrace will be as complete as my resistance had been.

"This world is a world that has embraced defeat, destruction, before its time. *Their foot will slide in due time.* But that time is not now. I will not call this laziness that pervades us, this comfort that has become our purpose, this pursuit of nothing greater than the fulfilment of desire, this ignorance of the pain we lower down upon the necks of the powerless of the world, the work of God. No. This time in which we live, this time in which we have decided that greed will be the central tenant of success, this is a time of men, not of God.

"You are addicts in a world of addicts. But, go forth proudly, because you, at least, have confronted your disease. You, at least, are strong enough not to allow your foot to slide before that time in which it will be due."

Pastor John's jowels shake as he speaks. His pointed finger rattles above his head as if he is conducting an orchestra.

When he is finished, Riyad leads me back to the coffee.

We pour two cups of thin brown coffee into styrofoam cups and add plastic spoonfuls of non-dairy creamer.

"So?" asks Riyad.

"So, yeah, good stuff," I say.

Riyad looks disappointed. "Did it make you consider any of the choices you're making in your life?"

"Oh, uh..." I choose honesty. "Not, really. I don't really consider myself an addict, Riyad."

His eyes roll wide. He points at my black eye. I remember that I told him I got it while drunk.

"Right. But, seriously, this is an anomaly for me. It's been a strange week."

"Do you want to tell me about it?"

I think of the black room with Flanders' head emerging from the glowing blue tube for the first time since I left the trunk of that car. I have no idea what is real and what is not. "No, I don't think I'm ready to talk about it."

"Come on. If you don't talk it out, you'll never make progress."

Pastor John is walking towards us, stopping to shake hands with each member of his congregation as he approaches.

Maybe, I think, religious people could understand. They're used to crazy stories. They believe in supernatural stuff, right?

"Riyad," says Pastor John, that finger that had recently been wagging at the front of the room much bigger at such close range. "I see you've brought us a new slab of liver to throw on the grill."

I don't like the sound of that.

"Yes, sir. I picked this one up in Lebanon, just a little tadpole."

I like the sound of that even less.

Pastor John looks me up and down as if he is trying to decide something. "You had lunch, boy?"

"No, sir," I say. I always feel young and under-dressed in the presence of clergy.

"Mmm hmmm," he says. "Why don't you eat with us today."

Us?

He drives a Prius. I would have expected a Cadillac, or at least an Olds Mobile. The Prius feels like a toy under the palms of the preacher. "50 Miles per gallon," he says patting the dash.

The music is low and holy. His big fingers tap the steering wheel along with the rhythm.

I am in front. Riyad is in the back. Pastor John takes an occasional break from humming to look at me and smile. I force myself to return the smiles, though I imagine they look as fake as they are.

"Where you from, Tommy?"

"Chicago."

"Oh boy, big city kid, here. What has you traipsing through Missouri?"

"I'm, uh..." For a moment I forget. "I'm on my way to a funeral."

His eyes soften. "I'm sorry to hear that."

I believe him.

"Who, if you don't mind my asking?"

"My stepmother."

"Were you close?"

Does it matter? "Not particularly. Not in these last few years, anyway."

He lets my response stew in ambient noise and then, "Well that's a shame."

I wonder if it is. "Yeah."

"Is your father handling it well?"

"I don't know."

He looks askance. "Have you spoken with him?"

"No, sir."

He nods as if he understands everything now.

A few minutes pass before he pulls into a long driveway lined with tall, skinny pines. They make me think of Christmas.

The house is a good distance back from the road and mostly covered from view by dense rows of trees. The house itself is a small new construction cottage of red brick with half a basketball court in the driveway. Bicycles are strewn around the lawn. A dog, a beagle, jumps in and out of a kiddie pool. I can hear children shouting in the back yard. The smell of charcoal permeates the area, mingling with the scent of pine and the cleanliness of the fresh air.

We step out of the car and walk towards the backyard. There are tents and makeshift wooden shacks strewn around the large plot of land. A picnic table and a large grill stand in the middle of the yard. The smell of food on the grill gives me a massive and undeniable hunger. It has been ages since my last meal.

Pastor John rests a surprisingly gentle palm on my shoulder and guides me towards the grill.

"Are you a carnivore, Tommy?"

I start to shake my head and change to a nod halfway through. "I try not to be."

"Well, hope you aren't disappointed in our fare. We tend to stick to the vegetable around here."

I could eat anything at this point.

"We farm it all right here on the premises and cook everything fresh. No one really misses meat when you're eating this good."

The food is amazing. Grilled corn on the cob. Veggie burgers made from vegetables grown on the premises. Potato Salad with a fresh mustard dressing. Apple pie. I eat like a horse. Pastor John was right: I do not miss the meat.

The people seem happy for the most part. Foreign to me. They sing, call each other brother, sister. They seem genuinely interested in me. It creeps me out, but at the same time I feel bad about being creeped out by them, because they are earnest and sweet in the way I have known few people to be.

"Brother Tommy," comes a voice from the picnic table, "Will you pray with us?"

My God. My greatest fear realized. "Ummm..."

"C'mon." The pressure comes from all sides. "It won't kill you."

I am not sure.

I catch a glimpse of Pastor John who shrugs to signify that there is no fighting it, and nods encouragement.

I feel like the only sober person at a karaoke bar.

I enter an ever-enlarging circle of swaying bodies. There is this strange low hum that arrises, not so much from any one person consistently humming, but from a series of disorganized grunts and moans that seem to overwhelm the grunter at unexpected moments. I feel that I am the only one not swaying, and when I try I am always going in the wrong direction. I feel like a kid playing an instrument for the first time, but then I feel like the instrument.

"Ooo ja ja may comta," comes a voice from my left causing me to jump to the right, almost knocking over a pregnant women with stringy black hair and a chin that seems to have over-stepped the natural human length by an inch or so. She smiles and pushes me back into the rhythm of the sway with a light push of her shoulder onto mine. "Comba bayh likkka likkka morandyyyyy-ahhhhhh. Samdha samdha jing jong hubbha hubbha liiiiiiiinnnnnddddddadada." What the hell? A woman on the far edge of the circle barks like a chihuahua. The Pastor has his eyes closed as he sways in tune with the others. "Makkha makkha juroney srifff srifff ploooooooaaaaaaaaaaaaaaaaah." I see that this is not a joke, or a vocal exercises for some intelligible prayer song that is coming. This is the main event. The woman to my left nudges me again with her shoulder and I try to grab the rhythm, but when she does it again I realize that is not what she wants. "pray," she mouths to me. I look up and see that the eyes of the whole group have centered on me. They are urging me with their nods to contribute. I shake my head. A voice from the far left begins, "Mranda singlar tchoney loney brar brar brar badalllakah swingdlumm yarrrrrrr." Shouts arise from various points on the circumference. "Whoa. Whoa. Whoa." A man raises his hands, and the hands of the people on either side of him, and begins to jump and flail like he is at a swing concert. He screams at the top of his lungs, and a psychotic shudder wiggles through my nervous system. I am scared at this expression of something naked, something sublime, something that may be misguided, but also seems somehow real. A woman breaks her contact with those at her sides, throws her body to the ground and jumps and twists like an eel on the beach. To me this is insane. To them it is holy. I am filled with the desire to laugh. It comes on slow, crawls up from somewhere deep in my belly and tickles my upper lip. It will not be stopped. My gut convulses and my esophagus itches. My eyes tear with the effort to suppress, but all in vain. The laughter busts out of my gut like diet soda from a bottle filled with mentos. I laugh so hard I nearly scream. At first the others take it all in with a sense of excitement, then, as it slowly dawns on them that my joy is coming at their expense, the air floods out of the circle. There are strong hands on my shoulders and I am being led away, the rejuvenating sounds "wikawallibijooomarkakaka," fading into the distance.

I compose myself on a couch in the living room with Pastor John.

"This was a little different for you," he says.

I nod, wiping tears from my eyes. "You could say that."

"Looks silly?"

"You could say."

"Well, I guess I can imagine it would from the outside," he looks thoughtful. "Hell, maybe it is silly." He chuckles. "Maybe most things people do are."

I nod in agreement.

"The thing is, in a world where everything's silly, maybe it's the one who ain't afraid to look silliest that wins out. I tend to think people look silly driving around in Hummers, talking on their iphone, lacing up their nikes, without realizing they're walking billboards. Without realizing they're choking themselves slowly, torturing kids on the other side of the planet, radiating their own brains."

I nod.

"All back to addiction, idn't it? Even me in my Prius."

"Listen, I tried to tell you before, I'm not an ad..."

"I know, I know. I've heard it all before. I'm not an addict." He scratches at the gummy veneer of his coffee table. "Thing is, I don't believe you. We're all addicts, son. This is a society built on addiction. It's inescapable. The best you can do is realize it."

"You know what makes capitalism work?"

Money, I think. I say nothing.

"Anyone who finds themselves in a position to change it is too rich to remember why they'd want to. You find your enemies, and you make 'em rich. That's the long and short of it. News is the same. Reporters want the story, well, they gotta pay those Columbia Journalism school loans somehow. You can always use a persons ambitions against them. It's only the ambitionless that I fear. Those types don't tend towards the political. Most anyway."

He scrapes some of the waxy surface of the wooden tabletop under his fingernail. It leaves a light brown trail on the table's surface.

"Follow me," he says.

I stand up and follow him down a dark, carpeted hallway towards the back of the house. There is a nightlight plugged into an outlet halfway through the hall that illuminates a portrait of Jesus that might have been painted by someone's grandmother.

When he reaches the end of the hall, he pushes open the door. "Welcome to my past," he says.

I step into a dark room. He closes the door. I have a flashback to Flanders floating in his blue orb. My pulse rises and I think I might scream.

The light flicks on. The walls are covered in newspaper clippings. Headlines spanning 30 years of history each accompanied by a photo or a series of photos. Vietnam to Desert Storm. The 'by line' of each reads a different name.

"What is it?" I ask pointing in a circle.

"Look under the photos."

Each photo was accompanied by the name John Sinclair.

"Pastor John Sinclair," I say.

"Bingo."

I walk around the room. The photos are familiar. Not because I have seen these in particular, but because they are familiar subjects. Broken men, scared children, strong women, burning homes, huts, villages, toys. All our saddest cliches.

"You learn a lot about power in places like that. I'll tell you what, it's as blind as a drunk, and I ought to know cause I was as drunk as they come soon before or after shooting most of those. A blind man taking photos of the damage done by other blind men. Don't get much sillier than that." He tapped his knuckles against one of the photos, a teenage boy scowling on the streets of East Timor. "It's all part of the same addiction. Hunger for more comes from the same fear of nothingness. You don't want to be empty, so you fill yourself so full that all the 'you' is diluted. When all the 'you' is gone a person will cling to whatever happens to be left like it's life itself."

"How can you have seen what you've seen and still believe?"

"Hell, I believe because I've seen what I've seen, boy. All that suffering can't possibly be meaningless. I won't let myself believe that."

The sun is setting. I thank the Pastor for the food as Riyad and I climb back into his truck..

"You get in touch with your father. Family is all we have in the end." He hands me a business card. "You get in touch with me if you need anything at all." He winks.

I tell him that I will, though I am sure that I will not.

Riyad does not speak to me much until he drops me off in the lot of a truck stop in North Tulsa. I think my laughter offended him.

5

Him

It took Eli's father nearly three years to die. It started slow. A twitch in his left eye. Forgetting Latin words while delivering the Eucharist. He had performed mass thousands of times, and he was still a young man. Forty-four. Not old enough to be forgetting. He was not a drinker. Not anymore. He had given it up when he turned forty and woke up on the church lawn, chalice in hand, a pile of regurgitated wafers laying six inches from his head. No one had spotted him, thank God, at least no one of much consequence. Georgia in the early 60's was still hostile territory for a Catholic, and they would have used any excuse they could to have sent him packing. Well, two people had seen him. The widow's grandchild, Ronnie had spotted him, and even helped him up into his quarters at the back of the church. And, Eli. Eli had watched from his upstairs window as Ronnie helped Dimitri into the cottage. Eli's eyes were more curious than disappointed, and that day was no exception. He squinted at Demitiri as is if he were encased in glass and placed under the lens of a microscope. Dimitri decided then and there to quit drinking.

For four years Father Dimitri's head was clear. Eli noticed that his smiles seemed to be set more deeply, like he was pulling them up from his diaphragm. The greenhouse went through something of a renaissance. Dimitri found new flowers, and those that had begun to wilt began to thrive all over again. They were close in those four years in a way that had been impossible before, and would become progressively more difficult in the last years. But, for that while they were a family. Dimitri read with Eli each night. Eli helped Dimitri write his homilies each Friday for the coming Sunday. They wrote them on Friday, practiced on Saturday and Father Dimitri performed the final product in front of the congregation.

"Where do they come from?" Eli had asked on a Friday afternoon.

Father Dimitri chewed on the back of his pen, a habit he had taken up since quitting smoking. "I don't think they come from anywhere."

"What do you mean?"

"I think they've always been there, waiting for the right series of events to unleash them."

"But you write them?"

"Do I make the plants out back? Do I create a tulip?"

"Yes."

"No. I create a circumstance in which a tulip can grow."

"But it wouldn't be there if it weren't for you."

"Maybe not *there*," Dimitri said pointing in the direction of the greenhouse, "but, it might *be* nonetheless."

"In some other garden?"

"Maybe."

"It's good to cultivate, because you give things the opportunity to grow, but you're never responsible for the existence of what's grown. A homily is the same. You cultivate. You make space. But, that space isn't yours, and neither is what grows there."

After a few months, Dimitri began forgetting which plants to water at what intervals, and the once luxurious greenhouse behind the little A-framed church—the one Father Dimitri liked to refer to slyly as his 'Cathedral'—began to look like an overgrown lot that happened to have been encased in glass. Plants that had never been planted found their way into the once well-kept environment. Dandelions grew. Dimitri seemed to like the wild growth. He would stand on the back porch and gaze into the gathering brush behind the glass that had grown opaque with debris as if he was watching the birth of the universe or the unfolding of some equally magnificent mystery.

Eli, now thirteen and having spent a year taking care of the increasingly absent-minded Dimitri, decided to take over the job of tending the garden. One day, while Dimitri napped, he put on gloves, brought his spade and his hack saw, and set about clearing the unwieldy growth that filled the once serene space. He yanked at the long vines that had grown intertwined with each other and clung tightly to the stems of weeds and flowers alike. He pulled up root structures, trying to parse the desired from the unwanted, invariably unrooting some of the plants along with the weeds. The dirt was richer than he remembered it being. There was a strange pleasure in the sensation of pulling a plant from the ground and shaking the soil loose from its sinewy roots. They looked like drawings he had seen of the human vascular system. They were not altogether different, he supposed. He thought of roadmaps, too, for some reason, or the paths of rivers. He thought of mazes winding their way through the material of time: roads both taken and untaken. He thought of all the processes of travel through life, grasping desperately for the next drink of water, the next bite of something nutritious, the next lesson that will lead to real nurturing growth, the next mistake. He thought of how random those paths were. He thought of the Dr. who had come recently. Of the name of the disease he had spoken, long, foreign sounding, inscrutable to Eli. He thought of the process the doctor described. The pathways of Father Demiri's brain would slowly erode. All those tendrils, as delicate as the roots of an orchid, would steadily rot, along with everything that had come to be associated with Dimitri's personality. He would cease to sleep as the pathways that had forged over forty years of life began to be erased. It was something like time travel: an unravelling of the past. He would grow delusional, violent, maybe. He would cease to produce melatonin. His body would eat itself. The doctor said his facial expressions would provide the illusion that his personality was still in there somewhere, but this, he assured Eli, was just muscle memory: patterns from a lifetime of smiling with a preference for the left side of the cheeks and lips, raising an eyebrow when he did not know the answer to a question. It was a genetic disease. Just one slightly irregular gene and the whole plan came apart. The odds were fifty-fifty for anyone in the genetic line. It was the first time Eli really worried about his own parents. What gifts had they left in his DNA.

Eli woke Dimitri and brought him out to see the garden when he had finished restoring it.

Demetri stood silent, mouth agape as had become the custom. His eyes surveyed the garden, the colors ordered, the heights uniform, the little pebble pathway cleared, the vines manicured and positioned along through their various paths, the picture of intention.

He smiled for a moment, then shook his head. The tears that streaked across his cheeks did not seem to spring from a joyful source.

"Don't you like it," asked Eli?

Eli gazed upon it as if it were a burial at sea. "I don't know."

No one in the town seemed to have a memory for anything pre-reformation. "Are you Christian or Catholic?" was a question Eli heard on weekly basis. "Both," he would say. The inquisitor would invariably shake their big smiling head, "Cain't be both 'em at once."

He was not the proverbial baby in a basket, but something not far from it. There was only one Catholic church in Macon, Georgia in 1953, when the newborn Eli appeared. Father Dimitri gave the homily to the dozen or so regulars each Sunday. There was no nun. There had been one. In the year leading up to Eli's birth. Months before Eli showed up, she disappeared. There were whispers of an Ashram in Punjab, a parish in the most provencal regions of El Salvador, some said she had defected to Cuba, or stolen away with a Fancy Frenchmen who had been in town setting up an outpost for an up and coming cheese trade that never up and came. When Eli arrived, the rumor was that Father Demetri was starting up an orphanage. Only the widow was smart enough to deduce the truth which was that the nun had given birth and sent the boy to live with his father. It was a very small orphanage that consisted of only Eli's lonely cot in the attic above Father Demtiri's chambers behind the church. Though Father Dimitri called it his 'cathedral,' it was not much more than a brown wooden A-frame with a pair of two-by-fours joined together in the shape of a cross adorning the apex.

Father Dimitri marveled at the boys deep green eyes. "He has the eyes of a wise old man," he said, holding the boy high up in front of him.

The widow scowled at the comment. "Granted, he has intelligent eyes, but wisdom's in the deployment of intelligence, and this boy has yet to deploy anything." She grabbed the boy and held his body close to her chest, leaning his head back to look more closely. "It is tempting to call him wise. Then, I've never been one to give in to temptation." She glared in Dimitri's direction.

A Jesuit, Father Dimitri had come to Macon after a long line of 'begotten by's' had led from the Ukraine and Ireland, to Southern Texas, and a generation before his own birth, Philadelphia, to start a school that offered the best education to the town's poor residents. For the most part, not even the poorest would take a free education if it came attached to the word Catholic, let alone Jesuit. Few of his few parishioners—mostly displaced New Englanders, or old stock from Louisiana—had school aged children. Father Dimitri taught Eli at home along with 2 other pupils: Laura Sanders (who's grandfather would make a fortune in Fried Chicken) and Franklin James, who's father was a lawyer from Boston who had been sent down to oversee the still tenuous desegregation of the Macon school district.

One day when Eli was seven he asked, "Father, what is a Jesuit?"

Father Dimitri put on his favorite expression: a squint that encompassed everything from his chin to his hairline, not sparing lips, nostrils, ears or anything in the region of the eyes. "Well, Eli, one day a scientist, a palaeontologist... Do you know what a palaeontologist is?" Father Dimitri knew full well that he knew the meaning of the word.

"Of course," said Eli, who's few possessions were covered in images of dinosaurs.

"Well, a palaeontologist came back from the holy land and stopped in the Vatican. 'Your eminence,' he said to the Pope, because that's what we priests call the holy father among other things, 'your eminence, we have found the bones of the lord and savior Jesus Christ.' Well, the pope was shocked and he turned to his three advisors, who happened to be a Franciscan, a Dominican and a Jesuit. The pope looked to the Franciscan and asked, 'what do you think?' and the Franciscan replied, 'your eminence, oh glory of glories, this beautiful discovery will shine a light through the ages and fill every spirit with with joy in the knowledge that they are not alone in this Universe, for the man Jesus lived and died for their sins and was summoned back from the dead as a sign of new and everlasting life.' The Pope turned to the Dominican and asked 'And you, Father, what thinks you, sir?' The Dominican frowned deeply. 'Your eminence, this is a travesty.' The Pope looked distraught. 'But, why, sir?' The Dominican threw his arms into the air and nearly shouted, 'because, my noble friends, if his bones are here, then there could have been no resurrection. The very mystery of our faith is a sham if his earthly body deteriorated into this that you now lay before us.' The Pope looked gravely concerned. Even the Franciscan looked a bit perplexed. 'And you, brother,' said the Pope to the Jesuit, 'what, good sir, do you think?' The Jesuit, looking confused, scratched his beard, 'do you mean to tell me there was really a Jesus?'"

It was not immediately clear to Eli how the joke illuminated the character of a Jesuit. But with time he would come to understand the difference between the blindly faithful, the skeptically faithful, and those that were faithful in spite of seeing just fine. It was impossible, he decided to be without faith. Even faith in nothing was faith. A belief in Science, a belief in a system based on the ability of the human senses to come to finite truths about the nature of reality, time, the universe, that was perhaps the most far-fetched of all the faiths. A belief that knowing was impossible was an equally binding ideology. If one was bound to have faith, Eli decided at an early age, he was not going to fight it. He had been born, or delivered soon after birth, into this strange pocket of Catholicism—the world's most historically successful faith after all—and it seemed it would suffice to meet most of his spiritual needs. But, Father Dimitri was also a man of science, and as such, he spread his faith around. He often said, "It is within humanity's power to exponentially increase their infinitely meaningless knowledge every single day, and furthermore that it is their absolute responsibility to do so."

Father Dimitri built the greenhouse behind the church when he first arrived in Macon. The residents joked that he spent more time shepherding his crops than his flock. He retorted that his plants outnumbered his congregation, and so merited more of his time, energy and prayers. Despite his eager spirit, his early ignorance to the needs of the botanical world became local legend. The widow lived in the old colonial estate a few miles from the church. She was one of the few non-Catholics in the neighborhood who stooped to interact with the town's new clergymen. She brought him a basket of homemade cloth roses, which, much to her amazement, he proceeded to plant and water for nearly a month without ever coming to the recognition that the plants were artificial. Rather than destroy his illusion, she had her teenaged grandson, Ronnie, a boy who seemed to have a permanent aversion to shoes and shirts, uproot the fake plants in the middle of the night, and replace them with real rose bushes. "That man's thumbs are redder than those fake roses," she took to saying when he was nowhere near ear shot. Father Dimitri, if he noticed the change, never let on.

With time, though, his thumb grew greener. He planted vegetables, fruits and herbs, all of which found their way onto the dining room table throughout the Summer and Autumn, and into jars for the Winter and Spring. He experimented with exotic plants, too. The back left plot, furthest from the door, and most hidden from the casual passersby, was filled with the mixed results of his efforts to cultivate orchids.

By the time he was five, Eli knew how to test the PH of soil, how to trim a plant for optimal growth, how to fertilize and water two-hundred different species each with its own set of idiosyncratic needs and desires.

When he was not tending to his plants, he was reading. He took mostly to religious books, moving slowly through the Bible, the Koran, the Vedas. Slowly, he tired of the strange, two-dimensional myths of religious texts, and by the time he was 15 he had turned his reading further afield to the poetry of Rumi, and Khalil Ghibran, the novels of Herman Hesse, the Confessions of St. Augustine, and especially the complete works of Shakespeare. Shakespeare's works were like ivy that spread from humble roots through the imagination, covering every available surface. Macon's public library was his second home. He went almost every afternoon, and afterwards he laid under a lunging green elephant leaf in the greenhouse and flipped through the pages of whatever the day's book happened to be, pausing on occasion to trace the veins of the plant's undercarriage from its stem into the outer provinces of its foliage. He thought of how similar his own body was: a series of passageways delivering fluids, pumping chemicals that were derived from the Earth, water and the Sun. The plant was also like his mirror, breathing in, even thriving on, the very toxins that his body dispersed with each exhale.

He never attributed this perfect symbiosis to God. He never said that God had made the plants. For Eli, that was reductive. God was the interdependence between the plants body and his own. God was the process that bestowed information with meaning, the subtle shift from the anxiety of a dream to the narrative it became soon after dawn, the incalculably mysterious transition of genetic material into patterns that prescribed the physical world, that locus between one person's mouth and another's ear where minds meet and reproduce meaning. God was the juncture between the concrete and the abstract, the thinking and the thought.

For his part, Father Dimitri never, not even in the early stages of his dementia, seemed angry with God.

"God's as much a madman as a Saint, Eli," he said. "I may lose my words, I may lose the ability to turn shapes into a world, but this reality will, one day, disintegrate from before each of us, and the day that it does will be a good day. A beautiful day."

Eli was not sure.

6

Her

They took the car to San Diego. Kim drove. Straight West on I-80. Iowa City. Des Moines. Omaha. They did not stop until the Rockies. Denver. Strange intermittent home to some of Twentieth Century America's most improbable literary fame. Kerouac. Ginsberg. Cassidy. Kim loved the beats. He imagined himself stealing cars, smoking "tea", taking on lovers without stopping to consider the flippancies of gender.

Adam and Kim kept the car fuelled by stopping when need be and finding a cafe or bar that would let them play songs for change. They were in no hurry. Kim had nearly a month before he had to report for basic training. He wanted to try on the identity of a burgeoning beat before enlisting... and who knew, maybe he would find himself before arriving at the base. Maybe he would go AWOL before he even started training. They were a pair of earnest young poets positioned against society like a body strapped against a hospital bed. Kim could tell that Adam thought of himself as a young Chet Baker. It was the way he did his hair. The way he never said no to a drink or a cigarette, or anything else that happened to be offered. Adam was a nihilist, or a sensualist maybe. Adam wanted everything in quantities that were self-diluting. Pleasure upon pleasure evicted pain from the neighborhood until pain finally tired of its nomadic displacement and started squatting on pleasure's couch. The two had become indistinguishable. Kim was a dabbler. He wanted to try everything. He wanted experience. And experience, even the experience of excess, is something that can thrive in small doses. If there was some organizing virtue behind Kim, it was a need to see for himself. He wanted to see what it was like to be high on psychedelics, but he also wanted to see what it was like to steer an aircraft carrier, to fly at mach 3, to write books, shake hands with presidents, live with bedouins, eat yak… To see all of that, one had to have a clear head. As some buddhist somewhere once said, and his father often reminded him, the key to a happy life is to walk a million miles and read a million books. He was only about eleven when he realized that reading a million books would be impossible no matter how hard he tried, never mind walking a million miles, but still, it seemed like the principle was sound, and no really great goal was ever one that could be finitely accomplished. The greatest goals were those that propelled people into the future knowing full well they would only take a few steps of the journey within the limits of their own time on Earth. Kim knew that for Adam drugs and drink were ends in themselves. They were not experiments or experiences but freedom from those things. Adam lunged himself towards annihilation with a casual abandon that seemed like he was flicking all of reality a limp-wristed bird. So, Kim would have to free himself from Adam. This trip would be the end for them.

Kim joined the Marines because he wanted to travel, he wanted to study, he wanted to see things that hitching the countryside, smoking pot, playing music, couldn't offer anymore. There was no 'movement'. There was no community. If you were into cock rock and cocaine there was a scene in LA. Seattle offered some interesting possibilities, but it all rung a little cynical. Besides, with Japan on the grow, Europe on the mend, Russia on the decline, it was already clear, to Kim anyway, that the future lay outside of the borders he had become accustomed to. This was before the Eurozone, before China rising, before India the superpower, before NAFTA, before terms like globalism and free trade were on the tips of every preteen tongue. Kim had no way of knowing how the world would change, but he knew change was coming, and he saw the Marine Corps as a bridge to elsewhere. Fifty years earlier he may have gone to Cuba and fought with Castro, but now? Who to fight with now? Why fight at all? The short answer was, his father.

Kim's father, a slender old Korean man with jet black hair, perpetually wrinkle free clothes, and an unhealthy obsession with Greek mythology, had fought in the Korean war, crossing and recrossing the 38th parallel for two years as the US backed South advanced on and retreated from the Chinese and Soviet backed North. He was 16 when the war had begun. After the war he had gone to the United States to live. Kim never understood why his father had waited until he was in his early forties to marry and have children. He never understood how such a traditional old Korean man ended up marrying a young blond tax attorney. He never understood anything about his father accept that he revered above all else the experience he gained in the war, an experience that he almost always referred to through allegories to the Greeks. He never spoke of it directly, just like he never spoke of his life in Korea directly, only answering direct questions with indirect references to Apollo,

Orpheus, Achilles, or Ariadne. But, it was always clear he could never fully respect someone who had not seen battle. Kim wanted his father's respect, and quite simply that was how he found himself on his way to basic training.

"How's a fag like you gonna make it in the Marines?" asked Adam.

Kim stared at him from between his long flanks of hot pink hair. "How's a fag like you gonna make it as a jazz singer?"

"Isn't that, like, uh, some kind of prerequisite?"

"Was Chet gay?"

"Probably. Sometimes. He was every other kind of degenerate."

"Are you calling gays degenerate? You? Seriously?" Kim feigned anger.

Adam smiled out of the side of his mouth that faced the passenger side window. "If the ruby red slipper fits."

Kim knew that Adam took a special joy in infuriating people, so he did his best to act infuriated. "You're an ass."

"Don't you know it." Adam turned up the radio as "Unskinny Bop" by Poison faded out and "Nothing Compares to You" by Sinead O'Connor started to track.

Kim liked the song, nonetheless he rolled his eyes and stuck-out his tongue. It was a dismal era for music. The big hits as of late had been things like "Don't Worry Be Happy", and "I Wanna Be Rich," The New Kids on the Block and the definitive demise of Billy Joel filled the airwaves alongside Wilson Phillips' hits and Michael Bolton's stardom. The strangely soured optimism of George Michael was everywhere, though his sexuality was still a matter of debate, as for that matter, was that of one of music's few bright spots, Freddy Mercury and the incomparable Queen. M.C. Hammer and Vanilla

Ice were yet to be fully and forever entered into the realm of comic reference. Michael and Janet were the incestuous king and queen of pop. Milli Vanilli existed. And then there was Prince. Prince was a saving grace. The one that might rightfully succeed Queen. The one that brought theatricality tinged with artistry. He was not another coke fiend hack, shouting racist and homophobic tripe from his Reeboks. He was not selling a gimmick, though he certainly was adorned in his fair share of accessories. In Prince resided the slim hope that music might still have somewhere to go that was not entirely driven by the cynical rattles coming out of the Pacific Northwest.

"Nuhthiiing compares. Nuh-thing compares. Too-you," Adam screamed at the top of his lungs.

"Save your voice, Sinead. We're gonna need to gas up in Denver."

"How far are we?"

"Not very. Should be less than an hour."

Adam ran his fingers through Kim's hair and Kim felt, for what would be one of the last times in his life, at least the last time for a couple of decades, the last time before he would, as a middle aged officer who had spent the better part of his life hiding his sexuality, meet a woman named Eve, that he was being touched. Not some semblance of him that had to be maintained for a military career, not some duty bound collection of nerve endings and skin cells, and synapses forged under enemy fire, but him.

"We're gonna have to shave all this off, you know?"

"I know," he said smiling. "I'm ready." But even as he spoke them he doubted the validity of the words. It is strange that some things have to be stated before they can feel uncertain. Feelings about some things, like love and maybe death, as long as they are allowed to remain amorphous, floating in the ephemeral cloud of projection, can remain solid as fictions. But once spoken, the rattle of vocal chords against consciousness lets them be known for whatever they really happen to be: sentiments somewhere along the spectrum of full or empty. The moment he said the word 'ready', the moment he felt it loft emptily from his tongue, was also the moment that he knew he was embarking on a very long predetermined path. He could see exactly where he was heading, but nonetheless could not change course. He knew at that moment that he was not ready at all. He knew that he was betraying his love, abandoning Adam to the hell that hovered around his vices in favor of a life that would always be someone else's. But, the papers were signed, and he knew what happened to those who looked back.

7

Her

Denver was where it happened. They played at a little coffee shop on 5th Street. Kim pulled the keyboard out of the Volvo and dragged it into the cafe which wreaked of some horridly artificial incense covering the usually pleasant aroma of freshly roasted coffee beans. The music in the coffee shop was new age. Indecipherable instruments played slow scaleless patterns. The walls were covered in airy pastel ribbons. The tables were nearly all empty. A couple stared into each other's eyes in the corner. A student sat before a thick highlighters stained volume. The owner's name was Bill. Bill was tall and thin and wore tight white jeans. His shirt was a blue so light that it might have been white too. His hair was blond and overgrown. It fell over his forehead, but then swooped back up for an inch or two as if just the tips were reaching towards the static magnetism of some invisible balloon. His wide smile exposed slightly yellowing teeth. It was his eyes that Adam would remember, though. They sat above that smile but might as well have been a galaxy apart. The corners of his mouth could raise and raise, but never a sparkle from those deep blue rings circumnavigating the stoney pupils. Adam would look hard into them even as he was pinned to the ground, a hand gripped hard around his neck, legs forced to either side of him by sharp elbows pressed into the back of his knees, his testicles held painfully against his pelvis to expose him. That stupid wisp of weightless blond hair dangled over his forehead all the while. Those eyes telling him that even this torture was joyless.

"Hi boys," said Bill, a wild smile emanated from his mouth and was reflected in his eyes.

They offered shy, polite nods.

"Coffee?"

Kim shook his head. Adam nodded.

"We were wondering if we could play here. I play piano. He sings," said Kim.

"Hmmm...." Doubt spread across his face like an easily quenchable thirst.

"We're on our way to San Diego. This idiot enlisted," said Adam touching Kim's head with feigned affection.

"Ah. A war hero to be."

Kim cringed. "God, I hope not. I just want to travel, you know, see the world, maybe get some of that G.I. Bill action."

"If you want to travel, you ought to have gone into English teaching. Joined the Merchant Marines. You, son, have signed up to fight wars. A volunteer killer."

"Well..." He didn't really have any decent response. It had never occurred to Kim that there might be better ways to see the world.

"Nothing to be ashamed of, son. We've had soldiers longer than we've had language." He ran his index finger across the front of his upper teeth. His incisors were a little too long and sharp. "Hell, they say prostitution's the oldest profession? Well, I say it's soldiering." He pushed up the sleeve of his T-shirt revealing a USMC tattoo.

"Not setting a very high bar, really," interjected Adam.

"You have no idea just how high the bar is, son, until you've had your head up against it."

Adam's was the first to break eye contact in the staring contest that ensued.

"Well, anyway, it seems that you boys are in a different business for the moment. So, what can I expect to hear this evening?"

Kim could hardly contain his excitement. Adam could hardly summon any.

"Well, sir, we play all kinds of stuff," said Kim.

"Sir? I'm impressed. But, please, don't impress me again. Bill. Billy. Wild Bill. W.B. Wild William. No more sir. Por favor."

"We'll drop the sir if you'll drop the Spanish," said Adam.

Bill contemplated the offer. "Trato hecho compadre."

"Dios mio..." said Adam.

"So aside from 'all kinds of stuff' what do you play?"

Kim surveyed the pastel wall coverings, overflowing ash-trays, un-bussed tables and gum-impacted shag carpeting.

Bill noticed him inspecting the area. "May not look like much, but we're kind of a local institution."

"Well, we play jazz standards. Some depressed rock tunes. An original or two."

"Can't pay you much."

"We just need a tank of gas and a meal."

"I can do you one better."

"How's that?"

"Tank of gas, a meal and a place to lay your pretty little heads."

"I hope you're not thinking of your lap," said Adam.

"What do you think, I'm some kind of pervert?" Bill's smile widened under those unchanging blue eyes.

He gave them thirty dollars and said they'd have to make it work for food and gas. They could come back and play at 9 that evening.

They had a few hours to walk the streets and find some food. Bill had recommended a place for burritos big enough to share. They had great carnitas, he said.

Kim spotted a trinket shop on the way to the restaurant.

"I want to get you something," he said.

"Get me something? Like what?" Asked Adam.

"Like something. Something that makes you mine.'

"I don't want to be yours," said Adam through a smile.

"Too late, slut."

"How do you figure?" Adam said, laughing now.

"I figure because when someone gets inside your mind, you can never really get them out. We're always going to be connected. Like intertwined electrons mirroring each other across galaxies. So, maybe you're not quite mine, but I'm definitely a shareholder."

"That's actually kind of sweet. So, I own a little Marine," said Adam.

"Just a little."

"Well, where can I unload my stock, man? I am broke with a capitol B."

"You can't sell this stock. You take it to the grave."

"Hmmm..." Adam kicked at a leaf that was rotting in an almost melted snow pile that slowly deteriorated near the edge of the sidewalk. "So what are you gonna get me?"

"What are we gonna get us, you mean?"

"Okay. Us."

"Let's see."

They opened the door and walked into the store. There were little elephants carved from jade. Bright stones with no value whatsoever. Earrings in the shape of dream catchers. Adam picked a pair of the earrings up and showed them to Kim.

"Hideous," said Kim.

"Practical, really. If you're gonna lose a dream it'll probably be coming right out your ear, so it makes good sense if you ask me."

"I didn't."

"Can I help you boys?" The man was old, and seemed to be of Middle Eastern descent.

"We're looking for, well, a symbol of love." Kim said the word 'love' in a deep baritone.

He looked at them over the top of his glasses one of the lenses of which was cracked down the middle, and whistled a random note. "Love?"

"Or some such," said Adam.

"Or some such," repeated the man. He seemed to think it over for a minute and then laughed. "I guess it's always 'or some such'." He walked towards a glass display, "Rings, I suppose, would be too traditional?"

"And too expensive."

He abandoned the glass display with a dismissive wave and pulled out a cigar box.

"Quite smoking years ago, but they still make great storage."

"I can see that," said Kim looking past the man at a wall fully covered in cigar boxes piled one atop the other.

He opened the box in his hand, grimaced, and headed for the wall. "Hmmm..." He looked at Kim. "Bring me that chair there." He pointed to an old wood chair with a green leather seat that sat behind the register. Kim brought it to the wall of cigar boxes.

"Do you mind?" he said to Kim gesturing towards the chair.

Kim stepped onto the chair.

"That one there," he pointed.

Kim reached for a box.

"No. No. No. To the Left. The other left. A little farther. Down a row. A little farther to the left."

Kim was stretched to his full length, the tips of his toes barely on the chair.

"That's the one."

He slid the box out and facilitated all of those above it as they descended one spot in the order.

He put the box on the counter.

The old man opened it. "Here we have it," he said pulling out a pair of shiny silver pins.

"What is it?"

"What are they you mean?"

"..."

"Pins. This one is the Lyre of Orpheus. This one the grapes of Bacchus. Once upon a time Neil Cassidy gave one to Ginsberg and wore the other himself. You can guess which was which."

"I'd rather you just told me," said Adam.

"You, then, will wear this one." He pinned the lyre on Adam's peacoat.

"What is it?"

"Have you ever read Milton's 'Il Pensoroso'?"

"No, sir," said Kim.

The man looked him over knowingly. "And this one for you." He put the grape pin on the lapel of his shirt. "L'allegro and Il Pensoroso are two interlocking poems written by Milton about two different approaches to poetry. You could say two different approaches to life. The first abandons itself to the flesh, finds the muse in pleasure, sensuality, booze, the whole lot. Where the first is rolling around down in the gutter, in a world that can be a little too real," he gestured towards his crotch with his left hand, "the second lives up in the tower, in ideas, dreams." He maintained his left hand in place, pointed his right finger tip, like the nozzle of a pistol, against a temple, "in a world of ideals." He stood there looking ready to recite a perverse rendition of a nursery rhyme. Kim half expected him let loose with the first lines: 'I'm a little teapot short and stout. Here is my handle. Here is my spout.' "The thing is boys, the dick falls an organ short without the brain. And the brain without the dick, well, it's gonna wind up a few thousand generations shy of man's first abstract thought."

"So, the grape's are kind of a dick?" asked Adam petting the little silver pendant. "Nice."

"In a manner of speaking, the grapes are a dick. But, it's a mindless dick. A directionless appendage. An erection gone mad with the power of a king who's killed off his best advisors. A junky who's never read a book. A cause so lost it doesn't even know how to enjoy the sheer bliss of it's only emotion: orgasm."

"And the lyre?" asked Kim.

"Ah, well there we've found the lonely old man who knows everything but how to elicit pleasure from his own balls."

"I don't have that problem," Kim said smiling.

"Not yet," the old man said, a foreboding glare leaning over the crack in his lens.

Kim, nervous, felt his hair. He wondered what it would feel like once all the follicles had been reduced to sharp little nubs.

"You could think of that hair your rubbing as an hour glass. See where you find yourself when the hours half gone. See where you're at when the last strand drifts to the ground and your time's run out. Everyone's got a little balance when they're young. The challenge is to keep the balance throughout your life. Not too slide too far into one abyss or the other. To keep one hand solidly on your cock, while the other rubs a throbbing temple."

"Hmmm..." Adam said. His own temple was throbbing less than that other member. "Which was Ginsberg's?"

"lyre," said the old man. "Let's just say he had to learn to howl, but, he had it pretty well balanced there by the end. Cassidy was all cock. Led to the slaughter by his own mindless balls."

Kim thought of another Lyre. He heard his father's voice reciting the myth of Orpheus in Korean. Every night before bed he recounted Orpheus's journey into hades. His recovery of Euridyce. The fateful glance back into the darkness. He had the knowledge, but he lost his love again. It must have been later that he was ripped to shreds because of the beauty of his music.

8

She

No one was there for the concert, but they played anyway.

"I've already paid you, so I should at least get to hear a few songs," said Bill.

Afterwards Wild Willy bought three six-packs of Old Style tall boys.

"I don't really drink much," said Kim taking a can and struggling to crack it.

Adam had his half drained by the time Kim had his opened.

"I'm glad you boys happened through. I don't get much company," said Bill through a wide, wild smile. He slid a hand off of his own thigh and onto Adam's.

Kim excused himself and climbed the creaky staircase to the bathroom. He stood over the toilet, but nothing came out. He did not really have to pee. He could still hear his father's voice. Kim did not speak Korean fluently, but over the years he came to understand it. His father always recited the myths in his native tongue, his breath wreaking of scotch, a smell he learned to associate with kisses and the sound of the Korean language. There was a wrought-iron vent on the bathroom floor that opened above the living room.

"Just a little drop of that in your beer, and you'll be sailing all night," said Bill.

Kim knew that Adam would take whatever was being offered. No matter what it was. He always took it. He did not know, however, that Adam had accepted on Kim's behalf as well.

Kim awoke in a dark living room. There was a cat pawing at his chest. The low steady hum of its purring might have put him straight back to sleep if the cat hair on the couch had not irritated his allergies. His tall can of Old Style, still nearly full, stared at him from the coffee table. He tossed the cat to the ground and headed for the restroom to rinse his eyes to avoid their becoming a red puffy mess that would render him incapable of helping with the drive to L.A. He felt groggy beyond reason. His limbs were heavy. He lumbered at each step towards the stairway, fumbling through the dark. He left the light off in case Bill slept with the door open. He stepped onto the creaky wooden staircase, clinging to the old handrail, the screws of which felt as if they might yank free from the stucco wall. He pulled himself up to the second step, minimizing the creak by putting more weight on the handrail, but bobbling back when the handrail gave, making a still louder creak. He hit the third step and the fourth, sure now that he had awoken everyone in the house, but driven on nonetheless by a relentless bladder. Light infused the dark hallway through a slightly cracked door. He approached the landing with soft steps. He pulled himself up the last stair and paused to see if there was movement inside, or if someone had fallen asleep with the light on. He could see almost nothing, but he registered that even after he finished his ascent the the sounds of creaking wood bounced around the house's spacious, decrepit innards.

The sound of a moan seeped through the dark and intrigued him. Was it someone dreaming? Someone crying? Someone fucking? He waited for a sequel that would help him register the meaning of the first sound. The sound of wet lips meeting. The sound of a sniffle. Some indecipherable mumble. What came was another moan of equal ambiguity. It sounded muffled. Through a pillow? A hand? Something fell from a low height creating a dense thump. He moved towards the cracked door, his bladder screaming, his eyes beginning to burn from cat dander. He ran a hand through his own overgrown hair, remembered briefly, again, that it would soon be gone. He peered into the room and saw the lyre pin attached to the lapel of Adam's discarded pea coat. His stomach sunk back down to the couch where he had been asleep moments earlier. His pulse pounded into his eardrums. The moan extended, vibrated, contorted the air around Kim's head as it turned into a muffled poem fluctuating between stressed and unstressed syllables, communicating more articulately than words would ever dream of. He stared at the lyre as it bounced up and down with the fall of each stress. He was mesmerized by Adam's voice. He could not turn away, even as his every faith was being shred before him. It was as if he was involved in a gaper's block at an accident sight where he was the victim. There was a morbid joy in being party to his own betrayal. He moved closer to the door. He peered through, saw Adam's foot lifted over a shoulder, an elbow pressed tightly into a knee. He stepped closer. A hand held tightly over his mouth. The moan was muffled by a hand. Adam liked to have his mouth covered while he fucked. His eyes were locked onto Bill's like small planets fixed on some larger body they were forced to orbit. But, the hand. Something was wrong. There was something between the fingers. Then the eyes, they broke their orbit and found Kim's in the hall. They were scared. And between the fingers. It was that rich shining burgundy that makes humans queasy when it seeps out of its containment. Kim was thoughtless. Empty. Reactive. A vessel for impulses that were sourced somewhere deep. Internal or external, it was beside the point. They were forces that were remote from his consciousness. He shoved the door open, moved quickly towards the bed. What was in his hand? Where had it come from. Bill turned from Adam and barely had time to register Kim's presence before the tip of the umbrella accelerated past his eye socket and into his brain. He slumped, and gurgled, and said, oh shit man, which sounded so inappropriate to the occasion, and Kim twisted the umbrella, and there was a terrible sound like water being squeezed from out of a head of lettuce, and Adam's moan became a sort of psychotic staccato chuckle as some of the contents of Bill's head dripped onto his chest, and he fell from the bed to the ground. Kim picked up the peacoat before the puddle of mess could expand to dirty it.

9

They

Will was watching television. Some reality program. Celebrities who had fallen from grace living in tight quarters with retired zoo animals.

"We need you ready for the debate, Will," said Karen.

"I'll be ready."

"Nothing lasts," said Karen glancing at the screen.

"Some things do."

"Well, not for them, not fame, not wealth…"

"Wealth can last. Power has lasted. For generations. Resources. It won't be oil forever. It was gold once. It's even been tulips. It will be sunlight. Celebrity. Genes. Even neural pathways. We're on the brink of a thousand paths to fortunes that will dwarf any that history has seen. Lasting fortunes."

"And what about economic equality?"

"Equality is a fantasy. In a world where energy is free, labor practically unnecessary, wealth consolidated, there will be no place for equity. With increased life spans we will want to be sure that population growth is controlled. With a complete understanding of genetics, we will eliminate disease, stupidity, even abject poverty will be obviated. We can do a better job than democracy at curing the worlds problems. An orchestra needs a conductor, not a hundred musicians playing their whims. But, inside the conductor is another orchestra, a brain, an identity composed of a thousand well tuned impulses."

"So, you nominate yourself conductor?"

"Not me. Not now." He looked at Karen, his eyes begging her to understand him. "I'm not describing the future that I want Karen, I'm describing the future that I see coming whether we like it or not."

10

I

The voice comes from across the gas station parking lot. "Boy, you luckier than a three-legged dog with two peckers."

George is my stepmother's ex-husband. He was a strange addition to the family that sort of came along with Sue when she married my dad. They grew up in the same small Oklahoma town. They were neighbors from birth more or less, and even upon divorcing it never seemed to occur to them that they might create some distance.

My luck, that which has just been compared to a dog with a missing limb and a proliferation of genitalia, is based, in his mind, on the fact that I had bumped into George in a Git n' Go parking lot, and he can offer me a place to sleep. I would not normally consider this luck, but I am dead tired, and I have no idea what other family or friends were even still in Tulsa, so I take him up on it.

"Shame about Sue," says George in a way that lets me know that was all he would be saying about the issue. His brow compresses with all the force of a Dog trying to comprehend the functionality of a telephone. Death was too much for George to contemplate, so he swept it aside. It was too much for any of us. Maybe his way was the most honest.

He puts one of his big, rough hands on my shoulder and ushers me towards his truck. He has to move tractor parts out of the seat to make room for me. He is in the tractor parts business as he is fond of telling those that cannot assimilate that information from his hat which read "George's tractors." To say that George is "into tractors" is a massive understatement. He owns a distributor which provides parts to just about every farmer West of the Mississippi.

The stereo in his truck is broken. We ride along in silence marked by the occasional gratuitous exhale until finally George decides to venture an effort at conversation. "How's the old man?" He says it without any hint of a grudge. They got along, he and my dad. I never understood that.

I nod as I think of my response. "Good," I say. "I don't know." I draw a smiley face on the window in fingertip grease. "It's been a while since we talked."

George nods. This is not new information for him.

"I just don't get it," George says staring out the window.

"What?"

He only shakes his head as a response.

"So how's the big city?"

"You mean the Second City. The Windy City. It isn't the big one."

"If it's bigger than OKC it's the bigg'n to me."

"Good. Busy," I lie.

He nods. "Idle hands."

I look at my hands. Soft other than the calloused fingertips from guitar playing. My nails are unclipped. Cuticles dry and stringy. George's hands are big and calloused with a line of grease that blackened the moon-shaped slivers at the tips of his nails.

"Still playing your rock and roll?"

I nod another lie, though I guess if you count playing in the living room for yourself and your non-plussed girlfriend to be rock and roll, it is not exactly a lie. Then, I guess Missy is not my girlfriend. I feel the phone in my pocket. Still no call.

"I always tell my friends I know a rock star from Chicago," George says.

I rarely tell my friends I know a tractor magnate from Oklahoma, I think.

George's house is in Catoosa, the town where I was born. It is a few miles outside of Tulsa on Lynn Lane, a road that's lined with small farms and stables. In the Spring it is all weathered brown fence posts popping up from grasses so green you could be in Ireland. Late Summer, like it is now, it has all turned brown and crunchy like someone spilled a giant box of cereal over the whole state. It is late as we pull onto the gravel driveway and the distinct crunch of tires grinding together hundreds of tiny stones breaks through the steady throb of cicadas. The cicadas seem to accentuate the heat. They remind me of long games of hide and seek I played with my cousins, or late night kisses from the neighbor's niece during a game of Truth or Dare.

George's dog, or one of them, runs alongside the car as it heads down the drive towards the house he likes to tell everyone he built from scratch. It is more or less true. There is a lawn jockey in front of the house, and a tire swing that I remember playing on as a kid. I hated that lawn jockey as a kid. Still do.

Inside is a disaster. George is a collector of all things mechanical. There are old stereos ripped to pieces, half assembled carburetors, the remnants of a septic pump, disassembled pistols that must have been sixty years old. The only thing the house doesn't have in it is food. No one in my family, not that George was exactly family, ever seems to be capable of keeping food in the house.

"Hope you ain't hungry," says George carrying two tumblers and a bottle of Black Label.

I am starving. "No. I'm fine."

He pushes the gizzards of a Victrola off of what was once a coffee table with his booted foot and sets the tumblers down on the grimy surface.

"Ice?"

I shake my head, more or less aware that there iss no ice in the freezer and if there is there would be no telling how many years it had been idling.

He pours the whiskey, takes his down in a gulp and pours again.

I take mine in two gulps and feel a little ashamed.

After repeating that process a few more times George stands, exhales deeply, stretches his arms and says through a yawn, "Well chief, I...am...bushed." He points to a couch that is buried in wires, metal and grease. "You go on ahead and burrow in their however you see fit." With that he heads to his room.

I look at my sleeping arrangements, pour myself two more shots, and go to work clearing a space on the couch.

She was there in my dream again. Sue stood over a garden filled with her usual cantaloupes, cucumbers, and tomatoes. She held a spade in a gloved hand. She wore that stupid hat with the wide-stretching brim, covered in earth and beaded sweat. She smiled.

"What's it like to be dead?" I asked her.

"It's not like this," she said gesturing towards the garden. "It's like the opposite of this."

11

Him

They passed unevenly, the three years of illness, as years of illness often do. At times they dragged. The tedium of long dark days in bed, slowly turned to bouts of sleeplessness and outbursts of violence. Good days were days when Father Dimitri stammered to himself in a corner, seemingly connecting words and phrases with no prejudice for their relevance to one another. Eventually, he was connecting syllables that scarcely even made words, and later still, sounds that it would have been difficult to define as syllables. At other moments, time seemed to fly by. Weeks would pass without anything that could truly be considered a self-conscious moment. Eli felt like a nurse in a war zone, running from tragedy to tragedy, but he only had one patient. His life dissolved into the illness, his consciousness was completely co-opted by the genetic deformity that had commandeered both their minds, both their bodies, both their wills. As his sense of self drifted further, and his body became more feeble, Eli began feeling more like a gardner than a nurse: watering his patient, providing the right balance of nutrients, testing the temperature, and various chemical indicators of health. In the meantime, the greenhouse was left to its own fate. The wild overtook the cultivated. The tended the became madly lush.

For the first two years, there were more moments of clarity than not. The third was another story.

It started with one book, and ended with another. It was one of his favorite corners of Macon's library where he found it. He had sat on the floor in front of one of the racks, absorbed in the musty smell of brittle-paged volumes, afloat in the mere prospect of being encompassed by the millions of words that constituted the collective memory of humanity's intellectual history. There were names that were grander than anything biblical: Mellville, Voltaire, Dostoevsky, Aristotle... Not that he had read any of them. They remained distant and untouchable. Things he suspected would one day be meaningful, when he was grown and the world made sense.

When he was younger, he spoke frequently of 'maturing'.

"When will I be mature?" he asked Dimitri.

"Never," said the priest with no trace of a smile. "You're not a cheese." The trace began to show itself. "You're a pudding."

"I wish I was," replied Eli.

"A cheese? A stinky gouda?"

"Yes."

"Why, Eli? Why would you like to be a stinky mound of molded milk?"

"I want to be mature."

"No, Eli. People don't work that way. We just go through phase after phase of imperfection. We're never quite edible, thank god."

"Why be thankful for never being finished?" Eli asked.

"Well, because if you were finished, you'd be eaten up."

For the time being he steered clear of the intimidating names he saw on the shelf behind Dimitri's desk, knowing that somewhere in the distant future they would be able to provide the answers to all his most festering uncertainties.

Eli had a habit of reading books backwards. Maybe it was a looser attachment to linear time that manifests itself more strongly in youth, but more likely it was just impatience. He could not bare to read a book without knowing where it was headed. He needed to know if there was a tragic end in order to appreciate every sweet moment leading up to it. Maybe in adults the signs of genre allow us to inuit where we are heading, easing a bit of the shock. Kids have to cheat. Or, maybe it has more to do with children being so far from the anxiety of their own ending—and so near the anxiety of their beginning—that they still have the audacity to rush.

The first book was poking out from under the shelf. The binding was green leather, and the name *West is the Only Way* was printed in gold. The authors name was O'Dea. Donnan O'Dea. He had never heard the name. He had never seen it shining from the spine of the volumes on Dimitri's shelves, or those in the Macon Public Library. No reason to put him off for some later date when, he was promised, he would understand it all better.

He opened the book to the last page and read the last line: *As the city burned behind him, Dick ran West.* Who was Dick? West from where? What city burned? Cairo? London? Atlanta? Starting at the end did not answer any questions at all.

It had been weeks since Dimitri had slept a full night. His eyes were wide and animal-like. His hand shook violently, and even the smile that he wore to convince those around him that everything was fine, twitched and unnerved. This was not the end, the doctors had assured. The intensity would deepen cyclically. He would recover and degenerate in unpredictable patterns.

Eli stepped inside with soft toes. He hoped that Dimitri would be resting, though he feared his hope was foolish.

"Eli muh-eye pud-ding," came the voice in its strange new relationship to syllables.

"You sound like a horse," said Eli not daring to look up at him.

Dimitiri smiled wildly. "A ho-arse, I uhm." His body thrashed towards the wall, then recovered with an exaggerated dignity. A stern focus showed on his face as he gathered himself for an exercise in precise pronunciation. "Wud you hu-ave?"

Eli looked at the book. "A book," he said looking towards his feet. "Just something I found in the library."

Dimitri took it into his hands and, devoid of all intention, waved it cautiously from side to side. The weight of the pages flopped away from the cover, and the stress made a tear at the top edge of the binding that looked like a lightning bolt.

"I uhm su-uh-orry," he said, his eyes looking briefly red and brilliant.

"It's okay, Father."

Dimitri, put a forceful hand on Eli's shoulder and tried to pull himself up from the bed.

Eli pulled back and watched Father Dimitri fall down onto the bed.

He opened the book to the first page of the last chapter. The line that ended the story was strongly with him: *As the city burned behind him, Dick ran West.* He wanted to know where it began, but he was not quite ready to treat life as a story that moved like an arrow. He would go just a little further back in time, catching a more complete glimpse of how it ended before moving all the way back to the beginning. He began to read:

Maybe if her father hadn't seen the paint that trailed up from her belly button and peeked over the collar of her blouse everything that happened later could have been avoided. But, he did see the paint. Maybe if he'd chosen to believe her excuses—that she'd bumped into the freshly applied paint of an elevator—life could have moved on as it always had. But, who paints an elevator's wall yellow? A yellow ochre that invoked the omnipresent tone of Oklahoma fields. No, he couldn't have believed her.

He'd seen that color. Over and again, he had seen that exact tone. It wasn't from the fields. It was the very same paint. He had seen splotches of that exact hue. It took him a minute to remember where. And even when he had recalled, he waited a minute more to let suspicion take root. It was the boy from the painting contest. His hands. Underneath his nails. It might have been a coincidence. It might have ended right there. But one more memory would not let him loose.

It was when she had come to visit him in his office. That brush of hands, almost unnoticed. The cringe on the boys face. The look, ever so instantaneous, of nauseas reprimand. The playful glint in her eye. Her father had chosen to ignore it then. But now, the color of the paint washed over him like something irrefutable.

The other book, the one that ended the year, was one filled with prophecies.

12

I

I wake to the sound of George's riding lawn mower doing laps around the massive stretch of yard that leads from his front door to Lynn Lane. Lawn care is a favorite Oklahoma pastime. I step over the shell of a Dynaco tube amplifier and lean out the front door. It is only eight or so, but the humidity is already in full effect. George is, as always, in jeans, boots and a long sleeve plaid, with his baseball cap, perky and informative, resting atop his head. I had not noticed the night before how old he looks now. The bags under his eyes have become defined, irrevocable. They hang from his face like the film that forms on an old custard.

He cuts the engine.

"Morning Sunshine."

I salute him for some reason.

"You want to hit the canteen?"

Breakfast. My stomach is screaming about the whiskey it absorbed on empty.

George jumps off his mower and starts for the truck. There would be no shower. No change of clothes.

His dog, or one of them, follows us back up the drive, his bark accompanying the same sound of gravel crunching under wheel.

The air conditioner is out in George's truck, so the windows are rolled down. The hot air blows against my face as we pass mile after mile of horses milling through brown fields. Where the fields end, the pawnshops begin. After a while the pawnshops become car dealerships, banks, strip malls with big box stores and chain restaurants. Tulsa.

When he pulls up in front of Annie's, my stomach, already screaming, starts to thrash. If things are anything like they used to be at a quarter to nine on any given day there was a fifty-fifty chance my dad would be here. I know I will see him at the funeral, but I am not ready. Not yet.

We walk in. I see him there. His balding gray head rounder than I remember. Chewing and smiling in the middle of a group of business associates. It enrages me. I charge him. Fists swinging. I punch a jaw that is padded by a cheek full of pancake. His dentures crack and he spits blood on the table. I stand above him laughing

Or...

I see him. Pathetic. Mourning. He sits alone with a cup of black coffee in front of oatmeal that his doctor told him was his breakfast destiny if he wanted to live to retirement. He is thinner than I recall, and his hair is still full with the remnants of its deep black color still apparent. He is alone. I sit. We eat together in silence.

But he is not there. I am bound to a meal of door watching. I hope in equal parts that he walks in and that he does not. I feel violent, morose, and full of anticipation with every swing of the heavy wooden portal.

I order french toast.

George does not order. They know what he wants. Two fried eggs. Ham. Potatoes, smothered and covered. Rye toast with orange marmalade.

Orange marmalade makes me think of Paddington Bear in his little blue raincoat and yellow hat. London must be a dreary place for a bear, culinarily speaking. Sue read me those books. Or maybe my mom started that and she just continued it.

The waiter looks like Will Rogers. He has narrow Eastern European eyes, and a dark Native American complexion. I want to see him doing rope tricks. It seems indignant that such a man would be relegated to the distribution of breakfast meats.

I get up to go to the bathroom.

The waiter stops me as I near the door.

"Your Tammy Shell's boy?"

He knew my mom.

I nod.

"I knew your mom."

I nod.

He looks like he is running through memories. I hope they were not lovers, but something about his smile, which is at its base a kind smile, tells me they were.

"We were pretty close back in high school, actually."

I nod.

"She helped me with Spanish."

I nod.

"Always wanted to ask her out, but never worked up the nerve."

I breathe.

"Must a cried a week when she ran off with your pop."

I smile.

"How's ol' George?"

I shrug.

George throws a scowl in our general direction, and the waiter seems to return a softer sort of scowl.

"Well..." he says reaching into his pocket, "you need anything you give me call." He hands me a business card: Lean Rogers, rope show. There is an email address, lean@leanrogers.com, and a phone number. "Stage name," he says. He extends a hand. "Rusty." Rusty Rogers seems like a perfectly good name for a guy doing a rope show.

My dad never shows up. I think that is a good thing. I am not ready to see him today.

George has an extra car which he lets me borrow: a 78 Volkswagen Rabbit. The driver's side door doesn't open and reverse is kind of tricky. It works, but it takes love, George explains. I climb in the passengers door and scoot over the emergency break to lower myself into drivers position. The car is positioned with the front bumper six inches from the garage door. Love, I think, as I try to cram the shift stick back and to the right. The transmission lets out a thick grind, but the stick will not slip into reverse. George comes out and reaches over me to the stick.

"Push the clutch for me."

I do as told.

He grabs the stick and slides it all the way right, then back a centimeter to the left and glides it down.

"Just a little love."

Off I go.

It has been years since I have spent time in Tulsa. The funeral is tomorrow. I don't have many friends left here. There is Tanya, pronounced like tan, as in to sunbathe, with a yuh, at the end. She was my neighbor when we were kids. She was the first friend I ever applied 'best' to. She was the first girl I ever kissed. Though it was as a friend, she said. I was 14 the last time I saw her, but I know she is an insurance agent for Wells Life thanks to the omniscience of facebook. The office is in a big building near the Warren Center. I could surprise her for lunch.

I drive past the statue of the giant praying hands that pop out of the ground in front of Oral Roberts University. As a kid I always wondered about the man attached to those hands. What did he eat? Who fed him? Did he pull his hands down at night when nobody could see him so that he could tend to his daily chores? The campus behind the praying hands looks like a dated concept of Oz: gold shimmering towers that had not aged with grace.

I drive up to the Warren Center and pull the rabbit into a tight spot between an F-150 and a yellow Hummer. It's a corporate park. In these most dedicated pockets of free market America, most green spaces are property of one corporation or another, or the product of philanthropy. It was fine during the boom years, not to mention in times when public perception was important to leaders of industry whose names were tied to their products. These days CEOs need to show that any move they make improves the bottom line. Donating a park or museum to the city of Tulsa did not often fit the bill.

A little stream runs under some pines. I cross a small arched wooden bridge to get from the parking lot to the entrance.

I feel dirty as I enter the printing lobby. My hair is not long, really, but in Oklahoma I am a full-throttle hippy. There are also only two modes of facial hair here: clean-shaven and fully grown. How people actually grow beards and mustaches in Oklahoma is a mystery, because there is no lenience on the growth period. Essentially, the only time to make a change in grooming is if you find yourself briefly unemployed. Two weeks vacation might due, if you happen to be a prolific generator of whiskers. My five day shadow is a clear dereliction of personal grooming, signifying to anyone versed in the grammars of Oklahoma that I am a junky, drifter, or worse still, a yankee. Also, I do not tuck in my shirt. This is another detail that signifies to the locals that I am no good. Sorry. I cannot for the life of me see the purpose of tucking in a T-shirt. If it is a button down and a tie is required, I'll bow to custom, but otherwise I see no purpose. Still though, in moments like these, in places like these, my $100 dollar jeans, overpriced all stars and Mission of Burma T-shirt do not carry the cultural capital that they do in Chicago, at least not for a thirty-year-old.

"Hi, can I haelp you?" comes a voice that implies talent in the creation of peanut brittle and fudge, from behind a face that implies serious dedication to tanning salons, and hair that suggests a deep admiration of bleach. The strange juxtaposition of hair and skin tones make her look like she is under a black light at a rave.

"Yes, ma'am." I say ma'am here in Oklahoma. Old habits. "I am looking for Tan-yuh Samuels. She works with Wells Life."

"Are you a friend of Tan-yuhs?" She says with what seems to be authentic and excessive excitement. An excitement that I fear is intended to cover up what is actually a deep suspicion about the under-dressed, full-grown adult that stands before her, tattooed and unshaven.

"I am. Do you know her?"

"Well, 'course, honey, everyone knows Tan-yuh, poor thing." She gestures at her belly with two fingers, puckers her lips and widens her eyes.

Pregnant? Fat? Appendicitis?

I nod.

We stare at each other smiling and waiting.

"Ummm..."

"Oh, right, doll, you head on up to 6. Right out the el'vator and folla that to the end of the hall."

The walls of the elevator are all mirrored, making the ride something like being in a funhouse. I see myself a thousand times snaking off into the distance. I never wonder which is the real me. I am the one who moves an infinitesimally minute fraction of a second before the rest. Not that I can see it, but I know it. Maybe, I think, if I was in here for years I would forget which was me, but for now I have it down pat. I touch my face and so do my minions.

DING. Six.

I step into a bright, sunlit hallway which wreaks of a new tan carpet, the energetic fibers of which resist collapsing under the weight of each footstep. The walls are just off white enough to be soothing-homey as opposed to cold-modern. There are paintings. Shapes in pastel that look like they may have been created by sponge.

I reach the end of the hallway. The door on the right says Tanya Samuels. I hear her on the phone.

"No. No. Yes. Of course. We always strive to. Always. No. We're not always successful, but we... right... No. I disagree with that evaluation. You... You... You... Again, I disagree with that evaluation and I don't think it's... I'm... You... Uh huh, you know what why don't you just go eat a big ol' bag of shit." CLICK.

Enter Tommy. She is still staring, a bit fumed, at the phone in its saddle.

"We need to work on your customer relations," I say.

She looks up ready to pounce, but softens and then smiles. "Tommy?" She looks surprised. I am surprised she recognized me after more than a decade.

When she stands I see her abdomen is disproportionately large.

"You're," I begin pointing at her stomach.

"Yeah," she says with a bright smile. "Eight months."

"Wow," I say. In a strange, maybe juvenile, way, I always thought we would end up together. She was my first crush. My red-headed neighbor. My freckled prototype for future relationships. In another, more realistic, way I always new we would not end up together. We were friends. Also, she was three years older, which means a lot in adolescent years, and leaves a sort of lasting impression of a maturity gap. Also, the race thing. Her parents were cool, I guess. But, this was still Oklahoma.

In a flash it all comes back. Sleepovers, board games—Trouble, Life, Hungry Hungry Hippos, Operation, Trivial Pursuit, Monopoly, Chutes and Ladders—Tanya and Adam using me as a doll to dress like a girl, learning to whistle, her coming home from gymnastics and teaching me to do a cartwheel, her dad—a doctor—taking out the stitches after my father dropped me in a neighbor's pool, the night she offered to teach me to kiss, which was the night of my first kiss, then I remember the night, not long after, when I saw her kissing Adam. It was the ultimate betrayal to a 12 year-old. Briefly, standing here now I wonder if I am totally over it. I decide that I am.

"So, you're due soon?"

"A month."

"My God," I can't think of anything to say. "That's... weird..."

Her look is justifiably askance.

"Not... you know what I mean... it's weird that we're having babies..."

"We're having babies?" Farther askance still.

"Not literally, we, but, you know, people from the neighborhood, of our general age, members of this friendship. It's just..."

Her head levels and her grimace becomes a smile. "I know what you mean."

"Thank God. I'm not so sure I do."

"Are you nervous?"

"Always."

"Don't be. It's so good to see you. What the hell are you doing here?"

I shake my head and shrug off her question. Where to begin?

Her freckles have entrenched with time, and the red of her hair has, perhaps with the help of a talented stylist, deepened and become nearly brown. Her maternity dress is solid black.

"Is there a daddy?"

Askance returns. "Of course there's a daddy, whaddaya think?"

"I don't know. Frozen pop. It's common these days."

"Geez, Tommy. "

Geez, indeed.

"Oh God, you're here for the funeral." She takes my hand. Her grip feels familiar and warm. "I was so excited to see you I totally forgot about Sue. It's terrible."

"It's okay."

"God, Tommy. It's not okay. It's terrible." When she says it for the second time, I realize it's true. "How are you?"

I nod. I have no idea how I am.

She looks me up and down. "Still the rock star."

Hardly. "So, tell me about the daddy."

"You mean the frozen pop? Later, you'll meet him. His name's Mick. That ought to be enough to get you through to dinner time, no?"

"Is that an invitation to dinner?"

"It is indeed Tommy Shells who sells smells in dirty wells." Ah, the nicknames of youth. I resist the urge to give her back a Tan-yuh the spaniel whose last name is Samuels. She notices that I will not reciprocate.

"Well, listen..." She grabs a pad of paper. "I have a ton to do before I go on leave, so I'll be skipping lunch for the next couple weeks..." she writes something on the pad. "But, you come to our place at seven O'clock tonight." She hands me the paper with her address on it.

"Seven," I say.

"Seven," she confirms.

The face-painted-at-a-rave receptionist bids me a fond farewell as I pass the desk.

"Did you find Tan-yuh?" She is applying a deep shade of lipstick that remains nowhere near dark enough to overcome her tan, increasing the overall impression of a photographic negative.

"I did."

"Ain't she just about ready to pop?"

"Indeed. She's quite ripe."

She twists the lipstick back into its shell and pushes it into a tiny purse that cannot hold much more than the lipstick and maybe a credit card or a stick of gum. "Well, I sure do hope you have an awful nice day, sir," she says pushing her lips together in what is either a kiss or a pucker to spread her lipstick.

"You too."

13

I

Back in the Rabbit I struggle to find reverse. The noise of grinding gears reverberates through the parking lot, attracting stares. The F-150 to my left is gone, but the full glory of the bright yellow Hummer still stains my field of vision on the right. A man across the parking lot in full cowboy garb from boots, to Lees, to buckle, to tucked in denim shirt, to fully-articulated mustachios, to aviator style Ray Ban's, to what would have to be at least a five-gallon hat, laughs through a cigarette—probably a Marlboro. After completing his chuckle, he tosses the smoke and heads towards me.

I fight to get it in gear before I am forced to suffer his humiliation.

He is coming closer. He puts a hand in the air.

"Hey there, bud."

Hey, I mouth silently.

"Sounds like transmission trouble."

I nod.

"You wanna pop the..."

It slides into gear and I begin to back out of the spot.

He lifts his hands in defeat and backs away from the car, still watching as I pull away. As I reach the exit of the parking lot, I look back and see him getting into the giant yellow abomination.

I decide to drive downtown to waste time until the evening. Downtown Tulsa is a mixture of oil boom success and its hollow aftermath. There is promise without fulfillment like so many American cities. It has been abandoned commercially speaking. It is not a city center in the classical sense, though many businesses maintain offices there, and the office populations support a handful of restaurants. I drive past the civic center where I saw Muppets on Ice with my mom and dad when I was 5 or 6. Trippy to recall Grover and Ralph skating around, leaping into the occasional triple axle, opened mouth smiles fixed on their shag carpet craniums.

I remember that my grandma Lil, my Dad's mom, worked down here. She had immigrated from Ireland by herself at the age of 12. Her parents had died there from what amounted to hunger, though the actual cause was disease brought on by lowered immunity, and her fate looked grim should she have stayed. She worked in an agency that provided Tulsa's homeless with meals, showers, cots and, if they wanted it, confession. I do not remember much about her other than her accent and that she loved the color brown. Her skirts and blouses were always brown. Her shoes, also, were always brown. Even her wallpaper, I think, was brown. Come to think of it, her maiden name was Brown. Lilly Brown. Ironic, that she was so angry at my father for choosing my mom. I guess Brown was a color that worked for everything from pantsuits to surnames, but not so much the skin of your son's spouse.

I drive by the shelter where she worked. There are not many people out front. I see a woman, whose age is impossible to define, in military fatigues leaning against a shopping cart and smoking an extra long cigarette. Her hair is cut short and her face is covered in growths. She reminds me of that old Renaissance paintings where the face is made of fruit. I can't remember the name of the painter.

I park the Rabbit and get out of the car. I walk across the lawn of the church, remembering grandma Lil standing in front of this very building handing out boxed lunches. Her accent had faded somewhat by the time we were born, but she never sounded like an Oklahoman. There was always a curve in her inflection towards the end of a phrase.

I do not remember her well, because I left Oklahoma for Chicago with my mom when I was ten and we seldom went back. She was, I think, a big part of the reason we left, a big part of the reason my mother and father just could not make it work, a big part of the reason my mother decided Oklahoma was not the place to raise a mixed-race boy. I remember little things: banging on the piano in her living room, eating brussel sprouts at Thanksgiving and spitting them into a napkin while I thought no one was looking, and of course, never, never, never touching her walls. I remember the gold chain that attached to either arm of her octagonal framed glasses and hung behind her neck, below the line of her silver bob.

I missed her funeral. I remember that. My father would never forgive me for that. We had a concert. I was twenty. It had been years since I had seen her. Maybe now, ten years later, is the first time it has felt real. Grandma Lil was my grandma. I loved her dearly and I missed any chance I might have had to know her. I even missed the goodbye.

The church bells begin to ring out their longest chime of the day. It is noon. I walk across the lawn and sit on a bench. A man is flopped drunkenly onto his own lap. He is unshaven, gray-whiskered, his shirt stained by unknown muck. This is the man I have come to to find. I sit on a bench as the sixth or seventh chime rings out across the burnt lawn of the churchyard. The man rustles a little as my shadow extends over him. A priest pokes his head out of the oversized wooden door of the church and then pulls it back inside as if he is the cuckoo of a cuckoo clock. I bend down and touch the brittle burnt grass. It snaps under my fingers. The man's head rustles and he looks up to meet my gaze.

"Tommy?" he says as if he does not fully trust the vision of what may well be a drunken hallucination.

"Hi Dad," I say.

His head falls into his arms and his whole body convulses under the weight of its effort to hold back tears.

We drive the rabbit in silence back to Annie's. They are famous for breakfast the Oklahoma way: biscuits and gravy, fried eggs, sausage patties, hash browns, white toast and grape jelly. It is lunch time by now, so the only real question is which meat do you want under your barbeque sauce: brisket, ribs, chicken, pulled pork. This is the way Summer smelled to me as a kid. My Dad orders the brisket. I order a large side of cole slaw, another of mac and cheese, and, finally, some bread with barbeque sauce. It does the trick. Pastor John got to me…

We sit in a booth of curved wooden benches covered in a thin red laminate. A roll of paper towels sits on the table and a little bowl filled with individually wrapped baby-wipe-esque hand towels. Dad rips one open and wipes it across his face and hands. Cleaning away the dirt under his eyes reveals saddle bags of nearly the same darkness. His beard is fuller than I remember it. Whiter. His salt and pepper is almost all salt.

"I ain't homeless, if that's what yer think'n."

I shake my head. His words arrive to my ears a fraction of a second earlier than the aroma of Gin. The scent was familiar. It was the scent of goodnight kisses before we left Oklahoma. It was the scent that filled my imagination during slur-rife phone calls in my adolescence. It was the smell that accompanied stammers as I carried him to his bed at night when I would visit in the Summer.

"I got the same house as ever, over there on 91st."

I nod. "I know." I did not know.

"I got money."

I nod.

"Lunch is on me as a matter of fact."

Thank god, I think, brushing my hands across empty pockets.

"It's just..." he pushes the brisket around its basket with a look of disgust on his face.

"What, Dad. What is it?"

He pulls at the whiskers on his cheeks and it makes his whole face sag downwards. "I just, can't go back there since Sue's gone."

"I can go with you if you want."

He looks up at me as if I had threatened to strike him. He shakes his head fiercely. "You?" he says. "You wanna come back to the house with me?"

"Yes. I do."

He shakes his head. "I haven't heard shit from you in ten years, Tommy. Not a goddamned word."

In another moment I might have gotten angry. I have not heard shit from him in ten years either, I might have said. You are my fucking dad, I might have said. You are the fucking grown up, I might have said. You are the fucking drunk, I might have said. You are the one who left me alone at my own mother's funeral, I could have said.

But, not now. Now he was broken all on his own, and it would do no good for either of us to hurl mounds of salt at each other's gaping wounds.

"Well, where do you want to go?"

He looks out the window. Traffic on Yale zooms by, old Chevy trucks, little red Jettas, the occasional classic convertible. "I don't know. I just can't be home. Not until after the service at least. Not until after tomorrow." The sun is amplified by the glass window of the restaurant. Thick, articulate beams peek through the window and expand as they reach out for surfaces to saturate in pure, angelic light. The dust in the air is fully visible where it floats through the fully-stretched arms of the sun, reminding me that the world we live in, the air we breathe, is always more complex than it looks, so complex in fact that it would be pure insanity to be fully aware of it. Sanity is ignorance. Thank God for ignorance. Without it we couldn't know anything.

"I can take you to your sister's place."

He grunts. "That just ain't happen'n." I forgot about the fights that came after their mother died. Who got the clock that stood in the entryway, the piano that I had banged on so many Christmas mornings, the house itself where each sibling's memories intermingled and more importantly departed from one another. The fights, which I had only heard about second hand, were never about the things. They couldn't have been. They were about the memories. The right to build the memorial to their shared adolescence.

"George's?"

I cannot imagine that staying with his deceased wife's ex-husband can possibly appeal to him.

He nods, a pensive expression drawing his beard in tight around his puckered lips.

But, then what do I know.

I drop my dad at George's.

The dog runs alongside the Rabbit all the way down the drive. I stop next to the lawn jockey: a black man with exaggerated lips, white pants and a red jacket, holding a lantern. We look at each other conspiratorially. Fuck George.

"I'll be back later. I'm meeting Tan-yuh for dinner," I say to my dad who is climbing the short stairway to the entrance.

He nods with an expression that says, 'typical.'

I will not be guilt-tripped by this man. Not today. "I made the plan before I even ran into you. I won't be long. Just dinner and back here."

"We have a long day tomorrow," he says as if I'm still nine and we're planning a road trip to the Grand Canyon. As if we ever did that.

I nod and start trying to grind the stick into reverse.

14

Him

When it finally ended he moved to the University of Wisconsin to study Organic Chemistry.

He arrived on campus like a ghost a month after the death of Father Dimitri. He had barely spoken to a soul in over a year with the exception of those who had passed on Sunday to offer their prayers. In his entire life he had only one friend other than Father Dimitri: The widow's grandson, Ronny. He had never had a friend near his own age that wore shoes and a shirt, let alone one that would be heading to college.

Frederic Wasson had few friends himself, well, few male friends. "Alo," he said on their first aquaintance, "I em Fredereek."

"Eli," said Eli extending a hand.

Wasson's handshake was firm and masculine, where Eli's was timid and boyish.

"Well," said Frederic, "I em going to unpeck a little as we get to know each other, do you mind?"

"No, not at all," said Eli. "I'll do the same." Eli threw his luggage onto his hard, thin mattress. His possessions barely filled even the meager suitcase. He had a suit, an extra pair of slacks and shirt, a couple of ties, a couple pairs of socks and underwear, a bulb from the greenhouse so that he could plant a little piece of home nearby. That was it.

Frederic opened one of many boxes, exposing the first layer of what appeared to be a massive collections of books. Eli had never owned books of his own. He had utilized the library extensively, and Dimitri's books, of course. He had even borrowed from the widow, who allowed anyone she deemed worthy unrestricted access to a collection that easily exceeded that of the local library, on occasion, but he had never really considered books as something that could belong to him. They seemed like mysterious and independent entities, with lives of their own, transmitting information from user to user on complex journeys through the world. Books could not be enslaved to the service of just one private individual.

Frederic spotted Eli coveting his collection. "Feel free, of course, to borrow anytheeng you please."

Eli was caught off guard. "Oh, thank you. I, uh..."

"My father is a very successful publisher." Frederic sounded almost apologetic. "So, I have many books."

"How did you get them all here?"

"Ah, well, we live in New York. My father brought me by car. And, he left the car." He smiled at this last bit. "So, feel free to borrow that as well."

Eli looked over the titles, all in French.

Frederic seemed to read his thoughts. "I have others in English."

Eli nodded.

"So, what will you stew-dee?

"Organic Chemistry."

Frederic's eyes widened. "Wow, the makeup of this phy-seecal world. Nothing bigger than that."

Eli had never heard a French accent before. "And you? What do you study?"

"Ah, well, I study the opposite from you. I want to be a linguist. The makeup of our non-physical world. That world we make of language."

Eli had never considered the relationship of language to reality before that moment. Language had always quite simply been a tool for communicating information, and he probably had not even put much thought into its role in that capacity.

On the very first night Frederick brought what would be the first of many girls home. A cute girl. Tall and lank with long brown hair and tortoise shell glasses that sat on the bed-side table staring at Eli as he tried to ignore her muffled moans.

He tried to think of it as a purely biological process to keep his own biological reaction from showing evidence be-neath the sheets. It is merely the process of spreading genetic material, promulgating the species, he thought. But, there was something much more mysterious that tugged at his conscious-ness and his erection all at once. Why did it excite him? What remote process caused titillation in him as his roommate and this wonderfully long-limbed girl rubbed their jeans and their genes against one another. And further, considering that there was clearly, or likely at least, no real reproductive intent, why did these two bodies still produce so much ecstasy when put into contact. What was the role of pleasure in fucking? It was as mysterious as trying to parse the meaning of the dream he had deep in his sleep later that night. He dreamed that it was him on top of that girl, that it was his anatomy communing with hers. It felt familiar and right, though he had never so much as seen, let alone touched a naked woman. How could his imagination know? More importantly, why did his mind feel the need to convert his desires into stories that he watched in his most unconscious moments? Was he taking some sort of pleasure at being a voyeur of his own secret self? How did pleasure result from stories? How did urges and desires cross boundaries of bodies and minds? The birds and bees buzzed through his mind, only it was more the bees and the flowers. The process of pollination. The mysterious movement of vital materials. For thousands of years they must have been inscrutable the way in which plants passed their genetic material. Hell, it was inscrutable how humans reproduced. Was there something similar happening in the process of abstraction? Was there some physical reality that allowed this image of his roommate fucking to communicate to his mind and then to his groin? How did his vision, his imagination, become physical desire?

Frederic brought them home many nights. They were tall, short, thin, full, dark, light, foreign, domestic, funny, serious, smart, sweet, loud, quiet. Frederick was not indiscriminate, but nor was he overly particular. And, every night, it was the same. Eli lay in bed thinking of his greenhouse, of planting, of the bees buzzing about, of seedlings falling into nearby soil, of all the processes accidental and intentional that took place in a garden. For a time he could keep his mind isolated this way, but eventually the moans would peak and his body would give in. He would role onto his side so that his tumescence would not grow too apparent, and as quietly as possible rub the skin of his penis against he skin of his fingers, before slipping into another dream where he had replaced his prolific roommate.

It was near the end of their first semester as roommates that Frederic invited Eli to go camping.

"So, how about it Eli? You. Me. A couple girls I know. We can light a fire. Cook. Drink. Maybe swim naked in the dark. Go crazy."

Eli nodded in his best effort at cool, trying, and failing, to conceal his excitement.

When the day arrived, they drove out to the woods in Frederic's car. It was a Volvo station wagon that easily fit the camping gear.

"So," began Eli, timidly averting his gaze from behind his thin, round, silver-rimmed glasses. "How do you know Frederic."

Mary Ellen, who sat in the back with him, answered. "We," she said gesturing to Christine whose deep brown hair seemed to find its natural habitat in the wind of the open car window, and whose eyes hid flawlessly behind large aviator lenses, took a long pull from a thick joint, "are in a seminar with Frederic." She paused, looked upset with herself, then continued. "God, seminar, I hate that word."

"Why?"

"It's so... fucking misogynist."

"Really?"

"Seminar. Duh. Semen. Inseminate the students with seminal works. It's like the professor is just walking into the room and cumming all over the students brains, breeding thoughts where there were none." She said this last bit gesturing like a conductor standing, grandiose, before an orchestra.

"It's a metaphor, no? A biological metaphor, that's all. The sperm enters an egg, something new and unpredictable, something that is more than the sum of its parts, is born. Like an education, sort of. Ideas populate minds which sprout in unpredictable ways," said Frederic

"Well, I think it's offensive."

"The biological process of insemination is offensive to you?"

"Well, yeah, sort of. It sort of makes the brain, the egg, the lesser of the two. The brain is this passive lump that's acted upon by all these spoogily nutritious ideas."

Eli nodded an uncertain agreement. He had never thought of soil as lesser than seed. Who was to say the soil was not more an actor than the seed? That the seed was not ensoilenated as much as the soil inseedinated? Did any of this happen in language anyway? Maybe to focus on the words was to miss the point?

"Does it matter how we say it? Isn't what we mean to communicate more important than the words we use? I mean obviously it's important to be concise, but does it always have to be political?"

"Yes," she said without any glimmer of doubt. "It is always political. What you mean cannot be separated from the words you use. More often than not people don't even know what they mean until they say it. The words they use form their thoughts as much as they are formed by them. They say a thing. Then they keep saying it, refining it. Speech isn't the end result of thought. For most of us it's the process. And, yeah, it's a political process. So, when you presume that all the information is in a squiggly little sperm, and that it's given to the egg, you make a political decision to value male over female. And a prof isn't in the classroom inseminating his students—though what he's up to after class may be another matter—he's facilitating a conversation which forms him—or her for that matter—as much as it forms the students."

The image of professor Samuels ejaculating massive clouds of material onto the pupils in his lecture hall ran through Eli's mind making him laugh out loud a little, before frowning at his own mental trajectory. He struggled to control his thoughts. They seemed to go in every direction with little or no concern for what he wanted them to do. He shook his head trying to physically pull the thoughts back in line.

"What's funny?"

"Nothing. You don't want to know."

"Of course I do. I always want to know."

Eli shook his head. Christine passed the joint back to Mary Ellen and she took a long smooth drag. Eli shrugged as she handed it in his direction. She smiled as the smoke slipped through the cracks at the corner of her mouth. She had thin moist lips that were a little bit paler than pink. All of her coloring seemed a few shades shy of the norm. Her hair a little too blond. Her skin a little too light. The blue of her eyes like a strange translucent sky. Looking at her moist lips made him lick his own, and then he was thinking about kissing her, of climbing on top of her and sucking all of that smoke out of her mouth and testing her theory about the metaphor so entrenched in the university seminar.

She smiled like she knew what he was thinking and this made him nervous.

"Take it," she said still holding out the joint.

He had never smoked before.

"Take it and I'll give you a seminar while Freddy drives." She said it like one of his Chemistry teachers offering some very mundane bit of data.

Her laugh broke through her lower lip, which she had squeezed between her teeth, before he could summon a response. "But no math, OK?"

Mary Ellen shook her head in a way that left Eli very unsure as to where the joke began and ended.

He nodded and took the joint.

He sucked in the smoke and tried his best to hold it, but it fought back and sent him into a fit of coughing that he could not suppress. The others all laughed as he coughed through burning lungs. When the fit was over he was laughing along with the rest. His head felt like a helmet that someone had fastened too tightly.

He couldn't stop smiling.

"I was just kidding, you know," she said with an exaggerated frown.

"I know," Eli said.

She whispered, "you can kiss me if you want to."

He leaned in to kiss her, and she pulled back. She laughed a little and he lunged towards her again.

She made a tisk tisk sound and pulled back a bit towards the door. "Not just yet Mr. organic chemistry. Just be patient. We're going out to the woods to take the world apart."

Eli felt like the world had already fallen apart.

It was dark when they got to the lake. Frederic, or someone, had a flashlight. The beam of the light shot across the emptiness of darkened woods, briefly illuminating spheres of the trunks of trees, and the occasional reflection from an animals eyes. Leaves and twigs crunched under Eli's feet as he searched with his hands through the dark. He stumbled onto one of Mary Ellen's—or maybe it was Christine's—feet, and ushered out a reactive apology before grasping for the flesh again. His grasping was requited by a tongue searching deep into the cavity of his mouth. He tumbled to the ground entangled with the body he had encountered in the dark. How much time had passed? Had someone built a fire? There was a fire burning in the distance. His lip was being sucked into the mouth of the body before him. He forgot the fire. His pants were opened, discarded. He felt flesh against his own. Friction. He would have smiled, but it would have been insufficient. His pleasure extended beyond joy, deep into the excruciating. "Fuck," said the voice. "Fuck." Was it his voice? "Fuck." There were fingers on his back now, scraping. He rolled over, and a new set of lips pressed against his. Were the Mary Ellen's? Christine's? Frederic's? A hand pulled his chin forward. "Stay with me," a voice said. A twig dug into his back. Dirt gathered under his downturned palms. He grasped at the grass beneath him as he breathed in the light of the moon.

Later there was a fire. Frederic had made it. They all sat around it, naked and giddy, mosquitoes attacking their sensitive bits. Christine still wore her glasses. "We should do this everyday," she said.

"You can't have cake for every meal," said Frederic.

"Why not?" asked Christine a faux pout planted firmly on her face.

"It wouldn't be so sweet."

"You're a fucking conservative," she said.

"I'm a realist."

"You're a relativist."

"A conservative relativist?"

"Worst kind."

Eli stared into the flames. The wood that was once the very trees around him disintegrating into the air. He thought of Father Dimitri.

Mary Ellen noticed his eyes trailing the uplifting smoke, "Where does it go, Eli?"

He shrugged, "Up."

"And then?"

"Back down."

"Like everything else. Round and round and round and round and round and round and round and round and round." She stood and continued as she began to twirl, "and round and round and round and round and round and round and round."

Christine also stood and began to spin, though much more slowly. Frederic lay back, his penis flailing onto a thin hairy thigh, and looked up at the stars.

"Mary Ellen," shouted Mary Ellen.

"Why are you shouting your name?" Eli heard himself ask.

"Because Frederic is staring at the stars, and I want them to to know what I am called in case they are paying attention."

"Stars don't care about names," said Christine. "They don't even care about their own names. Alpha Epsilon 465, Gamma Beta 56. They're big hot bursts of energy. They're orgasms with no brain attached."

"What a waste," said Mary Ellen.

"A waste? Why?" Responded Christine.

"What use is an orgasm without a brain?" She chewed on her lower lip. "Especially one that big."

"The whole point of an orgasm is to forget your brain. Brain's are nature's biggest mistake. The nervous system developed its own little tyrant. I'd rather be a star, cumming all over the universe with no need for a name." She held a hand over her invisible penis and aimed it all around the campsite. "Like a giant insterstellar bee."

"Bees have brains," said Eli.

"But their brains just fool them. They don't know about the task they're really setting about."

"Neither do we," said Eli. Maybe it was the mushrooms. It must have been the mushrooms. Eli felt like he could hear the stars in their deafening and dumbfounding process of converting fuel into energy and expelling it into the emptiness. The rumble was almost too much to bear. He thought of that process sending its energy through the cold emptiness of space, heating planets, feeding plants, feeding animals, powering all the conscious and unconscious life and lifelessness in the universe. He thought of words, waves floating through space from mouths to ears, and assumed they were no less deafening.

"Mary Ellen!" she shouted again.

The words burst forth from her star and nourished his planet.

The flames died down as the sun came up. The four naked bodies had huddled into two sleeping bags, but the mosquitoes had found their way in. Eli awoke with his erection pressed tight against Mary Ellen's back. She pulled him towards her. Her bad morning breath became almost instantly appealing as she let out a light moan. "Shhh," she said to herself as if she would be embarrassed if the others woke. Eli wondered why it mattered.

Everything smelled of smoke. It was cold and dewey. Eli was covered in little red spots where his blood had been sucked by puny straw-nosed beasts, but he didn't care. He wondered if the bugs would pass along the gene that had killed Father Dimitri. No. Bugs did not pass along genetic diseases. Besides, the mosquitoes were beneath the complexity necessary to suffer from that particular fate. He closed his eyes and had a brief glimpse of himself as a middle-aged man, insane from lack of sleep, muscles atrophied, cheeks collapsed around the cavern of his mouth, eyes bloodshot and paranoid, ass toneless and scabbed over from too many sleepless hours in bed. He shook off the strange blend of memory and projection and breathed deeply of the Wisconsin lake air.

"What were you thinking?" asked Mary Ellen.

"Nothing."

"Boo," she said. "Unfair."

He tilted his head instead of asking a question.

"After all that we've been sharing it's not right to shut down your most intimate parts. This is about communion."

He looked up at a tall pine tree that swayed so far that it might snap at any moment. "I was thinking of my father," he said.

She picked up a pine cone and rubbed her index finger over one of its points. "Okay," she said. "That's a start."

15

Him

Watson and Crick had broken the ground over a decade earlier when they realized that people were essentially written into existence by millions of tiny typists who wrote and rewrote the same message generation after generation. Well, almost the same message. They were artists these typists, and despite a hegemonic system that did its best to demand conformity, that ushered them harshly towards their fate, they could not help but indulge in the occasional flourish. A new use of an old word that slowly morphed into a word all its own.

His teachers did not seem to understand the direction he was heading in. They could not see the value in comparing language, a pure invention of culture, completely relative and without any essential structure, to genes that unconsciously acted out their destinies. Language was messy, unpredictable, meaningless other than as a tool of reference. Genes were the stuff of life. They were not referents, but the 'its' that needed so much referring to. Language was ephemeral goo trying, sloppily, to anchor itself to some always escaping truth. Genes were truths in themselves. They were not language to be interpreted, but maps that led to fate. Not even maps, they were the roads themselves, and they only led in one direction.

Eli intuited early on that things were not so cleanly distinguished. His professors accused him of being reductive, of mistaking similar patterns for proof of identity. He knew that rather than himself being reductive, it was they who had too acute a view of the world. Patterns were everything. Similarity was more often than not, indeed proof of ancestry, of identity. This was one of the lessons of evolution. Language was not only a process that benefited from handy metaphors to genetics, it was the rightful heir.

Words made truths. Words were truths. Words caused actions. Words changed worlds. The Bible, the Koran, constitutions, Shakespeare. Words revealed and formed thoughts that took shape in the neocortex, which rested on the mammalian brain, which rested on the reptilian. It was not reductive to claim it was all related. It was obvious. A protein sent a signal across the wall of a cell, it was received by a receptor which was equipped to handle many different signals, the signal was then interpreted by the cell and translated into action. His professors took pause at this word: interpretation. It was action and reaction, they said. Nothing more. But Eli knew that the beginnings of greater cognitive feats existed right there in that moment when the receptor received the signal and acted in a given way. It was not predestination, but the very foundation of freedom. There were ways that one was expected to act, there were actions that should be taken, but the possibility that there would be some divergence from the norm was what really made the whole system function. Life was not based on all of the rules being followed, but on the vitality that was inherent in breaking ranks. Language, likewise, would fall into obscurity if it were not for the fact that it constantly stepped outside of its own well-trod boundaries to push the edges of human abstraction. Language was an organism, plain and simple, and it inhabited people just like a bacteria that needed our bodies as a habitat in order to spread, morph, thrive.

Dr. Simpson looked over the top of his glasses, "You want to do what?"

"I," Eli paused trying to think of the best way to package his proposal. "I want to study the connection between language and genetics."

"You mean the origin of human capacity for language?"

"Yes, well, no..."

Dr. Simpson angled his view even deeper over his glasses. "Well, what then?"

Eli began to gush, "Religion is a linguistic bacteria, ideology in general maybe, it's an organism that travels from person to person through words. Words can inspire us to change global attitudes. Shakespeare colors our thinking about love, death, revenge. Machiavelli, or Sun Tsu about power. These are ideas, transmitted like genetic material from generation to generation, and it's not just a matter of linguistics, it's biology. Biology will tell us why we have a need for narrative, why our brains rely on so much constant contextualizing and how that contextualizing might lead us to fatedness, or to freedom. Words have been used to control people, to dominate their minds and bodies. They have been used to liberate people. They emerge and morph and regulate."

"Eli," Dr. Simpson looked amused, "this is all fascinating material," his amusement turned to judgment, "for a poet. This is a biology department. We don't study religion, ideology, love... We study science. We have a method that is built to protect us from our own subjectivity. The things that stir in us are chemical, and obviously the ways in which they emerge from our bodies results from the chemical history that our bodies arise from, but to claim at some level that the stirring itself is paramount to consciousness, to claim that what human communication in all its complexity is no more than a difference of scale from the interaction of a peptide at the barrier of a cell with some enzyme is, well, to say the least a little unfounded. There is a difference in quality between a word, ink on a page, sound waves vibrating towards some unwitting ear, to be interpreted according to a conscious member of some conglomeration of cultural traditions, and a primordial message written in DNA."

"But, Dr. Simpson, you just said it yourself: *Message, Written.* Your own words prove the connection."

Dr. Simpson started to look irritated. "Those words are metaphorical. You interpret them to your liking. Something a receptor in a cell cannot do, by the way. There is no interpretation, no preference, in a cell. To attribute human qualities to an automaton is fallacious."

"Humans are made of automatons. That is my point. At their roots the processes make room for choice, for freedom, but it's the exception, not the norm. Consciousness in the form we experience it is an outlier, and language is trying to lead us back into the cave, back into the shadows. It's aim is to regulate, normalize. Humanity is in this weird little window in which we have sort of taken over the system. Through language, we're driving the process. We're storing the information, writing our own script. Only we don't realize it."

"It sounds to me as though you'd be happier in Linguistics, Political Science, Philosophy."

"No. The whole point is that it *is* biology. This is where I need to be."

"Well, I'm sorry, Eli, but in this department you'll have to read from our script."

PART 4

1

ME

Eve emerged from the body of Adam, or so the story goes. A rib. Cultured from the bone of her thoughtless predecessor like an Edenic experiment in CRISPR technology. Frankenstein before Frankenstein. Dolly the sheep before Dolly the sheep. The clone always goes astray in these stories. The first sign in Eve was vanity. She stared into her own reflection in the river after a long day's work. Adam had never bothered to notice himself, his body. It just was. But, she did. She saw herself and she liked the wild hair and untamed eyes. He had never noticed his mind either. He was aware of the tree at the centre of the garden. He was aware that it held all the secrets, yet he was never tempted. He never wandered past the tree, his gaze lingering a bit too long as he pondered the mysteries of god, the enormity of heaven, the strangeness of being… Eve was Lucifer's target because she was curious. She ate the fruit. Knowledge was intoxicating. The world shook as it split in two, its essence drifting out beyond its material. Sin gave impulse to that first planetary mitosis, soma lifted above sema, the mind departed from its home, the body. Satan's daughter Sin emerged, motherless, from her father's body just as Eve from Adam, just as the world from the earth, culture from nature. When Satan raped his daughter, Death was born. When Adam and Eve eat the fruit, death enters the world. Death is the price of the body, the body the cost of knowledge. But then, the body was already there... Adam just failed to notice it. The planet too, was already solid beneath the feet of its inhabitants. The night was there to contrast against the day. God was there to delineate the human. And so were the animals. Difference did not emerge with sin, only the ability to reflect on it, to know it, to suffer in all of its tensions and contradictions. To become human was to have one's vision split, to forget that the mind and the body were always one planet, to ignore that gender was an optical illusion, a refraction under the lens of time that allows us to see the whole divided into its constituent parts. The mind became a microscope that deceived us into thinking we were outside looking in, forgetting that the virus we peered into came from the blood coursing through us.

Love divided from lust as our vision split in two. Adam and Eve, intoxicated from the fruit, fall into each other's arms, take of each other's bodies. They had done this before. What was different now? It wasn't the body. These two bodies had been joined before. The body was doing what it had always done. The mind, though, was on its own trip now, taking in the bodies before it as things to be used, things to be had, things that were objects apart from the sensual self that consumed them for its pleasure.

What would it mean to put nature and culture back together? What if they were never apart because the Fall itself was just a sleight of hand?

2

Us

Kane's eyes wandered around the warehouse as if he had lost track of where he was.

"Are you okay," asked Tommy.

Kane let out a one syllable laugh, followed by a deep inhalation. "That's a big question, Tommy." He dragged a foot through the dirt that covered the cement floor. "Are you okay?"

Tommy thought for a moment. "I would be if…"

"If what? If I wasn't here? If your grandfather wasn't your grandfather? If you weren't you?"

"That'd be a start."

Kane took off his glasses and rubbed at eyes covered in burst blood vessels. "No."

"No?"

"No, Tommy. It's not that easy. It's not about you. It's not about me. It's not even about humanity, really."

"What then?"

"Have you ever heard of the Heliamphora?"

Tommy shakes his head.

Kane stares into the distance for a minute, running his hand through his greasy hair before returning to his train of thought. "It's a pitcher plant. A plant that evolved over countless generations. It's leaves rolled into cups. It developed a little valve to release overflowing rain water. They don't have their own digestive system, so they rely on bacteria that lives symbiotically on their leaves to digest their prey. Millions of years of playful trial and error all leading to this plant becoming a perfect piece of engineering."

"Unless you're a bug."

"Unless you're a bug. That's right, Tommy. The whole thing is just a matter of perspective. The whole thing. The whole living system, infused with signs and symbols from top to bottom. Evolution… It doesn't care if you're alright. It doesn't care if I'm alright. All it cares about is continuing. Becoming. Becoming a Heliamphora. Becoming that…" He turns his head towards the orb, the light extinguished, the body quivering ever so slightly.

3

I

Tanya lives in Broken Arrow, a small town on the edge of Tulsa that might be called a suburb if Tulsa did not already feel like a suburb, making the title redundant. I get to her house just before eight, pull into the driveway and watch the screen door swing open. It must be her husband, Frank. Frank is taller than I had imagined, and darker complected. His hair is in a long ponytail, and his black button-down tucked into jeans the bottoms of which are, in turn, tucked into black snakeskin boots. His complexion is dark. I can't tell at first if he is latino or Native American.

I pull the Rabbit up behind their boxy green Volvo.

Frank comes walking towards me with a wide smile on his face.

I reciprocate by smiling widely back at him and wonder if my smile seems authentic. I hope it does. But, smiles almost always feel fake to me when I am wondering whether or not they look real. How stupid. Of course I want to smile at the husband of one of my best friends. Of course it is authentic.

Then I am just pissed that I waste a moment that is joyful wondering if I seem to be enjoying it.

He walks up to the driver's side window as I gesture awkwardly towards the other door, then scoot myself across the passengers seat to slide out.

He walks around the front of the car, sliding through the narrow gap I have left between my front bumper and the rear of their Volvo.

"Sorry," I say. "Guess I cut it a little close."

He shakes his head. "Not to worry."

Tanya's face pops out of the front door and shouts something that I do not quite catch.

"It's okay, baby. I can greet our guest while you finish up the pilaf."

He rolls his eyes in my direction, bringing me into his world of domestic familiarity.

I smile, this time without wondering how it comes across.

"Frank," he says extending a hand.

"Tommy," I say extending my own.

His shake is hearty, but not offensive, and his eye contact direct without being overbearing.

"Tan-yuh's making pilaf," he says dropping his hands back to his sides.

"Nice."

"You're a veggie she tells me," he says with no trace of recrimination.

"Yeah," I agree, averting my eyes. Am I?

"Cool."

That is a first for me in Oklahoma.

The pilaf is served. Frank has also made some mysteriously sauced chicken that smells really good and makes me doubt my commitment to the cause.

"Tommy's a musician," Tanya says to Frank.

"You've mentioned that," Frank says smiling in my direction.

"Frank is an artist," says Tanya to me.

"Really?" I ask. "What's your medium." I hope that does not sound as dumb as I think it does.

Tanya rolls her eyes. I am not sure if it is at my question or the coming answer.

"Semen," says Frank unabashed.

"Wha..." hmmm. "I mean... can you clarify?"

Frank smiles a smile that lets me know he is used to awkward responses to his reproductory fluid art, which makes me feel a little better about my own awkward response.

"Photography, really. I'm a photographer, but lately I've been sort of caught up in shooting jizz."

I nearly loose my mouthful of pilaf, but I maintain and manage a polite nod.

"I used to shoot the grander things. Mountain tops. Craters and Canyons. I worked for National Geographic on a couple jobs. For a while I was all about the Milky Way. The big picture, you know. And then one day I just got tired of the big picture, and I decided to go for the minutiae. A glass of water. The patterns on a fresh scab. I got a little Whitman with the blades of grass for a spell. Just trying things out. One thing led to another, and, uh, well, now I photograph that more familiar milky way."

"I married a perv," says Tanya.

"No, it's not like that... I mean, I know what it might look like, but, it just seemed like something so fundamental and yet so uncharted, ya know? Something that most guys wipe off and toss in the toilet on a daily basis without really considering it. Something that's half the list of ingredients for a human being and more often than not it just ends up making some old sock crusty. I guess I just think it deserves better."

Hmmm. Maybe? No? Why not?

"When did you start?" I ask.

"About 8 months ago," he says smiling and gesturing towards Tanya's belly with what I notice to be a well manicured hand. "I was reading Moby Dick." He says in way of explanation. "There's this scene where all the characters have their hands in the blubber of a sperm whale. Just got me thinking. If the baby's a boy we're calling him Herman," he says through a twisted smile.

"Can you believe he teaches seventh graders?" asks Tanya.

"Really? What do their parents think?" I ask.

"Shit," he says, "let's just say it's not the first line on my resume."

"It will be soon," she says.

"Why's that?" I ask.

"He has a show at the Stamford. It's bound to be in all the papers. Parents are going to find out and he's likely to lose his job."

"Is that legal?" I ask.

They shrug in unison.

"Fine by me. I'll head back out on the trail."

Tanya clutches at her stomach. "Not fine by me."

"I'll show you some work after dinner."

I ponder.

"After dinner is right, Frank. Good lord," says Tanya.

Frank clears the plates as Tanya and I linger at the table.

"Coffee?" Tanya offers.

I shake my head as does Frank.

A round of sighs crosses the table.

"So, Tommy, tomorrow's a big day."

I take it as a signal to leave and start to stand. "Oh, right, I'll get out of your hair."

"No, dummy, I meant for you, the funeral."

I sit back down. "Right. I've been trying not to think about it too much."

"Have you seen your dad?"

"I..." for some reason I begin to feel choked up, like someone is belting me repeatedly in the diaphragm. It is as if I cannot get air until I agree to release the floodwaters I have been restraining behind some internal dam. "I... ran into him today." I have not cried publicly since I was ten. I am trying to keep the streak going, but I feel myself losing the battle. "He... uh... he's at George's, just, uh..." the seal breaks and the tears start pouring out of me. I start with my dad and work backwards. I tell them everything. About the gun I had pointed at Mickey, about Mme Trouché, about the strange letter from Sue and the mysterious goons coming after me, about Buddha and Bear, about the letters from my great grandfather, about Flanders and about Stamford, about my band and about Missy, about the fact that I do not even know if Mickey and Eve are dead of alive. I leave out the bit about the dark room and the blue orb and the man who might be a vampire... I still can't convince myself that it was real, and even if it was, I would be asking a lot of someone to believe me. I am already asking a lot.

As the tears drain out of me, I begin to feel calm and whole. I remember being a kid and crying until I was so exhausted that whatever it was had dwindled in comparison to the exertion, and I just lay there, spent on my tear and mucous covered pillow case, completely recovered, completely safe, some invisible embrace induced by things having been as bad as they could be, and the knowledge that, at least in the short term, things could only get better.

Tanya and Frank are seated at either side of me. I can tell they have no idea what to do or say. I can tell they are wondering if I am suffering from some type of post-traumatic stress. I can tell they are hoping that when the tears end, I will tell them that I made it all up. To forget everything I said and just go back to the way things were yesterday, before I made my surprise visit.

"What do you need, Tommy?" says Tanya. "We'll help however we can."

"Absolutely," Frank agrees.

I get back to George's later than I had expected. The lights are out and the dog does not chase me down the path. There is another car, an unfamiliar car, a little hatchback that looks to be more or less brand new, parked in the driveway. I walk inside and see my dad curled on the couch where I had slept the night before. There is a dim buzz at the back of the house, so I head towards it. I walk down three steps that lead into the den and see two heads, a man's and a woman's watching the news.

"Eve," I say.

She turns slowly. "Tommy," she says. "Thank God."

Mickey turns, too. His face is bruised on his right cheek, but otherwise he seems okay.

"Mickey, Jesus Christ, I'm so fucking sorry." I feel the tears coming again.

"I've seen worse," he says with a smile. "Besides, you didn't have a choice, and we're all still here. Bygones."

Eve stands and walks towards me. She hugs me with the strong arms of an older brother. "We're both just glad to find you in one piece."

"What now?" I ask.

"Now we focus on the funeral."

"What happened to you two?"

"They took you away and left us there in the woods. I untied Mickey and we stumbled to the road. An old lady who thought we'd been in a car accident picked us up and brought us to the hospital. We convinced her that we'd be fine if she just left us at the door, then we high-tailed it back to Mickey's place to borrow a credit card from Teri."

"Teri?"

"Mickey's mom, Mme. Trouché."

Wasn't Teri what they had called my guardian angel in the warehouse? She didn't have the same voice...

"Then we rented a car, and here we are, "she pulled at the bottom of her skirt, readjusting her position. "And you, what about you, how did you get here?"

"I woke up in a truck stop in Lebanon."

"Lebanon?"

"Missouri."

"Right."

"Got a ride from a tucker, bumped into George and here I am."

"Here you are."

"Here we all are," said Mickey. "But, what the hell to we do to make sure we're still all here tomorrow and the day after that."

It was a good question. Unfortunately none of us had a very good answer.

Eve pushed some hair out from in front of her eye. "First we get through tomorrow. Then we make plans."

4

I

The church is at the top of a hill in a wooded area that was unfamiliar to me as we arrived. It is small and dark, favoring aged and polished wood surfaces. The light enters enters through thick stained glass bearing no discernible images. The stations of the cross are represented abstractly. I imagine this is an Oklahoma Catholic's best effort to accommodate those abundant locals who condemn icons. It is not quite an icon if you can't tell what it is supposed to be, right?

The crowd is thin. Sue is in the box at the front. A priest speaks, but I do not understand a word he says. My dad is sitting two places away from me, Eve is sitting two places in the other direction, Mickey by her side. My dad has cleaned up respectably, a well-trimmed gray beard, neatly combed hair. I even smelled cologne in the car on the way over. No one had spoken, but the cologne was evident. Dad is wearing a suit which reminds me of better times when the gin was confined to the hours after 6 pm. It was probably some time around the divorce that alcohol infiltrated his lunch hour. That is when the violence started. Dad does not have the power behind him that used to make the outbursts intimidating. He is beaten. Aged. Even if he were to raise his fist, it wouldn't cause anyone to cower. He is thin and brittle now.

Dad stares towards the front of the room, but it's hard to tell if he is seeing anything. It feels wrong that no one is going out of their way to support him, to comfort him, but there is no one left. George, maybe, but George is not the comforting type, and besides, this is the love of his life laid out in the coffin, too, though he would never let on. There is a reason he never remarried, never even dated after they divorced.

My father is not a bad man. He loved Sue well, and, truth be told, she had her own drinking problem, which is why they complimented each other as well as they did. He is a good man in his way, and I think everyone in this room knows that. But, it is hard to watch a person disintegrate before your eyes if you hate them, much more so if you happen to love them. It may be funny to see your best friend stammering to the cab on the odd Saturday night, but it is decidedly tragic to see your brother, sister, father, mother, lover stammer away into oblivion each and every evening, as the left eye grows ever more twitchy and the hands extend their shaking steadily farther past the breakfast hour. The people that loved him most stayed the farthest away. Eve and I were proof of that.

My father is not crying. Nor does he stand and speak. No one speaks other than the priest.

There are footsteps at the back of the church. The priest looks up. Everyone turns their heads towards the back of the room.

Missy.

Missy in a black dress, tattooed shoulders exposed, three inch heels making her all of 5'5".

I cannot believe that it is her. I stand and walk towards her, pulling her by the hand out into the church's entryway. I kiss her and she kisses back.

"What are you doing here?" I ask.

"Taking initiative. Meeting your family."

Okay.

"I missed you," she says.

I missed you too, I think.

I smile and pull her back into the church, where we sit, squeezing each others hands, bodies filled with the strange blend of ecstasies brought on by love renewed at a funeral.

Eve throws us a knowing nod, careful not to demonstrate any joy given the circumstances.

We all return our eyes to the front, to Sue, to the body of Sue, resting in that final pose, interlaced fingers on her diaphragm, eyelids, dusty and too white with the standard over application of coverup.

I remember her garden from the summers of my youth. The watermelons, the tomatoes, the cucumbers. I remember the basketball court right beside it placing the vegetables at great risk in the event of a missed shot. I remember Sue watching us from the dining room window, behind which she regularly sat at table piled with page after page of… I never knew what… yellow legal pads filled with choppy phrases, phone book pages ripped from a thousand different Tulsa phone booth editions, bulky folders filled with copies of city council minutes, business cards taped to ruled paper, and a thesaurus, of course. It was the most mysterious corner of the world to me, that pile.

I always wanted to be a reporter, like her, until I dropped out of college and music had its way with me.

I wonder what she would do in my position. I wonder how she would get out of this mess. Her body laying there, I guess, is a good indication that she didn't know how to solve this one either.

I wish she would she sit up and tell me what to do, tell me what they want, what I should give them, who I should go to, how I should escape.

She sits up. She looks at me. I am not scared. It is just Sue.

"Tommy," she says, that same playful curl in her upper lip, the same wise ass glimmer in her eye.

"Sue," I say.

Missy nudges me. I look at her and realize I had spoken out loud.

"Sorry," I say to Missy. "I'm…"

Missy pulls on one of my earlobes and kisses the air.

I look back to Sue who is chuckling at me.

"What're you gonna do, kiddo?" She asks.

"I don't know," I say, this time careful to keep my imaginary conversations at proper imaginary sound levels.

"Neither did I," she looks around at the coffin she is now perched on the side of. "Obviously."

"I'm lost, Sue. I don't know what the hell any of this has to do with me. I don't know what I can offer these people. I don't know why they have an interest in Jared, who, by the way, I never even met. I don't even know... shit, I don't know anything, other than that I'm being threatened by a glowing head floating around in a blue orb, and that it has something to do with my great grandfather's paintings from nearly eighty years ago."

"Have you ever seen his paintings?"

I have, but I lie. I lie to an imaginary ghost… "No."

"Go see the paintings. The scene of the crime."

"What?"

"Always go to the scene of the crime."

"How are his paintings the scene of the crime," I ask.

"Jeez, Tommy, it's just an expression. Plus, you're asking an awful lot of questions to your own hallucination."

She has a point.

Sue is incinerated. We watch as the casket, body carefully positioned inside, is propelled along a conveyor belt that reminds me of a grocery store check out line. Except, the other side of this register is a wall of embers that convert into flames the second the front edge of the casket enters. We watch through a window as her body and the expensive box it was packaged in turn to ash. Technology can buffer us from brutality for a good while, but come this day, and come it will, reality will slap us all in the face. Goodbye, Sue.

The plaque on the wall where her ashes were interred read: "The story can never be outrun, but she wore herself out trying to keep pace."

Missy and I walked back to the Rabbit hand in hand.

"I liked the epitaph," said Missy. "A good writer's epitaph. Who wrote it?"

"I don't know. Sue, probably…"

Missy's Senior project in college had been driving around the country photographing the epitaphs of writers and artists. It was almost published in a book, but the little press that had planned to release it went under before it could be printed.

"Gone are the living, but the dead remain, and not neglected; for a hand unseen, scattering its bounty like a summer rain, still keeps their graves and their remembrance green."

"Who's that?" I ask.

"Longfellow, buried in Cambridge, Mass. Always one of my favorites."

"It's beautiful."

"I know," she says.

"Why epitaphs?" It occurs to me how strange it is that I never asked her before, even while she was driving everywhere, developing prints, putting together the book that was not to be. How could I never ask?

"They're poems, but better because they have real stakes, you know. They may be the world's most concise art form. You have to fit a life, an ethos, into just one little square. Maybe twenty words to let all posterity know how they should remember a person."

"I never paid enough attention." I mean to Missy and her work, but I imagine she thinks I mean to epitaphs, which I do not bother correcting, because it is equally true.

"They are the best proof that art is an effort towards immortality. A failed effort, but still..."

"Hmmm..."

"The stone the builders rejected?" She asks.

"Who's that?"

"Guess."

"Stone Phillips?"

She chuckles. "Not dead, smart ass. Try again."

"Jimmy Hoffa?" I don't know if he has a memorial.

"Interesting. No. Jack London. Glen Ellen, California"

"Ah."

"So we beat on, boats against the current, ceaselessly into the past."

"Kerouac?"

"Ooooh no, but decent guess. Fitzgerald. Rockville, Maryland. They wouldn't let him be buried where he wanted to be, beside his wife, at first, because of his 'unsavory' writings, but they moved him later."

"Ouch."

"They're together now, that's what matters," she grabs my hand and squeezes.

"I guess," I say, putting my arm around her and pulling her shoulder against my rib cage.

"Curiosity did not kill the cat."

"Sherlock Holmes?"

"Not a real person, jackass."

"Still got to bury him someplace, no?"

"Good question. No. Try again."

"Newton," I guess.

"Studs Terkel," she corrects.

"Makes sense."

I unlock the passenger side door of the Rabbit and slide through as Missy tries to control an embarrassed laugh. "Nice ride you got here."

"Only the best, my love, only the best."

I grind it into reverse and we set off down the hill.

A couple of miles from the church I notice the yellow Hummer in the rearview.

"Shit," I say.

"What?" asks Missy.

"You see the yellow Hummer behind us?"

"I fucking hate those things, why don't those guys just get themselves inflatable junk like Flip Wilson?"

"I think he might be following us. I saw him the other day in the parking lot of a friend's office."

"If he is following us, he's not very stealth."

"I'm not sure he's concerned with stealth."

The Hummer pulls up along side us at the next light. I cannot see through the high, tinted windows. I wait for a crack in the window, for a pistol to emerge, for the door to open and Buddha to pop out. My pulse is pounding its way into my esophagus.

Missy touches my knee, "Why would anyone be following you?"

The light turns green and the Hummer speeds ahead.

I exhale. For now at least, we are okay.

"Why would someone be following you," she repeats.

"I need to take you somewhere," I tell her.

5

Him

They'd met in graduate school in the early 70's. Karen was at Harvard studying law. Eli was doing his doctorate in Biology at MIT. They both loved theater. They met in the waiting area auditioning for an amateur production of *A Midsummer Night's Dream*.

"Is this your first time?" Karen asked. He was timid, standing in the corner like a potted plant.

He nodded and mumbled something unintelligible.

"Are you an actor?" She prodded.

He shook his head.

"So not here to audition?"

"More a fan, really."

So, he could talk. "Fans don't have to audition, you know."

"Sets, maybe… I thought I might be able to help building sets."

She nodded. "Sets."

"I'm good with plants. I thought…" He trailed off and averted his gaze.

"Plants." She shifted her head so that it was nearer his line of sight. "Well, this is certainly the right play for that."

He looked back, hope in his eyes, and offered the briefest hint of a smile.

"Do you like Shakespeare?" She asked.

"Everyone likes Shakespeare."

She was uncertain about his assertion, but also unwilling to challenge him. "I love Shakespeare."

He smiled again, this time for a fraction of a second longer.

"You can never pin him down. You can never say just what it is he thinks, you know?" She put a hand on his forearm and his muscles convulsed at the contact. "I love that he can stay with the question, the uncertainty…"

"The irrationality…" he added.

"The irrationality…" she repeated.

"He doesn't pretend to think that humans are any better at making decisions than plants or animals. It's all just action and reaction, cause and effect…"

Eli did make the sets. Karen played Titania. Every night she stepped onto a stage embraced on all sides by flowing vines of ivy and dotted with potted ficus. Every night he watched her fall in love with an ass, and then, when the play was over, he watched her go home with one. Will wreaked of privilege and the absence of any semblance of an original thought. Eli disliked him immediately.

It was Karen who had invited him to dinner that night. Eli could tell that Will was annoyed that he would be joining them, which was probably the only reason he ultimately agreed to go along.

The show had gone well that night. Eli watched from backstage as Karen became the queen of the forest. Her fingers were long and thin. He watched as she ran them across the leaves of the Pothos he had weaved across the set, imagining the veins in the leaves to be those on the backs of his own hands. He imagined his fingers, sinewy and botanical, expanding to meet her, intertwining like roots deep underground. They melded into one structure and sprung towards the sun.

They walked together to the restaurant. It was dark and modern and specialized in Eastern European food. Will's uncle Mulroney had chosen it, Karen told him. Uncle Mulroney was already seated when they arrived at the restaurant. He was old. It was difficult to pinpoint exactly how old because there was a vitality in his eyes that belied the dry, wrinkled skin and wispy, white hair.

He did not stand up, but nodded from his chair by way of introduction, never breaking eye contact, a curled lip revealing a disarming boyishness. He was sickly thin. A cane with a silver apple for its handle leaned against his chair.

"Karen," he said. His voice was surprisingly young.

"Uncle Flanders," she said moving close to his cheek for a kiss.

He put his head close to her neck and lingered in her aroma.

"This," she said putting her hand on Eli's shoulder, "is my dear new friend Eli Kane."

"Kane," he said. "Strong name."

"Eli is studying Biology. Not a bad set designer either," she said winking in his direction.

"I love the theater," said Flanders, inhaling the air around him as if it were a snifter of vintage bourbon.

"Eli has created a living set. Totally covered in plants. It's amazing, really," said Karen.

"Is that right?" Said Flanders looking across the room to the waiter. He pointed to the nearly empty bottle of wine and snapped his fingers. The waiter nodded. "I got a little head start as I waited for you."

"Sorry we're late. Eli has to move all of the plants into the atrium of the theater so that they catch the morning sun," she explained.

Flanders seemed displeased with the explanation. "I have never had much of a green thumb myself," he said. "Always too much of a late riser."

"Where is Will?" Asked Karen.

"He should be here momentarily."

But Will never did arrive. First one bottle of wine disappeared, and then another. All the while they discussed in great detail Eli's emerging theories of plant communication. Fuelled by the wine, he explained to Karen and to Flanders how the signals received from the sun and transferred into chemical energy were similar to what happened when language encountered consciousness. "Light and reason," he said, "have long been held in a metaphorical relationship, but now we can see," he paused and started again, "I can see, that it's so much more than a metaphor. Light is reason. It's story. It's God."

Flanders rolled his eyes and took a big sip of wine.

"God," he began before pausing and staring into his glass as if it were a particularly dense poem. "I find that God is whatever one decides it is."

"And so is reason!" Added Karen. "If you learn nothing else in law school, it's that."

"Touché," said Flanders grinning.

Eli leapt into his explanation. "That's really just the point. It's like the play we're doing. It's meant something different to everyone who's watched it for 400 years. It changes the people who watch it, but they change it too. Each new version, each new perspective pushes the play to become something new.

And it matters... It changes us... It's evolution! Just like a plant's genetic material is cross-pollinated or hybridized, the play is also part of an ecology. Reason spreads its roots through our ecosystem, but it's not predetermined. It's a story we haven't finished telling. An evolution."

Karen's jaw hung open. "My god, Eli, I've never seen you like this!"

Flanders stared into Eli's eyes. "And what is the story we should be telling, Eli?"

Karen spoke before Eli could manage. "A better one. A story of equality, empathy, vision, progress. We can make this world a better one."

"Is that right, Eli?" Asked Flanders.

Eli nodded. "I hope so." He squinted under the weight of the wine and the difficult calculations that went into an accurate answer to Flanders' question. "Most often I think it doesn't particularly matter."

"Go on," said Flanders.

"I mean, the story is so much bigger than us. The motions so far beyond our consciousness. Progress in an evolutionary sense is a series of mutations that are way outside the purview of consciousness. Consciousness is likely just one accidental outcome. Our intentions seem important, but it's just an illusion. When I say that botany is a story, I am not trying to humanize the plant. I'm trying to point out that we're no different than the plant."

Flanders raised his glass. "I'll drink to that."

The dreams started that night.

Karen was always there, costumed as Titania, the vines that covered the set flowed seamlessly in and out of her vascular system, as if she was a puppet whose strings extended never-ending in every direction. Eli poured water from a rusted metal can into the red soil beneath her. When he looked down at his feet he could see the flesh of his calves variegate and reach into the ground. The roots ascended from his legs and consumed his body little by little. His consciousness simultaneously faded and expanded as the vines climbed closer to his torso. The sinews intertwined as Eli lost track of himself. His pulse elevated as his face disintegrated, he clung to his image as tightly as he could, but it always eluded him. A scream crescendoed in the back of his body and his whole being tensed, chlorophyl pumping through every vain. A magpie flew above them dodging in and out of the web created by the vines that reached ever higher into the sky, landing only to rip at the flesh of a dead mouse. His breath became a pulse and he disappeared into something horrifying and orgasmic.

6

I

The Stamford Museum is an old Italian Manor. It was imported in full from some Italian village in the 20's after the elder Stamford made his fortune in oil. He had planned for it to be his residence, but as his empire grew, he moved West to California and left the villa to the city along with its collection of renaissance and baroque paintings. The city added a hefty collection of Oklahoman and Native American art, and the Stamford became one of the Southwest's most complete museums.

It stands on a hill, its pillared facade a regal reminder of big oil's cultural and political standing. It is a place I remember fondly. It is the first art museum I ever went to. My mom brought me here. We would walk the halls staring at paintings of saints and angels floating in mid canvas. I thought they were aliens with their strange halos and levitating poses. The painting I remember most was the man holding a platter with a severed head. I had not had much religious education. I had no idea who John the Baptist was. To me, it was just a grotesque message from a violent past. I thought of Robin Hood, King Arthur, and other cartoon histories relevant to me. They were just as real as John the Baptist. Just as real as Jesus.

I remember the Native American art as well. A painting called "the trail of tears" showed me something about the history of my own home. I asked my mom why the Indians were crying, and she said because they had to move to Oklahoma. What was so bad about that, I asked, Oklahoma was a nice place to live. Well, she said, they used to have the whole country, and little by little, it was taken from them. Why? So that we could build houses and schools and art museums like this one. We, who? Well, baby, we Americans. Were the Indians Americans? Yes and no. Mostly yes, but they were something more, too. Being an American was a complicated subject, I thought.

And then there was that other painting. The one I was related too. My mom brought me to stand in front of it. She told me that my grandpa had painted it. I had only met my grandpa once that I remembered. He had just been released from prison and came to our house. My grandpa Jared was a professor of art who had been contracted by an oil company to document exploration work in East Texas, which had, in one way or another, landed him in jail. No one ever talked about it. No one ever talked about him at all, least my mother. He was dark-skinned, which had surprised me. I knew I was of mixed race, I knew that my mother was darker than me, but somehow seeing my grandfather made it all real.

I loved my grandfather's painting. It was a couple, a black man and a white woman, crouched under the branch of a tree. They stared into each other's eyes and clasped hands. The eyes were what pulled you in to the painting, they were luminescent compared to the flat skin tones. In the background, deep in the background, was a fire. I did not know what was burning, not as a kid. I asked my mom. Hope, baby, she said. Hope is burning.

This is the first time I have thought about those trips with my mom since she died. Usually my memory is nothing more than a disjointed tool I reference when I need to recognize a face or remember the name of some old friend I bump into. Now it feels alive. A boiling pot of emotional connections to places, people, moments. Maybe it's Sue's passing, seeing my father again, standing here with Missy, the first person who ever left me and then came back, maybe it is walking into a museum where my grandfather's painting is proof that what we do can last, can speak for us even beyond our own limited time. For the first time I feel like my memories are not just part of me, but they are me. They are not my circumstances, they are my constitution. It is more a sensation than a realization. It pushes up from my center and makes my jaw shudder, my eyelids flutter, and I have to shake to get the static out. I am here. Now. It has been years since I knew what that meant.

I push Missy against one of the pillars in front of the museum and kiss her with every bit of energy I can summon from my toes.

"Well, Geez, Mr. Shell," she says, "I didn't know art turned you on."

"Neither did I."

There is a massive crowd outside of the museum. It feels like a carnival. There are people selling cotton candy, bottles of water, T-shirts, and miniature versions of the painting. There is a long line to buy tickets and we stand in it for over an hour before we are admitted. We walk inside and start through the halls. We rush past the Renaissance and Baroque pieces, past the Native American collection, and to the Oklahoma artists exhibit.

We push through the semi-circular crowd around the painting, until we can glimpse it on the spaces between people's bodies. And finally, there it is. Grandpa Jared's painting. The eyes peer out from the canvas just like I remember. They penetrate the onlooker, pulling the viewer into the canvas, and then pushing the canvas into the world. The deep green eyes of the woman and the tiger-striped brown of the man's. They are so much sadder than I remembered. Their arms are wrapped around each other as they hide under the protection of the branch. But, hide from what? There was no fire in the painting. The background was a simple pastoral scene. A small barn resting at the edge of an expansive field. No airplanes. Just blue sky.

"This is Jared Rowland," says Missy. "This is your blood."

I nod.

"Have you seen it before?"

I shake my head. "Well, yeah, but..."

"But what? It's beautiful. I feel like those eyes are prying inside me. They remind me of water in a Sorolla. They're briliant." Missy was always showing off.

"I know, but somethings wrong."

"Wrong?"

"Well, yeah, there used to be a fire in the background. Planes overhead. They were hiding from an attack."

"An attack?"

"Yeah, an attack."

"Hmmm..." she says. "Maybe it's just one in a series. I mean, maybe this isn't the very same painting, just a similar one."

"No, I remember this painting."

"It's been a long time, Tommy, maybe… I don't know, maybe your memory is a little off."

"The news is right… It's changing…"

I tap a guard on the shoulder. He turns abruptly to face me.

"Can I help you?" I think the guard is Vietnamese. Young. Judging by his accent he was born here. His hair willows up like Beethoven's or Einstein's.

"How is this happening?" I ask.

He shrugs. "Got me."

"Is it really the same painting? I mean, was it changed?"

"Changed? Just look at it. It's changing right in front of you."

"Yeah, but I mean like on purpose. You know, restored or altered."

He shakes his head and pulls at his hair. "Restored, no, not since I've been working here."

I turn back to the painting.

"But, between you and me," says the guard, "There's always been something weird about that painting. Even before all this."

"Weird?" I ask. "How weird?"

"It's always new, different, every time I look at it."

"What do you mean?" asks Missy.

He shrugs, "I can't say, I mean every painting changes over time, subjectivity blah blah blah, but there's something different about this one."

"Different how?" I ask.

"It just... I don't know... To be honest it kind of gives me the creeps," he answers with a masochistic smile. "Personally, I blame the lizard people… Of course, I always blame the lizard people."

"The, uh... Lizard people?" I ask.

"Yeah, you know, Lizards and Vikings... Ancient races that have fostered and decimated humanity throughout the centuries."

I can't tell if he's kidding, but if he is he has a great poker face. "I wasn't aware," I say.

His voice gets low and conspiratorial, "Oh, yeah, all very well-documented. I have books. I could lend them to you."

"That's, uh, that's alright, I am just interested in the painting for now."

"Suit yourself," he says in a normal voice before returning to his conspiratorial tone, "But I can show you things you wouldn't believe." He winks at me.

"Do you know if you have any more of his paintings," Missy asks.

"Oh yeah, lots. There's a whole mess of 'em in the basement. They say he was supposed to have an exhibit here. They brought all the paintings, but he died before they were hung. They've just sat down there ever since."

"Is there any way to get down there. To see them."

"Sorry. Off limits to the public. Sometimes a scholar can get special permission to go into the archives, but..." he looks us over, "...you two don't strike me as scholars."

"How about family?"

He shrugs and again pulls at his hair. I notice that he has a tattoo at the base of his neck that just peeks out over the collar of his shirt. "You family?"

I nod.

"Whatever you say, boss. Listen, I'm not really the one to talk to about this kind of thing. Stop by the front desk and ask for Dr. Sandy Snyder."

"Thanks," I said shifting towards the exit.

"Hey wait," said the guard. "You look familiar from somewhere."

"I don't know. I don't think we've met."

"I've seen you somewhere though." A flash of recognition widened his eyes. "You were the singer for the She Shells. Holy shit man, I loved you guys when I was in school. I still play your records every now and then."

I hope he does not play them backwards. A She Shells fan in Oklahoma? Must have been lonely school days. "You knew my band?"

"Of course, man. The She Shells were big around here. I have all your 7 inches. Shit, Tommy Shells is a relation of Rowland? What a world." He shook his head, and ran a hand through his Beethoven hair.

"Listen, maybe we can grab a beer sometime? How long you here? My friends would freak if they knew I was hang'n with you." He leaned in close. "And I could show you what I've been talking about."

I think of how to dodge him. "This is kind of a crazy time. Family stuff, but yeah if..."

"Just call if you have a minute." He gets out a piece of paper and scribbles his name and number. Vincent Tram.

"Alright. Nice to meet you, Vincent."

"Nice to meet you! Tommy Shells…"

As we walk away Missy whispers into my ear, "My little rockstar."

And I whisper back, "My little Mark David Chapman."

We stop by the desk, but we are told Dr. Snyder is not in. I leave my phone number and a short message that we would like to talk to him regarding Jared Rowland. The desk attendant gives me a business card with Snyder's information printed on it.

It takes us a few minutes walking around the parking lot to realize that the Rabbit is no where to be found.

"Shit," I say.

"My suitcase," says Missy.

"We'll get you some clothes."

"No, I don't care about the clothes. I brought Rowland's journal. I was going to surprise you."

"You brought the journal?"

"Well, you asked about it last time we talked, and I thought it might be good for you right now."

"You have no idea how good it would be for me right now."

"Well, it's gone."

"It is indeed," I say.

The police come and go in the space of half an hour. Not a lot of sympathy for a broke down Rabbit.

Vincent Tram is finishing his shift. He leaves the museum just as the cops pull away.

"Hey there," he shouts. "What are you two doing lingering around the parking lot."

"Our car seems to have been abducted," I say.

"Ouch," he says.

We all bask in an awkward silence.

"Well," continues Vincent, "It would be an honor to chauffeur the great Tommy Shells to... where do you need to go?"

"the Olive Barrel in Utica Square," I say.

"...Okay, to the Olive Barrel in Utica Square."

"The wake is at the Olive Barrel?" asks Missy.

"Welcome to Tulsa."

Vincent nods and pulls at his high stack of follicles.

Vincent plays the last disk we made before Zack moved to Portland. It is probably three year old now.

"So you're the one," I say.

"I'm the one one what?" says Vincent.

"The one that bought our last album."

"Afraid not, my man. I haven't bought a CD since Napster. Vinyl, I'll pay for. If it's digital it's fake, and if it's fake it's free. That's what I say."

I have never really listened to my own albums. It's embarrassing to be with others, a spectator of yourself. Performing I can handle, but not this.

Vincent drops us in front of the Olive Barrel. I promise him to call for a beer sometime.

The crowd is gathered around the bar inside. I see Dad and George chatting in a corner, Eve and Mickey on the other side of the bar. Rusty, the rope wrangling clown is there, too. A large number of what I assume to be Sue's journalist friends are bunched near a fake fire place. Sue's parents have both passed. We walk towards dad and George.

Dad looks better today. Stronger. Maybe it is for the sake of the crowd, or maybe the crowd has translated into some kind of strength.

He smiles as we approach. "So this must be the famous Missy," he says. "I was so happy to see you come in this morning."

"How are you holding up Mr. Shell?" she asks.

"I'll make it. Part of life, as they say."

"Yeah, the last part," says George. "Bum deal if y'ask me."

"Well, as usual, no one's ask'n you George. Death's 'bout the only reality I can rely on these days, and when something's that close to you, you may as well make friendly with it," Dad says.

"If that's what you call friendly, I'd hate to see meet your enemies," says George. "I'm sick of it. Get to a certain age, build up a life with every bit of vinegar ya have in ya, and all the sudden you ain't doing noth'n but watch the ones you cared for drop." George must have had quite a number of drinks. I've never heard him talk so much. "No, I'll tell ya, I'm tired. Tired. You tell me, what kind of sick old designer makes a roller coaster in which you're miserable on the way up *and* on the way down?" George rubs the thin hair on his very round head. "Anxiety and fear. Those are the phases of life."

"Anticipation and fulfillment, might be another way to call 'em," Dad says.

"Fulfillment? You find this fulfilling? That's just sick."

"George, I think you ought to take a seat at the bar and collect your thoughts," dad says.

I imagine now is not the time to tell George about the Rabbit. He opens his mouth halfway as if he is about to say something, but decides to take dad's advice and heads for the bar.

Dad puts his hand on my shoulder. "Tommy," he says, "thank you for yesterday. You will never know how much it meant to me to see you right then, right there."

I feel the faint urge to cry.

"I'm so happy to see you, son. I've missed you and Adam more than you would probably believe."

"I know," I say. "I've missed you too, dad." I realize that it is true as I say it.

He looks like he is also trying not to cry.

Missy starts to walk away in order to give us privacy.

"No, don't go, Missy," says dad. "You're family." He puts a hand on her shoulder and one on mine and leads us to a small table.

The journalists, all of Sue's friends, are gathered opposite. Dad fixes a glare on them. "Those bastards have a lot of nerve to show up here."

"Why? Aren't they her colleagues?"

"She went to every one of them for help. She knew this story was toxic. They did, too, which is why they left her to eat her lunch all by herself."

"What was the story, exactly, Dad?"

He shuts his eyes and breathes in deep before he speaks. "Sue had found letter's between your grandfather and an old friend. You know that, though. I gather from what Eve tells me that you've read the letters, or some of them anyway. Well, she had also found correspondences between Flanders and Stamford that put them smack in the middle of causing the riots. They more or less admit to conspiring to end the prominence of Black Wall Street. She found the article from '21 that proves that Flanders's paper called for the lynching in an editorial. She was going to publish all of that, and, honestly, everyone probably could have lived with it. But, then she found out about Bergman and the art exhibit that your grandfather was supposed to have at the Stamford Museum and started investigating. That hit a nerve with someone. That's when the threats began. That's when it was clear she was on to something."

"What, what was she on to? I'm lost here"

Dad leans in close. He whispered in my ear. "Bergman taught your grandad something. He did something to those paintings. They were... listen, I know this sounds crazy, but those paintings don't just show reality, they... They change it. And, somehow they're connected to the stamford family in a way that they find very threatening."

There is a phone call that night. The police found the Rabbit, but there was nothing in it. No suitcase. No journal.

Missy is tired, so I go to pick up the car without her. George drops me in front of the police station.

"You be alright?"

"Yeah, I'll come straight back home."

I walk into the station, tell the officer at the desk my name and that I am there about a stolen car.

He picks up the phone. "He's here. Yeah, the kid about the car," he says. There is a pause. "Uh-huh. Yeah." He hands up the phone. "Sit there." He points to a bench.

An officer comes through the swinging door and points at me. "Tommy Shell?"

"Yes, sir."

"follow me."

I follow him through the swinging door, out the back and into a parking lot. I am looking for the Rabbit, but I don't see it anywhere. And then I do see something familiar. The big yellow Hummer and its cowboy clad driver leaning against the door.

"Howdy, there."

I try to run, but my legs are kicked from under me. My vision goes blank as I feel the familiar sensation of the satin bag being pulled over my head, and then hear that familiar high-pitched voice. "Well, hello there, Tommy."

Buddha. Fuck.

A heavy-booted foot jolts my kidneys and I feel my own saliva pressed between my cheeks and the bag over my head. I cling to the sensation of moisture as my perceptions dull. It's strange to lose consciousness in the complete darkness. A subtle transition.

7

I

Coming to consciousness in total darkness is a different experience than fading out. Pure anxiety. You do not know if you are blind or paralyzed. You try to move your limbs, but you cannot see them to verify that they are reacting to your brain's commands. I put my hand against my face. Skin. No bag. Still, I see nothing. I move my hands all around me, but all I feel is cold hard concrete. A light emerges in the distance, or maybe it is just a product of my eyes adjusting to a light that was already there. It is blue. Dim.

"The world is full of moving parts," comes a familiar voice, "that must be fine tuned by us."

"Who's us?" I ask.

Flanders answers, "All of us." he exhales a profound breath. "Though, I suppose, there is a special sort of pressure on those of us in positions to orchestrate all the cogs in the machine."

"Is that what I am?"

He speaks through laughter. "Oh no, lad, you're much more than a cog. You haven't figured that out yet? If you were a cog we'd have long since done away with you."

"I guess that's comforting."

"It doesn't matter if it's comforting. I'm not worried about your comfort. I'm worried about the health of the mechanism."

"What the hell are you talking about? What the hell does any of that have to do with me?"

"You're grandfather's of a different mind than I am."

"Was of a different mind."

Flanders spends a moment hacking up something from deep in a lung.

"Listen, I don't want anything to do with any of this. I'm not out to get you guys. I don't even understand what this is all about."

"What were you doing at the Stamford Museum today?"

"Looking at my grandfather's painting."

"Did you like what you saw?"

"There's only one."

"Did it seem different to you than you remember?"

"It is different. Everyone can see that"

"But was it different than what you remembered?"

I do not feel as I have much choice but to play along. "Yes."

"Why do you think that is," he says, "why do you think art changes with time? It grows smaller, less dramatic as we grow larger and complicate the machinery of our own existence."

I am really not interested in my abductors philosophy of art.

"I remember reading Shakespeare as I child and feeling as though the plays were nearly infinite in what they offered. They were worlds that stretched beyond the edges of our own universe and never stopped expanding." a machine induced exhale interrupts his train of thought. "Now, I'm not so sure. Revisiting them as an adult I can't quite find those portals to the infinite. They're just plays. As long or short as they are.

The musings of a dead man. Art has that capacity when you're young, to transport. What happens?"

I rest my fingers against the cool concrete.

"Maybe it's too many years in the news business. Sending one-hundred-thousand words a day to press—that's publishing more words than the average novel each day, by the way—kills the mystique of stories on the page. Images, too. And don't tell me it's not art. We create a vision of the world, sell it to the masses. The only difference is, people believe the images we print to be reality. They react to it, each and every day. Can't say that about many novelists or painters."

"It's not that I don't appreciate your musings, but..."

"Impatient little bastard." He releases a short phlegmy laugh.

Another mechanical rise and fall of the lungs sounds out like an aerosol can releasing its spray.

Finally, he speaks, "I want you to destroy the paintings."

"Why? Why would I do that?"

"So that we let you live."

Fair enough. "But why don't you get rid of them?"

"We've tried. We can't. You are Rowland's blood, and only his blood can kill the prophecy."

"The prophecy?"

"The paintings are portals. Your grandfather painted himself back to 1921 and tried to stop the riots that led to Stamford Oils empire."

"You're fuck'n looney."

"Have you heard of Miguel Montcorte?"

I shake my head. He cannot see me, but he seems to grip that I am unfamiliar with the name.

"More popularly known as simply Montcorte."

The French priest. The mystic famous for his visions of the future that he painted from an asylum. "Yeah?"

"His son was one of the early settlers of New Orleans. He fathered a child with a slave. That slave fathered another child, and that one another. 24 years after emancipation, in 1889, that child took part in the Oklahoma land rush and staked a claim in what came to be Tulsa. His name was James Jones, and he named his son, born in 1900, Jimmie. No one knows for sure what happened to James, but after he disappeared Jimmie was adopted by the Rowland family. He went by his nickname, Dick. He was the was involved in the events leading to the Tulsa Race Riots in '21. He had a son of his own. With a white woman. They named him Jared. He was A painter. That was your grandfather."

"So, I'm related to Montcorte, is what you're telling me?"

"Yes."

"Uh-huh." What's to be said, really? This guys bonkers. "So, to be clear, you want me to destroy my grandfather's paintings, which are portals to the past, which only I can do, because I am a relation to Montcorte, so that you're oil buddy doesn't lose his empire in some alternate reality?"

"You're starting to catch on." Another mechanical rise and fall. "Not all the components of this world's mechanism are so straightforward as we'd like to believe. Consider yourself one in a long line of mechanics. You have tools that are necessary to keep things moving as they should."

"Who decides how things should progress."

"In this case it would be those with the fuel the machine needs." This time it sounds like he's hacking something up from his spleen. "Do it soon."

"I..." am fading out before I can finish my thought. I see something, a book, sliding towards me as my already dim surroundings fade entirely to black.

I open my eyes. A giant yellow boot is in front of me. It is attached to a giant jean-clad leg, which is attached to a solid abdomen, hefty shoulders, and a stiff neck, all topped off by a mustard-yellow hard hat nearly 80 feet above me. There's a giant penguin in overalls perched between his legs. The Golden Driller, and his oil-enthusiast aviary sidekick. They must have dumped me on the fairgrounds. There is a plaque near his feet that reads: "To the men of the petroleum industry who by their vision and daring have created from God's abundance a better life for mankind." The statue has been the symbol of Tulsa, of Oklahoma, for longer than I have been alive. Speaking of being alive, it occurs to me that perhaps I should be grateful. I think of the praying hands extending up from the ground in front of Oral Roberts. Maybe that is the Drillers day job. Maybe the mystery of where the rest of the man went can finally be laid to rest.

I pull myself to a sitting position and something slides off of my chest. It is a book. A journal. I recognize it immediately as Jared's journal, the one that Donnan had brought. My face hurts, but not as bad as the last time. I may have a cracked rib, but I'm not entirely sure what one feels like. In any case, it hurts to inhale. I breathe shallow choppy breathes.

Surveying my surroundings I see the Rabbit is parked at the far end of the lot. I pull myself up with as much care as possible and shuffle towards the car.

I open the passengers side door and slide over the stick shift, put the keys in the ignition and turn. It fights the good fight, but will not turn over. I try again with the same results. Finally, I see the gas gage. Empty. Some fucking luck. Out of gas at the feet of the Golden Driller. Me and Tulsa apparently have a lot in common.

I think of calling Missy, but it would just worry her more. I think of George, but that would mean waking him up, and he would worry everyone else. Dad?

I call Tanya.

"Hello?"

"Hi, Tanya. Did I wake you?"

"Tommy? Well, yeah, it is 4 am."

"Listen. I can explain later, but I'm at the fairgrounds. Out of gas. I need someone to pick me up."

"So, you call the pregnant girl who has work in the morning."

I hear a voice in the background, "Who is it?"

"Tommy," she says away from the receiver.

"Yeah, I guess I didn't think it through. Listen, I'll find someone else."

"No, Tommy, I'm sorry. Frank is on his way."

"Frank is on his, wha..." I hear Frank begin to say as she hangs up.

I stare at the journal. It's familiar. For years it sat on a bookshelf in our living room. The brittle brown binding stuffed between Missy's photo textbooks and my biographies of Chet Baker, Screaming Jay Hawkins, Patti Smith. It smells of musk and mold and as I open the cover I see pages that I am afraid to turn because they might break off in my fingers.

I've been working with Bergman for months now. He's pushing for my exhibition despite what they say at the museum. I think, in some sense, his advocacy of my work is his apology. As if by exposing the tragedy that's been forgotten here, his defense of the tragedies in his own country, those that he cannot quite allow himself to condemn, will be forgiven.

He paints gas cans, pieces of pipe, broken farm tools, old tractor parts and thinks that he is capturing the spirit of the worker, transporting the growing class of those who don't know labor into its greasy clutches.

Meanwhile, I paint Greenwood and all that it has forgotten.

He's told me to go there. To dig up mud, collect segments of bark, pull up blades of grass, stones, splinters from the sides of old buildings. To get the material, he said.

I make my tint, to what extent possible, with relics from the neighborhood.

I'm painting longer hours each day, longer than I've ever painted before. My body is exhausted, and I'm beginning to wonder if my minds not, too.

We played Debussey in the studio today. It was like flowing through some intermediate world. Brush strokes fluttering eyelids in some deep strange sleep. I have always confused sounds and sights. They say it's a disfunction in my brain… Maybe it is… When the music starts, the colors bounce around the room, and it's as if my mind becomes dislodged from the rational world. I feel myself expanding, becoming as big as the sky itself, and at the same time ceasing to exist at all. It's like I'm not a self anymore, just awareness of all these fluid sounds and shapes that for some reason we've come to call the world. And that's when I paint.

The world is emerging.

The one on the canvas, I mean.

Maybe this one, too.

It's become hard to separate one from the other. Bergman is pleased. He says this is a good sign, and he continues to push the folks at the museum to allow my exhibit. In the meantime he's contacted dealers in New York and Chicago.

I've begun to dream of the places I'm painting.

All day I stare into them, and when I finally close my eyes each night, there I am, not in front of the canvas, but inside it's frame looking out. It's an eerie feeling that I am being pulled in two. Half of me now lives in the greenwood I've created. I've come to know those faces and that time as well as I know my own. Often, when I look up from the canvas and see Bergman grinning or scowling at whatever inanimate artifact he has decided to paint, it's he, and not the subjects of my work, whose reality I doubt.

Figures in this world have taken on a ghostly hue. They are all the undead descendants of the betrayed. What debts we owe the past! How we should fear those we've wronged! How we should be weary of those we set about creating! The world is made and remade instant by instant, each of us architects of immense universes. We pull form from the Earth and as we do we reframe the past, realign paths to the future. Angry and grateful eyes locked on us from every imaginable direction. There is no escaping because time is the universe's best kept secret.

A knock at the window makes me jump, slamming my knee against the steering wheel.

Frank. "Little jumpy, I see."

"I guess."

"What the hell are you doing at the fairgrounds in the middle of the ni..." he stops himself "...morning?"

"I was dropped off here by some nice folks I met in St. Louis."

Frank offers an understanding nod and pulls a gas can out of the back of his truck. "Well, this ought to get you moving."

He pushes the yellow nozzle into the tank and slowly tips the can up.

"Make sure you fill up as soon as you get moving."

"I will," I say.

He hesitates before getting back into his truck. "I was thinking about your situation. How I may be of help."

"And?"

"And, how would you like to be my assistant. You know, help me set up the show at the Stamford."

"Why would..." ah ha.

"Assistants probably have plenty of free time to roam the museum, see what they can see."

"When?"

"Wednesday. Two days from what I would call tomorrow if the sun weren't halfway up."

"Listen, I'm sorry for pulling you out of bed. I really just couldn't think of anyone else to..."

He interrupts me. "Not necessary, Tommy, You're like family to Tan-yuh, and we all have to do shit we don't want to for family."

A beautiful sentiment? "Wow, I..."

"I'm just pulling your leg, Tommy. I'm happy to help."

"Thank you."

"Call me Wednesday. And try to stay out of trouble in the meantime." He peaks his head into the Rabbit. "That eye looks like hell."

"Believe it or not I'm growing accustomed to the beatings."

"Did you go to the police?"

"That's where this little adventure got started."

"Well, maybe avoid the police then."

"Yeah, that's my intuition."

"Shit, man. You've got yourself some mess here."

Missy is not happy when I get back to George's. "Where the hell have you been all night?"

"I wish I knew," I say.

"What is that supposed to mean?"

"It means I have no idea where I was. I went to the cops, who turned me over to some bad folks who want me to do some strange things, and I woke up on the fairgrounds next to a car with no gas, had to call a friend and wait for help."

Missy stands slack-jawed.

"I'm sorry. I should have called between the beating and the stranding."

"Why didn't you call us for help?"

"I didn't want to worry you."

"So, your method of not worrying me is to stay out until past 5 in the morning without letting me know where you are?"

"I'm sorry. I know I should have called."

Her glare becomes pity. "Are you okay?"

"More or less."

She rubs a finger over my swollen eye. It hurts.

"Does it hurt?"

"No," I lie.

"Do you want some ice?" she asks.

"No," I say, even though I would love some ice.

"I was really pissed at you," she says.

I nod.

"I couldn't decide whether to leave and be angry or stay and be worried."

"I'm glad," I say, "that you stayed… Not that you worried."

"You're lucky is what you are," she says.

I point at my face. "I guess you could call this lucky."

"Well, no one can have it all."

She leaves the room and comes back with a washcloth soaked in warm water with which she wipes my face clean.

"So, what are you going to do, Tommy?" She asks.

I still do not know. "I'm going to go to the museum and try to get some answers. I'm going to, I don't know I guess I'll do what they want me to... What else can I do?"

I am glad she does not ask what they want me to do.

"Can't we just go back to Chicago? Forget all this? "

I shake my head. "They'll find me. Wherever we go. I just have to see this through."

"And me?"

"I think you should go home. Wait for this to be finished."

She tilts her head and widens her eyes. "I'm supposed to go back to Chicago and forget all about this while you run around getting your ass kicked by some apparition's goons? I think not, Tommy."

"Well, you can't sit in George's house worrying about me either."

She nods in agreement. "I can come with you. Help you."

I am not sure how I feel about this. I want help, but how can I ask for help when I do not even know what I am doing. In order to delegate, first you have to know what is to be done, right Doc?

We lay down on the couch face to face. I pull at the skin on her cheek and she pretends to slap me.

"I spoke to your dad for a while this afternoon," she says.

I nod.

She pushes forward. "He's an interesting guy. A sweet man, really."

I nod again.

"Why don't you ever see him, or even talk about him?"

I want to tell her. I want to tell her about how I thought putting ice in your morning orange juice made it dangerously sour until I was fifteen and realized that it was the gin, not the ice. About how goodnight kisses wreaked of booze soaked whiskers. About how I fell from the roof of the car when he drunkenly put me there as a toddler while he tried to unlock the door. About finding my mom crying in the dark again and again. About how everything it means to be a man in

Oklahoma prevents your from connecting, from feeling, from opening up even to yourself. About a lifetime of little incisions that had become this unbearable wound that only had the chance to scab over when he was not around. But I did not tell her any of those things.

"I just don't know him that well," I say instead.

She squints for a moment, then frowns a little excessively. "You know, to me that sounds really cowardly."

"What, that I don't know him?"

"Well, yeah. Listen, I've spent the last 5 years trying as hard as I can to create the chance to know two people who for all intents and purposes sold me and my sister. Worse yet, they gave us away. Maybe I would understand if there was some profit involved," she giggles, "but nope. Just a gift. I owe it to myself to know who they are, at least. And you, you have this sweet, flawed, yes, but basically good, man right here, and you are afraid to know him."

I try to find a point of disagreement, but come up blank. "Yeah."

"Yeah? Is Tommy Shells agreeing with me? Without even putting up a fight?"

"I guess so. I just... I just... I don't feel like there's anything to know."

"He's a person, Tommy. There's always something to know."

I know that she is right, and I feel a deep emotion that I cannot pinpoint as happy or sad well up inside me, making my lip quiver and eyelids shudder, if just for a moment.

"I'm going to get some sleep, Tommy. It's been a long day.'

"You're telling me," I say.

But, I cannot sleep yet. I have reading to do. I open my grandfather's journal, and a letter that I had not seen earlier in the evening falls out.

Dear Tommy,

The old folks home at Clark and Roscoe is one of the mixedest of mixed blessings. On the one hand, it let's an old geezer remain in the city. An old man, if he's still mobile like me, can get out and take a walk around the block. Hell, if the weather is good, and the old man is up to it, he might even make it all the way to the lakefront. If an old man still has a little of the voyeur left in him, which I am proud to report this one does, it is not at all a bad spot to watch the young ladies either. If the old man likes their spiky pink hair and tattoos, all the better, but even if he doesn't, it gives a griper something solid to gripe about.

On the other hand, it's still an old folks home. There is at least a contingent of those who would have preferred to spend their twilight years in the suburbs with family than in the city alone. Well, I don't have any family, and I hate the suburbs. Of course, the Chicago Housing Authority, the same agency at the helm of massive success stories such as Cabrini Green, the Robert Taylor Homes, the Henry Horner Homes and the Stateway Gardens, is not known as a model of good upkeep. Hell, even that adds to the adventure. Nothing like an unlit vestibule to breed mystery. Good for an old writer's imagination.

The paint chips from the walls peel in planks the size of porterhouse steaks. The last time my apartment had a good painting was 15 years ago by volunteers from a local School. There are rats the size of cats and roaches the size of rats. Of course, a gentleman may learn to appreciate the company of any life form, no matter how unpopular with the rabble. Even the building's most unpleasant feature, the constant stench of an open sewer line, can be adjusted to with time. The heat works in the Winter and the electricity to power a fan in the Summer, so what is there to complain about? All of this is to say, Tommy, that I adjust well to my surroundings, and I don't bother a great deal with regret.

I am happy enough to be alone, and wouldn't trade my life in the city for anything. As a career garbage man—sculpting has brought me lots of opportunity in life, but never paid the bills—I have become well acquainted with them anyway.

Allow me to introduce myself: I was born in Dublin on New Year's Day at the turn of the last century, but I have spent the last 80 years right here in Chicago. The second millennial will be my first centennial, and, if human longevity is not to undergo any radical changes in the very immediate future, it will be my last and only. I am lucky not to be reliant on a cane. I don't move quickly, but for nearing one hundred, any movement is quicker than the average.

I am known in the neighborhood for few things: my accent, my polka-dotted bow tie, and my occasional foray into less lucid territory in my interactions with the local youth. I think I have a pretty good idea of how they see me. Miguel Montcorte has always been a favorite topic of mine. Marijuana another. I imagine I am also known as the weird old man who harasses the local youth into finding him weed. Glaucoma, is what I usually say if they insist on an excuse.

I bought some marijuana yesterday, because I had no interest in seeing the millennial, or my own centennial, stone sober. Years have past, nearly a quarter century, since I gave up drinking. Plus, weed is good bait for the young. I like to entice them up to my place to watch movies and talk. They always assume there is something creepy about it, but there isn't. My sexual existence came to an end around the same time I gave up drinking. Never quite figured out the connection there. As to why I invite the young: I just like their company. I prefer it to be surrounded by people who see forward rather than backward.

I'm sitting on a big red corduroy chair in my living room. My sculptures, metal and leather towers of geometrical shapes and primary colors, mostly made of things I pulled from the trash over forty years of working for the city, surround me. The closest to family I have left.

A rat just peeked it's nose out from under the stove. He stared at me. I stared at him. I smiled and the rat departed to its hidden layer inside the walls of this old building. Ingrate. What kind of animal can't comprehend a smile?

I have been smoking substantial amounts of marijuana today from an old wooden pipe. Nothing fancy. More discrete this way, or at least I think so.

There are flyers on my coffee table: "The Metro Y2K Bash!!! Florence Nightygown, the Golddercoasters, and the She Shells. Free Champagne at midnight if we're all still here!!!"

Three hours to go before I finally meet you, the last person in this world I might be able to think of as family. Not blood, obviously, but the blood of someone I considered my brother.

I cannot tell you how much I wonder what you will be like. I wish I had found you sooner, but I only just learned that my long gone best friend's grandson lives in Chicago. That he is a musician. I can't help but wonder if you see the world the way he did… And now, on this which so many idiots are insisting will be the last night of human history, perhaps we will meet. Better late than never.

Just so you know, I don't buy this whole end of the world business. Not even a little. But I will admit there is a static buzz in the frigid Chicago air as the sun heads down and the lights of Clark Street come up. Something is working at my nerves. I've been through the text. Montcorte said nothing about Y2K, about the world ending at the second millennial. There is no mention of some massive information failure leading to ultimate chaos. No, the end, I'm afraid, is still on the distant horizon. It will be a slow decline of community, a descent into cultural narcissism, an irredeemable selfishness that will eat away at the ability to care for others. The stage is set, but it will be a long way down the road. The plot is in place, but it would be too easy a resolve for some bad math to take us all out in the middle of a New Year's celebration. No, psychological tensions that plague entire races of beings don't end so conveniently. Whatever final absurd sentence precedes the last punctuation of humanity's masochistic third act will be both anticlimactic and grueling, like a forty-five year old drug addict finally recognizing the obvious and avoidable idiocy that guided two and a half decades of decision making. This? This is just millennial madness. A symptom of the slowly progressing disease for certain, but not yet the final stage.

I am going to take a little break, and finish this letter after a quick nap.

I am sitting at a diner now. I bundled up in my old wool winter coat and covered my hair with a fedora almost as old as I am, grabbed my stack of letters, an old journal and a copy of the novel I will not have the time to finish, and took the elevator 13 floors down to the ground. I live on the 14th floor, but it is a rouse since the building cleverly decided to skip 13. Renaming a thing doesn't change its fundamental unluckiness. The street is blanketed in snow. The sidewalks of the old folks home had yet to be shoveled. I shuffled along with great caution. A snow pile on Y2K will not be the end of me. I want to wake in the morning, the first day of my second century shared with the world's first day of its second millennium, capable of laughing at all the fools whose continued existence is also their disappointment. Of course, I know I won't. It is written.

That smell is in the air. I took it in with a big whiff as I left the house. The smell of Winter in a city. There is nothing like it. The cleanness of the snow, the slight tinge of smoke from the collected efforts of chimneys, barrel fires, and roasting chestnuts and yams on street corners. I still remember the way that Dublin smelled at the end of December. It wasn't so different except that my memory of Dublin carries the moldy aroma of an old photograph along with it.

I passed Wrigley Field on my way to the diner. I have never, in all these years of living just beside it, entered Wrigley Field. A loser is a loser, and I get little joy from watching a team that has learned to take pride in its failure. Plus, Cubs fans are the scourge of the neighborhood. The punks I like. The gays too. I don't even especially mind the yuppies that have piled in...

but, drunk yuppies. A line has to be drawn there. The moderately wealthy, shirtless and boring, chests painted, screaming incoherent slogans in deep, unintelligent rasps. It is vulgar. If for no other reason, I prefer Winter just because there is no baseball. Wrigley is most beautiful when it is empty.

The diner I am in is just in front of the Metro, the venue where your concert will be tonight. It is of the polished, permanently modern, black, white, and metal variety so popular in the 50's and so kitschy ever since. Pepper's. Believe it or not, I remember Pepper, the woman who opened it. We were lovers, briefly. She always smelled of bacon and strawberry milkshakes. Her fingers were dried out from constant dishwashing. Walking into the diner tonight I felt like I was smelling her again. I have no idea what become of her. She sold the place years ago.

The waitress just came to the table.

"Mr. Donnan O'Dea!" she said. She's a young red-headed waitress with freckles across every visible bit, which, if you have any of your grandpa in you at all, must lead you to assumptions about the invisible.

I slid my coffee cup an inch in her direction.

"Claire, my girl. How's yer New Year look'n?"

She poured the coffee fast and came to a quick stop just as the thin, dark fluid kissed the brown ceramic rim. "No outlook just now. I'll make plans in the morning if we're still here."

"You don't buy the old bit about the computer bug, do ya?"

"Mr. Donnan, do you really think I'd be pouring coffee right now if I thought this was my last night on Earth?"

"What else's to do?"

She winked. "I could think of a thing or two."

That made me blush. "Don't tease an old fella," I said.

"Never." She drew a circle on her pad of paper "So what's your outlook señor Moncorte? You're our local sage, after all."

"I'm no sage dear, just a bored old coot who likes a puzzle."

She rolled her eyes. "Hungry today?"

"No, dear, just coffee."

What an effusive spirit on this girl. It's like her soul is puking up smiles faster than her mouth can stretch them across itself. 50 years ago I would probably have asked her back to my place. 70 years ago I definitely would have. Jesus, 70 years ago... 70 years ago your existence was still 50 years in the future. Not even Moncorte could have predicted you, Tommy. How would he have put it: A young man, a generation removed from a battle between light and dark emerges from obscurity, takes the stage at the turn of the second millennium and evades global destruction by bringing the rock… Or, something to that effect…

I am going to write your grandfather now. I still write him letters, even though he's not around to receive them.

I plan to give you this journal tonight. I hope it serves you.

Donnan

I opened the journal to where I had left off and continued to read.

Immersion in the world of my work grows daily. I've collected records, photos, names, artifacts. The smells, colors, tastes, textures, even the songs of Greennwood are all inside me. The Tulsa of '21 is more my own than this one. I begin to think that perhaps I could talk to Sarah, tell her not to go to the police for whatever reason it is that she went. I wonder if I can warn the bankers and tycoons that their wealth, their well-being, is threatened. But, art is no intervention. I'm just a witness. I'm a photographer who collects moments that have ceased to exist, reconstructing scenes from their physical remnants.

My dream last night was tangible. It wasn't weightless and translucent like my dreams normally are. It was dense and fully rendered. I saw my mother and father under a willow at the edge of a field. They were lovers. I wanted to warn them that their world was conspiring against them, but I couldn't speak. I opened my mouth, but nothing came out. The dream itself may have felt substantive, but I was as ephemeral as any dream. A spectre haunting the past and nothing more.

Bergman has always said that art can change reality. Give it new form, he said. I always assumed he meant by changing minds we change the physical structures minds create. By broadening the possibilities of images, we force the broadening of notions. The mental and the physical unite in works of art. They effect each other. Alter each other. Violate and create each other. Reality pours from their union, their battles, like a child, or a scab.

A man came to the studio today. A young man with broad, shiny cheeks and round lensed glasses. He wore a green and brown tweed hat that was wet with rain.

He took a great interest in my work, he said.

I was unsure as to how he knew my work as it's never been shown anywhere.

All he offered in way of explanation was Bergman's name. Bergman didn't show up to the studio this morning. A note said he was feeling ill and wouldn't be in for a number of days. Perhaps, I thought, it was due to all the rain that has been falling.

The man looked over my paintings like a scientist examining a slide under a microscope. He held his thick-framed glasses a few inches from his eyes and perused each canvas. He seemed to take a particular liking to the one of my father in his prison cell.

He offered to buy it, but I told him it was unfinished. Next, he said a curious thing. "It will always be unfinished," he said.

"Like all works of art," I responded.

"Except that this one's painting you," he said.

I wondered for a moment if I wasn't dreaming. It's become so hard to know.

I paint each day, but never feel the collection is nearing its finish. The paintings, 12 in all, are on easels, mounted on the walls, or accessible on the floor. I paint them all at once, little by little. I prefer this to working on them one by one, because this way they will be more uniform. I want them to share seconds, minutes, and hours rather than days, weeks, and months.

There is a mirror in the barn that Bergman had been using for his self-portrait. I caught a glimpse of myself today and was shocked to find my own face a strange mixture of the distant and familiar. It was like seeing an old lover on a street corner in Budapest. Not that I've ever had that experience. At first, I thought my face was alarming because I had been staring so long at my father's, but as I reflected, I realized that it was the familiarity and not the difference that was off-putting. I've painted myself into the works.

It's me and not my father that sits with his love (my mother) on the edge of the woods. It's me who looks up in horror as the planes fly overhead and the homes collapse under the weight of bombs. It's me who runs scared from the flames of Greenwood's businesses. It's me who sits alone in the dark prison cell, eyes filled with fear of the lynch-mob outside of the prison. It's me who lies bloody, dead, with eyes like marbles, empty and staring into the one patch of blue Oklahoma sky that has emerged through the smoke plumes and jet streams. I've put myself in the middle of it all. As I move through the room, from painting to painting, I'm moving through moments, experiences that have been mine. I'm having them again. I never had them. They are not mine. I know they are not. But, I feel that they are. I'm no longer creating. I'm remembering. Is it possible to delve so far into a thing that it becomes a memory?

The man came again today. I asked him what he had meant by his comment that 'the painting was painting me.'

"Art is a biological process. A host invaded by a virus. Neither is fully responsible. Both simply share in an act that is not fully the will of either the object or the artist. All biology is a conversation. Art is no different. In this case the work has taken over the process. The virus has taken over its host. Not all biology is about cooperation."

I told him I didn't much like the sound of that.

"It doesn't matter if you like it," he said. "It's evolution."

I asked him what he meant, but he only repeated himself again, "You may have started this thing, but the painting is painting you now."

He offered, again, to buy the paintings on his way out. I, again, refused.

The third day with no Bergman. I decided to go to his house and check on him. I knocked on the back door for a few minutes, but there was no response. I went to the front and rang the doorbell. After three rings I heard a light rustling.

"Wait... wait... wait," came a voice through a fit of coughing.

A series of locks were undone, and, finally, the door creaked open.

"Jared," said Bergman. "What are you doing up at this hour?"

"This hour?" I asked. It was only seven in the evening.

He rubbed his eyes and explained that he'd been asleep, dreaming. He asked the time, and I told him. The overcast skies, he explained, must have confused him. It looked much darker, much later, than it was.

He invited me in. It occurred to me that this was the first time I had been asked into his house.

It felt vancant. Brown. It smelled of books and cigar smoke. I'd expected it to be filled with photos, knick-knacks from travels around the world, a globe perhaps. But, there was none of that. Just stacks of books, not even a shelf to hold them, and a couch.

He noticed me noticing the emptiness.

"It was all left behind," he said. I didn't need to hear anything else.

I stared at the piles of books. Pre-war German painters. A significant collection of German aesthetics. Goethe, of course. There was a large, leather-bound book with a gold emblazoned title. The author's name was Miguel Montcorte. I stared at the book for quite some while. I was unfamiliar with the author and couldn't translate the title Les Temps á Venir.

I asked him if he was well, to which he responded with a nod in the affirmative and a hacking cough that annihilated his affirmation.

He let himself fall onto a dusty leather sofa, and set a defeated stare on nothing in particular in front of him.

The clouds which had lingered all afternoon had finally become rain. It's been raining a lot lately. The drops pounding the roof helped to remind me that there was still a world outside of this empty room that seemed, possibly due to the planet-sized ego of Bergman, to have its own gravitational pull.

"What is it?" I asked him.

He told me he was unsure, but another coughing fit, this time producing red spots on his handkerchief, spoke more loudly than his proclaimed uncertainty.

"Have you gone to the Doctor?" I asked.

"What would be the point?" He responded.

As much as I wanted to disagree with him, I had to admit to myself that he was right. I sat down next to him on the sofa.

"How are your paintings coming?" asked the poor old kraut his voice straining to be heard.

"Always a process," I answered. "You taught me that."

"Finish them. Promise me you will. Those paintings will be important."

"They're just a bit of forgotten history," I said, feeling a little overly humble.

"Forgotten history is the most dangerous kind," he said to me. "It's forgotten history that's destined to repeat. Your works are an assurance that we can move forward even as we move in circles. That's the trick of time. We go 'round and 'round, yes! But, also forward." He spun his index finger around as he lifted it up towards the ceiling. "Promise me."

"I promise," I told him.

I thought of mentioning the man with the shiny cheeks who visited the studio, but Bergman looked tired, so I let it decay with all the other unsaids.

It continues to rain. I strung a tarp over my paintings to keep the leaky roof from allowing them to be water damaged and gathered them towards the center of the barn so that water leaking in from under the sides of the walls could not get to them. I feel like I am working in a small tent inside of a bigger one.

This afternoon I must have been more exhausted than I realized. I was working on the painting of my father in his cell, and the next moment, I must have been dreaming on my feet, I felt as though I was looking out from the cell rather than into it. My gaze was directed out through the bars into a dark hallway. I heard shouts from outside that contrasted sharply with the static-filled quiet in the dark building. I could hear the crowd gathering around the courthouse. I could feel static of their hatred piercing the buildings cold stone walls.

8

I

Missy wakes me from sleeping on the couch by pushing on my shoulder and making me bounce up and down. It's dark outside of the screen glass door in the den. I must have slept through the whole day.

"Wake!" she commands

I smile and rub what must be a mess of hair on my head. "What are you doing?" I say.

"We are making dinner."

"Who does *we* consist of?"

"You know. The family."

"The family, eh?"

"George, Eve, Mickey, your pop, and me, of course."

"Ah, the family." Odd to say, it sort of feels like waking up on some dysfunctional Christmas morning. I feel my eye. It hurts. My rib, however, feels slightly better, which, in my very un-medical opinion, must mean it is not broken.

Missy flops down on top of me. "Hey," she says.

"Hey," I say.

"Do you realize we haven't…" she lowers her chin and open her eyes wide, "in months."

She is right. I feel desire for the first time in a long time.

"I don't..."

"If we're going to be together, we're gonna have to work on fucking a lot more often. Like the end of that Kubrik flick when Nicole Kidman shakes Tom Cruise out of fantasy land by telling him they have to fuck—speaking of which, I don't think there's a woman alive who could fuck Tom Cruise out of fantasy land, obviously not Nicole Kidman anyway."

She has a point, well, two really, but one that seems more relevant.

"What I'm getting at is, we're still more or less young, and I don't care if you want to look at porn, or talk to invisible celebrities, or read comic books all day and jerk off thinking about Catwoman... As long as you can also function in this world... As long as we can still function."

I nod in full and eager agreement. "But..." I look towards the den's door which is halfway open. I can hear plates clatter and voices chatter on the other side.

"We can be really quiet, Tommy."

I cannot argue with that.

Her lip quivers in front of mine for a moment, and then she smiles at me, eyes locked into that strange portal that only opens for lovers. We have come home. This is family, I think. I push gently against her and we kiss.

She groans a little.

"Quiet. You promised."

She laughs. "Shut up and do your job."

Moments later we are at the kitchen table. I feel like the world has been asleep for months, like reality has been hibernating all around me, while I walked through it half-awake.

Something sizzles in the kitchen. I smell meat and garlic. It smells amazing, but I am afraid that I will not be eating whatever carnivorous creation it is, and I have a mighty hunger.

George steps out of the kitchen, "Hey our little vegetarian's out of bed."

Thank God he remembered for once. "Yes sir," I answer.

"What kind of man don't eat meat?" asks George in his blunt, half-joking way.

"I don't know George, I guess the kind of man that doesn't like to mix his misery and his pleasure."

"That don't sound like no man at all, if you ask me. Misery and pleasure are one and the same."

"How's that?"

"I don't know," says George, "You ever had a good habeñero salsa?"

"Probably."

"It's only good because it hurts."

"Last I checked, no animals died making salsa."

"Never can tell. Maybe they test it on llamas. Shit, now that'd be torture. These bolt guns they use on the cows. Phwooop. Millisecond and the whole thing's over."

"Lovely, George, just lovely," says dad.

"I couldn't give up meat," says Mickey.

"Why not?" asks Missy.

"I'm just a carnivore," he responds. "Through and through."

"It's not healthy," says Eve. "The body needs a little meat." She gives Mickey a sly glance. George grimaces visibly as he brings out plates of food. It's not clear whether he is responding to Eve's comment or the weight of the plates. Probably both. A giant pile of spaghetti in tomato sauce. Meatballs on the side.

"You can get almost everything the body needs from veggies and grains plus a multi-vitamin," says Missy.

Mickey nods, and then adds, "Or you could just eat meat."

Missy looks fed up, and let's out all in one breath: "The day will come when people look back on this time, when societies had the choice and decided to factory farm animals instead of lowering meat intake, when we decided to feed the few to their gluttonous whims instead of provide all with adequate and healthy diets, as totally barbaric and decide that his was without a doubt the most intemperate moment in all of history."

A collective whoa consumes the table.

"A little prophecy from the misses," says George.

I think of Montcorte.

George begins to dish out the spaghetti.

Mickey jumps in. "Big picture, I'm with you, but there are temperate and cautious meat-eaters who still live by subsistence and give their animals happy homes before their deaths, which is all any of us can really ask for, more than most of us ever get."

"Is that what you are? A subsistence farmer?" Missy asks.

"No. Granted, but I try to buy from respectable farms, at least," Mickey says.

Missy is quick to respond. "And that's decent of you, I'm just saying that one day you may look like the kindest manager of a factory that exploited child labor."

"Ouch," says Mickey.

"Or a slave owner," says Missy.

All eyes turn away from Missy and the table falls silent. Eve's eyes are closed as if she is holding back a seismic outburst.

I look to see who will go for the meatballs.

Eve is first, and she stares straight at Missy as she dishes them forcefully onto her plate.

George is second. He is oblivious to the tension in the air and cavalier in his portioning.

Mickey goes for the spoon. He dishes out three which puts him between the two.

Missy and I abstain.

Dad does not reach for the spoon.

Everyone watches him as he twirls the first noodles around his fork and takes a bite.

"Jerry? You alright?" Asks George.

"I'm fine. Why is everyone staring at me?"

George's brow is thoroughly furrowed. "It's just... you know... you're plate's a little light, if you get my gist."

"The young lady made the more convincing case." He winks at me. I smile.

After dinner we admire George's lawn care.

"That's one hell of a shiner you've got there, Tommy," says my father.

I swipe at a firefly that's hovering above George's lawn jockey. "Yeah, I guess so."

"Do you want to talk on it?"

"I don't know, dad. I don't think you would understand."

"Try me, kiddo. I may not look like much, but I been around the block a time or two."

I have never been close to him. It is hard to want to talk to him. Every time I almost open my mouth to talk an invisible punch to the gut keeps me quiet.

"It's okay, Tommy. I understand if you don't want to talk. I just thought I might be able to help."

"How? How can you possibly help?"

"I just. I just think I know what you're going through."

"What? What is it that I am going through?"

He grabs the firefly and holds it in his open palm. The little bug lights up in his hand and then flitters off towards the road. "Come with me."

I follow him towards where the cars are parked.

"Do you have the keys?"

I nod.

"Well, let's go."

"Where?"

"Home, Tommy."

I run back to the house, tell Missy I am bringing my dad to his place, and we set off.

Dad lives in a subdivision near 91st and Memorial. It is a small dark house made of brown stones and wood. The Christmas lights have been up year round since somewhere around 1986. I remember the neighborhood. I had my first bike here, my first skateboard, my first fist fight. I remember my mom and dad being together here, something which is almost impossible to fathom now. I remember playing on the lawn with the other kids as the sun went down. One mother after another would call the kids home for dinner, and then I would be in the yard alone, listening to the cicadas, talking to our Dalmatian, Colby, in front of an empty house that I was too afraid to enter. Eventually someone would come home, usually Adam, and we would go inside, make something to eat, something from a box with a package of powder, and fall asleep in front of the television.

He opens the garage door and pulls up the drive.

The house is silent. My mom took Adam and Me to Chicago in '88. Colby died years ago. Sue just days ago. Dad was the last inhabitant.

The smell is exactly what I remember. I cannot define it. It is just the smell of Dad's house. Nothing more particular. We walk straight to the back of the house, a room that had been Adam's. Now it was an office of sorts. Sue's work space, dad says.

There is a large book shelf filled with books, mostly non-fiction works by journalists: biographies of diplomats, histories of social movements, collections of editorials. There are a few journalism text books, a huge row of magazines, binders that probably contain clips of stories Sue wrote. On top of the shelf is a box. Dad steps on one of the lower shelves to push himself up high enough to pull the box down.

"These were your mom's," he says.

Inside the box are a couple of pictures and a big book with gold lettering on the binding.

The pictures are of mom with her father. I had never seen pictures before. Mom was light-skinned, but her father's skin was dark brown.

They are in some park. Roses all around them. Mom is young. Twelve maybe. She is smiling like I never saw her smile in the time we shared the Earth.

I grab the book. It is aged and brittle. *Les Tempes á Venir* by Miguel Montcorte. I flip through the pages, which are all in French. I studied French in high school, but I cannot even translate the title now. There are markings in pencil throughout the book, notes in two different handwritings, my mother's, I assume, and Sue's.

"Did you know what Sue was up to?"

He looks at his wrist where a watch would be if he was wearing one. "I had a notion."

I wipe a bead of sweat just as it is going to fall from my brow, but miss and it makes a round dark spot on the page. "Why didn't you stop her?"

"She was a reporter, Tommy. Her job was to investigate things she cared about. She cared about this story."

"How much do you know about the story?"

"Tommy, I've known this story since before I can remember. This story was your mom's, and so, it became a little bit mine. Now it's yours."

"Did mom know?"

"Of course she knew. She took you boys away to protect you. It worked. For years it worked. Damn near killed me, but you boys were safe. Until now, anyway."

"So, you divorced to keep us safe?"

"It wasn't quite that simple, Tommy. We had our problems, but foremost among them was that your mom wanted to get away and, well, I thought she was paranoid."

"You thought she was crazy?"

"Wouldn't you?"

Probably, I think.

"Her father, your grandfather had been locked up in the looney bin a couple of times, and wound up in jail."

"He was locked up?"

"Five years."

"What happened to him? Where'd he go when he got out?" I asked.

"I don't know for sure. I don't think anyone does. Last contact he made was a collect call from Arizona in '88, just before your mom left with you boys."

"So, how did Sue get into it?"

"Sue and your mom were friends, Tommy. Sue knew a thing or two about the family. She found the book you're holding when she moved in. She was already writing about Stamford and Mulroney. That had been a lifelong vendetta for both your mother and Sue. They were close. They started talking about in college before your mom transferred up North. Sue was working on a book about the race riots, and everything just started falling into place. At first I thought she was crazy, too. But, as the saying goes, when everyone around you starts looking bat shit, maybe it's you who needs examining.

"Anyway, there was enough doubt there for me to prefer you boys be safe and gone, than here and in danger." He covers his face with a shaky hand. "I swear it damn near killed me, Tommy."

I am not quite ready to comfort him.

"So, you believe it now?"

"Believe what?"

"This. Montcorte. That somehow the paintings can change things..."

"I don't know, Tommy. I don't know a thing about the paintings, or Montcorte, or Bergman, or any of it. All I know is, that someone mighty powerful believes it enough to have killed Sue, and maybe your mom and your grandfather, too. And I know that the painting on the news every night sure as hell seems to be doing something strange."

"You know about Bergman, too?"

"Sue was talking to him."

"Talking to him?"

"Yeah, he lives in an old folks home out in Broken Arrow."

"He's alive?"

"Barely, but yeah, he's till ticking. Creepy old fuck if you ask me. Taught at the university here for years, but finally got retired."

"Can I take this?" I say grabbing the Montcorte book.

He shakes his head. "You can take whatever you want, Tommy, but I wish you'd just get the hell back out of here. Go back to Chicago. Play your music. Forget about all this."

"I can't, Dad. And besides, I don't get the feeling that these people will just go away if I go back to Chicago. If they're crazy enough to think the paintings of a dead man can hurt their chances in an Oklahoma Governors race, they're not going to leave it just because I travel a couple states North."

Dad nods in agreement. "Well, what are you gonna do?"

"First, I'm gonna go see those paintings. Then, I'm gonna talk to Bergman to see if he can make a little sense of this. If they want me to destroy the paintings, I'll destroy them. I just want this over."

I turn on the radio in the car on the way back to George's house. A scientist is talking about the oil spill in the gulf. Stamford Oil. Of course.

The voice of the scientist says: "The ability of the environment to adapt should never be underestimated. What seems like, allow me to rephrase, what *is*, a tragic event right now, will right itself more quickly than we expect. It always does. That's not to skirt responsibility, just to point out an obvious truth. It's never as grave as we think, because we routinely underestimate nature. It's not static, not a body acted on, but an active contributor to a dynamic interaction moving in a direction far beyond our purview, and we won't do much to delay, let alone stop, that progression."

"If you're just joining us, first of all, welcome to you, and you are listening to myself, Sheldon Travers, interviewing Stamford Oil-employed scientist Dr. Eli Kane. Dr. Kane, So are you saying that what happened in the gulf is ultimately of no consequence? If so, it seems your company has chosen a rather callous representative to express their perspective."

"Allow me to put in another light. We tend to think that humans are the only beings that communicate in complex, symbolic ways, am I right?"

"I think it has long been accepted that other species participate in complex symbolic language. I'm thinking of the honeybees dance, the complex warning systems of prairie dogs, the lang distance sonar of whales, the chirping of dolphins, monkey's signing, the list goes on and on..."

"Fair enough, but would you allow that we don't tend to extend those capacities to the plant world?"

"Generally speaking, no, we do not consider plants to be thinking subjects."

"Thank you. And this, is what I propose needs to change. The totality of nature is communicative. Nature is currently communicating to us, and I mean that quite literally, that it is in dire straits, and we are deaf to its messages. As I said before, Nature is strong, Nature will persevere, so really we should be taking this as a good will effort by Nature to warn us. Make no mistake, this is a human crisis. Nature is just giving us a second chance."

"How so? You propose that the plants in the gulf, which, I would like to remind you, is what we are discussing, are thinking subjects?"

"In so far as we ourselves are, yes, however, my purpose is not to lower our understanding of the plant to that of our current understanding of the human, rather to question our understanding of the human as somehow superior. We are all one organism. The genes in a tomato are largely the same as those in you, or more to the point, the genes in you are not far from those of the plants that are currently suffocating in the sea. What that means is that there is no substantial genetic difference between you and any other living thing. Nothing special, so to speak. The only difference is what those genes got together and created. What they decided to create, in as far as we can talk about deciding. Those genes are the only thinking subjects, they aren't points on a map that draw a human, they are discursive units, and the human emerges from the nuances of the conversations they engage in. It's the same for plants. The human is not isolated, not above. That is a myth, and a dangerous one. When we hurt the world around us, we hurt ourselves. We do grave damage to our ability to survive in this world. If we continue to wreak havoc on our ecosystem, the conversation those little guys are having will not continue to work in our favor."

"So, clarify this for me. What are you saying?"

"That nature is smarter than we think *we* are. And that *we* are nowhere near as smart as nature. That the situation will correct itself if we refuse to correct ourselves, and that our tenure on this planet will soon have been short and sweet with a grueling and extended finale if we don't listen to what the world is trying to tell us."

"Thi... um... so, clarify Dr. Kane, are you speaking for the Stamford Corporation right now? When you say that the solution will be... our extinction?"

"It doesn't matter who I am speaking for. Consider me a spokesman for all the proteins of the world."

"That guy is off his rocker," says my dad.

"And about to be out of a job," I add.

9

I

Frank drives a little red pickup. A Chevy. He shows up at 8 am and honks in the driveway. I slip out of Missy's death grip and head to the kitchen. I think my dad and I made it back no earlier than 4 am.

"Everyone's sleeping, Frank," I say.

"Time to wake up and salute the sun, brother. Best part of the day."

"Seriously?" I say hopping into the passenger's seat and rubbing the crud from the corner of my eye."

"Yes, indeed."

George's dog, the one with one floppy ear, chases us up the drive, barking all the way.

I turn to look behind me and see a stack of frames, covered on top by a tarp.

"Here," says Frank handing me a plastic bag.

I look inside. There is a gray jumpsuit, a baseball cap with the O and U of Oklahoma University, and a pair of thick-rimmed black glasses with lightly-tinted lenses.

"That way they won't spot you."

Oddly, I had not worried about being spotted. "No false mustachios?"

"I thought about it. Believe me, I thought about it."

"What stopped you?"

"Costume shop don't open 'til 10."

"Ah," I say while trying on the glasses.

He points to two large steaming cups of coffee in the side by side cup-holders mounted to the dash.

"Thanks," I say.

"De nada." He grabs his cup and blows into the drinking hole like it is a flute. "So, what's the game plan here. I mean how do you intend to make your way to the paintings?"

"I don't know, Frank. I guess I'm just gonna feel it out today. See what kind of openings there are. Scout, as they say."

"But, listen, set up shouldn't take me more than today. You better get done whatever it is you aim to get done."

We carry the paintings to the door of the museum one by one. A curator meets us at the entrance. The crowd's in the parking lot are still asleep in their tents. A few early morning stragglers sip coffee on the curb, but for the most part the carnival is in repose.

"Mr. Littlehawk," says the man, "a pleasure to make your acquaintance."

"Likewise," says Frank extending his hand, "Mr...?"

"Call me Sandy."

"Sandy," says Frank. He seems to ponder whether or not the name is acceptable for a minute or two.

"You've brought your own assistant?" asks the curator.

"Yeah, I always use Biggles here. Wife's little brother."

"Biggles?" Sandy repeats.

Biggles?

"Nickname. You know, family stuff."

"Ah ha," says Sandy. "Well, let me send out a few people to help you unload your exhibit, and allow me to say now, we are very exited to have your work here."

The curator walks back inside and we headed for the truck.

"Biggles? What am I a beagle?" I ask.

"I was on the spot."

A girl and a guy in security outfits come out of the museum's front entrance a couple minutes later. The girl is tall and thick. The boy is Vincent Tram.

I lean the painting against my thighs and pull the brim of my hat down tight over my glasses in the hopes that he will not notice me.

He walks directly towards me, stops, looks at the photo that leans against me.

"What is that, Tommy, spooge?"

Frank rolls his eyes.

I say, "In a manner of speaking, Vincent, yes, that is spooge."

Frank objects, "That, my friends is human life at its most elementary. Well, half of it."

Vincent shrugs. "Whatever." he grabs a framed painting of millions of sperm cropped into the shape of a keyhole. "What's with the incognito thing?"

"Listen, Vincent, could you just pretend you didn't recognize me? This is a bit delicate."

He leans in close and cups a hand over my ear. "Are you here to take down the lizard people?"

I decide compromise is more effective than explanation. "In a manner of speaking, yes."

He winks. "You can count on me."

Once we get everything inside, Frank gets to work directing the crew in charge of mounting. Sandy is always nearby, guiding the process, offering Frank suggestions, vetoing the occasional placement for seemingly arbitrary reasons. Grown men discussing the placement of all this sperm makes me think of *Moby Dick*.

At a moment that strikes me as opportune, Sandy and Frank are distracted by an argument about sperm cropped in the shape of a whale, oddly enough. I excuse myself.

I wander the halls looking for something like an entrance to the basement. I pass the Oklahoma Artists gallery and see my grandfather's painting of the young lovers huddled under the tree. Since the museum is closed, there is no crowd around it. Vincent is in the gallery, too.

He walks near me, his head looking towards his feet. Without looking up he says, "End of the hall. 26573#. Be quick. Sandy is the only one here until opening."

I speed to the end of the hall, passing sculptures of men missing their fingers and penises. The woman are just missing their fingers. Lucky.

At the end of the hall is a door with an electronic lock. I press the code that Vincent gave me 26573#. There is a beep and the sound of bolts releasing.

I grab the door knob and turn it, then pull the door open, revealing an unlit stairway down into the basement. My pulse is climbing into my throat. I step onto the first dark stair, then the second, the third, each sending the sound of a footstep echoing off into the dark distance of a stone-walled structure. I feel the walls for a light switch, but so far nothing. Four steps, five, six, seven, eight. I feel as though I am disappearing into the darkness, the only thing keeping me grounded here is the sound of my own heartbeat that now seems to be beating in my eardrums. Nine, ten, eleven, twelve. I feel with my feet for the ground while clinging to the cool concrete wall at each side. Thirteen, fourteen, fifteen. Fifteen would be a fine place to stop. Nice and round. Not even, but a multiple of five. Usually I like even numbers, but I prefer fifteen to sixteen. Sixteen, seventeen, now I hope we make it to twenty. Eightee... no more steps. This is ground. Eighteen. Even. A pair of nines. Three sixes... well, that I do not like so much, but eighteen feels clean anyway. I feel the wall for a switch, but there is still nothing. My eyes are beginning to adjust ever-so-slightly to the darkness. I fumble off towards the left and large forms come into view. Boxes? Crates of some sort? I wander farther into the room. The boxes, or crates, or whatever they are, go on and on and on. There is a strip of emergency lighting along the base of the shelving units that hold the crates which allows me to see the names of the artist's whose work is inside. I look up above and see there is a system that seems alphabetical. The names of the artists. Bates, Becker, Byrd, Clarke, Christiansen, Clemmons, Cruz. I move forward and come to a wall, I curve around and head back, on the other side of the stack. D's, E's, F's, G's, I curve around again. There are no H's or I's, but many many J's. I go to the end of the hallway and turn again, and again, and again until I come to the R's.

Rowland, Jared. There they are. I pull at the crate, but it is too heavy to move. The front cover is removable. I pull at it and feel it slowly coming loose. Once I separate it from the box, I see some twenty canvases standing on end one after the other. I slide one out: a man with shiny cheeks and little round glasses stands in a room next to a plant with giant purple leaves. His hands are dripping a deep brown substance that is somewhere between blood and oil. Another is of an old man lying face down in the snow. He is wearing a green plaid hat and a blue and red striped scarf. Another still is of a boy on a stage playing a guitar. He looks like, no he is, well... me... I think. I am almost sure of it. How could that be? These paintings were painted fifty years ago. I flip to the next and it is the blue-lit sarcophagus floating in the dark room. This is the first time I have seen it without being knocked on the head first. Could this be validation of what I have been trying to tell myself was just a dream. I look for Flander's head, but the image is consumed by the light. There is a hint of human form at the core of the blue light emanating from the rectangular container. The image seems to shimmer before me, the edges of the darkness around me and the darkness within it blurring, I feel for a moment that I might have crossed some border, but between what and what I am not sure.

The sound of the door opening and the sudden penetration of light throughout the basement draws me back into my surroundings. I hear steps coming towards me. Whoever it is has a nasty cough. I push the paintings back into the crate and cover it as well as I can. The footsteps move from one end of the series of long passageways to the other, sounding more distant, pausing and coming nearer again. With each pause I know the feet are turning down a new hallway and that each is closer than the last. I climb up the metal rack that serves to store the crates of artworks. The shelves are sturdy and support my weight with ease.

The footsteps come closer still as I try to control my breathing. Being calm is the best thing. If they do not already know that I am here there is little chance they will spot me above them now... I hope.

The steps are rounding the last bend. I see the shiny tip of a big boot plant itself onto the concrete and swivel under a portly frame. He coughs again, this time with enough force to halt his progress. He bends and places his two giant paws on his knees as he hacks at something wedged deep inside some pulmonary pocket. His hair is stringy with grease, his shirt struggling to stay tucked in over a bulging, hairy belly.

A final push gives birth to a huge phlegm ball which he expels alongside one of the crates.

"Gotcha," he says to the gooey green expulsion, adding the first syllable of a laugh.

He straightens himself out, inhales deeply, and continues in my direction.

"Where are you, sir?" He says.

For a moment I think he is speaking to me, and I gulp down on my breath. But, I see that he is focussed on a yellow slip of paper that looks to be part of a carbon copy.

His vision skims over the shelving units and crates registering and discarding the name of artist after artist.

"RRRRRRRRR..." he says. "Here we are." He scratches at something at the edge of his bulbous nose. "And where are YOU, sir."

His words make me nervous. I bump my head against the ceiling and recoil beyond the edge to where I hope I am out of sight.

"Hmmmm," he grumbles.

I hear shuffling feet. He is looking around for the noise. He heard me. He must have.

Finally he speaks. "Ah. There we are Mr. Rowland." His cadence reminds me of Santa Clause.

I peek back over the edge. He is directly below me. The little dark circle made by the top of his head looks like the pupil in an eyeball completed by the broad white circle of his body.

He pulls the lid from the crate. "A bit loose, that one," he says.

He spreads the yellow page in between his paws and draws it close to his squinted eyes. "367LTZ. Well, alright then."

He turns back to the crate, sifts through the stack of paintings, leaning one after another from the left to the right and finally slides one out of the crate. I can only see the back of it as he shuffles back down the passageway, moving back and forth until he reaches the stairway, ascends and cuts the lights, leaving me to wait for my eyes to adjust to the darkness before I can attempt to get down.

How could it be? How could my grandfather have painted these? Painted me? Painted Donnan at his death? Painted Flanders in his… in his whatever the hell it is that he is in? He died long before any of this even happened. Before I was even born. It is impossible. I stare out into the strange fullness of the absolute dark. It is like sound underwater. Concentric circles of amorphous color fluctuate in the atmosphere, slowly becoming forms as my eyes become accustomed to their surroundings. The colors moving through the darkness are like a melody to me, and I feel it reverberate through my body, my consciousness, blurring the borders of my skin and the room that surrounds it.

I slide down the rack. My feet situate themselves one by one onto the concrete ground. I pull the lid back from the crate to see which painting he took. I find the painting of myself, of Donnan, of the man with the plant. The missing painting is of Flanders and his blue orb. But why? Where could he have gone?

I have to get out of the basement before anyone else shows up. I start down the dark hallway. Something crumples under foot. The paper. The carbon copy of the slip. I bend down to grab it and head through the maze. I am near the staircase when I hear footsteps from somewhere in the rows of shelves behind me. There cannot be anyone else down here. Unless, well, unless they were already down here before I came. The footsteps are coming closer. I want to know who it is, but I do not want to stick around to find out. I run up the stairway and push the door open a crack. I do not see anyone. I push it open a little further, poke my head out and look both ways. No one. The footsteps below are nearing the staircase. I go through the door and push it closed. When I turn around I am facing a sculpture of an Indian with his bow bent all the way back, arrow ready to fire. Always the Indian's with the bow and arrow. What a fucking cliché…

"Hey, Tommy," shouts Frank. His voice echoes so I am not sure which end of the long hallway it is coming from.

"Yeah," I say too quietly to be heard from either side.

"Tommy, you all right? Hey, get your ass over here and give me a hand."

I look one way, then the other, but I do not see him.

I head in the direction the Indian's arrow is pointing.

It dead ends at a big glass window that looks out over a wide snow-covered lawn. Snow?

I turn back in the other direction. It dead ends at what seems to be an identical window. Nothing but white horizons beyond it. It was near 95 degrees when we came inside. I touch the glass to see if it is a painting, or some clever exhibit. The glass is cold and my finger leaves a smudge. I put my cheek close and watch my breath create opaque circles of condensation. I draw a little smiley face with my index finger. I never pass another hallway. I never pass Frank. I never pass anyone. None of the art is familiar. Portraits. Men. Women. Children. Black. White. Red. Yellow. Just faces. I do not remember a hallway like this when I came in, though I was in a bit of a rush. I look.

"Tommy," I hear again.

I swivel 360 degrees, but there is no one.

I look at a face. It is a young black face, the texture so intricate that it seems almost alive. The cheeks seem to deepen and drop as I watch them. The brow grows entrenched. The hair recedes. The eyes dim, but achieve a depth that was not in their brightness. Someone said that the eyes never change, that the eyes you have when you are born are the eyes you have when you die. It is only the context around the eyes that changes the way they appear. I have to disagree with that someone. The eyes change moment to moment, and even more so over time. I do not know if they are windows to the soul, but they are surely windows to whatever is inside: the mind, the self, memory, experience. Eyes show strength, fear, love, sincerity, and as these qualities come to define character, they show us that too. Eyes are malleable in youth, stony in age.

The portraits are ageing before my eyes. I turn back to the window, the snow is gone. The grass is burned brown. There is a stream in the distance. I cannot tell if it is flowing or stagnate.

I look for the door to the basement, but that is also gone.

"Tommy!"

A jolt rushes through my body. I inhale sharply and am forced to cough. The light feels like it is singeing my irises. Frank's face appears before me, a skylight above it showing a cloudless blue. His face is steady in time. Not young, especially. Not old. But not moving either. A face to be trusted.

"Jesus, kid," he says.

"What? What is it?" I ask.

I realize I am laying on my back looking up. The carpet is comfortable. It reminds me of kindergarten. I have not napped on carpet in years.

"You were fuck'n out, dude," comes the voice of Vincent Tram.

"Out?" I ask.

"Cold, bro," says Vincent.

Frank nods. "Scared us shitless, man."

"Literally?" I ask.

"Did I literally shit myself? No smart ass, but damned near," he laughs a little.

"What happened?" I ask.

"We just, like, found you laying here," says Vincent.

"Can you stand?"

"I think so."

They help me to my feet.

"Listen, man, I should probably tell my boss, get an ambulance," says Vincent.

"No, I'm fine. I'm fine. I was just lost."

"Lost?"

"Nevermind."

They both look at me like I am roadkill.

"I'm fine. I swear. Let's just get out of here."

I look around the room. Frank's spooge portraits are mounted everywhere. It is actually kind of beautiful. Disconcerting, but beautiful in its own way.

"Jesus, Frank," I say pointing in an inarticulate circle to the exhibit as a whole.

He smirks. "Well, maybe not Jesus, but they're my own good works."

Vincent scratches at his Beethoven mane. "If that qualifies as 'good works' then even I'm a Saint."

10

I

I found the address to the Sooner Come Later Retirement home on the internet. The place looks rundown, but tolerable. Just upright enough to preserve the conscience of those who did the dropping off and occasional visiting, but unkempt enough to show that it is an economical place to stick a loved one for their last days. I wondered if Bergman had any loved ones to put him here, or if chose it himself.

"Shoot me in the face if I ever end up in a shit hole like this," said Missy.

"Well, if all goes well I'll either be dead or with you, so..."

"If you're dead it's because I shot you in the face for even considering letting us live in jar of formaldehyde like this. My God, I can smell rotting sex organs and we're still in the parking lot."

"I take it you're not totally comfortable with the prospect of ageing?"

"Truth told, when I was a kid old people made me vomit."

"Vomit?"

"When I was a kid, I said, Jesus."

"How old?"

"I don't know. 6 or 7. I was living in the states already, I know that. I was at a diner with my P's and my sis."

"And?"

"And, I don't know, I had never seen old people, at least not old white people. I was probably just meeting my grandma, or it was one of the first times I remember anyway. They lived in Florida. Anyway, she picked me up and was bouncing me up and down in her lap and that weird old lady smell overwhelmed me, and she opened her mouth to do one of those little 'ohhh yer soo cute' baby faces, and I saw her dentures wiggle and I just puked all over her."

"Ah, the compassion of my better half."

"I was a kid. Compassion's got nothing to do with it. Honest's what I was."

"Well, try not to dwell on their 'rotting' junk and you should be alright."

"Uff, don't even say it." She pretends to wretch on my sleeve.

A neatly-dressed man with long white hair and whiskers approaches us.

I look up and make eye contact which makes him smile a kind, but guarded smile.

He pulls a piece of paper out of little a bag hanging from a necklace and a pen from his pocket. He raises a finger to indicate that we should wait, which we oblige.

He writes, "I will thank you not to smoke."

"Okay, no problem. I, uh, don't smoke, so, you're very welcome."

Missy roles her eyes, even though I know she hates smoking, too.

He begins to scribble something else as we wait. "And thank you even more for stopping your walk," says the paper.

"Of course," I say.

He turns back to the paper. "And thank you for understanding our city."

"Well, I'm not sure I would say..."

He shakes his head and starts writing more, "And for understanding your obligation, and offering your privileges before being asked."

"Oh, do you, um, want..." I stammer.

Missy helps, "Money?"

He shakes his head violently and looks back to the paper. "This paper is recycled. I think it is important to recycle."

We both nod. Confusing, but hard to disagree with.

He writes, "Confess that you believed in God before you met her, and began to understand this only present."

"I'm, uh, afraid I don't follow..."

More writing, "Would you like to share a cup of tea and some of our privileges while I explain to you your responsibilities and perhaps begin to shed a light on the mysteries of death."

"Wow," says Missy, "that is totally not what I had in mind for this afternoon."

"Yeah, I'm sorry, sir, we are sort of in a hurry, and, well, maybe some other time we could have a tea, but now is impossible."

"Why?" he writes.

"Well, because we have an appointment."

"Who are you superiors," he writes.

"Our superiors?"

"Who is it that you prefer to this opportunity to understand and assume your responsibilities."

I do not know why I decide to tell him, "Martin Bergman."

He smiles a wide, crooked smile and points towards his chest with his thumbs.

We follow him through the unsupervised lobby of the retirement home and into an elevator that has seen better days. The buttons are numberless from age, half the light bulbs dead, the other half flickering. He presses the third button from the bottom on the left, but I could not be sure what that corresponded to. The elevator jerks its way upward to the undetermined floor.

The hallway is wallpapered in what may once have been a color resembling white, but has turned into the color of a water stain, a pale yellowish brown that seeped away from various points of origin in decreasingly tinted concentric circles. The carpet had been matted down from hundreds of thousands of slow elderly steps dragging behind their walkers and the solid rubber wheels of the various chairs and carts that helped the incapacitated remain mobile. The original color of the carpet is also tough to determine, but I would guess it had been a light maroon.

The door to Bergman's room is labeled with an H. Inside there is very little in the way of furnishings. An old radio with a German name sits on a glass-topped end table, a red leather couch with buttons at regularly indented intervals. A book shelf with a number of oversized volumes. Little else. There is a window that provides the rooms only light, which beams through the glass in a thick stripe, illuminating a roughly cubicle passageway of lingering dust particles. There is a white sheet covering one of the walls. A closed bucket of white paint sits at its base.

Missy's nose is scrunched as she surveys her surroundings. I skim the bookshelf. All the titles are in German, or at least those I can make out from the crumbling bindings.

Bergman walks to the kitchenette and lights a burner with a match. He fills a kettle from the faucet, places it over the flame and turns to us motioning with a hand towards the sofa. We sit.

"Mr. Bergman," I begin, "how long have you been here?"

He walks to the wall that is covered with the sheet and pulls it down. I see that the section of the wall covered by the sheet is bright white. Freshly painted, though at the edges I can make out fractions of words that have been covered. He picks up a black marker from the counter top and scrawls on the wall, "That is not important. Long enough. Not as long as I will have been tomorrow."

Missy whispers into my ear, "like talking to frigg'n Yoda, here."

Bergman shoots her a sharp glance and we both recoil.

He writes on the wall, "If I'm not mistaken, you have not introduced yourselves."

Missy says her name first, then I tell him mine. There is a flash of recognition, and he turns back to the wall.

"So, you've come to talk about responsibility after all."

"I'm not sure I understand."

"You've come to talk about art, history, nature..." he writes.

"I suppose so, yes."

"I'm no longer a teacher of the type you're seeking, Tommy Shells."

"I'm not looking for a teacher. I'm looking for information."

"Ah, information. I'm afraid I'm not much a source of that either."

"I just want to know what happened to my grandfather. I want to know what I have to do with his painting. Why..." I'm not sure how much to assume he knows.

"Do you know what art is?"

"I… ummm…?"

"Art is the first attempt of the human to make sense of nature through codification. Art is always the first stage of what becomes history. Art breaks ground and creates space where there was none for the alteration of reality. Art is the roadmap of the possible from which the rest of the world works. Da Vinci was an artist, of course. But also Edison, Curie, King, Ghandi, Wolfe, Wells, Parks. And, Napolean, Joan of Arc, Alexander the Great, Ghengis Khan. Even Hitler." He looks me directly in the eye as he says the last name. I cringe and he smiles. "Each saw a possible world and drew it to create a reaction in the the rest of us. The results were different. The intentions were different. But, each knew the relationship between art and reality." His eye is possessed by the twinkle of the fervent.

"And my grandfather?"

He turns back to the wall. "He knew. He had a responsibility to care for the world. Which is ultimately what creation is. Care."

"Do you know?"

"Do I know what?"

"What it means to care? How to care?"

The teapot whistles and he moves towards the stove.

He puts a cup before each of us and fills it with tea. I wonder briefly if it is poisoned. He looks at me as if he knows what I am thinking and sips his own.

He points at my tattoos and laughs, then pulls a handkerchief from his pocket, licks it and pretends to wipe the tattoos from my arms. I really do not like the sensation of being proxy-licked by this old guy.

"You don't like tattoos?"

He shakes his head vigorously.

Missy looks disgusted. "It's just art closer to home."

He shakes his head and sticks out his tongue through the gap between his missing front teeth.

Missy quivers like she is about to vomit.

I put a hand on her shoulder. "You weren't kidding."

"I told you," she says.

Bergman's whole body convulses silently in what I think is laughter.

"What happened to my grandfather?"

He stands and walks to the wall. "What happens to all of us?"

"Death? He died? I know, but why, of what?"

"What is death?"

"Ja-heee-zeee-us Christos on unleavened bread," whispers Missy.

Bergman shoots us another sharp look and, again, we recoil.

"I don't know," I say. "The end of life."

He nods and turns to his wall, "The end of creation. While we create we live. When we cease, we die. Even if our blood still pumps. Life is this and only this: the process of creation. The responsibility to create."

"Is he a Nazi or a Capitalist?" Missy whispers.

Bergman stares into us with eyes like railroad ties as he sets his marker on the counter. He sits, sips his tea, blows Missy a kiss, winks at me and flips us both the bird.

I guess it is time to go.

Before he can urge us through the door I look back at the book shelf. "What about Montcorte?" I ask.

He shrugs like a teenager answering his mom about where he has been all night.

"What's in the book?"

He pulls his wallet from his back pocket and slides a card out. He holds in front of my face: "Tulsa Public Library."

"Thanks," I say.

"I guess," adds Missy.

I am afraid he is going to use the tongue to make Missy wretch again.

11

I

We decide to take Bergman's advice and stop at the library on the way back to George's. Most of the books that show up in the card catalogue are biographies and commentaries. There seems to be quite a number grouped together so we head for the section that has the most info.

Missy asks, "So, you're related to this Montcorte guy?"

"That's what I keep hearing."

"And he's some kind of psychic or something."

"Or something."

The section with with books on Montcorte is in the basement. We take the stairs down. The first floor was quiet, but occupied. There is no one in the basement. The room is silent and filled with the musk of thousands of long unturned pages. There are a half-dozen biographies, almost all written after 1960. The oldest, the sensibly titled *The Life of Miguel Montcorte* is dated 1920 something. The last number is smudged. It could be a 0 a 3 or an 8. The author is listed as anonymous. It is by far the thickest, and all of the subsequent biographies cite it, and its mysterious author, as a major influence. Missy grabs a book of commentary on the veracity of Montcorte's predictions called Montcorte: Mystic or Charlatan?

We find a pair of chairs in front of child-sized desks buried deep in the stacks and begin to read.

It is unclear whether the figure of Miguel Montcorte, purported prophet and early defender of indigenous rights, is a historical personage or a fictional creation, the result of an elaborate rouse. There is such a person in the historical record. He was born in Alicante, Spain on July 14th or 21st in the year 1503. His father, Ramón German Ruiz Montcorte, was a glove maker who also kept sheep with which he harvested the wool for the linings of his gloves. The elder Montcorte was successful in his business and amassed a good deal of wealth which little by little he invested in expeditions to the colonies. This much is verifiable.

It is from the realm of legend that we draw the notion that the family home came to be filled with artifacts from the voyages to the New World that he financed: drawings of the bizarre inhabitants of far away lands, beasts with faces in their torsos, woman warriors as tall as four men, cannibals with pointed canines as sharp as wolves. Aside from the basic facts of his birth and lineage, Montcorte the prophet only enters the historical record in a biography by Miguel de las Canoes—an author equally mysterious to his subject—, appearing in the mid 1700's. The work refers to many previous documents that have either disappeared or never existed. Some speculate that the biography is actually an early novel blending history and fantasy.

The supposed biography states that Montcorte reported in his journals that the beasts in the images that his father collected came to haunt his dreams and that from a very young age he felt compelled to travel to these strange worlds to confront the creatures he saw in the drawings. He was unsure if it was to conquer them or to know them, but he was certain that, at least, he had to see them for himself. He spent his childhood, so the legend goes, running along the hillside beneath the hilltop fortress of Alicante, immersed in a world six-thousand miles away, battling the beasts in his imagination with a sword he'd carved from wood.

His father, again, according to legend (I will stop reminding you hereafter that the line between fact and fiction is blurred, simply know that all that comes down to us regarding the figure of Montcorte is dubious in nature, not least because we simply have an inordinately detailed account of his life given the period), had a penchant for telling stories which he insisted came from the sailors, traders, conquistadors and colonists that brought his goods to the New World and returned with the trinkets that so consumed him.

He told stories of cities of millions, of kings more mighty than the sovereigns of Spain, of gold so plentiful it could, and would, corrupt the pope himself, and of gods more powerful than the Christian God. These stories undoubtedly populated the young Miguel Montcorte's mind with fantastic worlds and beings that would obsess him throughout his life.

His father's success eventually earned the family some notoriety which in the days of the inquisition could be a mixed blessing, especially for a man spreading what could so readily be perceived as heresy. On two occasions his father was incarcerated, though in both cases he was quickly cleared and returned to his family after paying hefty fines. Montcorte visited his father in prison. He is supposed to have cried for days upon his first view of men, his father among them, in chains. It is said that one of his earliest visions came through those tears, in which he had a distant dream of a world in which it was unthinkable to apply restraints to another human being.

Montcorte's early education appears to have been conducted primarily by his mother, María Carmen Serrano de la Cruz. Very little is known about her other than that she was taken by the inquisition and executed in 1516, when Montcorte was just 13 years of age. Inquisition documents relate that she was accused of engaging in witchcraft. Montcorte, if legend is to be believed, learned certain peculiar rituals from her that involved the ingesting of herbs and long stints of quiet reflection which cleared the mind and opened space for a sight that Montcorte himself later described as visión alambrico.

The financial success of Montcorte's father allowed him to attain permission to study at Salamanca, where he began a course in Theology and Medicine. However, a shipwreck in 1520, when he was just 17, took a great toll on the family wealth and forced the young Miguel to abandon his studies. The following year, his father died leaving the family fortunes diminished to nearly nothing at all.

Miguel worked briefly as an apothecary, putting his uncompleted medical training to some practical purpose, but in 1523 he decided to satisfy his lifelong desire of journeying to the colonies.

He was disappointed by the world he found upon landing in the sugar plantations of Jamaica. There were no face-bellied beasts. No giant woman warriors. Only enslaved Taíno indians and Spaniards who would have been subjected to the Inquisition for their cruelty towards the natives had they been at home.

Montcorte's journal, while fictional or no longer extant, is referenced frequently in the biography. A reported entry from on the 15th of March, 1523, reads:

I never thought that I would have cause to curse any Spaniard as a tyrant, but now I see that, given the free reign of their desires, and the absence of any restrictions by a strong court of law, many of my countrymen are nothing but. I have witnessed cruelty against a humble people that fits no model of Christian charity. The Taíno are abducted from nearby islands, as a good deal of the locals have already been massacred or given over to disease and brought here to work the fields. They are unenthusiastic workers, as they are not a people that give over easily to bondage, and being in such a state breaks their spirits. I am told that their abduction often involves the burning of massive tracts of forest, as the Spaniards are afraid to enter the jungles and prefer to make the jungles disappear. I came in search of inhuman creatures, monsters, other worldy beasts. I found them in my fellow countrymen.

Montcorte left Jamaica shortly after his arrival, upon hearing of a priest, Fray Bartolomé de las Cassas, who was working to found a new type of colony on the coast of Venezuela based on cooperation between the Europeans and the Natives.

Montcorte befriended Las Casas, and became dedicated to his cause of creating a new kind of colony. One of the many reasons scholars have been led to doubt the veracity of tales about Montcorte is that the reported friendship is never mentioned in the extensive writings of Fray Bartolomé de las Casas, though this is by no means definitive evidence.

Montcorte's training in medicine and experience as an apothecary came in handy in America. He worked to ease the diseases of the Natives, often diseases that were brought on by the mere presence of the Europeans. Montcorte, of course, was not aware of this, and attributed it to the Indian' s 'weaker constitution'. His remedies were of their time, and ultimately rather ineffective. He was prone to offering his patients bleedings, and treatments with herbal remedies that would likely have often had deleterious effects. He is said to have considered taking religious orders, but for unknown reasons, he never became a priest himself.

"Hey," says Missy.

I look up from my book. "What?"

"This guy predicted some pretty wacky stuff."

"Wacky how?"

She points to a page in her book. "He said that Mexico would be separated from a great power by a mighty river and that many would suffer, like the jews before them, as they tried to escape slavery across the desert beyond it."

"That doesn't sound so wacky."

"Wacky 'cause it's true."

"What else?"

"He said, hmmm, let's see, he said" she flips a few pages. "Ah, here we go. He said that gold lust would turn towards a darker substance more indicative of the nature of desire. That the substance of human desire would fill each breath, eventually choking entire nations on their own greed."

"Can't argue with that."

"No you can't. Spot on José. Way to ir."

"That's redundant."

"What is?"

"To ir."

"Why?"

"Ir is already 'to go'. It's like you're saying 'to to go'. Redundant."

"Look who paid attention in high school after all." She flips a few more pages, "and, uh, that, yeah, California would fall into the ocean. Why's it always California? What do these seers have against avocados?"

"Anything oblong. Pears. Mangos. Dan Akroyd."

"Dan Akroyd? Really? You couldn't do better than that."

"It's true. Montcorte predicted the unprecedented commercial success of Uncle Buck."

"Shut up." Missy pokes at the cover of my book. "How's our anonymously authored history coming along?"

"Supposed history, more like. Alright, I guess."

"Supposed?"

"Yeah. Apparently, Moncorte, or at least what he's credited with having done in his life, is maybe just a story."

"What about the prophecies?"

"I don't know. Did you see anything in your introduction?"

She scrunches her nose. "I sort of skipped the intro." She flips back to the books beginning and lays it out in front of us.

The first few sentences of the introduction say it all:

These prophecies were first printed in English in 1946 after having been uncovered in a library in the Northern state of Keopanti during the second World War. They are claimed to be the translations of a Belgian colonist, Henri le Port, who traveled aboard a French slave vessel to Haitii, where he unexpectedly came across the ragged Spanish documents. The translation, performed in 1798, traveled back to Brussels with le Port. The fate of the original, if it ever existed, is unknown. Some suspect that the prophecies were constructed as a stunt to perpetuate the success of the strange book—novel or biography—about Montcorte that had been printed some 40 years prior. This belief is supported by the fact that le Port subsequently translated Montcorte's biography into French and oversaw its publication to much personal gain. Still others believe it is evidence of the existence of the man the biography depicts. Either way, the prophecies and their dubious accuracy have held generations of imaginations captive.

"Well ain't that a humdinger," says Missy.

"Yes, ma'am," I say.

12

I

I bring Missy to Annie's for dinner. It's the most Tulsa place I can think to show her. Rusty, the Will Rogers look alike, is our waiter.

"Hey there it's Sharon's boy again," he says with a smile.

"Rusty." I say it like a question though I know that is his name.

"You got it," he says smiling. "And who, might I ask, is this lovely young thing?"

I can see Missy grinding her teeth. "Missy," says Missy before I have a chance to interject.

"Nice to meet you, Missy. I'm an old friend of Tommy's mom."

We share an unwanted silence. I wonder how long we have to wait before I can ask for menus.

"Oh," says Rusty, "here y'all go." He throws place mats on the table. They double as menus. "Do you know what you'll be having to drink?"

"Iced tea," I say.

"Make it two," adds Missy.

"Nice and easy."

He heads off and we look over the menu together. The only options for a vegetarian are grilled cheese, fries, house salad. We both want all three.

"Order for me when he comes back," says Missy as she heads for the bathroom.

Rusty comes back to the table with two iced teas.

"Here ya'll go," he says as he places them on the table.

"Rusty, do you mind if I ask you something?"

"Shoot, partner."

"You knew my mom well?"

"Well as anyone, I guess." He screws up his face. "Was a long time back, though."

"Did you..."

A loud whistle like one from a steam engine blows.

Rusty rolls his eyes and tips his cowboy hat. "Hold that thought."

He swings around towards the bar, and moseys all bow-legged, jeans covered in the front by suede chaps, spurs clinking behind snakeskin boots. He pulls a lasso down from the knob of a leather saddle mounted over the bar and begins to twirl it above his head as the radio begins to play something by Aaron Copeland or Richard Rodgers—it could be from the score of Oklahoma for all I know. The rope swings up above his head as his eyes stay low, steady, and just a little too squinted. The song looks like a tornado of sky mauve, taupe and sky blue swirling through the restaurant. The rope drops from above his head to around his feet but never ceases its perfect twirling rhythm. He puts one foot out of the circle and then back in, then the other makes the same manoeuvre. He hops out and back in with both feet, and just as quickly, has the rope up above his head again. He throws it towards a couple of guest, but retreats before it lassos them. The whole room breaks out in applause. Just then the bathroom door opens and Missy steps through. There is a pick up in the speed of the choppy violins that brings to mind a wagon race on some green and brown frontier. The trails of color shoot across the room like jackrabbits. The rope lofts high across the dining room and comes down around Missy's unsuspecting shoulders. Cowboy shouts fill Annie's as Missy is pulled in a chop-stepped spiral towards Rusty, who has hopped atop a table. Just as she reaches his feet the music reaches its crescendo, the colors converge toward the ceiling like a foreboding storm cloud of soft evening tones, applause overtakes the room, and the palette, already invisible to everyone else, fades for me too.

Missy slithers out from the rope's tight grip and, in what seems to be a cheerful daze, sits back down.

"Wowsa! Did you order yet?"

"I think our waiter was otherwise occupied."

"Indeed he was. What a talent. What a bizarre and pleasant ability to possess." Her eyebrows go crooked. "Unless you're a calf, I guess."

"Or you, for that matter."

"Or me, for that matter! too true. That is a first, I must say, I've never before been roped."

I smile and wink.

"Hardy har. Not like that. Though, come to think of it..."

"No ropes."

"Prude..." she says.

After Rusty has rehung his rope, he comes back to the table, pen and paper in hand.

"Sorry, Miss Missy. I hope you weren't offended."

"Offended," she says, "are you mad? That was prime time fun. You can lasso me anytime, cowboy."

"Well," I start to say.

"Did you all decide on what you wanted to eat yet?"

Missy orders. "We will both have grilled cheese, fries, and side salads with... hmm... honey mustard for me, please."

"And for you?"

"Blue Cheese. Oh, and barbeque sauce on the side, please."

"Alright folks, I'll get that right out to ya."

"Thanks," we say in unison.

Rusty starts towards the kitchen, but doubles back, "You was just about to ask me something when the show started."

"Yeah. It can wait. whenever you have a minute."

"Let me drop your order in and I'll get right back."

I nod.

"I think he used to date my mom," I say to Missy when he is out of ear shot.

"Rar!" she says. "Go mom." She mimes a lasso above her head.

We finish our meal and ask Rusty for the check.

"On the house," says Rusty.

"No. That's not necessary," I say, though it really is. I have no cash, and I cannot keep mooching off Missy.

"Your mom was a good friend. It's the least I can do," says Rusty. "Listen, I didn't come back because I don't really have the time to do this conversation justice while I'm working. I'm off in 15. Can you wait around?"

"Of course," says Missy while I consider our options.

I nod.

"We'll wait outside," says Missy, grabbing my hand and leading me to the parking lot.

Rusty tips his hat to Missy and winks at me. Just then the bell rings and he heads for his lass-o.

Missy leads me by the hand across the parking lot to the little patch of grass that stretches along the road between the concrete of the sidewalk and the street. "Our own little park," she says.

"To bad we already ate, or we could have a picnic."

The moon is full.

"Ah, look my little poet, a full moon for you to fawn over."

"Oh no. I learned my lesson. I'm not going to get sentimental with you anymore."

She puts on a big frown. "No? Why not? I like sentimental."

"You could have fooled me."

She gets on her tip toes, brushes a finger over my lips and then kisses me. "I like sentimental very much. Just not when you're only sentimental because you're drunk"

"Understood."

When Rusty comes out of the restaurant we are sitting in the grass by the side of the road. He comes towards us with the same moseying steps he used inside.

He gives us his Will Rogers smile. "Well, you two kids found a nice spot to recreate."

"Not to shabby," says Missy.

Rusty takes off his cowboy hat revealing a head of hair that's fairly matted with sweat.

"Not that I don't admire your choice of location, but as I work here, I might like to get some distance between us and the restaurant.

"Fair enough," I say. "Where to?"

Rusty looks down the road. "There's a little bar at 41st and Yale. You wanna foller me?"

"You bet," says Missy pretending, for some reason, to draw a pistol from a holster at her hip and pop off a shot.

Rusty pretends he's been hit in the chest, and does his best Liberty Valance stumble, but recovers before he falls. "Alright then. Let's get."

The bar has a couple of pool tables and plays new country greatest hits on the stereo. Paisley, Brooks, Jackson, that kind of thing. I used to say I hated new country. I think I was just expected to. Hank Williams and Steve Earl were fine, but Alan Jackson? The truth is I like it.

Rusty orders with fingers. He holds up three digits. Three beers, Coors, and three shots, Wild Turkey, are plopped before us.

"I hope I'm not being presumptuous?" He says to Missy.

"Not at all, Rusty." She picks up the shot. We follow suit, clinking glasses before throwing it back. The second one is in front of us before the first is emptied, and we put it back with the same speed.

"So," says Rusty wiping away a whiskey induced grimace, "you want to know how close I was with your mother."

"Yes. I do."

"Do you mind if I ask why?"

"It's a long story," I say.

Rusty seems to accept this as reason enough.

"It's just, everything with Sue, seeing all this family... I guess I'm feeling nostalgic," I say.

Rusty nods as he slugs his Coors. "Well, we were pretty damned close, Tommy. I would have liked to have been a lot closer to tell you the truth." With his index finger, he draws an invisible circle around the base of his glass. "But, she was always hung up on your dad. God, she loved him."

"Were you friends even after they married?"

"We were friends right up to the end."

"The end?"

"Chicago. I came to visit when you were all of six years old. I doubt you remember that."

There was a glimmer of a memory. Adam and I were on the carpet watching this ten-gallon-hatted figure twisting balloons into the shapes of giraffes and dogs.

"Were you...?"

"Involved?" He stares for a minute and exhales. "No."

"But you kept in contact all those years?"

"Here and there. I never went back to Chicago. She was here a couple of times. There were letters. Phone calls. Friendships can be tough to service as you get older, but that doesn't make them any less meaningful." He paused as we all took a third shot of Wild Turkey. "How old were you? When she..." People never liked to say that last word.

"Died?"

He nodded.

"Seventeen."

"Must have been hard."

I feel a familiar tension push its way from my stomach to my tongue. "Honestly, she was barely around anyway, so, yeah it was hard, but I can't say that life changed much." I am embarrassed by the anger that is welling up inside me, but I cannot stop it.

"She worked a lot, your mom."

"Is that what you call it?"

"Well, yeah, what the hell do you call it?"

"Doing anything she could to stay away from home."

Rusty squints. "No. No, Tommy. No. She worked her ass off so that you would have someone to look up to. So that you'd have some food. So that you could go to good schools."

"And all she had to do to make that happen was disappear from our lives."

He nods. "That was a consequence, I imagine."

"At least with Dad I always knew where he was."

"Listen, your dad's a decent man, but I've been in the same places as he has a lot of these years." He looked around at the bar. "This being one of them. You didn't miss a damned thing."

"So..." I say hoping to move the conversation in a less frustrating direction.

"So..."

We all three take a nervous sip.

"There's something you should know," he says all of a sudden.

Missy and I look at each other and back to him.

"Her thesis... Jesus, I've never breathed a word of this to anyone." He slugged half the contents of his pint glass.

"What about her thesis?"

"Well, Rowland, her father. She became sort of obsessed with him towards the end, and I've always had the feeling that, well, I don't know, but that somehow he had something to do with her death."

"How? What do you mean? He died years before mom."

"I know. I know it sounds a little loopy."

"A lot of things have sounded a little loopy lately," says Missy.

I nod my concurrence.

"Well, listen, about six months before she, you know."

"Died," I say for him.

"Died," he says. "Well, she called me talking about her thesis and how it had lead her to this old fella living in Chicago at the time."

"Donnan?" We ask in unison.

"Donnan, yeah. That sounds right. You know him?"

"In a manner of speaking," I say.

"Well, she said that this guy, Donnan, was an old friend of Rowlands, and she found that he was living in Chicago, so she contacted him. He was a sweet old man, according to her. He made a living as a garbage man, because his sculptures never sold well, though he was something of a literary celebrity, at least in certain circles. She mentioned these sculptures that he made and decorated his apartment with. He made them out of garbage, and your mom was a sucker for anything handmade. She took a liking to Donnan, and, well, I guess they formed something of a friendship there towards the end. But, something changed in her around then." He compressed his brow like he was staring at an equation he just couldn't solve.

"What?"

"I've never been able to figure it exactly. It was like... well, she just seemed to get paranoid a little. She started to call at all hours, send me on strange errands. She had me pulling records down at the city hall one day, and telling me to forget I'd ever seen them the next."

"What records? Do you remember?"

"It was a long time ago, Tommy."

"Anything?"

"I remember they were newspaper articles from the 20's. They were mostly about the race riots, but there were one or two about Stamford Oil projects. Mostly, she wanted me focussed on the Tulsa Daily, but she wanted me to look at City Hall. She said I couldn't trust the Daily. To tell you the truth, I was mostly just worried about her. She wasn't holding it together so well. I told her that the last time we talked. I told her I was worried sick. I told her that she needed to get a grip. That she'd lost herself in this dissertation garbage, and that if she couldn't step back, she might be lost for good." His eyes are getting glassy, but he does not seem like a cryer.

"What did she say?"

"She said I was right. She said thank you. She said she'd come to Tulsa the next day and we could put this whole thing to rest. She... She said she loved me, and then she hung up the phone." Now he is crying, and embarrassed about it. "You can't know how much it hurts to hear someone say what you've always wanted to hear them say and know that it was coming from somewhere desperate. I think somewhere in the back of my mind I knew she wouldn't come."

"And what happened. Why didn't she come?"

"That was the last I heard from her. A month later she was dead. I don't know anything else, Tommy. Not a thing. Other than that I should have done something when I had the chance. I shouldn't have waited around for her. I should have driven to Chicago when she started losing it, and I should have taken care of her. I let her down."

I do not know what to say to him. I never know what to say to people who are crying. I put a hand on the back of his neck and he covers my hand with his own, squeezing it into the pulsations that accompany his tears.

I cannot remember much of anything from that time. Not her working. Not her being at home, or even her being away. I barely remember my bedroom, or our kitchen. Like it is all just some show I watched on television.

"Thank you, Rusty."

He looks up from under the brim of his hat. "Get his book," he says. "She seemed to think it all had something to do with his book."

"What book?"

"Donnan's."

PART 5

1

Me

The were all transfixed on the painting. Missy and Tommy, Will and Karen, Eve and Mickey. Even George, even Tommy's father, even Madame Trouché back in Saint Louis, and Pastor John in Lebanon, and Buddha and Monk, and of course, the near-corpse of Mulroney Flanders, floating in its blue orb, even he was watching the news as the world saw what might be magic, or what might just be some sleight of hand by an artist, or a savvy media player like Mulroney Flanders. Donnan would have been watching had he been alive, and Jared himself, too. Bergman did not have a television, not one that worked anyway, and if you asked him, he wouldn't have admitted this, but every time he walked through the lobby of the retirement home, he let one eye drift towards the screen to see what was still becoming of his greatest student even years beyond his death. Rusty was a full-fledged devotee. He drove past the museum on his way to and from work and said a silent prayer as he did so. Sue would have reported on the story, though always as a skeptic. Something was certainly happening here. Something.

2

He

Donnan closed the journal and tucked it under his arm. He shoved a stack of letters into an envelope and addressed it to Sue Shells at her address in Tulsa. He took another sip from his coffee and watched the snow fall on the gathering line of celebrants. Cars moved slowly through the snow covered streets. Headlights illuminated snow flakes making the whole world, at least that part of it in his field of vision, look like a disco ball was revolving in slow motion above the streets.

"More coffee Mr. O'Dea?" asked Claire.

"No, dear. I'm going to a concert."

"Really?" The freckles on her face bunched when she scrunched her nose. "Which? Is Paul Anka in town or something? Or are you more a jazz man?" She giggled.

He pointed to the line across the street.

"Wow. Hip old guy, huh?"

He winked, and this time she blushed.

On his way out he dropped the envelope into a mailbox. He went behind the restaurant to fill his pipe once more before the show. He could hear music pouring out from inside the venue already.

In the alley he found he was not alone. A man in a cabbie hat and a long black wool coat stood nearby. He was more than half Donnan's age. 65, maybe. Nothing to sneeze at unless you were hours away from completing a full century.

Donnan thought of leaving, but then thought again. Who was going to hassle a man about to turn one hundred on New Year's Eve of the year 2000 for smoking a little weed? He pulled out his pipe, packed it and put his lighter to the bowl.

"Out in this weather for a smoke?" Came the voice.

Donnan smiled, inhaled, held, and offered the pipe to the other man.

The man looked at the pipe for a second too long before accepting it. "What the hell. It's New Year's, right?" He took the pipe and applied a steady thick-lipped suction. "Not bad. At least I don't think it is. To tell you the truth it's been a while for me."

"It's never too late, or so they say."

The man's cheeks were smooth and they shined like freshly washed window pains when he smiled. His eyes were a profound green and seemed to run a thousand miles deep before stopping dead against a brick wall. His hands were bare, red from the cold and scaly with psoriasis. "It's never too late," he repeated. "In my line that dictum rarely holds."

"Is that right?" Donnan did not really have an interest in prolonged conversation tonight. As the man stepped closer, Donnan picked up the distinct aroma of raw meat that had gone bad.

The man nodded for what seemed to be altogether too long. "I'm sort of a truant officer. Everyone I deal with is too late."

"Truant officer? I didn't realize they still had those."

The man nodded. "They don't. Not really. It's a self-applied title. A metaphor maybe…"

Donnan felt the need to move on. "Well, if you don't mind, sir, I'm meeting someone."

"Right you are. Well, Mr. O'Dea, you have a pleasant New Year."

Donnan could not recall telling the man his name. His memory was generally pretty reliable, too, though at 99, pretty reliable had its weaker moments. Then, of course, there was the marijuana. He nodded a goodbye and shuffled carefully over the snow covered alley towards the street.

Before he could get all the way out the man shouted from the far end of the alley, "You say hi to Tommy for me now, Mr. O'Dea, okay?"

"What in Christ's name?" Donnan said under his breath.

The man had turned and was nearly out of the other end of the alley. He was sure he had not mentioned Tommy. No one knew about Tommy. He began to shout something, but the man was nearly out of sight. There was no running after him. He was liable to break a knee or worse if he tried running. The man's words rattled him though, like waking up after a bad dream with only a vague recollection of what had been so disturbing.

Inside the Metro was loud. It was one of the few times Donnan could remember regretting that his hearing had not suffered more in the process of ageing. The second band, the Goldercoasters, was still playing. They had a strange organ-based sound, with a cute half-asian girl singer. A cute fully asian girl ran busily around the stage snapping photos. She lowered herself onto one knee and shot up towards the musicians to make their short frames appear slightly taller. He wondered if this was the girl, Missy, who had called him. She had said 'I'll be the little Asian girl on the stage', but here there were two. Of course, one was just half-Asian. He had said 'I'll be the only 99 year old going on 100 that night.' He was right.

It was 11:00. Tommy's band, the She Shells, would be the next act, the last act, planning to play through the New Year. He went to the bar and ordered a beer. He hardly ever drank anymore. His doctors had made sure of that around the time he turned 80. But, he never went to rock concerts either, so this was clearly a day for exceptions. The waitress was pretty, with piercings in too many parts of her face to count. Her smile was soft and shined right along with all that metal. The Miller Light that she gave him was thin, too light in color, and too high in price, but he was pleased as he drank it since it was his first beer in many years.

The second band finished with a loud crash of symbols and some keyboard gibberish. There was silence on the stage and then movement. Amplifiers were rolled off, the keyboard and drums scooted to the sides. New equipment filled the spaces. The crowd hummed along with a tune played over the PA system. Donnan could only make out the words "I wonder if he talks like an ordinary guy."

A DJ came out on the stage. He was fat and goateed. His walk was obnoxious, over-exaggerated bends of the knee, a hand extended up in a fist as if there were some power that he were speaking against.

"Chiiiicaaaagooooooo!!!!" He screamed.

The crowd screamed back at him.

"What can we say this almooooost Neeew Yeeeaaaars Daaaaaaaaaaaay!"

They screamed some more.

"Let's give a huge round of applause to the Goldercoasters, huh?"

A huge round of applause followed his command.

"And now for the may-ene event, right?"

Right.

"Look out for champagne at midnight, and if we're all still here in the brand new year, don't forget to keep tuning in to the morning meltdown on KPP."

Tempered screams.

"So now, without further ado, please give a full blown Chicaaaagoooo welcome to your hometown heros and mine, the second millennium's soon to be greatest act in rock and roll... The SHEEEEE SHEEEEEELLLLSSSSS."

Without delay the guitar began a choppy series of dissonant chords. The DJ left and, and no one replaced him on stage for a moment. The chords came at unpredictable intervals and each was accompanied by nervous, nearly erotic shouts from the audience. This was rock and roll foreplay. Donnan had never been a great fan of rock, but he could understand this tension. The drummer walked onstage from behind a dark curtain and joined the guitar in its intermittent strikes leaving the impression that what seemed random was actually intended. Slowly the chaos swirled around a theme and arrived at a rhythmic, steady drone. The bass player came out on stage and joined the drummer. She plugged the bass in and joined the steady trot. The guitarist made himself visible and a huge splash of sound led them all in a new, faster direction, into the middle of which emerged a spinning singer with a guitar slung on his back. Tommy?

The music came to a sudden halt. "Is that a disguise?" He asked the crowd. "Or are we all just lost tonight?" Tommy flipped his guitar around from his back and began a Chuck

Berry-esque lick that faded into something much more in tune with the lackadaisical hipness of the day.

"S-s-salvation for the trees, shot from cameras at your knees." He sang looking down to the girl Donnan assumed was Missy, bent on the stage shooting up at him. "But you're dressed up now, dressed up, to hide your face." Donnan couldn't make out all of the words. "I lose a dollar every minute, but if you're ready to say sorry, we can all just keep pretending life's a costume party."

He looked a lot like Jared, especially the eyes. His skin was light. His grandmother was white, and his father too. His hair was the kind that tended up in tufts, like smoke escaping a chimney. Einstein hair.

He moved from side to side in short steps in a way that reminded Donnan of Jared standing before a canvas.

The second song began and Tommy limited his gyrations to his left leg. The song was slow and steady.

"Shut the fuck up about the moon already. I ain't another painter obsessed with yellow halos, I just wanna draw you into all of my disguises."

It was fun, for Dr. Kane, to watch the old man shuffle off confused. He might not remember if he told me his name, he thought, but he'll know damned well that he didn't tell me Tommy's. He rubbed a shiny cheek with a scaly red hand and giggled, which gave him a start. The sound of his own laughter always made him cringe. Why was that, he wondered? How could my own sounds of joy also make me shudder? People, thought Dr. Kane, are altogether too complicated. Plants keep life simple. Biological processes acted out, not reflected on. If a plant could laugh, it would never need to wonder why it did. It would never need to fear its own laughter, either. Of course, a plant wouldn't need to laugh, because to laugh would mean it had confronted some sort of irreconcilable contradiction, or some strange juxtaposition, and what, to a plant, could that possibly be? To plants, the world was rarely abstract. Or maybe it always was. Maybe there was no difference. They communicated. Constantly. They were beings as invested in communication as humans. They spoke through shapes, colors, reactions. They warned predators, invited lovers, attracted those who may benefit from their nutrients with aromas. Was that abstraction? Anyway, they weren't so damned paralyzed by the need to consider each communicative action they took, to bring it from the material to the ideal. Basil never wondered why it tasted so good. Apples never pondered how they traveled so far to populate the Americas. Tulips never questioned how they brought the Dutch economy to its knees. Corn did not ask how it convinced Americans to get so damned fat. This, to Dr. Kane's mind, would be their fundamental evolutionary advantage in the long run, unless, of course, we could learn from them, learn to emulate their ability to react, and use our own abilities to consider in more limited and focussed ways. The perfect society would be one in which humans honored plants as much as their own consciousness. A society in which life was precious for its physical presence as much as its more abstract constructions of economy, wealth.

He stepped over a snow bank at the end of the alley and went into the diner for a cup of coffee.

"Back again," said the red-headed waitress.

"Yes, ma'am." He smiled his widest, truest smile.

"Coffee?"

"You know me already." He thought of all the debts humanity owed the coffee bean for its ability to block adenosine which makes us sleepy. Or, should. Kane didn't get sleepy anymore. It had been nearly 10 days since he last slept more than an hour or so consecutively. He figured the process had begun. He couldn't be sure. It might just be anxiety about the disease's eventual onset triggering symptoms. Caffeine: blocking adenosine increases the firing of neurons, creates an inner brain state of emergency and ups adrenaline output. The marijuana that he smoked with Donnan was still pumping through him too. The cannabinoid receptors in the hypercampus, cerebellum and basal ganglia were being tricked into thinking they had been activated by the neurotransmitter anandamide when really they were being impeded by THC. He felt light now, but paranoia would be coming. The coffee may even make it worse, but it also may combat the effects of the THC. It was a toss up, really.

He looked up at the church across the street. Old and Catholic like he liked them. He had not been to mass in over a month. He could feel his sins clinging to him like a thick layer of sap, dripping down his limbs, preparing to crystallize if he didn't slip into a confessional at some point soon. 11:30. He should get back to the old folks home to be sure he was there before Donnan.

3

I

The morning after our meeting with Rusty we head for the library. I pull the Rabbit down George's drive and the dogs run alongside barking all the way. The cicadas are in full blare in a heat that makes 9 am feel like dead noon. We are looking for Donnan's book. The yellow Hummer shows up in the rearview as we head West on 11th Street. A yellow Hummer, or the yellow Hummer? I should have memorized the plates. I will this time. It's a Missouri plate. Shit. Farmland gives way to increasingly more planned subdivisions, entropy in its suburban sprawl phase. I keep looking into the rearview mirror.

"So you were born out here?" Missy asks. "For reals?"

I glance from rearview to road, ignoring her question.

"Tommy Shells. Born in a barn."

The truck is still there.

"Makes sense when you think about it."

I look at her, briefly letting my faux anger overtake my fear. "What?"

"Well, you never could iron a shirt, match a sock, wash a dish... Need I continue?"

My eyes go back to the rearview. The tinted windows of the Hummer give no indication of who is inside. I can guess.

"What?" asks Missy. "What is it?" She turns to look behind her. "The Hummer?" she snorts. "I hate those douche bags, too. I mean seriously, how completely lacking in self-awareness do you have to be to think that anyone doesn't see the inverse relationship to Hummer ownership and neural firings per second." She pushes the power button on the radio. Springstein. "And that, I'll have you know, is not the only inverse relationship."

I look down from the mirror and towards her.

"There are others."

I nod.

"Anatomical inverse relationships."

I nod again, forcing her to be explicit even as I know exactly what she means.

"The cock, dumbass. The cock is smaller in idiots who drive those giant yellow monstrosities." She throws her hands up, defeated.

I take a right on Mingo, hoping, no, willing, the Hummer straight on, or left. No such luck. The Hummer is trailing us closer after the turn. I accelerate to the maximum, but the maximum barely tops fifty, and the Hummer is only forced to follow us even closer. Coming up on a red light. I prepare to run it. Ready for the big chase. But the Hummer pulls off into the parking lot of a Git n' Go.

"Bye, asshole," says Missy.

I nod in agreement with the sentiment.

I flip around and take 15th Street towards downtown.

The Library is empty other than the old librarian who reminds me of a Sesame Street mock up of a librarian with his wispy grey hair, little square glasses, argyle sweater-vest, and long, curved nose.

He looks up at us as we enter, offering a nod, a sly smile. He puts on 20 years when he smiled.

We bypass him and head down to the basement. We walk to the computer, do a quick search which yields nothing. No Donnon O'Dea. No *West is the Only Way*. I do a search on the internet. Nothing. How is that possible? Even a book out of print would have some trace in the digital age. It was unthinkable that a writer could just disappear. Not even a distant niece making mention in a blog. No other Donnan O'Dea that happens to be a professional snooker player or a chef at an Irish gastro pub in Shanghai. Something. There has to be something.

We went back upstairs.

"Excuse me," Missy says to the librarian before I can summon the words.

"Yes? How might I assist you?" His accent is thick and rural.

"We're looking for a book."

"Well, you're on the right track." He snickers at what was clearly a joke that had aged well. "Anything in particular?"

"West is the Only Way."

The librarian's eyes go bleary, seeking something locked down a deep dark passageway in the basement of his brain, and recover lucidity as he finds it. "O'Dea," he says with something of reverence in his voice. "Now, there was a beautiful book."

"Do you have it?" I ask, pulling him out of a moment savoring whatever memories he had related to the novel.

"Did. I can tell you that much. I haven't so much as thought of it in a few decades. Certainly not one of our top movers." His fingers set to typing something on the keyboard in front of his screen. "Hmmmmmmmmmmm..." he extended the sound as long as it took him to type, even pausing for breaths and continuing. He finished by tapping a couple keys at long intervals with his index finger from an exaggerated height. "And… Nothing."

"Nothing?" Missy asks.

"Nothing?" I repeat.

"Not a thing." He says screwing up his eyes as he continues to search the computer screen for some sort of clue. "Strange, too. We should have some record at least of having had the book. But nope. I'm sorry."

"But you remember it?"

"'Course I do. Mr. O'Dea even came through on a book tour. I had coffee with him. Nice fellow. Nothing like Donnan the character from the book."

"There was a character named Donnan in the book?"

"Yeah. He was an early partaker of the metafictional."

"Can you help us get our hands on a copy? We really need that book."

"I wish I could, son. Not a lick of information pops up here though. I don't even have an ISBN to search for in the library of congress, and in theory I should have a record of every book there is whether we have it or not. Have you tried looking online?"

I shake my head as we back away from the counter.

"I'd lend you my personal copy…"

My eyebrows raise.

"…but it went up in the twister a couple years back."

And they fall. "Thanks anyway."

I crawl through the passenger side door and into the drivers seat. Missy gets in and shuts the door. The Hummer pulls up slowly, pressing its bumper against her window. The drivers side door opens. Buddha. He smiles like an old friend who is happy to see us.

"Tommy," he says in that squealing voice. "We've really got to start meeting in nicer places. I don't know, take the kids for pizza or something." He stands by my window as he shouts through the closed glass.

"I'm afraid we don't have any."

"Shame, really. Kids make life worth living. You two should think about it before you get too old. Well, maybe that's really too great a concern for you two: getting old." He makes a circling gesture asking me to roll down the window.

I do.

"Alright, out we go." He grabs me under my armpits and hoists me through the window. "You, too."

Missy flips him the bird.

He smiles in return and pulls her from the car.

We are both in the back of the Hummer now. Blindfolded as always. There's no Bob. No Frank. No Al. Just Missy and me. Buddha listens to Enya or something maddeningly similar.

"What brings you to the library?" asks Buddha. "Doing a little research?"

I roll my eyes, which is pointless because of the blindfold.

"I imagine you won't find much. Not real popular, Mr. O'Dea, these days."

"Seems to be the case," I say.

"I've never been a big fan of historical fiction, myself," says Buddha. "I say keep the fiction and the history very cleanly separated. Donnan went and wrote the story of things as they happened. Hell, even before they happened. Now, had he been a historian, people may have just ignored him, or at the very least we could have put out a contradictory account. But, stories have a way of getting peoples attention don't they. Achilles is a hell of a lot better remembered than Democritus, right?" He snapped his fingers. "Best place to expose the facts is in fiction, I say, and we can't have that, now, can we?"

4

They

Will rubbed his eyes with the edges of his palms. "Jesus, Karen…"

"Yep, we're in it," She said.

The television behind them played the scene over and over. The press, herded behind the onlookers, the religious, the progressives, the merely curious, all of whom were there to see it for themselves: the painting that had mysteriously altered while under lock and key in the museum basement. The crowd gathered around the Stamford museum where the painting had been given a new prominent position just inside the main hall, waited for something, some semblance, some subtle shift: Tulsa's own *Mona Lisa.*

"They'll figure it out sooner or later…" said Karen, making circles that traced a knot in the wooden desks surface.

"Figure what out?" Will asked.

"What it is that Rowland was painting."

"And?"

"And, what he was painting was the moment that your family destroyed his. A moment that history has conveniently forgotten," she said. "A moment when your family embodied everything that people hate: mean spirited capitalism, unmerited wealth, oppression of the have-nots by the haves, privilege apropos of nothing other than a last name, a bit of genetic right-place-right-time solidified into an unassailable advantage by violence. And his family, they were all the other stuff. They were noble in the face of a vile nobility. That is the moment that he painted."

"It was also a moment in which our families were untied."

"How beautiful," she said pushing the faded red nail of her index finger into the knot as if it were a button meant to release some noxious gas. "I'm sure the voters will be enamored with that classic American tale, in which, might I remind you, you're family disowned their own daughter, not to mention the son that was the result of the affair, and any knowledge of and or responsibility for the events of that day. People died, Will. Lives were destroyed. An entire community was wiped off of the map, and the potential for wealth, growth… Hope, Will… Your Grandfather destroyed the economic hope of a generation of black people. He destroyed fortunes that might have changed decades of human experience."

He sat on his desk, put his hands on his knees and exhaled as if conceding. "So, I take responsibility. I say I'm ashamed of my family's past. It would be the truth."

"In Oklahoma?" She lifted her finger from the knot for the first time since they had begun to talk, and then smashed it beneath her palm. "You are going to come out against the Stamfords in Oklahoma? You're going to disinvest in the company that is your heritage… The company that is the heritage of all that violence? You're going to tell a bunch of rednecks, that what you're family did was wrong, that you detest the racist roots of your wealth, that you detest the genetic lottery you happened to win, simultaneously reminding the few liberal stragglers, not to mention the black and Latino voters, or those who that haven't fled this state anyway, that you are the kin of everything they hate AND give all of the closeted racists as well as those who let it hang out there in the open, that you are quite possibly a closeted liberal yourself, ashamed of your sons of the confederacy lineage?" She exhaled and scraped at the tables surface with her nail. "Sounds like a great idea, Will."

"Well, what do you suggest, Karen?"

She looked out the window, over the monument and thought, like she always did, about the violent interruption of that day, about the bodies, the sirens, and of how radically different that here was from this one. "Pander. Just like always. You say just enough to make the left think you might not be the devil, and let the right think you're just paying lip service to a constituency you cannot win without."

He nodded, stuck between relief and embarrassment. "And the painting?"

"What about the painting?"

"What do I say?"

"What can you say? Don't say anything."

5

In 1921, Dick worked as a shoe shine boy in downtown Tulsa near the Drexler Building where the black shoe shiners were allowed to use facilities. At breaks he would wonder to the corner of 7th and Main Street, a little West of the stretch known as Cherry Street. He had been told time and again that he would be wise to stay West of the Cherry Street district. "West," his father would say, "is the only direction you need to remember." But it was North that was usually on his mind. North Tulsa's Greenwood borders had limited him to movement in his own city, but that was just fine, because he only wanted to go further and further North. They could have South Tulsa, and everything beyond it, as long as he could head through St. Louis and keep on moving.

Businessmen wandered through regularly to have their shoes shined. He developed the ability to play dumb: always happy, always positive, always grateful. So long as he remained well within those confines, his days passed without much trouble.

"Morning, Sarah," he said as he boarded her elevator.

She was new in town. Working as an elevator operator in the Drexler Building. The colored bathrooms were on the top floor. She was thin, blond and exceedingly nervous for someone who played it so cool.

"Why good morning, Dicky. Busy day?"

"busy, enough. I've already shined thirty-five shoes today."

"Thirty-five?"

"The war," he said in way of explanation.

She understood.

"You Ms. Page?"

"Traveling all day long and never getting anywhere."

"Up and down, round and round. It never stops," he said wearing his most earnest expression.

"There're worse directions than up and down," said Sarah, wearing an altogether different expression. She smiled sideways as she reached across him, hit the lever and they started for the top. "Dicky, I've been thinking about going to a concert at the Greenwood Tavern this Saturday."

"Is that right?"

"It is."

"Well, I hope you enjoy yourself, you know you're always welcome in our part of town."

She nodded. "Dicky, I was wondering if you might be interested in joining me."

"That's an awful nice offer, Sarah, but you know I can't do that. That don't pass even in Greenwood."

"Maybe we could meet up after?"

"Sarah," he said shaking his head.

That was all he needed to say.

Patricia Stamford also liked to go the Greenwood Tavern. The music was the best in Tulsa. Not the same old country and Western of South Tulsa bars, but a regular stopping point for stars like Bessie Smith, and Louis Armstrong.

Dick and Patty didn't meet at the bar.

They were both there that night watching a local group called the Deep Green Divers, but they stayed at a distance. They always stayed at a distance.

Patty watched form across the room as Sarah danced close to Dicky, and Dicky sent an apologetic half smile across the bar. She smiled back.

"When are you going to come home with me Dick?" asked Sarah.

"It's not likely tonight," said Dick laughing.

"One day, Dick, I'm gonna take you home."

The trumpet waddled through a solo and everyone in the crowd, everyone but Dick and Patty, got low with the music. They rationed their eye contact over the tips of their cocktails so as not to be spotted. Illegal booze was one of the draws for whites to greenwood during prohibition. But, even as they mingled, they kept mostly to their own sides of the dark bar like boys and girls at a fifth grade dance: curious, but not enough so to overcome the precautions that had been hammered into them for generations. Every now and again someone, almost always a white girl, would cross the line for a few moments of complete abandon, returning to a giddy pack of friends.

Dick and Patty couldn't afford that sort of exposure. They waited until the music died down and the crowd thinned. They walked out of the bar in opposite directions, making a particular scene of saying goodbye to all the necessary parties. Patty hopped in a cab that would take her around the block and out of sight of her friends. Dick walked around the block in the opposite direction. There was an apartment that they used. It was an abandoned apartment above an auto shop that a family friend ran. He had given Dick the keys so that he could paint in peace.

He went in the front, she came up the back staircase, after entering through the alley.

"What are you painting, Dicky?" She asked when she came in.

"You. Like always," he said taking her hand.

He grabbed a brush from a plastic cup that sat on the lip of his easel. He dipped it into a glob of blue that remained on his palette and dragged the brush along her forearm.

The sensation made her shiver and close her eyes. He put the brush against her collar and moved its tip towards her breast line.

"Dicky, you'll ruin my shirt."

"Your daddy can buy you another," he said.

"But I can't very well go home all blue, can I?" She bit down on his neck almost drawing blood. "Don't you like it?"

He pulled free of her grip and grabbed another brush which he dipped in yellow. He lifted her shirt and dragged the bristles across her belly. "There. Now you're not all blue."

She let out a gasp that was somewhere between a laugh and the first hint of an orgasm as he pushed a paint covered hand down below the waist of her long wool skirt.

On other occasions they would meet at the Orpheum. Dick was obsessed with the movies. He went at least three times a week. He loved the feeling of being alone in a theater, of losing track of himself in front of the screen, nothing but dark curtains and empty seats around him, like being in the middle of the ocean. There was something sublime about the theater, something that connected one to all the universe, the vast history of story, that strange uniquely human space that shouted across generations, centuries, millennia, and connected us to an ancestry grander and more united than we, from within our limited individual perspectives, could ever suspect. She would meet him for matinees on weekdays when he was off work. They would always choose an unpopular film, something that no one else would want to see. They would buy tickets separately and take their seats a row apart. Dick knew the projectionist. He was a solitary man who practically lived in the booth. He was not the type to talk even if he had anyone to talk to. Once they were sure that no one else was coming they would move close to one another, touch hands, breathe in the story together. Her favorites were the vampire films. They made Dick uncomfortable. Real life was scary enough.

She suspected it for all of the usual reasons: a late period, nausea, increased urination… The body was full of ways to let its inhabitant know when things were wrong, she thought, then doubled back on her own process and corrected "wrong" to "off" and then "off" to "different" and then "different" to "changing"… It's beautiful, she thought, while her eyes became red and swollen, and she knew that no matter what she felt, no matter what she wanted, this was a crisis. Her family would not accept this. Her father would sooner kill her than be the grandfather to a bastard of mixed race.

"Dicky," she said to him a few days after she knew.

"Patty," he said to her.

"Do you think we could ever…" She let it hang there in the dark air above the mattress that lay on the floor beneath them. There was an easel in the corner of the room with a few rudimentary shapes painted in primary colors.

"Ever what?" he asked her drawing with a finger in the air above him.

"Ever… anything?"

His finger stopped mid stroke. He turned his head towards hers and squinted his eyes.

"I mean... anything! Christ, will we be able to walk together outside? Live in the same house? Go to a restaurant? Have a..."

"Have a what?" he asked.

"A... family." she said rolling away from his gaze.

He went back to drawing his invisible picture. "Not as long as your daddy's a Stamford and we live in Oklahoma."

"And what if we didn't?" she asked.

"What? Live in Oklahoma?"

She didn't respond, she just stared at the ceiling.

"But, we do live in Oklahoma."

"I'm pregnant Dicky."

He looked towards her, focussed his gaze on the side of her face as she looked towards the ceiling, seeming to investigate the possible messages hidden in the cracks and stains that emanated from the light fixture.

"That's..." he started, but it went nowhere. "That's..."

"Impossible?" She asked without shifting her eyes.

"Amazing," he said, more worry in his voice than anything else. "It should be..."

"It should be..." she repeated.

His eyes lit suddenly, and he rolled her form her side until she was facing him. "We have to leave! We'll just go!"

"Yes! We'll just... leave!" She rolled back around to face him. "We could go anywhere. North to Chicago, or Detroit, Cleveland... Or Paris, maybe! We could be together. Free. Public. No one could tell us what to do."

"Chicago... I always dreamed about Chicago. But, I think you've got it all wrong Patty."

"Why? Why can't we go and paint our own future up North?"

"We can go. We can paint our own future, but not in those places. There's work up North, and a black man can get by...

Maybe even a white woman on her own, but you're dreaming if you think they're going to take us in as a couple. It's just more of the same, Patty."

"Then what?"

He smiled and looked the invisible painting he had finished in the air above them. "West."

"West?" she asked.

"West is the only way," he said. "I'm not saying it will be easy. It won't. I'm not saying everyone will understand, or that they'll pave our way. They won't. I'm just saying that out West, we have a chance, and that's all we need."

"West," she repeated to herself. "West it is."

They needed money and fast. Patty figured she only had a month or so before her mother and father would be bound to notice. She hoarded change from the grocery shopping, stole her fathers cigarette money, sold as many linens as she imagined she could without them being missed.

Dick took every extra shift he could, shinning shoes from 6am on most days. He imagined each shined shoe as a step towards San Francisco. He saved every cent, looking towards the day when they would be free.

Sarah Page got onto the elevator every morning around nine. She pulled the hem of her long dress a little higher than necessary when Dick entered, and smiled as if they were in the midst of sharing a secret. Dick pulled the gate closed for her, and she lifted the lever sending them skyward.

"So, Mr. Dick, when are you going to take me dancing?"

"Ms. Page, I will take you dancing when Tulsa turns into Paris."

"Well, that doesn't sound soon, Dick."

"No, ma'am, it probably won't be soon."

She looked towards the floor, frowning. "Maybe we can find some place private."

Dick averted his gaze until the elevator came to a stop and he pulled the gate open. "Ms. Page," he said as he stepped into the hallway.

The following day she asked again. "So, Dick, have you decided on a date?"

"For?"

"To take me dancing," she said as if it were obvious.

"Why, no Ms. Page, I have not," he said.

And the following day again.

"I can't just wait forever, Dicky."

His patience was wearing thin. "I'm afraid, Ms. Page, you just may have to." He smiled in an effort to dull the edge of the comment.

"I'm not fond of waiting, Dick," she said inching closer to him.

"Now, Ms. Page, I can't," he said pushing himself as far into the corner of the elevator as his frame would permit.

She put her hands on his wrists.

"You can't what Dicky," she said slowly moving her face closer to his, "dance?"

The elevator came to a halt and he side-stepped her abruptly opening the gate and practically leaping into the hall.

"Bye then, Dicky," she said, still in the tone that they shared some secret, only now, Dick felt that the secret was hers alone.

Willard Stamford loved his only daughter above all else, and he watched her closely. It was not easy for Patricia Stamford to get out of the house, let alone get all the way to Greenwood. Her father was known in the community, and as a result, so was she. There home in the Riverview district was one of Tulsa's largest. Riverside Drive hugged the Arkansas River and all the modesty of the downtown skyline at least leant itself to the imagining of some emerging glory. The money was there. The oil fields of Oklahoma had made this little city the global headquarters of the world's most profitable industry, and the oil had come hand in hand with banks, theaters, museums, restaurants... All this newfound wealth needed places to spend itself and people to spend it. Greenwood was all of ten blocks away, directly North of the humble towers that had sprouted on the other side of Cherry Street. It was not easy for her to climb through her bedroom window onto the roof that covered the porch, and to climb across onto the extended branch of the magnolia tree that spread itself across the lawn, and to shimmy down its trunk in a dress and dancing shoes. But, she did it. She covered herself in a black coat, with a dark hat, the brim of which did some work to shade her face. She walked along Denver Avenue to Seventh Street, then took that to Detroit Avenue and crossed the darkened downtown to East Archer where the little apartment above the mechanics shop was. She passed the Orpheum, where Dick would spend all of his time if he had it his way. Once on Archer Street people stared, but no one said a word. She moved quickly through the gazes, and ducked into the gangway along the building to the wooden stairway at the back that led up to the entrance.

Inside, Dick was painting. He was obsessed with the Impressionists, Monet in particular. He avoided the details and sought forms only in their broadest outlines, but obsessed over light and movement. There was something timeless about Impressionism specifically because it didn't aim to capture a moment in all its gritty detail. Impressionism seemed, somehow, to let the moment exceed its own confines and refer to universal things. He was painting an image of the neighborhood, he told her as she gazed over his shoulder.

"Greenwood?" she asked.

"Yes, this very corner. Archer and Detroit," he said pointing towards the front window which was covered in brown paper and masking tape.

"What's so special about this corner?" she asked, smiling.

"What's so special about any corner?" he responded. "It's the one I've seen more than any other. It's probably changed as much or more than I have over the years, but I never stop to notice." He painted a fine yellow ochre line of burnt grass onto the canvas, and then mixed the paint with crimson. "It's sort of an eternal corner. Everything changes, but it's the same old space."

She pulled him towards her, and his brush painted a stroke of yellow mixed with the deep red across her coat. She ignored the stain, looking instead into his eyes. "You know there's a contest for young painters at the Stamford. Five hundred dollars for the winner."

"Five hundred?"

"We could get away with that money."

He closed his eyes tightly. "Will they accept an entry from me?"

"From what, a painter?" she laughed.

"A black painter," he said.

"Of course they will, Dicky! My father wants to help Greenwood. He wants to help the black community. Especially young artists."

"But, not those, I imagine, that are going to father his grandchildren…"

Her expression became formless, like his painting. He saw her, but briefly, he could not grasp her, did not know her.

Then she came back into focus, the light drawing the lines of her features sharply against the greying walls of his studio. "No," she said. "Probably not." She moved towards him. "But, he won't know, will he?"

They moved closer. He removed her coat and then her dress and put his hand, still holding his paintbrush, on her bare stomach, leaving fingerprints of yellow ochre mixed with crimson all across her belly.

"I love you Patricia," he said.

"I know Dicky," she said as she moved her lips up towards his. "We're going to be happy. In San Francisco."

And even though she did not say it, did not parrot back that phrase that has become almost as powerful as some biological union, he saw it in her eyes and felt it in the way that her lips moved against his, and knew it to be true.

The contest was on a Saturday night. It seemed strange to Dick that a contest like this would happen after dark. Dick walked the three miles to the Stamford in paint-stained trousers, carrying his canvas depicting the corner of Archer and Detroit in yellow ochre and crimson—the dried grass and the brick facade—carefully underarm. The other participants, 15 in all, were mostly white. There were two other black painters, one a woman. He looked to them as if they were sharing in some conspiracy and they looked back with the same understanding. He nodded, polite, to the white contestants, but avoided maintaining much eye contact. Eye contact could be a dangerous gesture in Oklahoma.

The paintings were set up on easels around a grand salon. Most were realist and religious in nature. Images from the bible: a burning bush, The Sermon on the Mount, the crossing of the Red Sea, Mary Magdalene, Doubting Thomas… The black woman's painting depicted the moment in which Moses was found by the Nile in a basket, only the baby was dark-complected, and the Nile looked surprisingly like the banks of the Arkansas River. Only Dick's painting lacked a human presence. Willard Stamford himself wandered from easel to easel, looking deeply into the canvases as if he were trying to breathe them in, to drink them, or consume them in some other way.

"Young man," he said as he approached Dick's canvas. He knew Dick by sight at least. His office was in the Drexler Building, and Dick had often shined his shoes. While he may not have been much for elevator small talk, they had shared the same small space at least twice a week for a couple of years. "You seem to have forgotten about Jesus." He winked at Dick and Dick smiled nervously. "What have we here?"

"It's a corner in Greenwood. Archer and Detroit. It's where I paint."

Mr. Stamford looked upon it as if he knew it, as if it were a painting he had seen, appreciated, a thousand times before. "And why, might I ask, did you decide to paint a corner in Greenwood?"

"It's what I know," he said. "I've seen that corner every day of my life. I've watched it change with the seasons. I've seen it burn down and be rebuilt. I found a litter of kittens in the sewer there…" he pointed to a darkened portion between the grey of street and the yellow of grass, "…when I was nine years old. That's where my father fell for the first time before we realized he was soon to pass. I must have played ten thousand hours of baseball on that lot when I was a boy. I know that land. It's as much me as anything else in this world."

"And you're not one for religious themes, I see?"

"Pardon me for saying so, but, for me at least, this is a religious scene."

"Blasphemy," said Stamford, winking again. "It's brilliant." He leaned quietly towards Dick and whispered, "This is what we need if there's ever to be such a thing as Oklahoman art. Someone who can break free from all of these zealots and paint something they actually know." Then he backed away and spoke in a louder voice. "Why is it so sad, this corner?"

"I don't think it is sad, sir," said Dick. "I think it's melancholy like the passing of time. It's lonely, like an unkempt yard must be. It's stoic, like an empty building has to be if it aims to continue standing against the erosion of decades. This building is not sad, it's joyous because it's alive. This building is like Greenwood itself, like the people of Greenwood. It has survived, and it may be tired, but it's not sad."

Stamford smiled and took in Dick's gaze for an uncommonly long moment before returning his eyes to the canvas and breathing it in one last time. That color, he thought. He knew that color. He had seen it recently, that mixture of yellow ochre and crimson.

"It's an accomplishment, Mr. Rowland, that you should be proud of," he said as he moved towards the next painting.

In the end, Dick won third prize, which came with a fifty dollar award.

Maybe if her father had not seen the paint that trailed up from her belly button and peeked over the collar of her blouse everything that happened later could have been avoided. But, he did see the paint. Maybe if he had chosen to believe her excuses—that she had bumped into the freshly applied paint of an elevator—life could have moved on as it always had. But, who paints an elevator's wall yellow? A yellow ochre that invoked the omnipresent tone of Oklahoma fields. No, he could not have believed her.

He had seen that color. He had seen that exact tone. It was not from the fields. It was the very same paint. He had seen splotches of that exact hue. It took him a minute to remember where. And even when he had recalled, he waited a minute more to let suspicion take root. It was the boy from the painting contest. His hands. Underneath his nails. It might have been a coincidence. It might have ended right there. But one more memory would not let him loose.

It was she had come to visit him in his office. They had ridden the elevator down together. The shoeshine boy was in the elevator with them. There was that brush of hands, almost unnoticed. The cringe on the boys face. The look, ever so instantaneous, of nauseas reprimand. The playful glint in her eye. Her father had chosen to ignore it then. But now, the color of the paint washed over him like something irrefutable.

Dick was ecstatic the next Monday as he walked down Detroit Avenue towards the Drexler Building. He knew that he had accomplished something, though he had not taken first prize. Fifty dollars would still go some way towards San Francisco. He stepped into the building, took in the lobby, which he felt he was seeing for the first time, its high ceilings and morose marble that aimed to exalt the muted brown and greys with gold leafing and trim. She opened the gate to the elevator.

"Ms. Page," he said.

"Dick," she replied. "I suppose nature calls."

She shut the gate, pushed the lever, and they began to climb, but as they passed the fourth floor she hit the emergency stop and the elevator ground to an abrupt halt.

"How about you take me dancing right here, Dicky?"

"Ms. Page, I…"

"Oh, Dicky, don't be a bore."

"I…"

She pulled him closer and lifted her dress. Looking at her, feeling her against him, he was excited. She was an attractive woman, and he had thought of moments like this before.

"I…"

"Do it Dicky. Come on," she rubbed her hand across the front of his pants.

He pulled back half-heartedly, but he felt powerless to remove himself completely. His body was drawn magnetically towards her even though his mind pulled him in another direction. He both wanted it, and was afraid of it all at once. He was afraid of his own desire. She tugged at his zipper and pushed her lips close to his.

"I…" The thought of Patty ran through his mind, pregnant Patricia who he loved, who loved him, and without thinking, without being able to think, he pushed her, and she moved away from him much harder than he had intended, her back slamming against the gate and shaking the elevator, she bounced off and slid towards the ground. He reached as quickly as he could towards the lever and put them into motion.

"I'm sorry Sarah, I… it's just… Patricia… she's…"

Her face was stunned as she lay on the ground, processing, not yet having decided if she was hurt, if she was in shock, or if she was fine. She looked like a three-year-old who had bounced on her butt and did not yet know whether to laugh or cry.

"…pregnant."

The door opened just as Sarah, laying on the floor, her dress raised above her waist screamed, almost involuntarily, so loud that everyone on the floor came running.

Dick jumped from the elevator and ran towards the staircase. He flew down four flights of stairs, through the lobby and out the door. He did not run North towards Greenwood, but towards the Arkansas River, towards where he hoped he would find Patty, who would somehow help him clear all of this up before it could get out of hand.

He hid in the bushes beside her house, waiting to catch sight of her. It was after dark by the time she passed, and unbeknownst to Dick, he had become news. His name was on everyone's lips.

"Pssst," he sounded from the bush.

She looked all around, "Dicky? Are you there?"

"Patty," he whispered.

She ran towards the bush and he came out into the open. "Oh, Dicky," she said, relieved to see him, but terrified of what may come. "What have you done?"

"I didn't do anything, Patty. Not a damned thing…"

"Then why? What is all this?"

"She… She just pushed herself on me and I… I shoved her away. She fell. That's it."

She embraced him. "I know you would never do what they are saying."

"What are they saying?"

"That you assaulted her… That you tried to…"

"God, no…"

"We'll go. Now. We'll run."

Dicky nodded. Yes, that was the only way. Run West and do not stop. Not ever.

"Patty!" Came a voice from the other side of the lawn.

"Daddy," she shouted.

"Mr. Stamford," said Dick. "I didn't do what they're saying."

"How do you know him?" shouted Stamford. Then it came clear. The yellow ochre paint on her jacket. On her skin.

He understood it all in that moment, and rage pushed up from his toes, gathered in the muscles around his jaw. "Boy, you better run fast."

"Daddy, no!"

Dick ran as fast as he could towards the River as Stamford rushed into the house and towards the phone.

He was caught that evening and brought to jail. The newspaper, the paper owned by Stamford's dear friend Mulroney Flanders, published an account that seemed to call for action, for vigilante justice, without calling it such, it seemed to call for a lynching. The crowd, armed and on edge, gathered around the courthouse, where he was being held. In Greenwood another mob formed, this one aimed to defend Dick Rowland. Every black man in Greenwood gathered their weapons and headed towards the courthouse, too.

Dick heard the shots throughout the night, and the planes overhead. He smelled the smoke in the morning and through the next several days. But he had no idea what was happening. He had no idea that he was at the center of it all.

Sarah Page disappeared from Tulsa in the midst of all the confusion and, because there was no one left to press charges, Dick Rowland was released. When he went back to Greenwood, it was no longer there. His neighborhood, his community, his life, had been erased from the map. Many of the families that had inhabited the area had already left to find protection with family members in neighboring states, or they had headed North. The men who had resisted in his name, as he would later learn, had been forced to flee, risk imprisonment, or worse. There was no way of contacting Patty. Dick had no way of knowing that her father had found out about the pregnancy and sent her to a convent in San Francisco. Yes, she made it to their destination, albeit in a way neither of them would ever have foreseen. He spent a week trying to find her, then a month, then a lifetime.

He stood at the corner of Detroit and Archer, the yellow ochre grass now a charred lot, carbonised remains on top of dirt, the crimson red brick fallen and scattered amongst shattered glass. His canvases, stacks of which had lined the walls of the studio above the mechanics shop, were unrecoverable bits of information, chemically transformed by flames from messages that he had created, stories he had aimed to send through time, to illegible bits and pieces of ash. He wondered briefly, irrationally, if he could, given enough time, piece it all back together. He would start with his paintings and move outward: The studio, the mechanics, each crisp blade of grass, restored not only to its original brown, but beyond that stale ochre to a rich vibrant green that would be worthy of the neighborhood's name. He would form the ashes into a community and spread that community beyond Greenwood's boundaries, across Tulsa, Oklahoma, the South, across the continent, the oceans and the world.

He tried to compare this reality to his painting as it remained in his mind. That painting with which he had tried to capture the evolution of the corner throughout his lifetime. He tried to recapture the impression of the corner as the light moved across the building in the early evening, as the grass stood perfectly still in the breezeless humidity. Here too, in this space itself, some sort of chemical change had transpired, and whatever this place, this corner, once was, it was no longer relative to its memory. It was something else. Something that history had changed forever. He knew it was beyond him. He knew it was all lost. He would never put it all back together. He would never paint again.

Dick looked at the smouldering neighborhood, and imagined what he had missed while he was locked away: the ravaging of Greewood by flames after the National Guard had dropped bombs onto his the homes of his fellow citizens, his friends. He imagined the flames consuming not only his neighborhood, but the entire city. He had decided to put Tulsa, at least the Tulsa of his imagination, on some enormous pyre, to excise it from his memory. So, he turned, and let the imaginary city behind him burst into flames. And, as the city burned behind him, Dick ran West.

6

I

The television will not stop. The whole country is obsessed with this painting that seems to shift of its own accord. I do not know what to think. I tell Missy that it's bullshit. It has to be. But, I am not convinced that it is. After all, Vampires are real. We are gathered around George's television. His old tube amplifiers and engine parts have been taken off of the couch and spread around the wooden floors.

"A painting can't just change," I tell her.

"A man can't live to be 140 either, but, you seem to be telling me that one has…" she tells me.

The crowds outside of the Stamford are epic. Thousands have gathered, and more come every day. The museum has set up a screen showing the view from a camera that is poised on the canvas.

"So that was our grandfather," says Eve.

I nod. "That was *the* Jared Rowland."

"Do you think it's real?" she asks.

I look at the screen. The painting adjusts like a slow motion video, like a hologram, the faces of the two individuals turn away form each other after a kiss, a biplane flies overhead and disappears from the frame, the city burns, and then the flames go out, the canvas shifts, as if a camera is moving across the burnt landscape of Tulsa. There are flashbacks that show Greenwood in better states. The Orpheum flashes upon the canvas, its lights glowing around the marquee. The Greewood Tap, its windowlesss facade, appears and fades away. The mechanics shop at the corner of Archer and Detroit, the beautiful ochre grass, overgrown in front of those crimson bricks. I felt like I had seen it before. I knew this corner. As the images shifted, one to the next, the paint seemed to crawl to its new location, like colorful worms creeping into their new forms.

"Maybe it's just a screen?" Says Missy.

"It's got to be," says George.

"It's paint," I say. "You can see it. It's viscous. Oily."

"I've never seen anything like it," says Mickey.

"Magnets," says George. "Usually when you don't know, it's magnets."

We all nod in unison because there is no point in correcting George.

George points to a bracelet that he is wearing that is, presumedly, magnetic. "This things keeps me off dialysis," he says. "Magnets," he reaffirms.

We collectively turn in discomfort towards the television. The announcer begins to speak. "Let me tell you, I've been as close as one can get and this thing is for real. I am hearing words like 'supernatural' and 'miracle' and 'alien' thrown around the crowd, and I don't know what to tell you. I'm not capable of confirming, nor of denying, any of these claims, but I can tell you, that whatever this is, be it a massive manipulation, a prank by that famous British street artist, or the real deal, what we are witnessing is indeed something special, something without precedent at least in my career. By no means do I wish to add to the mania that I am witnessing in this crowd, but wow, this feels big."

A disembodied voice from the studio speaks as the on camera announcer holds his fingers against his earpiece to hear over the raucous crowd. "So, tell us, from your perspective, from where you stand, what is this?"

"Well, the canvas is a square, about five feet tall. The paint seems to be crawling across its surface, shifting if you will to create a variety of images. The painting is mounted on the wall in the first gallery of the museum. The crowd is being allowed to pass through to see, spending a maximum of three minutes in the gallery before they are moved out and others come in. Most of the people are, upon leaving, getting directly back into the line."

"And what is the subject matter? What is the painting representing?"

"It appears to be producing images of the race riots here in Tulsa that occurred in 1921. These are images from the Greenwood neighborhood which was destroyed from the air by the US National Guard in the only moment in which the US military has bombed US continental soil. This is a bloody, and largely forgotten chapter of American history that is seemingly being brought back to our attention by this work."

"And, who is the artist? Who is Jared Rowland?"

"Jared Rowland was an obscure, but important figure in the post war era. A neomaterealist who liked to use, I am told, materials that included matter from the subjects which he painted. He was also, as it turns out, the son of Dick Rowland who was at the center of the riots that broke out here in Tulsa. Dick was accused of aggression against a woman by the name of Sarah Page, and brought to the courthouse where a lynch mob had gathered. That mob, however, was met by an equally determined group of African Americans from Greenwood, and the conflict between the two groups ballooned into a battle. During that battle, Greenwood, a center of African American wealth, once referred to be W.E.B. Dubois as Black Wall Street, was wiped from the map."

"And the particular painting? Do we know anything about it?"

"Well, it seems that this particular painting was, in its original state, a painting representing the corner of Detroit Street and Archer Avenue. It was, I am told, an effort by the artist to recreate an image that was previously painted by his father and destroyed in the riot."

"And what is the significance of this corner?"

"That is not entirely clear. It seems as though the corner, a prominent one in Greenwood, was important to the family in some way."

Eve looks at me and I know what she is thinking. I nod.

7

Him

The drive from the cabin on Grand Lake to Tulsa was about ninety minutes. Kane had made it many times. The great irony of his life, a career in oil, required that he be near Tulsa, but he could hardly bare to live in the city. The cabin was his compromise. He lived on the man-made lake just far enough away to trick himself into thinking that he lived closer to nature, closer to the world that he could commune with, closer to the plants. Of course, he knew it was a sham. Nature was both extinct and eternal. The nostalgic ideas that roamed around his sleepless head—of a world in which humankind had never abstracted itself into language, never slipped beyond the chasm outside the reach of the sublime, never fallen to a place where there was only the occasional glimpse of the thing in its chaotic, brutal, entirety—that idea had probably never been real. The built in contradiction was that one had to be abstracted into an observer before revelling in any position towards nature. Otherwise, a person would live in a constant and immediate state, filled with fear, excitement, exhaustion, hunger, but incapable of appreciating any of those emotions in anything resembling a narrative. The ideal of a perfect state of nature was not only impossible to recover, it was not worth recovering as it would require humanity, whatever that was, to cede its consciousness and meld into its surroundings. The other surprise was that nature was indestructible. When it all boiled down, nature amounted to the sum of all the matter in the universe and its transition through different states of energy, and as Newton taught us, energy cannot be created or destroyed. Nature was immortal. The particularities of human consciousness were what seemed to be running a risk, human consciousness was that strange quirk, desperate to prove its own value, defend its own terrain, that made humans unique and vulnerable all at once. Consciousness seemed to be in a constant struggle to inhabit matter, and in the case of Kane it was loosing the battle.

He drove along the hills that led from the lake to Tulsa, sweat pouring from his brow, staying within the lines more from habit than anything else. There were moments when it all seemed clear, the sky was above, the ground below and the two met on a horizon, a stage of sorts that seemed to house actions and characters that were always just beyond his sight. But, then, suddenly and without warning it would all loosen its grip on him. He would expand across the land, through the sky, he would become the horizon, and as he circled the globe, the planet itself seemed to dissipate into some substance that was much more everything than nothing. The blue of the sky became an arbitrary hue that blended seamlessly into the green of the leaves and the black beyond our atmosphere. Colors were all just tricks of light. In those moments he hardly remembered who he was, or what, or why it had ever mattered.

He felt that he moved up and out like a gas expanding across space. He saw the world as a child standing before an easel, paint brush in hand, preparing to create it all, preparing to put the strokes onto canvas that would once again bring form to the chaos.

7

I

We are standing at the corner. Eve seems to be breathing it in as if it is the first air she has ever really known, as if every prior breath had been stilted somehow.

"This is home, Tommy," she says.

I nod. I agree.

We are in a parking lot. There is a warehouse beside a road that lifts into an overpass. The grass shoots up from cracks in the concrete and is scorched by the sun before it ever gets to be green. There is gray everywhere and a silence met with traffic and the dull hum of insects. Greenwood is nothing of what it was. There is a small college campus, a baseball stadium, a burger joint, warehouse after warehouse, parking lots in every direction. It has been stripped of its human history. It has become something that seems to be consciously insisting that it remind no one of anything. At the same time, the memories overwhelm it. There is energy. We walk the streets that once housed our family, half of it anyway. We touch the concrete that was laid over the yards. We let the marquees of long gone theaters, restaurant signs, and shiny-lettered bank windows repopulate, if only in our imaginations, the landscape. The smells from kitchens long since burned to the ground seem to overtake those of exhaust and hot tar.

"I want to build something here," says Eve.

Again, I nod.

8

We drive to the museum. The crowd has grown into a carnival. People are selling T-shirts, holograms of the painting shifting from one image to another. News vans surround the area like covered wagons. We move as close to the entrance as possible. Vincent Tram is guarding the door. I jump up and down to draw his attention and he ushers us towards him.

"I can get you in, but only for a few minutes," he says.

We walk with him into the gallery. The room is large and bathed in light from white oak-framed windows at either side. The floors are made of ageing wood planks that create a polished path towards the canvas which sits at the far end as if it is the altar in a cathedral.

I remember the painting as it was. There were two figures: a black man and a white woman… My great grandparents. They were huddled together beneath a tree as planes flew overhead. They were there still there at the canvas's center, but miniscule now, nearly evaporated. Around them were figures, dark and light, they seemed to crawl out from the center of the canvas. They moved slowly like amoebas, working without end. They were digging, planting, sawing, painting and they seemed to be growing in number. Moving out from the center, they worked their way towards the borders of the canvas. As they approached it seemed as though the canvas itself grew larger and larger, expanding to accommodate the growing number of bodies that populated the scene.

There it was: Greenwood. There were the Cherokee, the Choktaw, the Irish, the Italian, the Czech, and the Polish immigrants that had been pushed from the coasts towards the Indian Territory as they helped displace the native population in the rush to fill the "open" territory. There were the black slaves that had been owned both by Cherokee and the immigrants, brought with them on the infamous Trail of Tears as they left their native lands and resettled in what would become Oklahoma. There was the war in which the natives sided with the Confederacy and had their own internal divisions before fighting their own civil war and abolishing slavery in the Indian Territory in 1866. There were the beginnings of Greenwood, where the slaves that were freed by the Cherokee settled. In 1889 came the land rush and the final historical displacement of the native population. They were displaced even from their haven. And then, relative prosperity. There were 30 years of growth: buildings went up and businesses developed. The white immigrants fought for and against the unionization of workers, the black population fought for their own separate protections. They swirled around the canvas, around each other, coming closer and then being flung farther afield, like magnets that intermittently flipped without impetus, rejecting what had moments before been pulled closer as if by gravity. All the while the edges expanded, the canvas grew, the space between the individuals grew, even as they moved faster and farther, collided and went spinning towards the margins like subatomic particles. It was unnerving, because it seemed mindless the progression through time, it seemed undirected, random, like watching a swarm of gnats. It made the tragedies seem incidental, the heroics senseless, the progress and setbacks meaningless outbursts from within a flurry of random activity.

"Is it…?" I ask.

"No," says Vincent.

"It seems like it's…" says Eve.

"It's the same size as it's always been," says Vincent.

"But," says Missy.

"I know," says Vincent.

"It's getting bigger. I can see it," I say. And it is.

Vincent holds up a measuring tape that he had in his pocket. "Same size."

The edges of the canvas, the frame itself seems to wave and shift between blurred and focussed, as if it is struggling to exist. It seems to be larger than the room that we are in.

"It's…" says Mickey.

We all agree.

9

I

We leave the museum. None of us know what to say.

"I feel like shrapnel," says Missy. "Like I'm just some pointless piece of some inanimate object, briefly infused with the spirit of an explosion."

"Maybe that's what we are supposed to be. Maybe it's destiny…" says Eve.

"My destiny is to fly across the landscape until I wound some poor unsuspecting soldier's ass?" she looks at Eve, mouth agape. "Nuh uh. No way, Jose…"

"It can't be what it looks like," says Mickey.

"Magnets," George reminds us.

"Maybe…" I have no idea how I will finish the sentence. "Maybe, it's right."

"What?" asks Eve.

"Maybe that's what it is…" I think of Faulkner, of the line he borrowed from Shakespeare: s*ound and fury, signifying nothing*. That line had stuck with me since high school. I never understood it. Never knew why it wouldn't let me go. "Maybe it's just us trying to make ourselves out to be more than we are. Maybe all these thoughts, all these intentions, are just gestures meant to disguise the fact that none of it is under control, none of it *means* anything, none of it is even real. We've just created it. All of it. Books. Movies. Constitutions. Birth certificates. Poetry... It's all just there to cover up the fact that we're basically unconscious projectiles, comets that get sucked in by gravity from time to time..."

"No," says Eve.

"No?" I say. I feel my face reddening, my cheeks tightening, my temples pulsing with impending tears. "Then what? what the fuck could it possibly be about? How the fuck do you explain what we just saw? How can all of that pain, all of that suffering, all of those deaths... All of those people from all of those places, thousands of years of experience... Thousands of stories, an almost infinite amount of perception, and thought, and pain, lead to this moment, this neighborhood, this... this... And they just burn it all to the ground..." I cannot hold the tears off anymore. My shoulders shudder, my muscles contract, I feel the mucous in my sinuses loosen. These involuntary reactions make me angry. Why bother? What use?

"It's not for us," Eve begins.

"Fuck.." I say

"...too understand," she finishes.

"No," I say through the moisture that has gathered in my nose, mouth and eyes. "No. That's not enough. Not this time."

"It has to be, baby," says Eve putting an arm on my shoulder. "It has to be."

Missy puts another hand on my shoulder. Mickey keeps his distance, but his eyes touch me in their own way.

"Some things ain't about understanding," says George. "Some things ain't supposed to be intellectual." He walks towards me. “This, Tommy,” he says, “This right here, what you’re feeling right now. Feeling. Not knowing. Not thinking. What you’re feeling…” he puts a thumb on my cheek and wipes the moisture away. “That’s the proof.”

The emptiness suddenly recedes. Like a child who passed through a tantrum, I feel strangely full, as if I am waking under a sunrise. I feel the hands, my sister’s, Missy’s, George’s, and each of them means something I could never express. Each of them is as big as that canvas, as big as the universe it aims to frame, as big as the borderless expansion that it never could. The tears are still coming, but now they are the source of a river that will bring life to some far away delta. Now, instead of nothing, they are everything.

10

Him

Kane pulls up to the museum just as they are leaving. In a moment of focus he recognizes them through some remnant of his reptilian brain. They make sense to him in some vague way. He knows, through the fog of sleeplessness and the grandiosity of a slowly dissolved sense of self, that they are important to some narrative he has long since lost. They are like the figures from the painting that had hung in his cabin, no more or less real, just inhabiting a different canvas.

11

Us

"And the rest I know," said Kane, pushing the tip of the gun into Tommy's side.

"And the rest you know," agreed Tommy.

The light from the blue orb was fading. It looked as though someone, Kane probably, had kicked the cylinder from its perch, disconnecting it from his power supply. The body of the man inside it was pale, weak, fading.

By the rest, he meant the arrival of the befuddled Kane in the parking lot, followed soon thereafter by the Yellow Hummer. Tommy did not remember how they abducted him. He remembered a scuffle, Sheila raising her voice, Mickey and Missy trying to calm her. A noise in his head as if he were inside of a bass drum. After the parking lot it was all dark.

"I don't have much time left, Tommy." Kane's grip on reality returned in waves that arrived at steadily less frequent intervals.

"I can't destroy them. I can't."

"You must," said what remained of the voice from the orb.

Kane ignored the voice. "I don't want you to."

"What then?"

"I want the other world, Tommy. We have to bring it here. That reality has to eclipse this one." His words were slurred.

The gun is pulled away from Tommy's side. "Do you know what powers life?" Asks Kane.

Tommy shakes his head.

"The Sun," says Kane, "is ninety-one million miles from us. Photons reach our eyes in eight minutes and twenty seconds. Plants use a hormone called Auxin to reach towards the light by stretching the cells farthest from the Sun's rays and causing the plant to lean closer, capturing its energy in their leaves and converting it into food. It's amazing isn't it?"

It is.

"Ninety-one million miles in a little more than eight minutes and the plant leans a few centimeters in order to make the journey just a little faster. Would you call that impatience?"

"Or competition."

Kane laughs a single dismissive syllable. "You see it differently, Tommy. You lean into the light as it refracts against the upper atmosphere and slants towards us, illuminating everything we've ever known, giving all of these brutal shapes, these otherwise frigid surfaces, appearance and warmth, beauty, viability. You, and your grandfather before you, see all the infinite possibilities that exist in that light and the world it feeds."

"But you work for them," Tommy looked towards the orb and the feeble body inside of it.

"They pay me, that's true. But I don't work for them. They burn it all down. Tiny hells in the chambers of their combustion engines. The remnants of life in brief bursts of flame all for a few moments of inferior energy. We have all we need in the light. We just can't see." His voice was weaker. Less certain. "I don't work for them, Tommy. I work for you."

The gun fell from his hand as Kane's breath quickened. Tommy turned to look at him for the first time, and saw a vacant stare focussed on the sky that peeked through a skylight above them. Kane blinked between shortened breaths, his eyes closing in a seeming effort to capture each glimpse, make its something permanent, steady. Kane's body fell to the ground, he leaned back against the trunk of a tree, his legs splayed out before him across the cold concrete floor. His head fell onto his shoulder, as his eyes opened and closed rapidly, until at last, they did not reopen and the breath stopped. Tommy waited, watching his chest, expecting it to fill with air yet again, but it never did. Exhausted, he fell onto the floor beside Kane and cried until he was asleep.

12

She

Karen had been calling Kane for hours. The new polling had come in and it was looking like a massacre. The name Rowland was on everyone's lips. The painting that was changing before the world's eyes was painted by the son of the man whose imprisonment had set off the Tulsa Massacre of 1921. A few days earlier, no one had even known that such an event existed. Those who did had referred to it as a race riot. Now it was a massacre. Someone had sent the article to the papers, and a letter proving that Stamford had colluded with Flanders to end the prominence of Black Wall Street. Worse yet, Jared Rowland was not only the son of Dick Rowland, but also Stamford's granddaughter. The oil was still pouring into the gulf. People were calling for billions in compensation to residents of the Gulf of Mexico. People were calling for reparations to the descendants of the families of Greenwood. People were calling for the heads of long dead industrialists. People were calling for a new world in which privilege did not arrive on the backs of the less fortunate. The name Stamford was spent fuel. The phone rang and rang and no one answered. Karen knew that was always the sure sign a campaign was over.

13

He

When he opened his eyes the infinite blue of the Oklahoma sky poured through the skylight. It seemed doubled and obscured, as if someone had placed a piece of sea foam green tracing paper over the baby blue reality. A second, slightly muddled sky, greener than the first, was layered on top of the one that had always been there. He thought perhaps he was seeing double like Hermia waking in the forest outside of Athens. This world had lost its sharpness, its certainty, he thought. The body of Kane still rested on the floor by his side, tranquil as the still air and the cloudless sky. He reached a hand into his pocket and pulled out his keys. The orb lay on the floor, but it had lost its blue glow completely, and there was no body inside of it.

Tommy left the warehouse through a giant sliding door and began to walk down the only path that led away from the clearing, through the sparse woods, brown grass crunching under his feet with each step. He walked, and walked until he came to a road, Kane's car was parked on the side.

14

Her

Sheila had been making plans. She enlisted Mickey and Missy to help her get the painting out of the museum. Frank and Vincent Tram would be the inside guys. Vincent could distract the security team, Frank could get them inside as part of the team setting up for the opening of his exhibit. They would wait for the evening, when the museum was closed to the public. The crowds remained in the parking lot, sleeping in tents in their makeshift village. But, at night they were calm like pilgrims after a long day's walk. It was easier than they expected to slip into the room with Rowland's masterpiece. Vincent brought all of the guards to another wing of the museum to investigate a noise. Frank launched a speech that would last ten minutes and keep the museum staff and attendees rapt in his seminal works. Missy and Mickey, dressed in white jump suits and matching hats, pulled the painting from the wall. This was a regional museum and a work that up until mere days ago had been virtually without value, so there was no alarm, no laser beams, no heat sensors… They removed it from the wall, covered it in soft cloth and walked calmly to Frank's red pickup which sat parked, Sheila in the driver's seat, at the museum's entrance.

15

Tommy met them at the corner of Greenwood and Archer. The sun inching over the horizon. The strange double sky a deep pulsing purple.

"Do you see it?" He asked Sheila as they pulled the painting from the truck. "The sky."

"It's beautiful," she said as they put the painting into a position aligned with the corner it depicted.

They all stood back from the canvas as Missy pulled the cover off to reveal the shifting surface, the faces of Tommy and Sheila's grandparents now graced with smiles.

The edges of the painting inched their way further into the world beyond the borders of the canvas. The sky above them shifted ever closer in tone to match the colors of the painting.

"I can't tell if the canvas is changing or the world," said Tommy.

"They both are," said Sheila.

About the Author

Timothy Ryan Day moved a lot as a child. He was born in Tulsa, Oklahoma. His mother brought him and his siblings to Colorado when he was 5 so that she could attend University. When she finished school they moved to Houston, Texas, then to Hephzibah, Georgia, and Augusta, Georgia. When he was 12 they moved to Chicago where he stayed through high school. Before attending university, he hitchhiked from Chicago back to Georgia, and briefly toured the US as a roadie for punk bands, writing poetry and stories along the way. He worked as a barista, bartender, waiter, parking garage attendant, picture framer, sandwich artist, and clerk in a second-hand clothing store before deciding it was time to go back to school. He studied in Iowa, Chicago, and Madrid before taking a teaching job in Shantou China where he lived for a year before moving to Arizona where he completed coursework for a PhD. All that is to say, his early life was an itinerate one, and all of that movement has influenced his writing.

The view of such wide swathes of the United States landscapes and the people that occupy them led him to deep considerations of what it meant to be from the United States. His international experience has only increased his interest in the tensions around American identities: Perceptions of

Southerners by Northerners, anxieties around race and gender, gaps between urban and rural dwellers, and the environmental and political crises that seemed to set the stage for the unravelling of so many seemingly solid identities. His writing emerges from the places he has lived and the people he has met, all trying to figure out how they fit into the arcs of the their historical narratives.

This book comes out of a complicated relationship with his first home, Tulsa. His father lived his entire life in the city, and trips back were a regular part of his youth. The race riots of 1921 were a sort of open secret in Tulsa. They managed to remain a spectre in the background of the city's life. When he went back for his father's funeral, he took a day to wander around the historic Greenwood neighborhood, stopping in the museum dedicated to the riots and imagining the place that Booker T. Washington had once called "black Wall Street." That trip set off an obsession with his native city's original sin, and began a process of thinking, writing, and researching that has resulted in this novel.

He works as a professor at Saint Louis University's Madrid Campus where his teaching revolves around an ecological approach to literature, and an effort to understand why it is we, as a species, are drawn towards narrative in the first place

Made in the USA
Middletown, DE
21 December 2020